OIL STREET

DOMILO

Also by Malcolm Hughes

Shandy
(available from lulu.com)

Moonrise Forest
(ISBN: 978-0-9556901-0-5)

Looking for the Backbeat
(ISBN: 978-0-9556901-1-2)

OIL STREET

MALCOLM HUGHES

DOMILO

First Published 2009

Domilo Publishers
Wallasey
07526474553

ISBN 978-0-9556901-2-9

Copyright © MJH 2009

Malcolm Hughes asserts the moral right to be identified as the author of this work

All rights reserved. No part of this publication may be reproduced, stored in or introduced into a retrieval system, or transmitted, in any form or by any means electronic, mechanical or photocopying, recording or otherwise without the prior written permission of the publisher.

Cover Design © Malcolm Hughes 2009

This book is dedicated to Kate Callaghan, a wonderful editor.

And to Kate Godsmark, a wonderful friend.

All men dream: but not equally. Those who dream by night in the dusty recesses of their minds wake in the day to find that it was vanity: but the dreamers of the day are dangerous men, for they may act out their dream with open eyes, to make it possible.

T E Lawrence

The man with the shaven head looked out on his home town.

All my life has led to this.

He sighed with relief when the thought occurred to him because it had been *his* thought; it hadn't whispered across the chilly, twilight air and settled in his mind after bypassing his ears.

Of course, everybody's life led to such a point any time they said those words. Still, it was true. After they'd heard the tape he'd left and spoken to Neil Judd, they'd see that his life couldn't have led him anywhere else. Neil would've read the journal by then and he'd explain everything to Andrew.

Now, it was just nice to look down on his home town—Seapool and The Rows and Oil Street.

Everybody in Seapool knew about The Rows but nobody, except maybe Neil, knew Oil Street like the man with the shaven head knew it.

"But even Neil doesn't know about 12 Oil Street," the man with the shaven head told the air, the air that no longer felt heavy.

Then he shook his head slowly, a small smile lifting the corners of his mouth because, now, he didn't have to think about that. He could just look out and see the town the way a bird did—he let his eyes shift from one area to the next and it was like gliding.

The sky was a gorgeous dark lilac over the bay; the same colour as his wife's eyes. He moved his own eyes east to the town limits and the motorway, where the green fields seemed to shrink back from the town: wise green fields. Redhill to the north and Blackhill to the south and he remembered Neil saying the hills and the Moss between defined Seapool.

Neil.

Neil knew so much and, if the man's life hadn't led him to this, it would've been good to talk to Neil again. But Neil was too good at what he did and there was Andrew to think about. No, the journal and the letter were safer.

He glided over Somerville Moss where it lay in the cleft of the hills, glanced at Laketon and then twitched his mental wings and glided back, past the industrial park and the shopping centre, back to The Rows. Back to Oil Street.

He filled his lungs with air that *didn't* feel like storm air, full of the power of the lightning. And there was no smell of old tin to it. And, thank God, the microscopic ants had stopped their maddening forays over his body.

Finally, he felt at peace, felt light again. Oh, finally light enough to...well, reach for that sublime moment one more time.

ONE

click...

'I'm taping this because my hand's swollen tight and I can't really feel the pen anymore. And I want to get it done because it's getting late. Go and see Neil Judd. It'll save you a lot of time. The shadow's stopped whispering and it's just standing in the cone of light from the standard lamp. It's waiting and I don't want to keep it waiting too long. Besides, it's all done now. Time to find that sublime moment between the sky and the ground again.'

Cottingham rewound the tape and then looked at the note they'd found stuck to the cassette recorder when they had walked into the house through the unlocked back door.

PLAY ME

And, like in *Alice in Wonderland*, you couldn't help but do what the note said.

"No sign of anyone, sir. Him or her."

Martin nodded. "Okay. Get SOCO here. Check with the station, see if there's any word of Anne Jordan yet. I've got a phone call to make." He pulled a pair of rubber gloves over his hands and picked up the phone with his right thumb and index finger. Then he gestured with his chin toward the living room door and his sergeant took the hint.

Four miles across Seapool, Neil Judd looked at the padded envelope on his desk, recognising the handwriting immediately. He frowned. "What the hell's this, Davy? A book?"

The phone buzzed and he picked it up.

"Hello Martin." Even as he said it, Neil felt the hairs on his neck prickle. He listened to the question, still looking at the envelope. "Davy Eliot's an old friend of mine, Martin. We've known each other since we were about four and had snotty noses and scabby knees. Why?"

In 12 Oil Street, Cottingham said, "Neil, I need to see you. Can you...'ang on a minute." He covered the mouthpiece of the phone and raised his eyebrows at his sergeant.

"We've found a body, sir. In the swings. It's a woman. Nothing to identify her yet. I...you'd better come and see for yourself."

Martin turned back to the phone. "Neil, something's come up...I'll see you later."

He put the phone down and stood up. "Right, show me."

*

In his office, Neil replaced his own phone and picked up the padded envelope again. It was from Davy Eliot all right. Neil knew the careful handwriting well. It was so neat and clear, it was almost print. Davy had perfected his style at grammar school because, once he'd heard Mr McKaig explain the basics of electricity, Davy knew that he wanted to be an electrician and he didn't want to run the risk of not getting an apprenticeship because he didn't have enough qualifications.

Davy's handwriting had always been what his primary school teacher had called scraggly and that same teacher had warned him about other children she'd known who had been failed on an exam because the examiner hadn't been able to read the answers. Davy had told Neil during the afternoon break that he thought the likelier story was that the examiner had just been too bloody-minded to make the effort.

So, once Davy knew what he really wanted to be when he grew up, the first thing he did was head to the library to find a book on handwriting. And he'd practised every night until his hand had ached; no bloody-minded examiner was going to get the chance to stop Davy Eliot from being an electrician. And an electrician was what Davy had become.

Neil took the contents of the envelope out and laid them on his desk. There was a blue-backed Diary, one of the thick A4 ones with gossamer-thin gold lines and no margins. On top of this was a sheaf of ordinary writing paper. Neil looked at these and saw his own name printed on the folded-over top sheet. He didn't unfold the paper and read, though. Instead, he closed his eyes and leaned back in his chair.

Was it coincidence that a police inspector would phone him about Davy at *exactly* the same time Neil received this, whatever it was, from Davy? No, Neil didn't think so.

"Something to do with Trisha," Neil said softly and rubbed at the scar above his right eyebrow. "Davy, I wish you'd come to see me again."

He leaned forward and unfolded the paper on top of the thick Diary.

Hiya Neil

I hate to do this to you but it's all I can think of so that Andrew will be able to carry on, so he'll understand. You'll probably have a visit from the police soon and I'm sorry about that, too.

The book with this letter says Diary but it's not really. At least it's more than just a diary. I suppose it amounts to a sort of written version of what I've been thinking about for a good few weeks as well as what happened to me over the last couple of years. When I was getting near the end, I remembered you and Mr Gibson in English Lit. He asked us why we thought people wrote at all and we all hummed and hawed but you said you thought it was because we don't really know what we think until we've written it down. I think that's right. Anyway, you know most of it but not all of it, not the most important part.

I started writing it because I couldn't bungee jump anymore. The reason I couldn't jump anymore, the accident with the girl, made me think about when I was a kid and I realised I hadn't really thought about that stuff for a long time. Even when me and Eddie and Frankie and you get together, we don't seem to talk much about what we did when we were kids. Anyway, I thought it might be a good way to fill up some of the hollowness inside me, which I knew would creep back if I didn't have the bungee jumping. Then it felt like I was writing it as a way of passing stuff on to Andrew. Just writing down the stuff we would have talked about if he wasn't in a coma, telling him about when I was a kid and the stuff we got up to. But, as I was writing, not every day but most days, I realised that I was trying to find a way of accounting for what happened with me and Trisha.

Like I said, I thought it was the girl's accident at the bungee jump that made me think about writing it. But, now, well, now I'm positive it was the shadow I saw at the accident that made me write it all down.

I think I still thought of it like Churchill's black dog or whatever it was he said but then the shadow started whispering to me and I knew it was real. And it made me remember things like they really were instead of how I thought they were. And, the more it whispered and the more it made me remember, the more substantial it got. The really weird thing, though, is that it looks like somebody I remember from when we were kids. The shadow's features look a bit like Mad George. Daft, eh? But maybe it's just me trying to give it a face I know so I can kid myself I'm not as scared as I really am. It doesn't work, though, Neil. God knows, it scares me to bloody death.

Anyway, it started whispering to me and making me remember how things really were. About Trisha and, well, all of my life really.

It was the look on her face in our wedding photo, I think. That and the look in her eyes when we made love that first time. I didn't see them for what they were, though. Not then. It was the shadow in 12 Oil Street that showed me the truth about Trisha. But you'll know what I mean after you've read the journal or diary or whatever you want to call it.

We like to think we live our lives in the light but we only know the light because of the shadows, don't we? I've lived all my life in shadow. No, that's not right. I've lived my life <u>shadowed.</u> It's just that I didn't realise it until recently.

When the shadow of 12 Oil Street started telling me things, started making me see my life the way it was instead of the way I remembered it, I thought the shadow had been with me since I was ten years old. I know better now; it was with me from a long time before that. But I'd already written about what happened when I was ten and it still seemed like the best place to start.

Anyway, now that it's finished and I know what I'm going to do, it feels more and more like it's for Andrew. He's going to need help when he comes out of it, which I still think he will. I really believe he will come out of it and that's what makes it easier for me, I think.

What I'm trying to say is he'll need help and you're the best. That's why I've sent this to you. You'll read it and you'll probably understand everything better than me and then you'll be able to explain it to Andrew. You'll be able to explain it and help him.
You've always been my friend and you've always been the best at what you do. I'm glad you're my friend and I'm glad Andrew knows you.
I'll see you, Neil.'

Neil put the pages to one side. Yes, something to do with Trisha. The police wanted to talk to him about Davy and Neil had been right, it had something to do with Trisha. But what the hell was all that about a shadow? Knowing what he knew about Davy, Neil was willing to put it down to some odd physical manifestation of Davy's depression but...well, there was something nagging at him, something about this shadow and Mad George that made Neil think there was more to it than depression, what Davy called the hollowness inside him.

Still, the overriding sense was that something had happened between Davy and Trisha and the fact that the police were interested made the other, nagging sensation take a back seat. For now.

Neil looked at the phone and thought about ringing Martin Cottingham and then shook his head. No, he'd wait for Martin to arrive and find out what he wanted to know about Davy.

Neil had seen Davy two months ago. It was the second time they'd sat in Neil's office at home and the last time he'd seen him. The door was closed and Joy Judd was in her own little office preparing a brief. The two girls were out and the place was very quiet. Even Dylan the dog was sleeping without growling. That second time, Davy had been talking about how he felt like his life was running away from him again, out of his control. The woman he'd been seeing for two months had just given him the elbow without any explanation or reason.

The first time they'd talked, it had been about the emptiness, the hollowness as Davy put it, that he was feeling after the enormous sea-change in his life. He talked then, too, about how it felt like his life seemed to be running away from him.

Neil thought Davy Eliot, even as a kid, had felt like he wasn't really in control of things. Of course, when you're a kid, it's basically true. Still, Neil had always thought it was more acute for Davy and probably the reason he'd ignored the teachers' advice to go to college.

Instead, he'd taken the apprenticeship as a spark; here, at least, was something he could control. Better still, it was something huge and powerful, nothing less than the power of the lightning.

That first time he'd called on Neil, Davy had talked about his father's death, about Trisha Eliot and how she'd shattered both her marriage and her husband by going out and taking a lover just for the sex. The look on Davy's face and the flat tone of his voice when he talked to Neil was awful.

The second time, after Anne Jordan had called it off without any explanation, Davy's face had looked almost as bad. And then, so soon afterwards, Andrew Eliot, Davy's son, had had an accident and was now in a coma in Seapool Hospital.

Neil had expected Davy to call him again, to want to talk again but there'd been nothing from Davy at all.

Neil rubbed at the scar above his right eyebrow again and then, with the same finger, rubbed at the thick, padded blue-back of the Diary. Whatever was written here, Neil doubted it would tell him that Davy's life was back on an even keel.

Neil opened the diary.

Sitting here in the living room of 12 Oil Street in the middle of the last decade of the 20th century, I can close my eyes and see the ten year old boy I used to be when the 20th century was barely half way through its hundred years.

I can see him with his friends, playing in the fenced-in field they called The Pit. The sun is shining brightly but the shadows are lengthening as the hot summer afternoon stretches towards evening. It's half-three and the four boys are playing Batman and Robin. The two boys who are the baddies are up ahead, leading the Dynamic Duo through the abandoned warehouses and derelict sections of Gotham City. The three huge, overturned bell-shapes embedded into the ground of The Pit are all these things.

Back then, when I was ten, we never knew what those massive iron bell shapes were. Now, I know they were the discarded crucibles from the old foundry that used to dominate Seapool long before the brake linings factory was built.

They lay in a line running east to west, much as Oil Street does. The first bell, as we called it, you came to when you climbed over the chainlink fence was the largest, the middle one, some three feet away, was smaller by about two feet and the last bell, another yard away, was smaller by about six feet. Beyond the smallest bell was the remains of the old lime pit, left over from the days when the field was part of the brickworks. The pit was only inches deep and barely three yards across but the lime was still a danger. It was there that I first saw real pain, real damage done to a person.

The bells were rough-cast, their sides pitted with ridges and hollows where a young foot might gain a hold, where thin fingers might gain some purchase. But, as the sides reached the top of the bell, as the shape rounded to what used to be their bottoms, those rounded tops became shiny. Not really smooth but no longer full of crannies where young feet and fingers could catch a grip.

Of course, we didn't have trainers in those days. We had plimsolls, pumps in the language of the four boys there that day. If you were rich, as we thought of it, your plimsolls were really tennis shoes, made by Dunlop with green flashes on their backs and with white laces. If you were like us and even if your dad was lucky enough to have a job, your pumps were black slip-ons with the elasticated patch across the instep. They were great for running but, on something as shiny-smooth as the tops of those bells, they could be treacherous.

There was a way to do it, once you'd climbed to the top of those bells, a trick to playing the game. Once you'd gained the top of the bell, you had about five or six feet of standing room on what used to be the bell-bottom. So you needed to back up until you were almost falling off in order to get a good run-up. Then you ran forward and jumped across that three foot gap and down to the next bell.

Of course, the next bell was just as shiny and you had to control your landing or you'd just go on running and fall off. Between the first and second bells, you'd just land on the hard, grassless soil. If you lost control on the third bell, the drop was less but that's where the lime pit oozed with barely a foot of hard ground between you and the dirty-white of its surface.

So, ten year old Davy Eliot is last up the rough-cast side of that first bell and his hands are stained with old, reddish rust. Almost exactly the colour of his hair, which is matted with sweat and hangs down across his forehead. He blows through his open mouth to clear the hair from his eyes. He gains the top of the bell and stands, looking at his three friends as they set off for the next bell and then he follows.

The two baddies are always one bell away and, as Davy lands alongside his intrepid buddy, the baddies yell back American curses like See ya in Hell ya bums!

"They're stuck now," Batman tells Davy as they stand on the middle bell. "They can't go forward cos of the lime pit and they can't come back cos we're here."

Davy/Robin nods sagely and The Dynamic Duo get ready to charge the two hoodlums. When they clear the gap between the bells, the fight will begin, complete with comic books sounds like Kapow! and Kerrunch!

The two baddies look back and see the two crime-fighters getting ready to jump the gap. Panic! The younger of the two baddies, Willie Blake, squats down and slides to the edge of the bell just as Batman lets out his fierce yell and jumps. The older of the baddies, Jimmy Fennel, grins and turns to drop over the leading edge of the smallest bell.

As Frankie/Batman lands, bending his knees to absorb the impact and control his forward momentum, Jimmy tenses his thigh muscles and leans forward.

And his smooth-soled pumps slip.

His slide turns into a leap, exaggerated by his thrust forward. Jimmy totters, arms flailing, fright turning his face dirty white, like the lime in the pit below him. Jimmy falls, unable to control his descent.

Robin/Davy lands on the bell in time to see Jimmy totter forward. He reaches out to grab Jimmy's T-shirt but Jimmy is too far-gone now and Davy can only watch as the erstwhile baddie heads for the burning lime.

And Davy's own smooth-soled pumps can't keep their tenuous grip on the shiny top of the bell so he, too, begins to totter forward.

Davy feels his own fright fill his body but, somehow, he manages to twist so he's pointed towards the rim of the pit. He pushes forward with his legs, forcing adrenaline-filled muscles to eke out one last erg of energy, hoping against hope that he'll gain enough height and speed to pass the edge of the lime-pit and land on the hard-packed but safe ground.

As Davy leaves the top of the bell he sees, on the edge of his vision, Jimmy fall into the pit.

Jimmy's scream is of fear first but then it turns into one of pain as the burning reaches through his jeans to his skin. But Davy Eliot, barely ten years old, can only spare a brief moment for this sound and the knowledge that goes with it.

Davy is in the air and he's reached that marvellous point where his outward motion has ceased and the downward tug of gravity has yet to exert its pull. Davy is poised between the sky and the ground at that brief moment when he's virtually weightless.

It only lasts a second in reality but it lasts forever, too. I know that now. I know it because, all these years later, that moment is with me and has been in all the years between.

Then Davy's falling and he grits his teeth for the impact. His ankles jar and his mouth opens and closes, his teeth nipping his tongue in a sharp vice. Davy rolls like he's seen the parachutists do in the Saturday morning matinees at the Gaumont Picture House. Then he's up, racing to see what they can do for Jimmy who's screaming in pain, screaming for help, screaming for his mother.

Jimmy suffered second degree burns to both legs and his hands were a mess with third degree burns. He was lucky not to lose the little finger on his left hand. It must've been bloody agonising. When we got to him, you could feel the heat baking off his legs and we watched as the lime ate through the material of his jeans. He'd only bought them the day before from Millers in Byron Row. They cost nineteen and eleven, cheap because the cotton was cheap. We could see the blue dye in that cheap cotton being bleached away. His hands and legs had big, angry splotches on them that looked like weird wallpaper. Frankie was the fastest runner because Neil wasn't there that day so Frankie ran for adult-help. Willie and me stayed with Jimmy, telling him it would be all right and not knowing if it would be. Jimmy spent two months in hospital and bore the scars all his life.

I remember it all like it was yesterday. I know Neil can do it all the time over anything but I've never been like Neil. The only reason I remember it so well is because of what happened yesterday.
If I'm honest—I suppose when you're writing stuff down mostly for yourself you can afford to be—
 bungee jumping seemed to fill some of the hollowness I felt inside after my Dad died. Thinking about it now, that seems like something else I'll be writing about in this book. But not yet because I'm writing about what made me think about writing in the first place.

I was at the Seapool Show. The weather was great this last weekend and the show pulled in the crowds by the thousands. I went yesterday, Sunday and parked in the car park, close to the middle of the three grassy dips. The bungee jump ambushed me as soon as I walked out of the car park.
It was there, right on the edge of the dip, thrilling people who were willing to pay the twenty quid. The sign-board at the jump told everybody that fifteen of that twenty was being donated to the Jasmine Hospice for the terminally ill. The queue was long

but worth the wait. I jumped twice, the last time just before they announced the final jump of the day, the weekend, the show.

It was almost eight o'clock and the sun was like a burnished copper ball on the horizon. It was really beautiful that sunset, all soft pinks and pale lemons and greens. I think it was that, the loveliness of it that made it easier for me to face the fact that I just couldn't afford to make another jump. So I just joined the crowd to watch the last jumper, smelling hot-dogs and vinegary chips and feeling almost like I did when me and my little gang were teenagers and used to spend our summers up in Laketon.

There was a spotlight on top of the trailer where they took the money and it seemed to freeze the crane and its platform and the crowd, creating a penumbra all around the area.

I stood there, my body still half-way between the sky and the ground, and looked wistfully as the crane hauled up the last jumper. It was a young woman wearing black cycling shorts and a bright pink T-shirt. Up there, the spotlight aimed at the platform, she was almost a silhouette, only her long blonde hair obvious in the light. She stood on the edge of the platform, facing backwards, her arms outstretched and I felt a shudder run through me. I thought it was the breeze getting up and just rubbed my bare arms.

The cheers, mixed with squeals, brought me back to the jumper and I looked up just as she stopped lying back on the air and started to dip down, body twirling. I watched enviously as the elastic ropes stopped her descent and she was pulled back up again, her body twirling the opposite way. Then it all went wrong.

The restraints snapped with a sound like King Kong clapping his hands and the girl, thirty or forty feet above the ground, fell. She was still twirling.

The screams rose and rose from the crowd but the girl's screams could still be heard above them, like the descant of a Christmas Carol. Her hair was flung out from her head and was highlighted by the spotlight. The contrast between the plummeting figure and the way the elasticated ropes were shooting upwards was terrible. Then she landed.

This particular jump had an inflatable landing pad and, normally, your head would touch it in the blue cross in the middle if you were tall enough. This descent wasn't normal. The crowd screamed again and then it turned into a sort of mass exhalation of relief as everybody thought the safety measures would work.

I saw her land and had a sudden, sharp but brief vision of Eddie jumping off the slide in the swings in Oil Street back when we were all about ten years old.

But instead of hitting the blue cross in the middle of the landing pad, the girl hit its edge. She bounced up and then came down onto the ground. Hard. She screamed as she landed on her shoulder and then screamed again, louder and higher until it was almost inaudible as she fell on her right arm. The crack was loud and clear because the crowd hadn't realised what had happened and hadn't begun to scream or groan again.

It was bedlam then as the operators dashed out of the trailer and the crowd tried to help the girl. The first aid tent was in the next dip and somebody went to get help as a mounted policeman came galloping over and cleared us all out of the way. I stood and waited until the ambulance arrived some five minutes later.

The girl was conscious but it was obvious by the unnatural set of her arm and shoulder that bones were broken. Her shocked face was the same colour as her hair. They put her in the ambulance with a brace round her neck and drove off with the lights flashing.

I have to own up here. I felt sorry for her but, selfishly, I felt sorrier for myself because the accident meant there'd be no more bungee jumps for a long time. At least round Seapool. And that meant I'd have nothing to fill up the hollowness inside me again.

I turned away when the ambulance drove off and that was when I saw the shadow.

The fear seemed to spike up from my stomach, right through my throat and peak in the centre of my forehead. It almost felt like anybody who looked at me would see a glowing sign above my wide eyes which said help or panic or something. I groaned and tried to look away but, as always, the shadow held me effortlessly.

It wasn't supposed to be there. It was in 12 Oil Street and it scared me there but I'd learned to live with it. Mostly. I think you can learn to live with almost anything. But now, seeing it out of the house, it scared me rigid. And all I could do was stand there and stare at it.

It was there, right on the edge of the penumbra and I knew nobody else could see it because it was mine. Not my shadow but mine in the sense that it belonged to me. I'd put it down to something to do with the way I was depressed. Why not? I saw it when I first moved to back to Oil Street after I left Trisha and God knows, I was depressed then. Depressed by what had happened and depressed by the strange dislocation I felt after leaving my home of twenty years.

But now it was in the open and I didn't understand why.

The person-shaped and -sized shadow turned on the edge of the penumbra and looked at me. It opened its arms as if it was waiting for me to run to it and be embraced. And the fear in me jagged up another spike. Then something even stranger happened. I saw vague features appear in the spot where I thought its face would be. This had never happened before. It had always been just a shadow. An impossible shadow, one where no shadow should have been but a shadow just the same.

And the fear in me started to fade. Not as fast as it arrived but it was fading. I stood there, staring at the shadow and trying very hard to make out its features because I had a feeling, something nagging at the back of my mind, that I'd seen a face like it before. A long, long time ago but the feeling wouldn't go away. Then I knew and almost laughed.

The vague face I could see looked a bit like Mad George. I hadn't thought about him since we heard he'd finally died when we were about seven or eight. And, on the heels of that, I realised I hadn't thought about much to do with when I was a kid for just as long and I thought about Eddie again.

The fear was gone now but I knew it was only dozing. Still, it meant I could drag my eyes away from the shadow and head away from the bungee jump.

I went home, still feeling sorry for both the girl and myself but, just before I went to bed, I remembered again how Eddie jumped off the slide and then, even more strongly, I remembered how Jimmy got so badly burned in the old lime pit and I thought about Mad George.

Just before I finally got to sleep, I thought I understood why the shadow had appeared out in the open. I think it was because I was sorry for myself, sorry that I wouldn't be able to bungee jump, sorry that there would be nothing to help me fight the hollowness inside me.

I went to bed and expected to dream about the accident and the poor girl's broken bones and her shocked face and I did dream but not about the girl.

I dreamed about myself.

I was standing at the top of the stairs in a house I knew but wasn't sure where from. I was standing there, looking down at a person-shaped and -sized shadow that stood at the bottom of the stairs. It

had no features but it was holding its arms wide, as if it wanted to embrace me when I finally worked up enough courage to jump.
I woke up freezing cold but sweating, almost positive that I was getting ready to scream. I lay awake until dawn finally slipped into the room and tried to work out why I'd had such a weird dream and, too, why I felt like I'd had the dream before.
It was when I was in the bathroom, my mouth full of toothpaste, staring stupidly at my reflection in the mirror, I remembered, vaguely, having a dream like it when I was a teenager—just another thing about when I was young that I hadn't thought about it for a long time. Even when I met up with Frankie and Eddie for our boys-night-out, we seldom talked about when we were kids.
I shook my head and spat out the toothpaste and suddenly heard my Dad telling me how we pass stuff on to our kids and that's what life was all about. And then I heard Andrew asking me if people really did have to go outside to use the toilet and use a big tin bath in front of the fire instead of a white one in a bathroom.
That was when I made my mind up to write about what's happened over the last two years or so and about some of the stuff I got up to when I was a kid. It's just a way of telling Andrew about his dad, a way of passing stuff on to him.
Maybe it'll help me fill up some of the hollowness inside me, too. Now that there'll be no more bungee jumping. I think that's why the shadow appeared in the open. I was depressed at the thought that I

wouldn't be able to bungee jump anymore, sorry that I'd have nothing to help me fight the hollowness.

And, yeah, I was scared by the shadow and if I couldn't jump, there'd be nothing to keep that fear away either.

I still think the shadow's got something to do with my depression and, who knows, maybe I'll be able to sneak up on writing about the shadow, how it scared me when I first saw it after moving into 12 Oil Street. If I can do that, maybe I'll be able to write it <u>out of me</u>, make it go away. If it does, I'll finally be able to tell Neil. He'll be proud of me! I've never told anybody about the shadow, not even Neil. Probably because of some ego thing, like when we were kids and couldn't let on about being spooked because it was sissy.

I don't know. I just feel a bit better writing this because at least I'll have something that might help me fight the gnawing sense of emptiness inside me.

TWO

Neil looked up from the neat writing and blew a long breath out of his pursed lips. He closed his eyes, his mind still full of the two jumps Davy had described, so similar and so different, so many years apart.

And something else, too. There was still something nagging at his mind. He was about to scroll through the archives of his incredible memory to find out what it was when somebody called his name.

"Neil?"

He blinked and focused on Sarah who was standing in the doorway. He saw the worried look on her face and smiled. "It's okay, Sarah, I'm okay. What's up?"

Sarah took a moment to make sure he was telling her the truth, saw the slow smile and nodded. "I've just had a Sergeant Robb on the phone. He told me to tell you that his boss will be here in about ten minutes. Neil, it's not one of our kids, is it?"

Neil shook his head. "No, love. It's something else. Don't worry, go and get your lunch."

Sarah smiled now that she knew Neil wouldn't be out looking for another absconder down in The Rows. She left the office.

Neil glanced at the diary and then looked away, the something in his mind still nagging at his memory. He knew he'd have to find out what it was but there was the question of why Martin would have his sergeant ring Sarah instead of Martin ringing Neil himself.

Neil swivelled his chair and looked out of the window and thought about it. He didn't need to be Sherlock Holmes.

"Martin's letting me know it's official," Neil told himself quietly.

Yes, that's what it meant. When Martin had rung before, it had still been unofficial. Now...well, now something had happened and Martin wanted Neil to know that it was official and he also needed to make sure the other police on the case knew that Martin wasn't playing favourites just because it was Neil Judd.

Neil turned away from the window, away from the way the sunlight played on the shed roof at the bottom of Blackhay's garden. He looked at the open diary on his desk. He had less than ten minutes to decide whether to tell Martin about it or not.

"I haven't read it yet," he murmured and slipped Davy's note between the open pages. He closed the book and put it in his desk drawer; for now, it was just a private matter between Neil and Davy Eliot.

He sat back and waited for Inspector Martin Cottingham. He thought about working out what it was about a shadow and Mad George that was nagging at him but then he decided to put it on hold; he needed to be ready when Martin arrived.

Martin Cottingham turned off the ignition and looked up at what he knew was Neil's office window. There was no sign of Neil looking out of the window but

Martin knew that Neil would know he was here. Still, Martin stayed in the car, thinking about Neil Judd and what was going to happen when Martin finally got out of the car and went up to the office.

Martin and Neil went back a long way. Back to when they were both new to their jobs and trying to make them fit. Neil had been looking for a teenage absconder from Blackhay, this unit for broken kids that Neil ran. He'd tracked him to The Jacks, without doubt the worst pub in The Rows—the town legend was that, if you wanted to have a pint in The Jacks on Saturday night, you had to go on Friday night, get beaten up, go back Saturday sporting the broken nose and black eyes, and you'd be allowed in because it was obvious you'd been there before.

Cottingham had been on a surveillance job, waiting for a dealer who had been coaxed into the open for what promised to be very lucrative partnership with another dealer from out of town.

What neither Martin, his under-cover sergeant inside the pub nor Neil knew was that Neil's absconder knew a friend of the local pusher and was there, not to buy drugs, but to get some money to be able to leave Seapool.

Neil had turned up just before the dealer. While Neil was trying to persuade the teenager to return with him, the lad's friend, the pusher and two other thugs started to threaten Neil. When the dealer arrived, he decided it would be best if this do-gooder-social-worker never saw the light of day again—it wouldn't have been the first time somebody had entered The Jacks through the front door and exited through the back door in need of medical attention.

It was a bad mistake on the dealer's part. Cottingham, sitting in the car outside, sensed something was turning bad—so many 'unknowns' arriving at the pub at a time when the place was usually more or less empty most afternoons, just added up to *wrong*. So, without any back-up apart from the under-cover man inside the pub, Martin decided to pull the dealer in. If it meant a lesser charge to prevent what his instincts were telling him felt like an impending bloodbath, then so be it.

When he entered the pub, the dealer was giving instructions about what should be done with Neil. Cottingham was barely through the door when Neil exploded. And it really was an explosion. It happened so fast that two of the thugs were on the floor and out of the game with two punches. The pusher had a broken bottle in his hand and the sergeant was already making for him. Neither the sergeant nor the thug had time to make another movement. Neil disarmed the pusher and broke his arm, nose and dislodged two teeth. He turned to face the sergeant, fists bunched, a terrible light in his eyes. The sergeant stepped back and only Cottingham's shout of 'Police!' stopped Neil from doing the man serious damage.

Later, when the uniforms had arrived and were getting the thugs into the van, the sergeant was trying to get the absconder in, too. Neil stood between them and persuaded the sergeant and Martin that nothing would be gained by arresting the teenager. Neil persuaded them that, really, the lad had nothing to do with anything.

To this day, Martin Cottingham couldn't quite explain why he'd been persuaded but he was glad he had; the lad was now one of the more successful drugs counsellors in the Northwest. All thanks to Neil Judd.

Now, sitting in his car and knowing he was going to have to ask Neil about David Eliot, about the possibility that Eliot was now a fugitive suspected of murder, Martin had a sour taste in his mouth. Neil was a friend but Martin was investigating what looked like a brutal murder and, sour taste or not, Neil would have to answer the questions Martin asked.

"Shit," Martin muttered and got out of the car.

Neil watched his old friend struggle out of his overcoat and sit down. He saw the frown on the older man's broad forehead and nodded once to himself; it was real, then.

"Neil...."

"It's okay, Martin. I know you're not struck on the idea but you have to do it. Best just to get on with it, mate." Neil told the policeman and smiled.

The sourness in Martin's mouth increased and then disappeared completely. He shook his head slowly, twice; Neil could make you feel better with a word or two and that honest smile. No wonder he was so good at what he did.

"David Eliot," Martin said, reading from his notebook. "About six two, about eleven and a half stone, about the same age as you. Lives at 12 Oil Street, probably auburn or ginger-haired but now he's shaven-headed?" He looked up at Neil.

"Well, I haven't seen him since he shaved his head but, yeah, that's the Davy I know. What's happened, Martin?"

"Neil, first off, I have to ask you a few questions. Okay?"

Neil rubbed at the scar and nodded.

"When was the last time you saw David Eliot? Have you any idea what his relationship with his wife was and do you know of any relationship between him and a woman called Anne Jordan?"

Neil leaned forward in his chair and put his palms on the desktop. "Martin, it'll probably be best if I just tell you about Davy and what happened to him during the last two years or so. It'll answer all your questions, I promise."

Martin looked hard at Neil. The policeman in him smelled something awry but Neil was Neil and you only ever got what he gave. Most of the time, it was what you needed and it was always the truth. Finally, Martin put his notebook on the desk and leaned back in the chair. "Neil, tell it any way you want to but I have to tell you, this is—"

"Official," Neil said softly but this time he didn't smile. "I know."

"Okay."

"Like I told you," Neil said and leaned back. "We were mates from the time we were four. Down in The Rows. We grew up together and went to school together. His dad died exactly two years ago yesterday and it hit Davy really hard. Him and George were close but they'd only really been close since Davy was about eighteen. Up to then, George was just the bloke who lived in the same house as Davy and his mum, warned him against the fire and the boiling water, the deep end of the baths and taught him how to saw a straight line and how to tighten a bolt the right way. Anyway, George was a joiner and a good one. He worked down in the flour mills and, when Davy decided he wanted to be a spark, going against all the advice from his teachers, George fixed Davy up with an apprenticeship in the mills. On Davy's eighteenth birthday, George took Davy down to the Bird in Hand at the bottom of Oil Street. He introduced him to all his darts mates as Davy, my son who's going to be the best sparks in Seapool." Neil smiled as he remembered how Davy had looked when he'd told him the story during that first talk they had after Trisha's adultery.

Martin nodded and waited for Neil to continue.

"And I think he probably was the best. Anyway, when he finished his apprenticeship, the mills were in the middle of that streamlining in the early seventies and there wasn't a job for Davy. It didn't matter. His reference was a blinder and the council took him on. Davy was doing a job he loved and doing it well. He was fancy-free, had money in his pocket and the telly was telling everybody that the foreign package tour 'ruled okay'.

"He went on holiday to Spain with another old mate of ours called Frankie Morgan. And Davy met Trisha Marie Martin." He looked at Martin and waited while the policeman made a note.

"Davy was smitten from the start," Neil went on. "But Trisha put him off and put him down when he tried all his best lines on her at the beach. In the end, Davy had to give it up and he trooped back to the hotel with Frankie, who naturally took the piss out of him something terrible.

"That night, Trisha was waiting for him in the foyer, wanting to know if he fancied trying to impress her one more time."

"Oh?" Martin asked and picked up his pen again.

"Yeah," Neil said and smiled. "That's Trisha. She likes being in control. It was *her* decision. Anyway, Davy fell in love during the next week and, when Trisha went home, he phoned her every night and never mind Frankie taking the piss. The last night, instead of getting legless, Davy spent his last pesetas on one of those sets of concertina postcards and wrote Trisha a love letter that he posted to her at her home in Crewe. When he got home, Davy took driving lessons and, before he passed his test, jumped the train every Saturday morning to spend the weekend there with her. When he passed his test, he bought a battered Mini and then drove himself down each Friday night. He proposed after six months and Trisha got a job as a telephonist in Oxborough. They got a house, got married and were happy." Neil paused and waited for Martin to finish making his notes.

"They found out Trisha was pregnant on her twenty eighth birthday and Andrew was born the day after their fourth anniversary. Davy saw him being born and doted on the lad from the moment Andrew opened his eyes." Neil chuckled softly. "To be honest, and Davy'd be the first to admit it, he spoiled the lad rotten. Still, Andrew didn't grow up spoiled. Turned into a smashing lad. He went out with our Nicole for a while when they were fourteen but you know what it's like at that age, all pride and peer pressure. They stayed friends, though." He took a long breath and let it out slowly. "I take it you know about Andrew?"

Martin nodded. "In a coma in Seapool Hospital," he said quietly.

"Yeah," Neil said. "Fancy some coffee?"

Martin nodded.

"Okay," Neil said when the coffee was made. "Things were great. Andrew was as bright as both his parents and he sailed through school. His mum got a job in a building society when Andrew started secondary school and she became manageress. Davy became Chief Electrician for the council. Then Davy's dad had a minor stroke not long after he retired from the mills, just before Andrew took his GCSEs. Then, two years after that stroke, George had another, massive stroke and died in his front room.

"For the next few months, Davy was bad but not in any obvious way. Most of it was sleepless nights and Davy didn't really think he was any different at all. But Trisha and Andrew noticed it and it worried them. In the end, Trisha came down one four-in-the-morning and had it out with Davy. Davy agreed to see his doctor who told him that people grieved in different ways and this was probably Davy's. Not long afterwards, Davy found something to help him." Neil picked up his mug and sipped at his coffee—he knew how what he said next was going to sound to Martin the policeman.

Neil put his mug down on the desk and looked at Martin. "He started bungee jumping. It stopped the sleepless nights and helped fill what he called the hollowness he was feeling after his dad's death."

"*What?*" Martin's face looked almost comical. "You're telling me that a bloke who wouldn't see forty again started bungee jumping and it helped him get over his father's death?" Martin heard the tone of his own voice and it didn't surprise him; the idea that Eliot would risk his life on a giant elastic band as some sort of grief management sounded like the kind of thing a man on the edge would do.

Neil smiled but he'd heard the tone of Martin's voice and seen the rapid calculation that had run through the man's brain and shown in his eyes for a blink or two. Neil knew that Martin was thinking about the state of mind of somebody who fought his grief by trying to outwit gravity.

"Think about it, Martin," Neil said. "Back when we lived in caves, when it was a toss-up between you eating your dinner or your dinner eating you, we lived on the edge all the time. Now, we buy our dinner ready-cooked and most of life's remote-controlled. There's no edge anymore, nothing to make us feel alive. Isn't that why your job, mine too, is such bloody hard work? There are too many people out there looking for that edge, the thrill in a bottle or a needle or the latest funny-shaped pill. I dunno, Martin, bungee jumping doesn't sound so bad."

Martin thought about it and nodded in agreement. Still, he couldn't rid himself of the thought that David Eliot might have straddled that edge a bit too long and finally fell over. He shrugged.

"Anyway," Neil said. "He'd found something in his life again. See, Trisha was beginning to go through a relatively early menopause and it hit her really hard. But Davy, like most men I think, suffered a bit, too. I don't mean physically. It's right women get the understanding and sympathy but Davy loved Trisha and, because he did, it was hard for him emotionally.

"Trisha wouldn't talk to Davy about what she was going through, she blocked him out completely. I think the big problem was that here was something that she had no control over. She knew it was going to happen but she still couldn't control it and that would make Trisha very angry, I think. And, given that it was the start of it, the fact that the symptoms weren't predictable at all added to the physical changes, I can imagine Trisha being really hard to live with. Davy found that bungee jumping helped him cope with the hollowness he felt, that had been there ever since George died and made worse by his wife's attitude over her menopause. It might've worked out, I think, if it hadn't been for the fact that Trisha decided she wanted more than the love and understanding of her husband. She found a lover." Neil finished off his coffee.

Martin sipped at his own, making another note, already seeing a motive for Eliot to become violent; it wasn't looking good for Neil's old friend, not good at all.

"She wanted sex, Martin. Davy found out when he phoned her at the friend's house where she was supposed to be having a girls'-night-in. He was ringing with some good news and she wasn't there. He knew when he put the phone down but he waited for Trisha to come home. While he waited, he finished off fitting the new light fitment in the living room. Trisha had bought it that dinner time and then spent all of their tea-time meal talking about decorating the room when he'd fitted the light. Davy told me it was the most she'd said to him in one go for about six months." He raised his eyebrows at Martin.

Martin nodded; yes, he could understand how deep the hurt would go after that. After spending months living with a woman who refused to allow him to try to help her through her menopause, wouldn't talk to him about *anything* much and then spend an hour talking about decorating, the little things marriages are full of, and then find out she was having an affair. Oh, Martin didn't need to be a psychologist like Neil to know how deep that hurt must have gone.

"Trisha admitted it straight off when he asked her. No denials at all. When she told Davy it wasn't love, just sex, you can imagine how he felt. He told her he'd been in the same house, slept in the same bed, if she wanted to make love all she had to do was tell him, touch him. That's when she hit him with the worst thing. She told him she didn't want love, she wanted *sex*. Then she got angry.

Probably because she felt guilty. It's the way she is a lot of the time. She can be the nicest person in the world, funny and warm, full of life, and she's really gorgeous but the world has to fit in with her. That seems to be the condition she makes." Neil shrugged. "She's likeable, Martin but only when everything's going well. She has to be in control of herself and any situation. So, she told Davy she *didn't* feel guilty. Why should she when she'd only been doing what he'd been doing all through that summer?

"Davy didn't have a clue what she was on about and asked her what the hell she was talking about. Trisha had checked his account in the building society and saw the money he'd spent on bungee jumping and assumed he had another woman. See, Davy'd never told Trisha, never told anybody, about the bungee jumping. He did it at the weekends and she worked one in three and visited her parents in Crewe the other weekend. She was never home to see him go, to ask him where he was going or what he was doing. She never asked him what he was doing most of the time anyway. Davy took it as part of the change and said nothing. Oh, there was probably some male ego there, some spite but not much. Trisha had let him know she didn't want anything from him, didn't need any help with her problems and Davy left it at that. He hoped she'd come through the change and be his wife again, the woman he loved just the way he'd always loved her.

"That night, when she accused him of doing what she'd done only sooner, Davy finally told her about the jumping. She blew her top. She ridiculed him for being a bloody macho man who couldn't cope with his own midlife crisis." Neil shrugged again. "Like I said, she can be cold and cutting at times. Anyway, Davy heard her, saw the look on her face and decided the best thing he could do was leave. He left the next day and moved into 12 Oil Street the day after that. For a while, he was like a boat drifting at sea. It took a while but Frankie Morgan and another old mate, Eddie Harper, finally got him to go out for a drink one night a week. It wasn't long after that when he came to see me and we talked. He just needed to talk to somebody and I've always been a good listener."

Martin smiled. "I know. Go on."

"Well, he got on with his life. I saw Frankie a couple of times and he told me they'd found a club in Laketon that did a sixties night and they were going and enjoying it. Frankie's wife left him a while back and he'd been getting into too many fights because he had all this frustrated anger in him. The night out did them both good. Davy met Anne Jordan at the club."

Neil poured them another coffee while Martin wrote it down. It was getting close to the end of what Neil had to tell. Oh, it wasn't all he knew but it was all he was going to say for now. Then, Martin would ask what few direct questions he still had and Neil would find out just what Davy had done. Or what Trisha had done. Or whatever. Neil wasn't looking forward to it but he needed to know before he read the rest of Davy's journal.

"Okay, Neil. Anne Jordan?"

"They went out for a couple of months and got on great. Nothing heavy, good laughs, good sex. Good times. Then, towards the end of August, they were at the club again and Anne finished it.

"She just came back from the toilet and told Davy she thought they should call it a day. Then she left. Davy came to see me not long after and I think that hollowness was back in his life. It was the not-knowing-why that did it. Anne Jordan didn't explain anything, gave him no reason for calling it off. I asked him if it hurt as much as when he found out about Trisha and he said no but it still hurt a lot. Then he decided that, since he'd done it once before in harder circumstances, he reckoned he could do it again and get on with the rest of his life." Neil drained his mug.

Martin looked at him and saw the faint shadow of pain in Neil's eyes. Martin knew instinctively that it had been Neil who had persuaded Eliot that he could get on with his life because he'd already done it once before in worse circumstances. It was what Neil did and what he was so good at doing.

"That was the last time I saw him," Neil said quietly and closed his eyes. "I heard about Andrew from Nicole who heard it from friends they both have. I expected Davy to call me again but he didn't and I never got in touch other than to send a card from us all saying how sorry we were." He opened his eyes and looked at Martin. "Something like that happens, you have to give somebody enough time for them to come to terms with it and learn to accommodate into their lives. You let them know you're there if they need to talk about anything. Or even just to go the pub or sit in the front room and watch them get pissed if they want to." Then he turned the chair and looked out of the window.

Martin looked at Neil's back, having an idea of what Neil must be feeling. Martin knew that Neil would have some idea as to why Martin was here and now Neil would be thinking about the fact that he hadn't been in touch with Eliot and how, maybe, things might've been different if he had.

"Okay, Neil. As usual, you were right, most of my questions were answered. Still..."

Neil turned the chair back again. The shadow had gone from his grey eyes, replaced by a bright winter's-day-shine. "I know," he said.

"D'you think it's possible that Eliot had a breakdown? After everything that happened and the way it happened, is it possible that he just walked a little too close to that edge and...fell over?"

"It's possible because he's human, Martin. You'd better ask the next question," Neil said, his voice hard.

Martin heard the edge but asked anyway. Because he had to. "D'you think David Eliot is capable of violence?"

"Yes, of course." Neil shook his head once at Martin's wide-eyed expression. "We're all capable in the right or wrong circumstances. But I don't think Davy *would* become violent enough to hurt anybody."

Martin took a breath and let it out slowly. "D'you think he could've harmed Anne Jordan? Is that possible that he was...I don't know, obsessed? Seems to me that he might have that sort of personality. With the bungee jumping and everything?"

"Same answer," Neil said shortly and then stared at Martin.

Martin had seen that relentless gaze before but never directed at him. It was unnerving. "Only one more question. D'you have any idea where David Eliot might be now?"

Neil frowned but his eyes never left Martin's face. "At work," he said slowly. When Martin didn't reply, he said, "Obviously not. No, no idea at all. Now, what's happened?"

"We're looking for Anne Jordan. She hasn't been seen for a couple of days and she should've been. She should've been in Scotland visiting her sister. And she should've been in touch with her ex-husband over something to do with a final settlement after the divorce. When we tried to find her, the neighbour told us about a man whose description matches David Eliot, who sat in a parked car outside her house for about half an hour just three days or so ago. Then he drove off and Anne hasn't been seen since. We found out from Anne Jordan's friends, presumably the ones she went to the club with, that she spent some time with Eliot and that they'd split up. Nobody knew why, only that Anne was upset. We tried to contact Eliot at work but his boss said he'd been sent home, that Eliot hadn't, and I quote, been himself lately. We tried to contact his wife, to see if she had any idea where he might be but she's not been in work for a couple of days. Her office put it down to Andrew being in hospital. We contacted the hospital but they haven't seen either David or Trisha since the consultant told them both he didn't expect Andrew to make any sort of recovery. We're assuming we missed Trisha Eliot between the hospital and her house. So, we went round to 12 Oil Street today and found a tape. Neil, it's... well, it sounds like somebody at the end of their tether." Martin bent down to get the tape from his briefcase.

Neil watched his old friend and knew that Martin was bending down more to give himself time to think something through than get the tape; he was taking just a moment too long. What could Martin be thinking about? Neil decided not to even try to work it out; he'd find out sooner or later.

Martin had always intended playing the tape to Neil but he was wondering if he should tell Neil about the body they'd found in the swings. As he started to raise his head, he decided to keep that back for the minute; they'd yet to identify the body and, besides, the policeman in Martin kept telling him that, while Neil had given Martin the information that Martin needed, there was more. Martin knew Neil well enough to know he wouldn't hear the rest until Neil was ready to tell it.

Martin put the cassette in the recorder and pressed the play button. He watched Neil's face as Eliot's voice, tinny but firm, came out of the machine. Neil listened and his face gave nothing away. Just what Martin had expected. When the tape finished, he put it away again.

"Doesn't that sound like a man on the edge?" Martin asked. "Or even about to fall off it?"

Neil didn't think that at all but, until he'd read the journal, he had nothing to give Martin as a substitute. He was about to tell Martin he had no real opinion at all when the bleep of a pager spilled into the short silence that had developed.

Martin grimaced and took the bloody thing out of his pocket; he hated them but Charlie Patterson was a Chief Constable who liked the idea that technology could make it impossible for his officers to be unavailable to him. "Cottingham," he said after picking up Neil's phone and dialling the number on his pager.

There was a long pause in which the frown on Martin's forehead deepened. "I'll be there in half an hour," he said and put the phone back in his pocket. "Neil, I have to go. Listen...I have the very strong feeling that you've told me exactly as much as I asked but not all you know. Or guess. Okay, I'll accept it because I know you. But, Neil, I'll be back and, if necessary, I'll take you down to the station." He raised his eyebrows.

Neil smiled. "Okay. And, if we end up at the station, maybe you'll tell me the stuff you haven't told me."

Martin said nothing. He just thought what he always thought when Neil said stuff like that; there were times when he was almost convinced Neil Judd was psychic. Then he stood up, nodded and left the office.

Neil looked at his watch. It was gone one. He had no meetings, no counselling sessions, nothing vital which needed doing this afternoon. He pressed the intercom. "Sarah, I'll be here all afternoon but, unless it's an emergency, I'd rather not have any interruptions."

"Okay, Neil," Sarah said and the intercom buzzed off.

Neil took the journal out of the desk drawer and opened it to the marked page but didn't start reading. Instead, he thought about what he'd told Martin. More importantly, what he hadn't.

Yes, he'd told Martin about how Davy's father's first stroke was followed by a massive second one that killed him. But he hadn't told him about what George Eliot had told his son when George was bedfast after that first stroke.

"My Mum and Trisha and Andrew were downstairs," Davy had told Neil during their first long talk. "I got there late Saturday afternoon after some overtime. My Dad was in bed and I went up to see him. After I asked him how he was, he told me he was pissed off he wouldn't be able to play for England cos the stroke had left him with a limp. Then he laughed and told me to take that look off my face. He told me I looked like it was me who was knocking at death's door. I tried to brush it off but I couldn't. Not really. See, it was true. Seeing him like that made me realise that, not just my Dad was getting old but I was, too. Anyway, he told me off in that quiet way he had and then he said something which has stuck with me, really stuck with me.

"He told me that things like his stroke happened so the human race learned how to live. It was part of how we learned to pass things on and how we learn to take what's passed to us and carry them for however long is necessary before we pass them on to somebody else. Like our kids. It was life and we lived it as best we could. That's what he told me and I'm beginning to think it was an almost perfect description of life. Then he told me to buck up cos he wasn't ready to pass on anything else just yet and he wasn't ready to pass *away*, either."

No, Neil hadn't told Martin that nor about the deep pain in Davy's eyes and voice when he'd told Neil how he'd been watching the live football on the telly when the phone rang to tell him George was dead.

"I remember wishing that whoever was ringing had waited another five minutes till half time. I'll always remember that, Neil, because it'll always hurt that I thought it. I'll always feel guilty about that. You know?"

Yes, Neil had told Martin how Trisha Eliot had barred her husband from her life during her menopause and then gone and taken a lover purely for sex. But he hadn't told Martin how Davy had looked, the bewildered and hurt tone in his voice when he told Neil about the way Trisha's menopause had impacted on his own life.

"She just refused to talk about it," Davy had told Neil not long after he'd been persuaded to get out and about again by Frankie and Eddie. "I'd wake up in the early hours and she'd be sitting by the window, fanning herself with a magazine or drinking another bloody pint of orange juice. I asked her about seeing the doctor, about HRT, about how it might help if she talked about it. She'd just half-turn and fob me off, tell me the doctor couldn't help, HRT wouldn't work cos of the trouble she'd had with the Pill. She told me it was happening and that was it, she had to learn to live with it, there was nothing she could do about it and talking wouldn't help anybody. I think she was angry, not so much with the menopause, although it apparently arrived early for her, because she knew it was bound to happen, but with the fact that here was something she couldn't bend to her own will. Still, I thought, it comes and eventually it goes and then maybe she'll come back to me, be the woman I'd loved ever since that first minute I saw her on the beach in Spain. When the flushes had eased off and she was sleeping through most of the night, I was still waking up, though." Davy had looked at his hands and closed his eyes, a faint blush touching his cheeks and Neil had simply waited.

"I was waking up because I was having wet dreams." He'd looked at Neil and shook his head, his embarrassment still evident in his eyes. "At first, I was just waking up with one of those monstrous hard-ons. You know, the ones you got in your teens when the bloody thing seemed to have a life of its own and throbbed like earache. I was waking up, gripping the thing like I was trying to stop it exploding. Which, I suppose, I was. I couldn't remember the dream that got me like that but I had to go to the toilet and masturbate just so I could get back to sleep. I spent a fortnight wondering if I was turning into a dirty old man, dreaming about the young girls at work or something worse like sadism or something."

"Davy," Neil had said quietly. "Married men still masturbate, even when their sex lives are pretty good.

And I don't suppose your sex life was much with Trisha the way she was."

Davy had smiled and nodded. "Yeah, I know but it was still embarrassing cos I couldn't remember the dream. Then, I woke up early one morning with another hard-on and remembered the dream. *All of it.* I wasn't dreaming about young girls or some porno magazine." And he'd blown his hair out of his eyes just like he used to when he was a kid. "I was dreaming about making love with Trisha. My wife was my bloody fantasy-woman. That's how much I still loved her, Neil. I was having wet-dreams about Trisha but it was a very specific wet-dream. I was dreaming about the first time we made love. Every single detail, right down to the look in her eyes when we both came in front of her parents' fire in the living room in Crewe. How her eyes softened and looked at me, so full of love and happiness. We just seemed to fit together so well. That first time will stay with me for the rest of my life. It was the closest thing to heaven I expect to get. I saw Andrew being born and it was amazing but it still comes second to that first time me and Trisha made love."

Davy had cried then, softly and deeply and Neil had let him. Then, wiping the tears away, he'd told Neil about the night Trisha admitted her adultery and her reason for it.

"To hear her tell me it was just sex was...I dunno, awful, it felt like somebody'd kicked me in the balls. I suppose, in a way, she did. I told her we could've made love any time she liked, we slept in the same bed. God,

Andrew was at college and we could've made love up against the bloody fridge and not been disturbed. It just got her angrier. It was about sex, she said, not making love. She said we'd made love when we were both ill or still covered in paint after decorating, when we were tired. And that was because it was making love. It seemed to make her furious that we, that I did it cos I loved her. She didn't want love, just sex. She wanted somebody to want her. She wanted somebody to lust after her and not think about *love*. Just sex.

"Then she accused me of having an affair during the summer and I told her that was crap, I'd never even *looked* at another woman since the day I saw her on the beach. It's true. I saw no reason to deny it. I even told her about having wet dreams about her, about the first time we made love. I thought...maybe it would show her how much I loved her. She listened but said nothing one way or the other. That's when I told her about the bungee jumping and she just went bananas."

Davy had shrugged and they'd finished off the beers he'd brought with him.

No, Neil hadn't told Martin any of that. Why? Oh, that was simple. The look on Martin's face when Neil had told him about Davy's bungee jumping was all it had taken to make Neil keep all of that back.

Whatever he'd kept back from Neil made the policeman in Martin look for motive. Hearing about Davy's pain, bitterness, sense of betrayal and the still-burning love he had for Trisha would have, to Martin's mind, been motive enough. Allied to what Martin considered Davy's weird way of coping with the grief after his father's death, it would have sounded like Davy was a man close to the edge. Close enough, as Martin had hinted, to fall off and do God knew what.

Oh aye, phrases like *'while the balance of his mind was disturbed'* and *'mental breakdown'* and *'violent episodes'* would be flung around like streamers at New Year's Eve.

"No," Neil said and looked down at the journal. "Not till I've read this. Besides, there's still Andrew to think about. The lad doesn't need any more shadows in his life."

And, on the heels of that, Neil remembered Mad George and knew why the idea of shadows went with the name.

Mad George hadn't been the only eccentric down in The Rows when Neil and Davy and the rest were kids but he'd been one of the more interesting from a kid's point of view. Of course, the old bloke wasn't an eccentric to them, he was just Mad George. Now, Neil knew exactly what the poor old bugger had been—a schizophrenic.

The man used to sit on the parapet of the bridge over the railway line and talk to himself. Hail, rain, shine, howling gale, he was there. He used to wear a pair of cord trousers that had probably been brown originally but had faded to a sort of no-colour. His shoes were always polished so that they gleamed. He wore a jacket with leather elbow patches but no buttons. His V-neck pullover was a muddy brown and he wore a frayed, check shirt with the top button always fastened, as if there should have been a tie but he'd mislaid it. He had a pair of fingerless woollen gloves and a flat cap that always looked like it was going to fall off the next time the old bloke moved but, somehow never did.

His face was long and always covered in four days of beard, long before the media had heard of designer stubble. His teeth were off-white, almost lemon, like somebody who'd recently given up smoking. Neil never saw him with anything in his mouth except his fingers when it was cold and he was trying to keep them warm. The man's eyes were amazing. The sort of green the sea looked like, far out in the bay in September when the sun was just coming up and the clouds were high and thin. They seemed to sparkle with some secret knowledge, even when he was shouting at himself or at whatever the voices in his mind were saying to him.

All sorts of myths had grown up around the man. If you were a kid, the best was the one about how Mad George, if he was in a good mood, would throw up into his cupped palms, show it to passers-by and then eat it. Neil had never seen the old bloke do that and, as far as he knew, none of his mates had seen it but it was a great story to pass round when you were all sitting in the swings and had nothing better to talk about.

What Neil *did* know and had seen and heard for himself, was the way Mad George held low conversations with somebody nobody else could see. Neil had seen this and heard this often but the only word that really stuck in his mind was the same one that stuck in all the other kids' minds.

Now, sitting in his chair in his office, Neil's incredible memory provided him with an image so detailed, it felt like it could actually be touched—Mad George sitting on the parapet of the bridge that used to span the railway line.

The bridge was still there but it no longer went over the railway line because the line was now the road into the Fender Tunnel and there was no chance of billowing, oily, steamy smoke enveloping you if you sat on the parapet. But in his memory, Neil could see that smoke as it curled up and made Mad George look like he was sitting in a cloud.

Mad George was muttering as Neil walked past him that long ago day. Neil stopped two yards away and looked at the old bloke, waiting for him to say the words he always said loud enough for the kids to hear properly. The old man cocked his head slightly, as if listening. Then he nodded and muttered for another few moments. Another cock of the head, slight nod and Mad George turned his amazing eyes to Neil and raised his eyebrows. His mouth opened slightly in an almost-smile, showing the edges of his almost-lemon teeth. He muttered something that was too low even for Neil to hear but then his voice took on a more normal level. "The Shadow knows," Mad George said and grinned, his eyes sparkling. Then he turned away and went back to his normal muttering.

Neil had smiled and then walked away; thinking he knew what the old bloke had been talking about.

"The old radio programme about The Shadow," Neil said now, a man who hadn't been six for a long, long time.

Yes, that's what Neil had thought the old man had been referring to and that was why Davy mentioning a shadow and Mad George had jangled the bells in Neil's mind. It was probably the same with Davy. Seeing his shadow for the first time out in the open, his mind had made the connection but without letting Davy in on the reason and Davy had provided the shadow with Mad George's features. It was the sort of thing the mind was so good at.

Happy to have worked it out, Neil focused again on Davy's journal. But, still, something nagged at him as he read, something about Mad George. Never mind, he'd deal with it later. After he'd read what Davy had written.

The trouble with wanting to write about when you were kid is knowing where to start. D'you go back to the first thing you remember or what? It's all very well deciding to do this sort of thing but you have to find a way in, don't you?
The thing is, thinking about it now, I really enjoyed being a kid. There were so many things that made being a kid a great thing to be. All the games and the long afternoons in summer and the way Radio Luxembourg faded in an out like conversation heard in a dream. Where the hell do you start?
Well, I suppose the thing that got me thinking about when I was a kid was seeing that poor girl's accident and what it made me think about was Jimmy getting burned and me jumping off the crucible in The Pit. But I've already written about that so maybe I should start with the other jump the accident made me think about. That was an accident, too.

Eddie had an accident jumping off something high. It wasn't long after Jimmy got burned and I had that first, wonderful sensation of being between the sky and the ground. Now I come to think about it, that's the place to start. With the feeling I used to get, still get, before gravity's noticed what I'm doing, when the outward motion's ceased and I'm just lying on the air, floating.
After that jump off the crucible, I wanted that feeling as much as I could get it. That's why I was the first to do a somersault off the diving board in Chamberlain Street Baths.

God, I can still see the looks on Neil's and Frankie's and Eddie's faces when I came up out of the water after doing the somersault. They were staring at me, wide-eyed and wide-mouthed. Then they all started clapping me and whistling.

That moment before the forward roll turned into a somersault and I hit the water didn't last as long as when I jumped off the crucible but it felt almost as good.

That was the last day of the summer holidays and then autumn came and all those great games we played—Japs and Commandos and Jack-shine-a-light in and around the swings. And we played football in the middle of the swings or just sat on the King's Crown and wished we could get the jerker up as high as the teenagers did. They could get it right up to the crossbar and it looked really terrifying and really great at the same time.

But it was the slide that fascinated me that autumn. Everything about it fascinated me in a way it had never done before. The height of it and the angle of the chute and the clanging sound the ladder made when we went charging up it.

Then Eddie's dad got the job in the brake linings factory and Eddie's mum decided to do the house out so Eddie ended up calling to us from his backyard to give him a hand with the mattresses she was throwing out.

We dragged the six mattresses over the fence of Eddie's back garden and onto the grass verge round the swings. Eddie was all sweaty as usual. He wore a sleeveless fairisle jumper, a hand-me-down from one of his five brothers. He wore it day in and day out, winter and summer. And his hair always stuck up, in my Mum's words, like Alfalfa. Neil asked him what he was going to do with the mattresses.

"Thought we could have some fun," Eddie told us all. "Maybe wrestle on them or use them like a trampoline or something. Just have a laugh."

And we did. We wrestled and put them on top of each other and used them like a trampoline and that's probably what gave me the idea.

"If we put them next to the slide," I said very quietly. It was probably because the idea felt so good, I didn't just want to blurt it out, it felt like I was still trying it out in my mind. "If we did that, we could drop onto them from the slide."

After some loud argument about my sanity, we sort of agreed to at least see what they looked like from the top of the slide.

When we were all on the platform, looking over the top of the waist-high cage, the mattresses looked like they'd make a good cushion and they didn't look too far down, either.

We started by hanging off the bottom ledge of the platform and dropping down. The drop was only about fifteen feet and we'd all been dropping from that sort of height since we were about seven or eight. It was Eddie, claiming the right because they were his mattresses, who upped the ante by hanging from the top rail instead of the bottom ledge. By the time the afternoon sky was going from bright to that gorgeous dark lilac colour that always reminds me of Trisha's eyes, the mattresses had lost a lot of their springiness but they still cushioned us pretty well.

I could smell tea-time, sausages and eggs and bacon and chips, when we looked down from the platform for what we all knew would be the last drop for the day. Neil was standing next to me and Willie was coming up the ladder. Eddie and Frankie were straightening the mattresses. I put my hands on the rail and looked down. Then I just stopped moving and stared down.

"Don't, Davy," Neil Judd said to me.

I turned to look at him but he just stood there, looking at me with the same relentless gaze he's got now. I was full of it, full of the idea, the remembered feeling I had from The Pit.

"Don't what, Neil?"

"Don't jump," Neil said simply.

I started to shake my head and then, before I said something to make a liar out of myself, I swung my legs over the rail and sat on the top of the cage. I was waiting for the fear to set in and stop me but there wasn't any. All I felt was the anticipation of the moment when I'd be between the sky and the ground. Then I just pushed off with my hands.

God, it was wonderful. That moment I'd been anticipating wasn't as long as in The Pit but it was longer than doing the somersault in the baths. Then it was all whistling wind and the sound of Eddie and Frankie cheering and Willie yelling that I was an idiot.

I thudded into the middle of the mattresses and there was no jarring like down in The Pit. I bent my knees and flopped over onto my side, just like the parachutists did on the Saturday matinees at The Gaumont. When I stepped onto the asphalt of the swings, I felt like I owned the world.

Frankie called me a gormless gobshite and Eddie told me I was bonkers and then Neil and Willie came down the ladder. Neil said nothing, he just stood there and looked at me. He does that now, just stands or sits there and waits for you to speak, like he already knows what's in your mind.

"Come on, Neil," I said to him. "I knew it'd be all right."

What he said then has stayed with me all these years. Not just what he said but the idea that he was just a ten year old lad when he said it.

"No," Neil told me patiently. "You _believed_ it'd be all right. Knowing and believing isn't the same thing."

Then Frankie slapped me on the back and called me 'Eagle Eliot the flying dickhead' and I had my nickname. They all called me that for the rest of the year. Except Neil. He called me Davy and still does.

We used those mattresses all through that autumn and right into early winter, had some great laughs doing really stupid stuff, the sort of stuff you hardly ever seem to do after you get to about fourteen and realise there are such things as girls.

Anyway, we didn't just use them on the slide. We dragged them all over the swings and, just before the first real fog of the autumn, we used them under The Dead Tree.

God, that's really weird. I used those capital letters without even thinking about it, the way they were capitalised in our minds whenever we talked about it.

We'd been climbing The Dead Tree, up to its creaking top branch, since we were about nine but, like the somersault and the slide, I was the one who broke all the rules and jumped off it instead of just hanging from it and dropping.

Thinking about it now, I think it was that which made Eddie do what he did that Christmas Eve. I know he dropped off the top rail on the slide first but I think it was because that creaking branch was a bit too much, even for Eddie. It was just a bit too possible that the creaking branch would just snap and send him tumbling into the branches of the other trees and do God-knew-what to him.

So he decided to do something that, from his point of view, was just as tough. Eddie found out the hard way, though.

It was Neil who saw that the mattresses weren't lined up straight.

We were all squeezing through the railings from my back garden and Neil saw Eddie on the platform of the slide and he went running across the asphalt.

"'Ang on, Eddie," Neil yelled. "The mattresses are all skewiff!"

But Eddie just grinned and yelled, "Geerronimoooo!" Then he <u>vaulted</u> over the top rail.

Neil was just too late in arriving and Eddie, all control gone with that yell, landed on the edge of the top mattress. I can still hear the crack of his leg and the second crack when his right arm hit the ground, protecting his face from the asphalt. And then his cries were the only sound you could hear and he sounded exactly like Jimmy had sounded in The Pit.

He broke both limbs really badly and he was in traction for a month in the hospital. His dad dragged those mattresses down to the council tip and stood and watched until they were burnt to cinders.
So we didn't have the mattresses to jump onto anymore and we went back to just playing the ordinary winter games we'd always played. Eddie got out of hospital and his left leg was always a bit thinner than his right leg. It's never bothered him much, except on cold days, and he even works on the oil rigs now.

I missed jumping, though. I know that now. That brief moment of being weightless stayed with me and I know I was always looking for it in stuff I did. When the summer came, the last one before we all went to whatever secondary school passing or failing the 11+ sent us to, I found that moment again.

We promised ourselves that, because it was our last summer before secondary school, we'd have a really good one and we did. The weather was great and we spent all day out in the sun.
Most of those days, we spent up in the outdoor pool in Laketon.

I was the first one to swan-dive off the third top board.

The third top board was really high. It must've been about thirty or forty feet above the blue water of the deep end. The two above it were only about ten feet higher and it was the third top board that told you when you were almost a teenager.

Instead of just standing there with your stomach fluttering and a booming sound in your ears whenever you looked down at the rippling water below and then having to look straight ahead, over the top of Lakeside Café at the Fender river so your knees didn't buckle and your legs go rubbery—when you could climb up the stairs and then just jump off the board, you knew you weren't a kid anymore.

We all jumped off it that summer but only me and Neil dived off it.

I did it first and then Neil did it and, like with everything, he did it perfectly. Still, the more I think about it, it's the look he gave me after he'd done it that I remember the most. That and what he said to me the day <u>before</u> I did it.

We'd been up there all day and it was about half three when we were standing on the third top board and looking down at the water or looking at the people in the big amphitheatre of the pool, watching the seagulls darting down and pecking at the bits of food left on seats. It was really hot and the water was really cold and the change when you hit the water was great. Anyway, me and Neil were standing there and I really didn't think I was thinking anything at all until Neil said what he said. Then I realised I'd been thinking about it more or less all day.

"Practise a bit more, Davy," Neil said. "Get it wrong off here and it won't be just a belly-flop. You'll split your bloody stomach open."

I remember just staring at him, getting ready to ask him what the hell he was on about and then I knew what he meant. I just nodded, turned round and went down the rubber-coated stairway to the springboard at the poolside. I practised swan-dives for the rest of the time we were there.
I was good at diving. I always kept my arms by the side of my head to protect my face when I entered the water, just like we'd been taught. Neil was the best athlete, the fastest runner, king of the football pitch, but I was the best swimmer. That's probably the reason I still love it.
The next day, we met in the swings and worked out that if we all pooled our money and walked the three miles to Laketon Pool, we had enough to pay for all of us to get in. We mucked about on the water-slides for about half an hour and then I went to the boards.
I can still see that sky, how perfectly clear it was, the soft blue of it and how the river, easily seen over the top of the pool's wall from the height of the board, looked so high and slow.
Then I looked down at the water.

There was nobody in the water immediately below the boards and there was hardly a ripple. The others were standing by the springboard, looking up at me. They looked very small. I nodded once and then balanced on the edge of the board, tensing my toes and lifting my arms up and out. I took a big breath and then dived.

It was—oh, like being the only person in the world.

It felt like I was just lying flat on the air for ages, seeing the slow, high river and one seagull doing what I was doing, just floating above it all. Magic. Then I was diving, heading down to the water and I brought my arms in and protected my head and went into the water without making much of a splash at all, body, arms and legs all in a line.

I climbed out and they all gave me a clap and then Neil went up and did it. When he got out, he looked at me and nodded and then we all went back to mucking about, just a little gang of pre-teenagers having a great summer holiday.

I've often wondered what Neil thought when he gave me that look and that nod. Maybe I'll ask him. He'll remember exactly because he remembers everything.

Neil Judd.

We were always together, bezzie mates, like we used to say. And he's still one of my bezzie mates. God, the things we used to get up to. It was Neil who was with me and Frankie and Eddie when we hawked the wood for my Dad's aviary.

God, yeah, I haven't thought about that for years. Maybe even since we did it. It's funny, remembering it now, I remember thinking I saw a shadow that night.
Yeah. Bloody hell, it's amazing how long your memory is. I know it must be because of Neil and his memory but until now, I think I thought it was just that Neil's was a one-off.
Those budgies. My Dad loved those budgies. I think he started keeping them and breeding them in the hopes of selling them and making a few bob but they ended up just as pets and their high-pitched twitters and squeaks were part of my childhood.
I remember him building the aviary for them out of all the scrap wood he could scrounge from work but it was never big enough for him. He used to sit in his chair, the crossword in the paper done, his pipe sending up those little blue smoke tendrils, talking about how having a bigger aviary would be the best thing. He thought he was talking to my Mum and she used to nod and mumble in the right places, the knitting needles clicking as she knitted me another jumper but I'm pretty sure she was just letting him talk, have his little dream. That's probably what made me think of getting the wood for him.
When they started to rip out the insides of the houses further up the street, I remember watching the families moving their furniture out and moving to the temporary accommodation and smiling to myself and thinking I could get my Dad some decent wood.

It was the October after I swan-dived off the board in Laketon Pool when we did it. Me and Neil and Frankie and Eddie waited till Coronation Street was on the telly so there'd be no adults out and about and then we got into the house over the back fence. When Paul Horne told me which house I could rent off him after I left Trisha, I remember smiling because it's the house we got the wood from. Life's funny like that, I suppose.

So there we were, with our torches and motley collection of tools. Me and Neil went upstairs and Frankie and Eddie stayed downstairs. We knew the place was going to be completely gutted because that's what they'd done to the other houses. We didn't have to worry about taking stuff the families would need when they moved back in.

Back then, the houses in Oil Street all had a narrow wardrobe fitted into the alcove in the back bedroom and that's where me and Neil were going. Frankie and Eddie were in the back kitchen, trying to get the big cupboard out from by the sink.

I nearly killed myself that night and frightened the life out of Eddie. God, it was funny.

I was in front of Neil, my torch pointed up at the landing when we climbed the stairs. Then, when we got to the landing, Neil told me to do the back bedroom and he'd do the front. So I lifted my torch to make sure the door was open and, as it was, I walked into the room.

I was following the line of my torch beam as it pointed to the alcove where the wardrobe was.

The workmen had ripped the floorboards up and I fell right between the joists.
I went straight down, heading for the tiles of the back kitchen.
Eddie was bending down by the cupboard, heard me yell, looked up and pointed his torch. He saw something dropping through what he thought was a solid ceiling, screaming like a banshee.
Eddie dropped his torch and legged it right out of the kitchen and right out of the garden and into the street, trying very hard not to scream for his mother as he went.
I landed on the tiles and felt the jarring all the way up to my neck. I sat there for a minute, feeling the adrenaline rampaging through me, making it hard to breathe, hearing my heart very loud in my ears and feeling it in my throat. I was sure I must've broken both legs and saw myself in traction like Eddie had been.
Then Neil came charging down the stairs and into the kitchen. He had his torch in his mouth like some commando and his fists were bunched, ready to fight whatever it was that had made the horrible screeching noise and scared the piss out of Eddie. Typical Neil, ready to thump anybody who was looking for it.

"Jesus, Davy," he said after taking the torch out of his mouth. "How did you get here?"
I pointed up and he shone his torch at the empty ceiling and shook his head.

"You okay?"

"Yeah," I told him and got up gingerly. My legs didn't collapse and there wasn't even much pain. "Yeah, okay."

"I suppose Eddie thought you were a ghost and took off?"

I nodded as Frankie came in.

"Shit," Frankie said. "We better go and find him before he gets all the kids in The Rows in here to have a look at the ghost."

When they'd left, I went back upstairs to finish off in the bedroom. I was very careful this time, looking at the floor all the way. I was bloody amazed when I saw my little torch just lying on a joist. I picked it up and then stepped on the joists until I reached the narrow wardrobe. I had one of my Dad's old screwdrivers and started undoing the screws on the hinges. I balanced the torch on the fender of the fireplace all the houses had in the back bedrooms and just got on with it.

When I'd got the first hinge off, I started to wonder what was keeping the others and then I sensed movement to my left. My heart lurched back into my throat and, in my mind, I heard Neil talking about ghosts.

I snatched the torch off the fender and shone it in the corner to my left. There was nothing there and I shook my head. I decided it must've been a rat, out on some foraging expedition from the mills. That was okay, rats were pretty shy and I didn't intend bothering it. It'd go away. I turned back to the wardrobe.

At first, I thought the sound was debris settling in the house after the minor demolition that had been going on all week. That's what it sounded like so I didn't take much notice. Then there was more movement to my left and the sound got louder. I didn't snatch my torch up this time and I didn't whirl round to look. I sort of stroked the knurled aluminium handle of the torch and rolled it gently onto the joist so it was pointed at the corner. I just eased my head round and looked at where the beam lit up the wall.

The room was half-lit by moonlight through the window and shadows flitted all over the walls, cast by the branches of the tree in the garden next door. My torch lit up a patch of wall where the striped wallpaper was all torn, right down to the plaster and I could see some of the lath behind it. There shouldn't have been any shadow there at all; there wasn't anything between the torch and the wall. But there was a shadow, right in the middle of the cone of light from my torch. It was as tall as me if I'd been standing up and as wide. It had no features or anything, it was just a shadow.

A shadow where no shadow should have been.

I sat there staring at this impossibility and the noise increased and I was certain it was coming from the shadow. It was a hissing sound.

Yeah, I can remember it perfectly. It sounded like gas escaping from a pipe.

Bloody hell. I'm not sure I envy Neil this sort of thing, being able to remember even the spooky stuff. But that's what it sounded like and I remember it felt like all the hairs on my body stood up straight and I felt really, really scared. For a moment, all I wanted to do was scream and jump up, run away, anything so long as I could get out of the that room and stop being scared by a shadow that shouldn't have been there.

And I could feel myself leaning forward, trying to hear the hissing sound better because I was sure it was trying to be a proper sound, like a voice. If Neil hadn't called up, telling me they were back, I'd've probably just leaned out too far and toppled through the gaps in the joist again. Only this time it would've been head first and I'd've broken my legs or neck for real on the kitchen tiles.

And the shadow faded away.

It didn't go pop or disappear with a puff of smoke, it just faded away. The way shadows do when light moves across them. And the noise stopped and then Neil was in the room, bending down to help me get the wardrobe out.

I didn't mention any of that to the others. Well, you didn't when you were a kid, trying to be tough and hard. The last thing you needed was all your mates taking the piss out of you because you told them something spooky had happened in an empty house at night. Sissy, we called it. Besides, I was there to get wood for my Dad and that's what we did.

His face when he saw it piled up in our garden the next morning was great. I think he wanted to tell me off for taking it but I could tell that he was already working out how to build the aviary, which piece of

wood he'd use for the door and which piece for the sides and the floor. He just looked at me and tried not to grin and then ruffled my hair.
We started building it that afternoon and he let me use his good tools and showed me how to saw a straight line and plane just enough to make things fit.
I can remember that afternoon without any effort at all. It'll stay with me all my life. It was the day my Dad talked to me as if I was nearly grown up for the first time.

It's tomorrow now. Well, the day after I wrote all that. Thinking about my Dad and helping him with the aviary was a bit too much. I started to think about what it was like after he died. What I was like. God, what a bloody awful time that was.
I'm tempted to write more about the stuff we did when I was a kid so I don't have to think about it but, like Neil says, the mind's a funny thing. It thinks about what it wants to think about, even when you try to think about other stuff. I know what he means now. I wanted to think and write about being a kid some more but I keep seeing my Dad, laid out in the front room after the doctor had been and signed the death certificate.
Anyway, when I started this, I said it might help me write things out of myself and the only way to do that is to be honest. You can't afford to be anything else when you write about yourself for yourself. Lying to yourself only makes things worse.

Dislocation.

Even written down, it looks sort of ominous to me. I suppose it's because it's the word Neil used when I told him how I'd been after my Dad died. When he said it, it summed up perfectly the way I'd felt and it sounded, oh, I don't know, all echoey and boomy in my mind.
Which was about the way I'd felt after my Dad died.
When I had a talk with Neil, not long after I left Trisha, I told him about how it felt like I was the wrong person in the wrong place. It felt like I was suddenly alone in a strange place.

When I stood in the front room of my parents' house, after I'd seen my Mum and left Trisha with her, I looked around the room and it didn't seem to be the same room I'd always seen. I looked at the bookshelves he'd built for himself, and the cabinet he'd built for my Mum that she'd filled with all his darts trophies instead of the china she'd said she wanted it for, and they just didn't look like things I knew. I ran my hands over the coffee table he'd made using some of the wood from my Nan's old upright piano and I cried and the room just didn't look the room I known.
It was only when I'd said goodbye to him and kissed his forehead that the room went back to being the room I remembered.

Still, that feeling of dislocation stayed with me and it must have been that which gave me all those sleepless nights after the funeral.

And dislocated is exactly how I felt when I woke up at three in the morning when all I could do was just lie there, wide awake, staring at the ceiling and waiting for first light to creep into the room.

After about a fortnight, I just got up and started my day four hours early instead of lying there. It didn't seem to affect me at work and I didn't feel tired and I didn't think I was any different at home. Trisha soon put paid to that idea, though. The night when she came down half an hour after I'd got up, we had the nearest thing to a row we'd had in years. She told me it was worrying the life out of Andrew and her, I was like a different person, I should do something, see somebody about it.

Thinking about that now, it seems funny that she said that to me. Not long after, not long at all, I said the same thing to her about what she was going through with the change and she more or less told me to mind my own business.

Shit.

There's that mind-thing again. I was writing about my Dad and now I'm thinking about Trisha and me splitting up. Then again, maybe it's not so funny. The feeling I had when I moved back to Oil Street was almost exactly the same as how I felt after my Dad died. Come to think about it, it probably started the night I found about Trisha.

I was sitting in the living room, the new light fitting looking all sparkly in the ceiling, drinking a cold cup of tea and trying not to think about anything, never mind what I was pretty sure Trisha was doing.

She came in and was surprised to find me still up. When she started going to her girls'-night-in after Christmas, it was just on Thursdays then, she never got home till after midnight and I'd be in bed. When she started going on a Tuesday, too, she was getting in the same time and I'd be in bed. So when she saw me still up, she was surprised.

When she opened the living room door, her face was glowing and her lovely eyes were sparkling even more than the light fitting which I'd nearly given myself a hernia putting up. Then she saw me and her face sort of—it was like it closed in on itself. And her eyes went from sparkly to narrow and questioning.

Seeing it happen like that, so quickly and, I'm sure, unconsciously on Trisha's part, it really came home to me that I was right in what I'd been thinking ever since I phoned and found out there hadn't been a girls'-night-in on a Tuesday. Ever.

"Dave?" Trisha said slowly, softly. "Is everything okay?"

I nodded and stared into my half-empty cup. Then I told her that her mother had rung to tell her that her only cousin, Sheila, was coming home from Australia for a month's holiday.

The life flooded back into Trisha's face and she squealed like a kid.

When I told her that I'd rung her at Barbara's to tell her but Barbara said she wasn't there, Trisha sat down on the arm of the couch and looked at the floor.

"D'you love him?" I asked and then it all got bad and then worse and I ended up telling her that it was probably best if I left.

I left the next day. I carried my workchests out and three black plastic bags full of clothes and the one suitcase I owned. It was the one I'd bought for the holiday in Spain when I met Trisha. I went to work and phoned my Mum and asked her if I could stay that night at her house and, because it's what mothers do, she said fine.
I spent the rest of the day wondering where I was going to live. I didn't want to live with my Mum because it would have been too easy. Just too simple to stay and become part of another couple, like I'd been for the last nineteen years or so.
I looked through the local newspapers and saw all sorts of houses and flats but I knew there was bound to be a time-lag between deciding on one and moving in and the temptation to stay at my Mum's would have been too great. Then inspiration struck when I saw the advert for Horne and Frost Estates. Paul Horne and Derek Frost are mates of mine from Somerville Grammar and they own a big estate agents in town. I rang Paul and asked him if he had anything I could move into right away. Like first thing in the morning.

"Er," Paul said and there was a long pause while he worked out why I was asking. Then, good mate that he is, he said, "To be honest, Davy, the only thing I've got right now is down in The Rows. In Oil Street."

A funny feeling hit me in the stomach, like butterflies only it spread into my head, too.

"I don't suppose you own my old house?" I asked him.

"No, mate. Number twelve it is. It's clean but it hasn't been lived in much so it's empty and a bit— musty I suppose the word is."

I told him it would be fine and arranged to pick the keys up on my way home from work that night.

My Mum asked what was up that night and I told her and she left it at that, never took sides or anything and she didn't object when I told her I'd be moving into 12 Oil Street the next day. I wasn't surprised.

Between my Dad dying and the cremation, I was sure my Mum was going to curl up and die herself. Then, at the wake, I watched her talking with all his old mates and she seemed to grow by the minute. I watched her and was glad. It was almost as if she listened to all the good memories they had of her husband and started remembering her own and then decided to go on living as a sort of memorial to my Dad.

She joined a Dinner Club at the local old peoples' home and goes on trips with them about once a month and she has her dinner there every Wednesday and she lives her life to the full. She seemed, oh, sort of lighter, like the weight of my Dad's death had been lifted and she could walk again.

I didn't want to put any weight on her by staying at her house. She wouldn't have said anything, she'd just have felt obliged to stay with me while I was there and not to do the things she was doing, the things that were keeping her alive.

So, the next day, I took my suitcase and workchests and plastic bags to 12 Oil Street and moved in. I remember thinking, probably because I still think it, that five plastic bags wasn't much to show for a lifetime and that moving into a house just fifty yards from where I was born and brought up wasn't far to have travelled in that lifetime.

Those first couple of weeks were strange. I spent the days at work, behind my desk, sifting through work orders and budgets and wishing I was back as a simple spark again. In between the paperwork, I just sort of sat in my office and stared out of the window, part of me thinking about when I was a kid and the rest of me thinking about how much stuff you needed to furnish a house and how I seemed to be eating nothing but tinned food and chips. Eventually, I got the shopping sorted and knocked a bloody big hole in my building society account by buying a cottage suite and a bed, a cooker and kettle and getting the phone put in and all the rest of it. The worst was having to fend off curiosity masquerading as concern at work when they all found out I'd changed my address and phone number.

But, like my Mum says, life goes on and, like my Dad said, we get on with it.
I told myself that's what I had to do but it was hard. In fact, I think I came close to just cracking up completely.
For a fortnight after moving in, it felt like I was going round the bend.
Up the wall.
Doolally.
Shit!
The word is <u>insane</u>.

THREE

Davy's handwriting ended and the page was blank to the bottom. Neil looked up from the book. The office was dimmer now and he reached across to the anglepoise lamp. As he reached for it, he heard the high-pitched squeal of a child drifting up from the garden below. He swivelled his chair and looked out of the window.

The Callaghan twins, Adam and Kate, were playing Cowboys and Indians, hiding behind the shed and in the small bushes. Kate was creeping round the shed now, her long, wavy blonde hair tied in a ponytail that she thought made her look like an Indian brave.

Neil smiled. The four year olds had been in Blackhay for a month and were just about getting used to it. Their mother had had a breakdown when her husband had disappeared without trace. It had taken a while for the twins to settle, Kate especially but, finally, they'd done it and now seemed to be managing to be kids again. They still asked every day about their mother but, once the question was answered, they didn't sit in the big telly room and brood like they had done at first.

And Kate didn't spend so much time talking to her invisible friend.

It was the only thing about them that went against the perceived and proven truths about twins; Kate talked to her invisible friend when she was thinking about her mother, not to her brother. It was almost as if Adam was too close to be able to help Kate through whatever it was she talked to her 'friend' about. Probably, Adam couldn't help because he had the same feelings, the same problems and worries and no answers. Neil was almost positive that Kate talked to her 'friend' and then offered whatever advice she was given to Adam.

Neil turned from the window, a thoughtful look on his face, his grey eyes looking at an internal landscape where Davy Eliot lived alone in 12 Oil Street and felt like he was going mad.

Was the shadow Davy's invisible friend? Given vague shape?

Why not? Being alone after nearly twenty years of marriage was a huge change in a life and dislocation was a natural state to be in afterwards. Moving house was traumatic enough when everything else was right but after leaving your adulterous wife, moving would be like being cast out into a strange world that you knew nothing of and which knew nothing of you.

Neil had the very strong feeling that, a little further on, Davy was going to write about how the shadow he saw in 12 Oil Street was actually something he liked having because it helped him convince himself he wasn't going round the twist.

Still, even if the journal confirmed that hypothesis, Davy didn't feel that way anymore; not according to the letter he'd written Neil and sent with the journal.

Why? At what point did the shadow stop being something that helped Davy survive the enormous changes in his life and start being something that scared him?

And there was still something nagging Neil about the shadow and the fact that it appeared to Davy in Oil Street first. Not just when he moved into 12 Oil Street, but when he was a kid. Oh, there was a certain corny, almost gothic symmetry in the fact they had hawked the wood from the house Davy was living in now but Neil felt there was something more. And why did he keep seeing Mad George sitting on the parapet of the bridge over the old railway line?

He scrolled through his memory again but there was nothing there. That meant that Neil didn't know what it was because he hadn't seen or heard about it; once he saw or heard anything, it was embedded in his memory like the die-cast on a piece of steel.

"But there's something," Neil told himself quietly.

He was tempted to just sit there in the fading light of the October afternoon and keep looking until he found whatever it was that was nagging at him.

But when he looked at the open journal, at Davy's handwriting, at the perfectly aligned left and right margins he'd produced automatically, he was tempted to turn to the last written page and find out when and how the shadow had changed from benevolent to malevolent.

He shook his head. "I need to read this. All if it."

Yes, he did. Whatever was nagging at him would have to wait. The important thing was finding out when the shadow stopped being friendly and to do that properly, he would have to read all of this book; when Martin had more to ask, Neil would need to know everything.

Those first three weeks after I moved into Oil Street were terrible. I was going through the motions and knew it but couldn't change. It was the shadow that made me change, made me realise that I was still alive and had a life to live.

I know how daft that sounds but it doesn't matter since I'm the only one likely to read this. And it's true. Neil would probably say it was my subconscious or unconscious, I've never known the difference.

Anyway, I think he'd probably say the shadow gave me something other than the air to talk to and that it was the talking that helped me get through those terrible first weeks of being on my own. He'd be right, too but Neil himself helped me as well.

Still, I never told him about the shadow, did I? I wonder why? Probably some holdover from being that tough, hard-as-nails kid who would never be sissy enough to talk about spooky stuff that bothered him.

It's no good trying to gloss over those first weeks on my own. Dead right. If I do, I'm likely to end up the way I was then.

So...big breath, Davy.

After the accident on the bungee jump, knowing that there won't be any jumps for me to use, I can see myself ending up half way round the twist if I don't keep writing this. If I don't write about how I was and how I got over it. I did it then and I'm going to have to do it now and if it means the shadow stays with me, sod it, I'll have it. Better that than turning into the local loony and having the mothers dragging their kids away from me.

That's what they did and, really, it's why I wrote about being a kid and the stuff we got up to.
That was the problem when I first moved back to Oil Street—I couldn't stand being stuck in the house with nothing to do but think.
The days, especially the weekends just stretched out in front of me like one of those roads in the American Midwest or somewhere. So I went out of the house and wandered round The Rows.
And I can see me doing that again because I can't go bungee jumping anymore. And the days will be longer now that it's summer. If I write about being a kid or just write what's on my mind, then I won't be out in the streets, scaring the mothers of the kids.
I can keep it in the house.

Those first three weeks, I felt out of place, dislocated like Neil said later. I decided the best thing to do was go out and, I dunno, find a place for myself where I lived.
So I went round The Rows and it was strange.
The place still looks like it always looked when I lived here as a kid but it <u>felt</u> different. Even Oil Street, where I lived till I was turned eighteen, felt different.
It's still the road that bends round the swings in an ellipse and then snakes through the centre of The Rows, like a riverbed. The water tower is still there at the half-way point where the row of garages sort of splits the road in two—the shops begin where the garages end.

Oil Street looks the same but the houses look different. Most of it's because of the renovations that were done the year before last, renovations I helped do.

They've got double-glazed windows now instead of the old sash ones. The roofs are tiled now instead of slates and most of the houses have got the satellite dishes on the outside walls. Still, that shouldn't have made it feel all that different. The postage stamp gardens at the front are still there and the back gates are still in the same place, alongside the sides of the houses, in the middle of the high board fences. And the railings in the back garden all still have the gap between them so the kids can squeeze through and onto the grass verge of the swings.

So why did it feel so different when I first moved back in?

Because I was different.

I wasn't a man who lived five miles away with his wife in a four bedroomed semi with a garage. And I didn't know what else I was if I wasn't that man.

I spent the weekends walking round The Rows, looking at the old places I knew so well when I was kid and ended up thinking about when I was a kid. There was nothing subconscious or unconscious in this; I was doing it deliberately, hoping that it would make me understand who, what I was now. All that happened was that I got lost in remembering when I was a kid and I ended up just standing and staring. At the water tower or the shops on Shelley Row or the place where the brake linings factory used to be or the new factory they've built on The Pit.

Mostly, I stood on the grass verge of the swings and looked at the equipment and the kids who were playing on it. Mind you, the equipment <u>has</u> changed in Oil Street swings.

The old swings, <u>my</u> swings, had the King's Crown roundabout and the Witch's Hat roundabout and the Jerker and two sets of swings, one for big little kids and one for the small ones. The ground everywhere was asphalt and there was nothing between the top gate and the bottom gate but more asphalt.

Now, the Jerker's gone and the two roundabouts have gone. There are still two sets of swings but one's made of what look like half-tyres and the other's just a lot of chains and one slat of green-painted wood. There is still one roundabout but it's only small and there's nothing like the narrowing bars meeting at a point above the seats like the Witch's Hat, nothing to climb up while you're waiting to be big enough, to be a teenager and swing the Jerker up to the crossbar. And, underneath the swings and the small roundabout, they've put down that safety stuff, that rubberised, cushioned matting. And there's a goal-sized wall either end of the swings now. When we were kids, our goal posts were coats and jumpers and a shot over the bar was adjudged by acclamation.

That's more or less what I was thinking while I stood on the grass verge the third Friday night after I'd moved back to Oil Street and then I looked across and saw that the slide was still there.

Is it me or is that illogical? I mean, they take down the Jerker and the two big roundabouts and put the soft stuff under everything for safety reasons but they leave the slide.

I think I must've said that out loud and that's when I noticed the funny look I was getting from the young woman who was pushing a boy of about five in the tyre-swing. I smiled at her which was <u>not</u> the right thing to do because she took the poor kid out of the swing and took him into a house on the opposite side of the swings, looking back at me over her shoulder. That sounds like I knew I was acting a bit odd then but the truth is, I didn't know it at all. I was still more interested in the fact that the slide was still there.

I went into the house and had something to eat and watched the telly but I was thinking about the slide. I went to bed and woke up on the Saturday morning and found I'd decided, apparently in my sleep, to take a tour of the local kids' playgrounds to see if they had slides.

I can write that and it sounds exactly like it was—an odd thing for a bloke well-past forty to do. But <u>then</u>, it never struck me as odd at all. It just seemed like a natural thing to do, to find out if the safety-conscious minds of Those In Charge thought slides were still an acceptable feature of a kids' playground.

Oh boy, you really were in a bad way, Davy.

Yeah, I know that now and it's why I'm writing this diary or journal or whatever it is.

I DO NOT WANT TO GET LIKE THAT AGAIN.

I did a tour of Seapool's Childrens' Playgrounds. That's what they're called now but when I was a kid, they were always The Swings and, in my grown-up mind they still are.

There's still one on the little patch of grass the council persist in calling Byron Park. There's a new one not far from the ferry, just behind the block of flats. There are still two in Seapool Park by the cemetery, The Big Swings and the little swings. I went round them all and stood off to one side and looked them over.

I didn't do it all in one day. I did it over the next two weekends. I did it so I'd have something to do instead of sitting in 12 Oil Street and brooding. I went to all The Swings I could find and did the same thing in all of them—I counted the rides and checked the ground beneath them and, with the swings that had been swings when I was a kid, I remembered what I did on the old swings. I remembered and then I commented on the obvious but strange fact that only Oil Street Swings still had a slide that was worth the name.

There's a slide in all of The Swings but none of them is really a slide. Play-chutes are what they are, more or less the same as the heavy plastic ones you can buy in toy shops for your back garden. They're not slides like the one in Oil Street. The chutes are about five and a half feet off the ground and the angle of the chute is shallow.

None of them come close to being the twenty-odd-foot monster of Oil Street with its shiny metal chute coming down steeply from the wooden platform.

Even writing it down, I can almost sense the slight contempt I feel for the new slides and it was certainly there in my mind when I was checking out The Swings during that horrible time when I first moved back here.

The trouble was it didn't <u>stay</u> in my mind.

I knew I was muttering to myself about it, about why They seemed to think the kids of Oil Street were less susceptible to broken bones than the rest of the kids in the town. That didn't bother me; I think I'd always known I'd end up talking to myself at least some of the time and talking about the slide and kids seemed a lot better than talking to myself about Trisha and all that.

It took a fortnight before I found out I'd been talking out loud elsewhere than 12 Oil Street. I'd been talking out loud while I stood to one side and looked at The Swings I was checking out.

I suppose I could've got away with it if I'd only been talking about the slide; I could've said I was so angry at the danger kids were put in or something.

I wasn't just talking about the slide, though. I was remembering out loud about being a kid and that's what scared the mothers.

And I don't blame them one little bit. I'm bloody sure Trisha would've been the same if there'd been somebody hanging round where Andrew played when he was a kid.

When the young mother yelled at me to bugger off in Byron Park and then nearly squeezed the life out

of her little girl as she dragged her off the see-saw and away from me, I could only stand there, stunned. As soon as I heard her shout, I knew what I'd been doing and I cringed. I nearly followed her to tell her I could never harm any child, I had a boy of my own and I'd spoiled him rotten when he was little.
God, the thought that anybody could think I'd harm a child was awful.
When Andrew was a baby, even when he'd grown up a bit, I still got those horrible flashes all parents get. I'd be sitting in my office or at home and suddenly have a terrible vivid vision of him getting knocked over outside the house or school. Or I'd see him lying in a hospital bed, all tubes and monitors and the doctor shaking his head. Worst of all, I once saw the coffin being slid along the runners at the crematorium, the purple curtain hissing along its track as it hid the moving coffin.
Jesus, just writing about it now gives me the heebie-jeebies.
I wanted to run after the young mother and tell her all that but I knew it would only make matters worse; she was worried but she had nothing specific to use to get the police. If I ran after her, that'd be all took to bring the bobbies in and the last thing I needed was to end up at the cop-shop, trying to explain. So I cringed and slunk away like the loony she thought I was.
I got home and told myself that was it, I'd just spend the rest of my life getting up and going to work and coming straight home and staying in the house until it was time to go to work again.

The shadow appeared the next day and, like I said, it saved me from going round the twist and it helped me get out in the real world again.

I was standing in the kitchen, stirring my tea and watching the kids playing on the swings. I was still thinking about how I used to do the same things when I was a kid but the smile on my face felt more sad than anything else. Oh shit, the truth is I was almost ready to cry and I didn't really want to stand in the narrow back kitchen of 12 Oil Street and cry so I went upstairs into the back bedroom.
I'd put my workchests in the back bedroom until I decided what to do with them and, rather than cry for old times, I thought I'd sort through the chests and see if there was anything I could get rid of, like broken saw blades or empty connector packets. The trouble is, the back bedroom looks out on the swings and I could still hear the kids laughing and shouting and I ended up looking at them through the window instead of sorting out my workchests. And the smile was back on my face and I could feel that lump-in-the-throat feeling and my eyes started to get hot in the corners. All I could think of was that if I was back home, with Trisha, I wouldn't be able to see the kids or hear them and I wouldn't think about when I was a kid and I wouldn't be the sort of bloke who made young mothers scared for their kids. When the first tear crept into the corners of my eyes, I told myself to stop it and forced myself to turn away from the window.

The shadow was just there. In the corner of the room where the wardrobe used to be before me and Neil took it out all those years ago. I didn't jump or anything. I didn't feel scared at all. I suppose I just decided it was a shadow thrown by the big tree in next door's garden. It was only later that I realised the sun was in wrong place for that.

Oh sod it, tell the truth and shame the devil. That's what my Nan used to say. The truth is I actually liked the idea that the shadow was there. I know it sounds daft but I can afford to sound daft when I'm the only one who's going to read this. Even seeing it for the first time then, I knew I'd end up talking to it. Thinking about it now, I suppose it was because I knew, being alone and, let's face it, lonely, I'd end up talking to myself. Having the shadow there meant I'd talk to it instead of just talking out loud. Probably it was so I could tell myself I wasn't going crackers by talking to myself. What d'you mean? I could ask, how can I be talking to myself when the shadow's there, listening to me?

Anyway, I looked at it and then bent down to sort through the workchests, thinking about being a kid and Trisha and my Dad. Not in any specific way, just the way we think about all sorts of stuff when our hands our doing something. When I picked up the test lamp, though, I began to think about Trisha particularly because the last time I'd used the lamp was when I put the new light fitting in. I heard again the way she went ballistic when I told her about the bungee jumping and saw again the way her face closed in on itself when she realised I knew.

And I started talking to myself about it, going through the conversation we had and asking questions of myself, of the shadow.

God knows how long I was on my knees doing that, just holding the test lamp in my hands and asking the shadow why it had happened, what did I do now, wouldn't it better if I rang her and asked her if I could come home.

It didn't seem such a daft idea, not really. Since I'd left, Trisha hadn't phoned me or anything and I'd been expecting her to. I'd really been expecting her to ring me and tell me she wanted a divorce. But she hadn't and I suppose I'd started wondering if maybe she'd changed her mind about everything.

<u>pride?</u>

That's what made me stop staring at the test lamp and asking questions. That word just seemed to pop into my mind. And I had to stop and really give it some thought.

Was it pride that made me move out, move into this rented house? Pride and jealousy? Yeah, of course it was but there was also the pain I felt, the hurt. I'm pretty sure, even now, that the idea of another bloke having sex with my wife wasn't the huge thing I'd been expecting it to be. Oh, it was there but, the more I'd thought about it, the more I thought it was the pain I felt that she'd cut me out of her life.

<u>if that's the case, maybe going back isn't such a good idea</u>

And I couldn't argue with that, either. After what Trisha had said and then done and then said to me about why she did it, it didn't seem likely she'd change her mind. But all that left me was living this sort of half-life. All I had was this dislocation, this feeling that the world was going on without me while I was alone and lonely in this rented house.

<u>go out with Frankie and Eddie like they've been wanting you</u>

I went downstairs to the living room. I picked up the phone and dialled Frankie at the little builders' merchants' yard he owns in Laketon. Frankie had been at me for the last fortnight to go out with him and Eddie for a drink. Just one night a week, just to get me out of the bloody house. I'd put him off with one piss-poor excuse after another and he'd let it go. I rang him that late Saturday morning and asked him when he fancied going out for that drink.

We ended up going out every Wednesday night. I swim for an hour in the leisure centre pool while Eddie and Frankie play squash. Then we meet up in the little bar and have a couple of pints of shandy and talk about all the important stuff blokes talk about; football, the weather, cars, our houses. All the usual stuff. That first time, of course, we talked about me and Trisha and what had happened and it was because we did, I ended up having a talk with Neil.

"It was Neil who sorted me out," Frankie told me that first night. "He saved me from getting killed one tea-time down in The Five Bars. He was out looking for one of the kids from where he works and I was in there. I'd been there for about half an hour when this gobshite bumped into me and knocked half my pint all over the place. It felt deliberate and I told him to watch himself. He stared at me for a minute and then walked off. Next thing I know, somebody's grabbed me from behind and swung me away from the bar and this bloke, a lad really, who'd knocked my ale over, hit me in the face. I just blew. I'd been doing that a lot since Jean walked out. I had a really short temper over everything. Anyway, I back-headed the lad holding me and butted the lad who hit me and then another lad smashed a bottle on the bar. I looked at him and the bottle and thought, aye aye, I'm dead here. Then this lad's on the deck and the other two are getting the shit beaten out of them. When it was all over, there's Neil looking at me like he's seen a ghost."

Eddie laughed and shook his head. "He didn't know it was you, did he?"

"No," Frankie said. "He just saw one bloke against three and decided to even up the odds. Anyway, my nose was pouring blood and it felt like it was broken and, typical Neil, he drove me to the hospital and waited for me to drive me back to pick up my van. He talked to me and asked me what the hell I was doing getting into fights at my age. And, like always, I ended up telling him."

Me and Eddie nodded, knowing what he meant; Neil's always been like that I'm glad to say.

"The thing was, I felt like I was all my on my own, me against the world. It wasn't the first time I'd got into a fight over nothing. Neil said it sounded like I wanted to hit Jean but, because I couldn't, I ended up trying to hit everything else. If I stopped thinking about how bad I felt, stopped feeling like a kid throwing a tantrum in other words, I'd probably stop acting like one. Jean was gone, living with another bloke, she was happy and wasn't likely to come back so hadn't I better get used to it? He was right and I did and I haven't had a fight since. You should have a talk with Neil," Frankie said and finished his pint.

I thought about it all the next week at work and I'd just made up my mind to talk to Neil on Friday night, when he rang me at work. That's so like Neil. It's almost as if he's psychic. He asked me if I fancied going round to his house and talk. Just like that. No apologies, no beating round the bush. I said fine. Then he made me laugh by asking me if I wanted him to get some Mackies and cider in.

It was what we bought when we were about thirteen. Eddie's house was empty for the evening and we decided we'd have a bit of a party. I was the tallest and got elected to go to the offie and buy the ale. I was that nervous, I asked for the first thing I saw on the shelves—Mackies stout and Bulmers cider. It was truly awful but we drank it all because we were thirteen and trying to be grown up. Till Neil mentioned it that Friday, I'd forgotten all about it.

So I went round and I talked and Neil listened. I didn't tell him about the shadow or the young mothers and me muttering out loud in the local swings but I think he probably guesses it, or at least the general gist. That's when he used that word, <u>dislocated</u> and summed it all up for me. Then he told me a lot of it was probably fear, that I'd spent so long being part of a couple, the thought of being on my own scared the hell out of me. More than that, the fact I'd waited so long to go out with Frankie and Eddie just showed how worried I was that I wouldn't be able to cope with being single again.

Out, swimming in all that shit again like when we were teenagers was how Neil put it. He was dead right, too.

Still, I did go out and started to enjoy it. Then the clocks went forward and I began to look forward to the summer because I knew the bungee jumps would start again and I'd have something else to fill my life, stop me from brooding about how much empty time I had on my hands.

Bloody hell, I'm tired. This writing lark knackers you. I'd better get used to it though. I definitely don't want to end up like I was after moving back to Oil Street and that's what'll happen without something to take the place of bungee jumping.

Maybe that's what I'll write about tomorrow. How I found out about it and how I ended up doing it and what it felt like.

Yeah, good idea Davy.

It's next Saturday now. Well, the Saturday after I wrote all that. I know I was going to write about the bungee jumping and I will but—I've got to get this down because it feels so good. Christ, I feel like a fifteen year old again. All the same flutters in my stomach and panic at the thought that it won't

work, she won't like me, she'll walk out half-way through the date.
Oh sod it spit it out Davy
Last night, I met a woman and spent all night dancing and talking to her and tonight we're going out for a meal.
Her name's Anne Jordan and she's got really sparkly hazel eyes and this way of smiling that makes them sparkle more.
Oh, bugger this for a game of darts. I'm leaving it there in case I jinx it or something.
If it goes all right, I'll probably spend pages on it and that'll be okay. Just not now. It feels too good to be true and I don't want to blow it.

FOUR

The rest of the page was blank but Neil would have stopped reading anyway. Mention of Anne Jordan brought Martin and his search for Davy right to the front of Neil's mind again.

The shadow had changed in Davy's mind from being friendly and almost welcome, to something he feared. Neil had begun to wonder if whatever had caused that change in Davy's view of the shadow had also caused him to slip back into that dislocated state.

And, worse, slip far enough to have gone through feeling down to clinical depression or even a full-blown breakdown.

But then Davy had written about meeting Anne Jordan and you could read the happiness there, the way Davy was buoyed up by the thought of seeing her again. And Neil stopped thinking about depression and remembered instead how Davy had been when he was going out with Anne Jordan.

Neil had seen Davy one night during August at the leisure centre bar. Neil had been playing five-a-side with the social services team and he'd gone up for a drink with two of them. Davy and Frankie were in the far corner. When the two lads with Neil left, Neil went and sat with his old friends.

Davy had been full of the new relationship and Frankie had told Neil to tell him sex was no good for your back and then went to get a round of drinks in.

"It's not sex," Davy had said and then grinned the way he used to when he was a kid. "Well, not just the sex. Sometimes we've just gone to sleep and that felt just as good. You know, waking up next to somebody else felt great."

Neil had smiled and nodded and was glad; the last time he'd seen Davy, he'd looked bad. He'd always been a fit lad, always looked well and healthy but the last time Neil had seen him Davy's colour had been poor and his eyes had been shadowed with deep lines delved beneath them. His voice, too, hadn't been the normal Davy-voice but flat and slow, as if he had to think everything over twice before he said it. Normally, Davy's voice told you all about the bloke— lively, meeting life head on, just like his dad had, full of enthusiasm. Seeing him in the bar that night had made Neil feel a lot better about Davy; he looked like he was back in the land of the living again and it was all down to Anne Jordan.

Now, sitting in his office, the lamp on, the wind rising outside and the twilight lowering itself slowly over Seapool, Neil shook his head slowly; he just couldn't see Davy harming, even *thinking* about harming Anne Jordan. When Davy had talked with Neil after Anne finished it, he was just puzzled and hurt, not angry. When he'd left, it was with the intention of getting on with his life again. He'd done it once, after Trisha, and he wanted to do it again.

No, Neil couldn't see Davy doing anything to Anne Jordan.

The sound of a car horn made Neil turn to look out of the window. Across the road, over the high hedge of Blackhay's garden, he could see the big house and it had all its lights on. A big white limousine was pulling into the gutter and there was a crowd of people gathering on the pavement. A woman in a wedding dress got out of the car and the crowd started clapping and cheering. It was obviously the break between the wedding breakfast for the family and the night-time reception for the friends, a chance for the bride to get washed, maybe change into her going away outfit.

Neil turned back, almost smiling, remembering his own wedding to Joy. Then the smile stopped and a frown replaced it and Neil was remembering another night-time reception. As he remembered, he looked at the phone on his desk. He picked it up and dialled Martin Cottingham's direct line at the station. As the ringing tone started, Neil switched the phone to the speaker. It was the only time he'd used the thing since getting it but he knew he'd want to walk around the room while he told Martin what had just occurred to him.

"Cottingham."

Martin's voice sounded tired, even through the speaker and echoey. Martin sounded his age.

"Martin, it's Neil."

"Decided to tell me what you didn't before?" There was no humour in the question.

"Not exactly. I've been thinking about Davy and Trisha and Anne Jordan. Will you give me a few minutes and just listen?"

"Neil, I...okay, go on."

Ten years ago, another old friend of Davy's and Neil's got married. Neil, Joy, Davy and Trisha went to the night-time reception along with a lot of other mutual friends. The party was good and, at the end, everybody was in the foyer of the club, ringing taxis or waiting for taxis, talking and laughing, the usual end-of-evening stuff. With that weird sort of mass-consciousness, the crowd in the foyer all moved to the pavement outside as taxis arrived and took people away. Neil and Joy were standing next to Davy and Trisha when the taxi pulled up. Davy started to lead Trisha to the open door when a younger couple, not known by them, dashed in front of them and headed for the taxi. It was the sort of thing that happens all the time and nothing to get worked up over. Trisha told the younger couple that it was her taxi, wasn't the driver using her name? The younger couple ignored her and Trisha went bonkers.

Trisha grabbed the woman's hair and dragged her back, plonking her down on her shiny-dressed backside on the pavement. The bloke turned, saw his partner on the floor, saw Trisha standing over her with wild eyes and clawed hands, decided he couldn't or didn't fancy hitting this woman so took a swipe at Davy. Davy stepped back out of the way and Neil got between them. The lad took another swing and Neil blocked his fist with his hand and pushed the lad away. The lad must have heard about Neil and decided discretion was the better part of valour. He helped his partner up and they moved back inside the club. Trisha glared at them as they went past and then turned and glared at Davy. Then she stomped into the taxi. Davy nodded at Neil and got into the front of the taxi.

"Trisha's never liked anything getting the better of her, Martin," Neil said when he'd finished relating this incident. "I don't know for sure but if Trisha found out that Davy was seeing Anne Jordan...well, she wouldn't've liked it. She's capable of having a go at Anne Jordan to make her point. Maybe you should be looking for Trisha. Maybe she found out about Anne Jordan and warned her off or worse. God knows, Davy wasn't trying to keep his relationship with Anne a secret. Just a thought, Martin. I don't like it but it makes more sense than Davy doing anything."

The pause seemed endless, filled with Martin's breathing. Neil waited, staring at the grill of the speaker.

"We don't have to look for Trisha Eliot," Martin said slowly. "We've found her. She was dumped in the undergrowth at the top end of Oil Street swings. She's dead, Neil. And a bloody mess. D'you have anything else to tell me?"

Neil sat down hard and looked at Davy's journal. There was still a lot of it to read. "No," he said simply.

"Right," Martin said. "You still have no idea where Eliot might be? Because, right now, he's my prime suspect in at least one suspicious death and, if we don't find Anne Jordan soon, maybe two."

"No," Neil repeated.

"Okay. Well, as you can imagine, I'm busy. I'll be in touch, though. Where can I get hold of you?"

"I'll be here for a while, yet. For quite a while."

The click of the disconnection was very loud as it came out of the speaker.

"Shit," Neil said as he turned the speaker off and replaced the phone. "What the hell happened, Davy? What the hell *happened?*"

He rubbed at the scar above his eye and began to read the journal again.

Some things are too big to be articulated.
I remember Neil saying that to Mr Gibson once in English. I think it was an answer to a question about Wordsworth or somebody who said they could only write about something a long time after the fact. Or something; English Lit was never my best subject but stuff Neil said or says has a way of sticking in your mind. Anyway, I never really understood it till now.
This thing with Anne is like that. I really do feel like a teenager who's cracked it with the Girls Grammar School's fifth form pin-up, much to everybody's amazement including mine. It's so big inside me, like the feeling I get between the sky and the ground, it's really hard to find words to describe it properly.
It's a week since I met her and I've seen her every night since and it just keeps getting better. We laugh a lot, that's part of it. We started off laughing at the club in Laketon where I met her and we've been laughing ever since. Sometimes, just sometimes, I think my Mum might be right and there's a God after all.

I went to work the day after the bungee jump accident, feeling a bit better because I'd decided to fill my time writing in this journal. Still, the fact that the shadow had got out of the house still bothered me a bit and, even with this journal, it felt like I'd still be living a sort of half-life without bungee jumping. Then, in the photocopying room, I heard the two girls talking about the club in Laketon and how it had a sixties night every Friday and how much they liked the music. I spent the rest of the day trying to get hold of Frankie and finally got him just before five in the afternoon. I asked him if he fancied it and he said great. We went on the Friday and I met Anne at the bar as soon as we got in there.

We were both trying to catch the eye of the barman but both his eyes seemed permanently fixed on the overflowing cleavage of the barmaid and, while we waited, me and Anne got talking. We hit it off right away. I didn't feel nervous at all, probably because she laughed when I made a joke about the bloody barman. She went to sit with her friends and me and Frankie plucked up the courage to ask Anne and one of her friends to dance. We danced all night and I walked her home after Frankie got a taxi with Anne's friend. I spent an hour in Anne's living room, talking about ourselves and it never crossed my mind to try it on with her. When I said goodnight and opened the front door, she kissed me and I asked her if she fancied going for a meal and she said she did. We went out on Monday and made love when I took her home.

See? There's all sorts of stuff, how I felt, what she said, the smell of her, all that sort of thing that I just can't write about. I think mostly it's because it's so good, I don't want to ruin it or put the mockers on it. I just want to enjoy it. Why not? It feels like a long time since I felt good or happy.

But I still feel like I should be writing something in this book. It's like I made a promise to myself and if I don't keep it, I'll be making a big mistake. So, what do I write about?
Bungee jumping? Yeah, bungee jumping.
I got the idea after having to do some real work, doing what I was good at, being a spark. Shit, I've just realised something. This is really funny. It was in this house, 12 Oil Street.
The council got a load of money from the EEC for urban renewal and they decided to renew The Rows. The money had to be spent in a hurry or the council would be capped by the government so it meant a lot of overtime and not enough people to do the job. I ended up on a gang of sparks doing the electrics in The Rows. It was a good little gang and Chrissie Springer is a good foreman. And the two young lads with us were good workers, not just looking for the next pay packet so they could get to the alehouse. I told them and they knew I meant it, that I wasn't the boss down here, I was one of the gang.
Getting to work on the tools again came at the right time for me. It wasn't long after my Dad died and the hollowness inside me seemed to be getting worse. Working with my hands, having people to talk to, helped a lot and I could feel the hollowness filling up a bit. The night I felt it fill up a lot was here in 12 Oil Street.
We were on a break up in the back bedroom and the lads were talking about white knuckle rides. It was March, just before the clocks went forward and we

just had the worklights to see by. Lenny Gordon was talking about bungee jumping and Chrissie, who's older than me, joined in because his son had just done one. I knew what they talking about because Andrew had told me and his mum about a gang of students who'd done one for charity.

"Wouldn't get me doing that for a big clock," Dean Noble told us all. "Nothing between me and the ground but a giant elastic band? Forget it!"
Chrissie said his lad told him it was the best thing he'd ever tried, better than all those fast rides. Lenny agreed, said that was why he'd done it, those rides were okay but they didn't last long enough.
Robbie Fisher nearly choked on his tea.

"I went on that new thing at Blackpool and it lasted too bleedin long!" Robbie said and we all laughed.
Then Lenny was telling us that he meant the good bits on those rides, the somersaults and things, didn't last long enough, that apart from those bits it was just going fast on a straight track.
While he was talking, I suddenly had a flash of Neil telling Mr Gibson that words were powerful things. I'd always known it intellectually but that night in the back bedroom of this house, I understood it emotionally. The conversation set off a domino-effect in my brain. I was looking out of the window and could just see the shape of the slide in the swings and then the word <u>somersault</u> went pinging round my brain. Come to think of it, that was the first time I really thought about what we did as kids, not after that poor girl had the accident the other

weekend. Anyway, I heard Lenny trying to explain the feeling he got from bungee jumping and I could hear the wistfulness in his voice. I knew he wasn't really in the room anymore, eating paste butties and drinking stewed tea, he was back doing the jump

"I know what you mean," I told him. "When I was a kid, there was a little gang of us who used to jump off high walls and things to get that feeling."
I'm not sure now that the others in my little gang did it for that reason but it was definitely why I did it.

"We used to climb a tree down there in those swings and jump off it onto a pile of old mattresses. We even jumped off the slide. Used to do it all the time," I said and smiled at the doubtful looks they were all giving me.

"Christ," Dean said and shook his head. "Every time somebody tells me about the sixties, I'm always amazed that any of your generation lived to see the seventies! If it wasn't drugs, it was sky-diving without a parachute. Me, I get vertigo if I look down too quick. Everything spins round. Sorry, you wouldn't get me near a bungee jump."
We laughed and finished our break and went back to work but that word, vertigo, joined somersault in my brain and they went pinging round together. Dean said he got dizzy. He wasn't scared of heights and he never shirked running up a ladder or anything. But he thought he had vertigo because he got dizzy if he looked down. Vertigo's a posh word for dizziness but it gives people more problems than that. I remember reading about a woman who had it and she said

there were times when she had an insane desire to jump off any high point she was standing on, as if something or somebody was standing behind her, prodding her towards the edge of the high place and all she could think about was landing on the ground however far it was below her.
While I ran cable that night, I kept thinking about that and about the slide and The Dead Tree and I felt a sort of dim warmth seeping into me. That's what it felt like—seeping, like warm water seeping through a crack and filling up the cavity behind.
Shit, it's happened again. Neil's right, the mind's a very weird thing.
<u>The shadow was in this house that night, too</u>.
I've just remembered that. Is that weird or what? I saw it all those years ago when we were robbing the wood and it was in the same place eighteen months or so ago. Is this bloody house haunted? Or is the shadow mine like I thought it was when I saw it up in Laketon at the bungee jump?
I don't know and I'm not sure it matters. With a bit of luck, now I'm seeing Anne, I won't need the shadow to talk to anymore and that's fine with me.
But it was definitely here that night I first heard about bungee jumping.
I was on my own in the back bedroom, my worklight draped over the top of the door. It was shedding enough light to see by but it filled the room with shadows. I was just putting the first screw in the socket when I thought I heard one of the others coming up the stairs. I looked towards the door and saw it.

The light from the work lamp shone directly into the middle of the room and there was nothing between the lamp and the middle of the room but air. And a shadow. It wasn't cast on any surface and there wasn't anything to cast it but it was there just the same. Free-standing in the centre of the bedroom.

I remember staring at it just like I did when I was a kid and, now, I wonder if I was remembering when I was kid but not realising I was remembering, if that doesn't sound too Irish. What I mean is that I can remember leaning forward towards that impossible, free-standing shadow. As if I was sure there was going to be some sound. Like a whisper. And maybe part of my memory that I wasn't aware of was remembering how I thought I'd heard a sound coming from the shadow when I was a kid.

It doesn't matter, I suppose. There was a real noise then. It was March and typically blowy and squally and a burst of rain splattered on the window and the gust moaned in next door's tree and I jumped a bit on the ladder. The wobble that started was enough to make me concentrate on the job and I went back to work.

I forgot about the shadow. Well, obviously, I've only just remembered it. But I didn't forget how the words somersault and vertigo went pinging round my brain and how I'd felt that warm seepage seeming to fill up some of the hollowness inside me when we were talking about bungee jumping. It felt good, that warm feeling of seepage and I began to think I might be on the way to getting over my Dad's death.

Ah shit, here we go again, thinking about Trisha.
It was right around that time that the change really began to hit her hard.
I remember one night when Andrew came home from working as a labourer for Paul Horne and Derek Frost. It was during the Easter holidays and I'd asked Derek if he had anything for Andrew and they fixed him up on one of their building sites. Anyway, he came home one Friday night, grimy and sweaty and grinning all over his face because it was pay day. He loved working and I only half-believed him when he said it was the money he loved. This night, he dashed in, gave his mum a kiss and the money for his keep and then rushed upstairs for a quick shower. I watched him dash out of the door and wondered out loud where the three year old had gone, the one I'd spent an endless summer afternoon teaching to tie his laces.
Trisha told me he was still there, that when he came across something he wasn't sure of, I'd see him again. I watched her face when she said this and there was real sadness and longing in her eyes and it suddenly struck me that when she said I'd see the three year old Andrew again, that's exactly what she meant, that I'd see him, she wouldn't. Trisha had decided that she wouldn't see him again because he'd outgrown her now.
It was part of the menopause, I'm sure and she suffered with it badly, developing nervous little foot-tapping tics and getting irritable all the time. That was when I knew how bad it was—she'd never

had those sorts of tics, she'd always been the most in-control person I've ever known. And she made it clear I couldn't help, that she didn't even want me to try. That's probably why I went bungee jumping.
No, that's not really true. At least not all true. I wanted to recapture that feeling I'd had when I was a kid, that moment between the sky and the ground. But Trisha being the way she was must've had some effect, mustn't it?

It was one of those marvellous late August days we get in Seapool when I saw the advert in the council's **WHAT'S ON IN SEAPOOL** booklet and that was all it took. I read the advert and heard the conversation we'd had in this house and I felt that seeping warmth again. I rang the number and they told me to get a medical certificate saying I was healthy. Dr Smye told me I was fine physically but he wouldn't swear to my mental state if I was going bungee jumping. I thanked him and laughed. Obviously he's never been in a gang like that little gang of mine.
As I stood on the platform before that first jump, I was wondering if it would feel as good as those jumps I used to do when I was a kid. Well, when I made that first jump, I thought it was every bit as good.
The two blokes on the platform were very professional and told me how the harnesses and ties and giant elastic bands were tested to this or that umpteen pressure and tension. They told me not to worry, just enjoy the whole experience. I barely

heard them. I was watching the young bloke who'd just jumped and the animated way he was trying to tell his mates how good it felt. I thought about how I'd felt stepping off the mattresses in the swings and smiled.

The bloke next to me was still talking, telling me what to do, to just lean forward and let gravity grab me. He didn't know what I was like when I was a kid.

I dived. I did a swan-dive, as near as I could all wrapped up in the harnesses, anyway. I was a bit disappointed at first as I kept my eyes open and looked at the sky. That moment I remembered from the swings and the baths just wasn't there. I was going down too soon and it was just that stomach-churning feeling you get going fast over a hump in the road in a car. But then the elasticated tie-ropes yank you back up again and the moment I was longing for was right there.

The ropes haul you up but the tension goes out of them almost immediately and for that brief snatch of time, before gravity woke up to the fact I was trying to fly, I was almost weightless.

For that tiny moment, I felt like I used to when I was ten years old. Unfettered and free. It was glorious.

I jumped again and asked the organisers if there was anything else like it available. There's a new thing, a bit like a cats'-cradle affair, fixed to the ground. I tried it and it was okay. There's eight points where something happens to your body as you're shot up from the ground but, mostly, it's just bouncing up and down. There is a point where you're almost weightless but it doesn't last as long or feel as good as the bungee jump.

I spent the early autumn last year going round the commercial bungee jumps and I even tried parachuting and one free-fall but they weren't the same as bungee jumping and I left them alone. The bungee jumping was my thing and it helped me get over my Dad's death and, I think, helped me get through the way Trisha was with me.

When winter came, the jumps stopped doing business but I wasn't too upset; spring always comes and then summer and then the bungee jumps would be back and I'd be back with them.

Then came Christmas and the new year and Trisha's adultery and I ended up down here in Oil Street and I really don't want to think about that again.

Well, no I don't but there's something that's just occurred to me, thinking about how it feels jumping and about finding out about Trisha.

When I asked her if she loved the bloke and she said it was just sex, she said something else, too. It seems to go with how I feel about jumping, daft as it sounds.

Trisha said she'd been feeling bloated and tired with the change but she also said she'd felt she was dead inside. I suppose that's what I saw when I saw that sadness in her when she was talking about me seeing the three year old Andrew again. She said that sex, just the act, nothing to do with love, made her feel like her body was alive again. That <u>she</u> was alive again. Or still alive. Something like that anyway. Knowing that somebody wanted her body just because he lusted after it made her feel like she wasn't dead inside and then the act made it more so. Of course, she said it in a loud angry voice but you could tell she meant it.

If I'm honest, I can understand that. I imagine it was a bit like I felt when my Dad had the first stroke. I saw him and realised that he was getting old but more than that, I was getting old, too. Nobody was going to make an exception to the rule for me. I think it must've felt a bit like that for Trisha. She was going through the menopause and all that entailed and life, to make its point, was letting her know that her only child was outgrowing her. Worse, there would be no other children to take that empty place, that hollowness inside. Maybe Trisha treated sex, the wanting of her body by some stranger, as a sign that she wasn't old yet. Not really.

Sex was how she filled up that hollowness inside her. Sex was how she knew she wasn't past it, wasn't old, wasn't closing in on death.

Bungee jumping, the way it makes me feel like that ten year old kid, was how I knew I wasn't past it, getting old, getting ready to die.

I suppose we all have to find a way of accepting the inevitable and we probably know we do. Still, it doesn't stop us from putting it off as long as possible, does it?

So, I was an estranged husband, living in the street I was born and grew up in, living a sort of half-life and almost going round the twist. But I had an eye on the summer, knowing the bungee jumping would be there for me and I could have that marvellous moment between the sky and the ground to let me know I was still alive. Then that poor girl had the accident and even that was denied me and all I could see were long days and nights with nobody to talk to except a shadow I've been good at making appear for a long time.

That's how I think of it—that it's something I've been able to make materialise since I was a kid. I think I might even have worked out why.

Maybe when my life is lacking something and I know it's lacking something, making the shadow materialise is what I do. People like Neil can sit down and write a poem or a song and it gives them something to fill out the days. I can't do that although I suppose by writing this I'm trying to. But I've never done it in the past and I think what I do, or did, is make the shadow come. When the days are ordinary, filled with, let's face it, humdrum stuff, we get sort of numb and don't notice the rut, the way our lives are humdrum. Then some massive change happens, like a woman's menopause, and we have to find something to do or see or talk to. Anything to keep the depression or the anger or madness away.

Or maybe not.

Shit, I'm just some bloke, some ordinary bloke who's trying to get on with his life the best way he can. Now I think I can do it with a smile on my face thanks to Anne.

The best of it is, I don't feel guilty about it. I mean, I <u>was</u> expecting to. Yeah, I told myself it was a stupid thing to expect. Why should I feel guilty when it was Trisha who broke the marriage? But logic doesn't always work when it comes to things like emotions and love.

When I wasn't thinking about how I was almost round the bend and making mothers worried for their kids, I thought about Trisha and I thought about what I'd do if I met somebody. Just thoughts that filled my head while I sat here and brooded and didn't think I was brooding. It was probably because Trisha hadn't been in touch with me except for the one time she rang to ask if I'd seen a solicitor. I told her I hadn't and waited for her to tell me she had but she didn't and said she was busy at work and she thought she'd wait until the end of the financial year was over if that was all right with me. She didn't mention seeing anybody else seriously and didn't ask if I was seeing anybody but she never asked me to come home so I just assumed she was happy we'd split up.

But it got me thinking. I thought, well, if she's still thinking that she doesn't want me, it's not likely I'll be going home and I'm still young. Sort of. What about if I meet somebody? And then I started feeling guilty just thinking about it. Amazing how being married for so long and never thinking about another woman can get you brainwashed. I hated the fact that I was feeling guilty but I couldn't seem to stop myself. I think I went to see my Mum and asked her what I asked because of how I was feeling. I asked her about guilt the night before her birthday.

She was going to Stratford with the dinner club on her birthday so I took round a big bottle of Guinness and a blackberry tart and some flowers, the little treats she'd always loved. She made some of her thick custard to go with the tart and we sat and drank the stout and ate the tart and talked. She wasn't drunk but she was a bit past sober when I asked if she felt different now than she had done when my Dad was alive.

"Not really," she told me and wiped the cream from her top lip. "Before I was married, I was free and easy and liked a drink and staying out late. I liked meeting people and talking. I still miss your dad. I loved him and if it was possible, I'd do it all over again tomorrow. If he came home now with his duffelbag over his shoulder and sawdust in his hair, it'd be great. But that's not going to happen and once I understood that, I had to make a decision. I could curl up and die or get on with my life. I chose to get on with my life because that's what he would've wanted. I don't feel guilty about it like some of them do at the dinner club. He would've hated that. He took life by the horns and loved every minute of it. He wasn't book-clever but he was wise in his way. After that first stroke, when he came home, he told me off for looking like I was expecting him to die that night. He told me that two people, like in a marriage, bring things to their relationship and share more than their beds. They share the weight they each bring to it but, when one of them dies, the saddest thing would be for the one left to try to bear the burden of that old double weight on

their own. He said memories had their own weight but it's bearable. The weight of a parted relationship, however it's been parted, is the heaviest thing in the world to carry."
She looked hard at me to make sure I got the point, to make sure I understood she wasn't just talking about her and my Dad but about me and Trisha. I nodded to let her know I understood but I it still took a while for me accept it.

Being with Anne has got me all the way round that hard corner of my life. There were a few moments when the resentment I felt for and about Trisha were hard to bear and probably made my life a bit harder to live.
The worst one was when Andrew phoned me here not long after I moved in. He rang to see if I was okay and I told him I was. We had an awkward fifteen minutes talking around why I'd left home and I realised he didn't know the real reason. Trisha had told him we were having some problems and needed some time alone. She had the good grace to admit most of it was on her side but Andrew assumed she was talking about the menopause.

"Women have it hard," Andrew said to me then. "They spend all that time suffering with periods and then, before it's over, they have to suffer with the menopause, too. It must be awful."
All I could do was agree. And, the truth is, I felt proud of him for saying it. I was proud that he was grown up enough to have thought it through and sensitive enough to sympathise. Still, I'm human and I

couldn't help feeling resentful because I'd suffered through his mum's menopause, too. Until I met Anne, I think I still was.
So, although there's nobody to ask me the question except myself, the answer to 'why don't you feel guilty?' is that I'm not guilty. I'm probably guilty of a lot of things but not of breaking up my marriage and it would be bloody stupid, an act of supreme self-pity if I let this chance with Anne pass me by because of it.

There. I feel better for that. But I'm still superstitious about writing about me and Anne. It sounds stupid but I don't care. There's only me knows why.

FIVE

Neil rubbed his eyes and stretched, wincing at the crackles in his spine. He got up and made himself some coffee and tried not to think about Davy and Martin and Trisha. Especially not about Trisha being dead but, of course, he couldn't think about anything else.

God, Trisha was dead. It was so hard to believe, to take in. Neil couldn't say he'd been fond of Trisha, not the way he was of Derek Frost's wife or Jon Featherstone's wife or Paul Horne's ex-wife. Still, he knew the woman and there were times when she was good company and Davy had loved the bones of her. And then there was Andrew. He was in a coma now and, from what Martin had said, the prognosis didn't look good but Trisha was his mother and there'd never been any doubt at all that she loved her son. If, when, Andrew did recover, the knowledge that his mother had died while he was asleep would be a terrible blow.

"And if Martin's right," Neil told himself quietly as he sipped the coffee and looked out of the window. "He might have to deal with the fact that his father killed his mother."

Was that really possible? Neil couldn't see it, not knowing Davy as he did but the fact remained that Trisha was dead and Davy had had something very close to a breakdown earlier this year. If the police knew about that, they'd feel they had more than enough motive for Davy to have killed Trisha. Add the fact that Davy's recent girlfriend, one who'd finished the affair, was missing...well, it wasn't surprising the police weren't looking for anybody else.

"I still don't believe it," Neil murmured. "And if I don't stop talking to myself, they'll be thinking about locking me up, too."

He sat down and looked at the journal. It was a thick book and, somewhere in it, Neil knew he was going to find out that Davy had had something very close to a second breakdown. The question was why and how it had happened. Surely there was more to it than Anne Jordan finishing their relationship? When Davy had left Neil's house, after he'd told Neil that Anne had finished with him, Davy had decided that he was going to get on with his life and Neil knew he meant it. Did Davy start falling apart after Andrew's accident? It was possible but Neil doubted it for the simple reason that Davy would fight anything like a breakdown because it would hinder Andrew's chances; the lad would need all the help he could get. The two things combined, in Neil's view, would be enough to make anybody angry, bitter, even depressed but not depressed enough to fall apart; the anger alone would be likely to stop that happening. So, what did that leave?

The shadow?

If Neil had had only the journal to read and use in trying to work out what had happened with and to Davy, he would have probably thought of it as an odd manifestation of Davy's dislocated state. Davy himself thought of it like that otherwise he wouldn't have looked on it as almost welcome. Certainly nothing to be scared of; Davy had even made a half-joke of it when he wondered if it was himself or the house that was haunted. But Neil had Davy's letter, too and the letter hinted at something a lot more definite than a grown-up version of Kate Callaghan's invisible friend. No, something...

Neil pushed back in the chair, frowning. His grey eyes, even in the dim light of late afternoon, shone with that bright winter's-day-shine. Part of him wanted to go on theorising about how Davy might have fallen into a clinical depression while another part of him wanted to get to the end of the journal as fast as he could; he wanted everything and anything he could get to defend Davy against whatever accusations Martin might have. But there was another, deeper part of Neil, a part his wife always referred to as the poet in him, which kept prodding him with an insistence that there was more to all this than a man's depression and a woman's anger. This part of him was open to anything in or out of the world and it had picked up on that half-joke of Davy's about haunted houses and had been linking it with whatever it was that had nagged Neil since he'd read Davy's letter.

Mad George and shadows and haunted houses. Not the sort of things a psychologist should give much time to but Neil wasn't just a psychologist and he never ignored the occasional nagging at his mind.

He looked at his watch. It was half past four. Downstairs, the telly would be on and the kids already back from school would be arguing about which children's telly programme to watch. The kitchen would be making a start on tea.

"And Paul should be still at his office," Neil said softly, still thinking about what part of him had been thinking about for the last four hours or so. He dialled Paul Horne's office number and Paul picked up on the third ring.

"It's Neil, Paul. Can you do me a favour and check back through your records. I want to know if you've still got a record of the previous tenants of 12 Oil Street. Going back, say, fifty years...yeah, I know but it's important. Cheers, mate." Then he rang home and told Nicole that he wouldn't be home for tea, possibly not home at all tonight but to tell her mother not to worry, he'd speak to her later.

Neil went back to the journal on his desk, turned the page and then just stared at what was written on it. He didn't feel shock or surprise, only a deep, weary sadness, sadness that Davy had been wrong.

Davy had thought that writing about how he felt being with Anne might jinx what they had. But not writing about it hadn't stopped Anne finishing it after all. This page, full of one angry word was proof.

Well, he'd known that. The important thing was to see if he could work out where Davy was now. If he could work that out, it could only help Davy with the police.

SHIT

SHIT

SHIT

That was really helpful, wasn't it? Really grown-up. Anne packed me in and all I could think of was to get this bloody book out and scrawl shit all over it, like a friggin teenager with a gob-on.

No, if I was really acting like a teenager, I'd rip the page out so it wouldn't remind me of it, of Anne calling it off and of me being a bloody middle-aged juvenile.

I'm going to leave it there so it'll remind me of how stupid I can be. Oh, it still hurts that she called it off and it means I'm back to being on my own in this house but I'm more confused than anything else.

I am now, anyway. When it happened I was just gobsmacked and then I was—not really angry but bewildered.

I just don't understand it. One minute we were dancing in the club, listening to The Beatles and the Stones and having the same great time we'd been having every Friday since that first Friday and then she goes to the toilet and comes back and, bang, tells me she thinks we should call it a day. She picks up her handbag and walks out. No explanations or nothing, just tara Dave.

Why? What did I do?

I don't know. I really don't know. I've spent the last two days, since I made a mess of that page, trying to remember if I said something or did something. Or didn't say something or do something. I can't think of anything one way or the other. God, it's driving me bonkers!

Bollocks!

Oh stop it, you'll end up writing that all over the place if you carry on. Just forget it, it's over. She said so.
Easier said than done, Davy.
Oh bugger this for a game of soldiers I'm going to bed.

Hello journal or diary or whatever you call yourself, here I am at three o'clock in the morning. It's cold and windy outside and I think I'm going round the twist. Again.
If it wasn't for the dream, I'd think I was back when my Dad had died.
I woke up, wide awake, staring at the ceiling, knowing I wasn't going back to sleep again. At least this bit's different. At least I can do something other than just stare at the ceiling. I can come down here and talk to myself with this pen and this book.
But that dream was weird. It was the same dream I had after that girl had her accident.
I was standing at the top of some stairs, staring out through the grimy fanlight over the front door. The moon was playing hide and seek with the racing clouds and the light from the bare bulb in the hall was a dingy yellow. I was bollock-naked and I was trying to work up the courage to jump from the top of the stairs to the bottom. I'd just about worked myself up to it and looked down—and there was a shadow at the bottom of the stairs.
I'm pretty sure it wasn't the shadow I saw in the back bedroom or at the bungee jump in Laketon. That shadow is the one I made up, for whatever

reason, and it feels sort of friendly or at least not unfriendly.

The one in the dream, the shadow at the bottom of the stairs had its arms out, waiting for me to jump so it could embrace me. It had no features and embraces, cuddles aren't usually bad things so why did seeing it there scare the piss out of me? Cos it did, it scared me so bad that I woke up only just in time to stop myself screaming. That would've been fun, wouldn't it? Waking myself up by screaming, alone in this empty house. I'd probably have just gone completely mad if that had happened.

I didn't wake up screaming but remembering that dream still makes the hairs on the back of my neck stand up and it feels like the cold outside is getting inside me because I want to shiver. That's why I'm sitting here and writing this. I want to try to work out what it means but I can't. All I can think of is getting hold of Neil and talking with him. Hell, why not? He helped me last time. He's really good at what he does. Yeah, I'll ring Neil and ask him if I can come round and see him.

Okay, I feel a bit better now. If nothing else, it helped me stop thinking about Anne packing me in without telling me why. I just wish there'd been a less scary way of doing it. Never mind, I'll probably talk about Anne, too, when I see Neil.

If Neil wasn't the way he is, if he didn't think God put him here to help fix broken kids, he'd make a fortune. All he'd have to do is go to the States and set up some office in LA or somewhere and he'd be a millionaire in about five minutes.

I told him about Anne and he listened. I can't remember what he asked me but I know there weren't many questions. It was just me, talking it through, getting it off my chest, coming to terms with it. The one thing that sticks in my mind is what Neil said after I'd talked myself out.

He asked me if Anne packing me in hurt as much as when I found about Trisha and I told him it didn't. Yes, it hurts but not like that. He just nodded and smiled that slow smile of his and told me that I'd got on with my life after Trisha and, he said, after my Dad died. If I could do it after those two horrible events, didn't I think I could do it now?

Simple, really. Well, for Neil it is. I've been trying to sort this thing with Anne out for nearly a week and it's just given me a bloody headache. Still, that's why I went to Neil and now I've got to do the rest.

I—'ang on, there's the phone.

That was Paul Horne. He was ringing to see if I wanted to make it legal. Living here in 12 Oil Street he meant. I've only been renting on a casual basis but it's the end of his financial year or something and he needs to know if I'm going to be staying, moving or buying. As soon as he said it, I knew it meant I'd have to make a decision and that it would be a big one so I asked him if he could give me a week to think it over. Being Paul, he said fine.

Maybe it's a good thing. It might be what I need to keep my mind off Anne, to give me the push to get on with my life like Neil said. Wait a minute, hold the bus. I've just thought, I didn't mention the dream to Neil. In fact, it never even entered my head to mention it. That's really weird. I went round there to talk about the dream didn't I? I know I thought I'd talk about Anne, too but I definitely thought about seeing Neil because of the dream. Why didn't I mention it?

I don't know. It doesn't matter. Deciding if I'm staying in this house or not is what's important and the truth is, I really don't know. I'm going to have to think very hard about it. I mean, renting or buying—what will that mean in terms of the rest of my life?

I feel sad. I feel tired. I feel, God I don't know what I feel.

This is two days later and I've sort of made up my mind about living here but the things that helped me make the decision made me sad and tired, too. It feels like it's the right decision but, still.

Big breath time again, Davy. Start how it started and maybe it'll make sense.

Frankie rang me at work yesterday to see if we were going to the club tonight. I started to say no but then I thought about Neil and about getting on with my life and said yes. For the rest of the day in work, I thought about whether I was going to move out of Oil Street or what. It was funny. I had to sign an order form for a load of tools and I suddenly thought about my Dad's old tools. My Mum told me to take them after I moved to Oil Street. For the rest of the afternoon, I kept thinking about them and where I should put them. I got home yesterday tea-time and saw that the door to the outside toilet of the house was ajar.

I looked inside to make sure no little toerag had been in to smash the cistern or the bowl and thought about Andrew's disbelieving look when I told him about outside toilets like all the houses in The Rows used to have. I had to explain that the houses in The Rows were built back when only Royalty had inside toilets and the rest of the population had to go outside to pee and learn to whistle. And if they wanted to have a bath, they had to haul the big tin bath in front of the fire and keep the door shut.

Anyway, I checked the outside toilet and closed the door and then it struck me that I could put my own toolchests in the toilet and keep my Dad's gear in the back bedroom. Of course, it means ripping out the toilet to make room for my gear and that was when I realised that I'd half-made up my mind about staying here. Ripping out the toilet would be me making a commitment.

So, I spent today going over that half-decision and trying not to think about going to the club. I met Frankie outside the club at eight o'clock and we went in. Anne was there with her friends.

Frankie saw her and asked me if I wanted to forget it and leave. I shook my head and we got the ale in. While Frankie went to the toilet about half an hour later, one of Anne's friends came over and gave me a bit of an ear-bashing because she said Anne was a right misery since we split up. I had to tell her that it was Anne who'd called it off and that seemed to surprise her. Marion said Anne hadn't said why we'd split up and she thought it was me. She said she was sorry for having a go at me and then went back to her table. I went to the toilet myself near the end of the night and bumped into Anne in the corridor. She looked at the floor but the corridor is narrow and we had to stop walking and turn sideways so she couldn't pretend she hadn't seen me.

I asked her how she was and she said she was fine but it sounded like there was a lump in her throat. I remembered what Marion had said about Anne being miserable and I thought, sod it, and asked her if she fancied trying again.

"Just forget it, Dave." Anne said and finally looked at me. "It's over. I'm sorry—just, let's leave it."

And she walked off before I could ask her why she'd called it off, what had I done? Not even the Beatles medley they finished the night with could cheer me up and by the time I got home, I was feeling really down, really confused. I stood on the pavement outside the house and told myself to forget it, it was over and I had a life to live and had to start living it now.

As I got to the back gate I heard voices coming from the garden and the adrenaline pumped into my bloodstream, making my stomach feel hot and my hands feel clammy. I stood with my hand on the latch of the back gate, wondering if I should cough or something, rattle the latch loud enough for whoever it was in the garden to hear and give them the chance to bugger off. But the flush of adrenaline I felt wouldn't let me. And then I thought of my Dad's tools, just lying in the back bedroom and I lifted the latch very slowly and quietly.

I walked up the L of the garden and the side of the house on the balls of my feet, breathing through my mouth, my hands bunched and held away from my thighs.

There were four of them, aged between eleven and fourteen or so, wearing expensive trainers and dark tops and jeans. They were looking up to see if a window was open.

"Sod it," the tallest said and spat on the floor. "Just kick the door in and let's get on with it. He's probably got some white goods and a video and telly."

<u>White goods!</u> They were talking about breaking into my house like executives discussing business expansion. And then something very simple pulsed and thumped inside me. It was fury, absolute rage. I stepped into the square of the garden.

"Kick anything round here," I said and my voice sounded almost normal even though my blood was pounding in my ears. "And I'll kick you over the river to bloody Oxborough."

They all turned to look at me but none of them looked bothered at all. I wondered if I'd made a mistake. Then I realised I didn't really care.

"Why don't you all just piss off?" I asked them pleasantly.

They seemed to re-evaluate things. They'd all been standing there with that sort of hipshot way they stand, their faces trying to look hard and old, arms folded across their chests. After I told them to piss off, I expected a load of abuse, maybe a threat or two, certainly a lot of spitting to show how not bothered they were. But I got none of that.

In fact, the two youngest started to back away towards the gap in the railings and their eyes were wide and their mouths were open. And they didn't seem to be looking at me. They seemed to be staring at something to my right. The other two didn't back up but their eyes were opening wide, too, staring at the same spot as their mates. The tallest one, the one who'd told them to kick the door in, gulped. I actually heard it across the ten feet of garden.

I was about to step forward, to make my point, maybe make another threat of my own but I didn't get the chance. The smallest one, who looked about eleven, squealed and turned round so fast he fell over his own feet. He stumbled up again and nearly knocked himself out trying to get through the gap in the railings. That was enough for the others. They all turned their back on me and fought each other to get out of my garden and into the swings. The last one through the gap was the tallest of them and he was that panicked, he got his shoulders stuck where the gap narrowed. He threw me a look of such, well, terror really. His eyes were like big marbles floating on a bowl of thick rice pudding. His mouth was open in what turned out to be a scream that sounded like it almost ruptured his throat. His head was shaking in some sort of denial and his legs started to give out on him. He slid downwards, crying now and one of his mates grabbed him and yanked him through. Even as he did it, this other lad was staring at me like I'd grown another head. Then he yelled something at me.

"Please mister! Please keep it away! Don't let it come any closer! We're sorry! We're going now! Keep it away from us! PLEEEEASSE!"

I just stood and looked at them.

They finally got the tallest lad through the bars and then they were all running like mad things towards the bottom gate of the swings. I began to walk towards the railing. I don't know why, maybe I was going to call to them, tell them not to worry, I wasn't going to get the police or anything.

That was when the shadow stepped in front of me and beat me to the railings.

The world seemed to stop. I seemed to stop. It actually felt like my heart stopped beating and everything looked blurred and then the low noises of the night went all echoey and boomy. I could feel my eyes bugging out like the eyes of the kids who'd just run away like the devil was after them. I opened my mouth. I don't know if I was going to scream myself or ask the shadow if it was real. It didn't matter either way because the light came on next door and the shadow faded, like shadows do when light moves across them.

The bloke next door wanted to know what all the noise was and I told him in a voice that seemed to come from a long, long way away, that I'd just chased off a gang of toerags and he said good and then went inside. So did I.

I made myself a cup of tea and some toast and just sat here on the couch and tried to work out what had happened, what I'd seen.

The thing is, the shadow, if it was my shadow, was grey, not the black it's always been before. And I'm beginning to think that means it wasn't my shadow, if it was a shadow at all. I mean, even at night, with no moon, shadows aren't grey, are they? No, didn't think so. Still, the terror in those kids was real, they weren't acting the goat, pretending they were scared of me. That scream was real and the way the other lad begged me was real.

What happened? I can't believe that the shadow is real. I <u>don't</u> believe it's real. Whatever I see when I call it up is just my way of having something to talk to so I don't sound like a loony. It's just a part of this, depression I suppose it is, that I'm in after everything that's happened. What must have happened is that something, the tree next door or the chimney on this house or something, threw a shadow and, my movement or the wind or something, made it look like that shadow was moving towards the kids.

They'd been caught, they were already keyed up thinking about what they were going to do and then I caught them and didn't sound like I was worried

about taking them on and then the shadow looked like it was moving towards them.
Yeah, that's what happened, their already-psyched up bodies got psyched up some more and their young imaginations went into overdrive and they frightened themselves half-to-death.
Okay, that's better. I can handle that. It feels right, feels like it's true. Good.
I'm glad. Now I can think about making sure my Dad's tools are safe. I'm going to ring Paul and tell him I'll rent 12 Oil Street for a year and make sure he doesn't mind me ripping out the outside toilet to store my gear there. I'll make a big chest and put my Dad's stuff in it. I suppose it'll be my memorial to him, sort of. I can put a good lock on the toilet and, no. What I'll do is get a good alarm system and alarm the house. Get some decent locks and some interior door locks and maybe a floodlight for the garden. Yeah, I like that. It means I'll be getting on with my life and I'll also have something to fill my time so I won't start thinking about everything all over again. Right, good, time for bed. I'll ring Paul on Monday.

It's Monday night. I've just had my tea and now I'm sitting here with the telly burbling in the background and beginning to think it's the world that's going round the twist, not me.
Life is strange.
I know that's a line from a sixties song but I can't remember which one. Neil would know. I could ring him and ask him and while I was doing that, I could

ask him what he thinks about the idea that the world's going round the twist.

Trisha rang me at work this afternoon.

I was busy for a change so she said she'd ring me later. She didn't and, to be honest, I was glad. It felt like I'd got away with something.

I don't know, there was something in the tone of her voice—never mind. The thing is, she rang me here, just as I got in. Jesus, it was like she was watching me or something. I closed the back kitchen door behind me and the phone started ringing.

She phoned to see how I was, she said. To see if everything was all right, she said. I told her I was fine, everything was fine. Then I found myself telling her that I'd decided to rent 12 Oil Street for a year and even told her about the toerags and how I was going to fit an alarm system during the next week. I don't suppose it's so odd, really. I mean, we've been married a long time and I haven't really had anybody to talk to about that sort of thing, the minutiae of everyday life, since I left her. It felt natural.

"Oh," she said and sounded genuinely concerned. Then she said, "Isn't that funny, I was ringing to ask if you could put an alarm in for me. There've been a couple of break-ins in the road lately and I was getting a bit worried."

See what I mean about life being strange? I didn't know what to say so she filled in the gaps and we talked around it for a couple of minutes and it turns out I'm going to be doing it next weekend. To be honest, I wasn't sure I wanted to do it but it seemed churlish to say no so I want to get it over with as soon as possible, get seeing my old home out of the way as soon as possible. It means putting off installing my own alarm for a week or so but that's okay.

In the meantime, I can rip out the outside toilet and get Frankie to take it away and make that big chest to store my Dad's gear in. In fact, I think I'll make a start now.

Sunday night this is.

I've been in long enough to have a shower and something to eat but now I've got nothing to do but think about what happened today. God, it's getting ridiculous. My bloody life is starting to be some corny Australian soap opera only without the sunshine and surf.

I got the alarm systems for Trisha and me yesterday morning at B&Q and spent the rest of yesterday reading the instructions so I could just get to Trisha's, do it and get away in a hurry. Trisha had other ideas. Christ, I still can't believe it.

She opened the door to me and smiled. She was wearing a patterned dress, low at the front with half-flounced sleeves. Her hair was brushed back off her face and she was wearing makeup. That was odd for a start; Sunday is normally the day she just slops around in jeans and one of Andrew's old baggy sweatshirts. I nodded at her and carried the boxes in and she went into the kitchen and started making coffee. I had to stop unpacking the stuff and drink a mug of coffee while she prattled on about nothing in particular. In the end, I just stood up and got on with

it. She followed me round for an hour and that's really unusual; when I lived at home and had something DIY to do, Trisha always found somewhere else to be. I just got on with it and let her talk. She didn't seem to need me to answer her anyway. After that hour, she disappeared into the kitchen and started making Sunday Lunch.
I stood on the ladder in the hall where I was fixing the sensor and stared into space, wondering what the hell was going on. I found out when we'd finished the pork and drank the tea and I'd cleared the dishes away. She wanted me to sit down and have another cup of tea but some internal alarm was going off in my brain and all I wanted to do was get the job finished and get out of there. I had the really barmy idea that Trisha was working her way up to asking me to bed.
And I was right. Christ, it was crazy.
I finished in Andrew's bedroom and was packing my gear away when she came in. I picked up my tools and turned around. She was standing in the doorway, smiling.
"Why don't you have a shower?" Trisha asked. "And I'll make us something to eat. I've got some wine in the fridge."
I mumbled something about wanting to get an early night, work tomorrow and walked past her. She followed me downstairs, telling me I had time for a shower, it was the least she could do to say thanks. I went into the living room to get my car keys and she'd lit the wall lamps and turned the telly off.

"Come on Dave, I'm not going to bite," she said but her voice was, oh, like it was after we'd started making love all those years ago; flirty and throaty at the same time.

I started to say something, God knows what, but nothing came out even though my mouth was wide open because Trisha just stepped out of her dress.

She was only wearing a pair of black lacy knickers under the dress. It was like some cheap porno film in a dive in Soho or something. But it was real, too and I think that's how I finally found my voice. Knowing it was real and knowing it just wouldn't work. I've changed enough to know that just having sex with Trisha isn't going to make things better. And I'm sure that's all it would've been for her. Just sex, nothing to do with love.

"Trisha, I—" I could feel my head shaking slowly, saying no.

Trisha's eyes blazed and she brushed her lovely dark hair back off her face angrily. She stood with her legs slightly apart, her hands on her hips, forgetting all about the dress that was puddled round her feet and the way her breasts jiggled as she spoke to me. Well, she spat at me really.

"It's that _tart!_" She yelled. "Isn't it? That bloody dyed-haired bimbo!"

I didn't know what she was on about. Honest-to-God, I had no idea. It never occurred to me that she meant Anne because I hadn't been going out with Anne for nearly three weeks. All I could do was stand there, shaking my head. It only made Trisha worse. She ranted at me about the bimbo and the tart and I just pushed past to get out. I fumbled with the front door lock and tried to keep all my stuff in my arms when Trisha finally got it out.

"Jesus, after what I told her, I don't believe she's still going out with you! She must be even more bloody stupid than she looks!"

It finally got through to me then. Anne admits to dying her hair and I suddenly saw what must have happened the night she called it quits. Trisha must have been there at the club and saw me and Anne. Oh, it'd just be like Trisha to see us and then make sure we didn't see her and it wouldn't have been hard. At the club we were too wrapped up in the music and dancing and ourselves and there's a little side room to the side of the stage where we never went.

"You talked to Anne?" I said to Trisha.

"Yes, I talked to her," Trisha told me and her eyes stopped blazing but there was a cruel curl to her mouth that looked like gloating. "I told her she was wasting her time because you were only using her as a stop-gap till I asked you back."

What d'you say to something like that? I still don't know even after going over it all the way home and in the shower and eating my tea and writing about it. All I could do then was turn away from Trisha and get out quick. At least she didn't follow me into the street

God, no wonder Anne called it off. Having Trisha buttonhole you in the toilet or the corridor or wherever would be bad enough. Having her in your

face, talking to you oh so quietly while her lovely dark lilac eyes blaze at you and look you up down would be terrible. Hearing her tell you that the bloke you're with is only using you to pass the time away until the woman who's got you pinned against the wall decides to take him back...
Jesus, Trisha could've backed off Hitler, never mind Anne.

Ah shit, I'm tired and not just in my muscles and bones. I'm bloody knackered in my head. I need some sleep.

SIX

Martin Cottingham was sitting at his desk, puffing at his empty pipe and staring into the middle distance. Everything they knew or surmised about the probable murder of Trisha Eliot was jotted down in the notebook that lay closed on the desktop. Martin was still no nearer finding David Eliot. Mind you, he thought, if Eliot was responsible for his wife's death, it wouldn't be so surprising would it? It was likely the man had done a runner and he could be anywhere in or out of the country by now.

In the next few minutes, Martin would have to issue the order to have all ports, airports and police stations in the country alerted to be on the lookout for David Eliot. But...

"But," Martin said aloud. "I'd still like to find Anne Jordan before I do that."

Yes, he would because he had a good old-fashioned gut feeling that not everything was as clear-cut as his sergeant would like it to be. And Anne Jordan was the reason this bloody case had begun in the first place.

Martin looked at the empty bowl of his pipe and cursed Charlie Patterson again for his 'suggestion' that senior officers should set an example about smoking. If he'd gone round to Neil's office straight from the mortuary, he'd be able to have a smoke at least.

Neil.

Neil had suggested Martin look for Trisha and he had meant in connection with Anne Jordan's disappearance. Of course, they'd already found Trisha Eliot and Martin had cut Neil off a bit short. What if Neil had been right about Trisha Eliot being more likely to want to harm Anne Jordan than Davy Eliot?

"Neil rarely says or does anything without a good reason," Martin informed his empty pipe.

True.

"So maybe I should take a closer look at Trisha Eliot."

I thought the whispers were my own thoughts. That's how sure I was that the shadow was just something I made up to talk to so I could tell myself I wasn't going round the twist.

They started when I started fitting the alarm to this house. It was two days ago. I'd been drilling holes and lifting floorboards and moving furniture, so I didn't take much notice. I was sure it was just me talking to myself in my mind while I worked.
After what Trisha told me last Sunday, I've been thinking about Anne on and off all the time. If the whispers had merely said things at random or talked as if I wasn't in the room, I might've thought they weren't something in my own mind but it began by asking me questions I'd been asking myself ever since Sunday night.
Like:

<u>Even if Trisha gave her some grief, don't you think you deserved an explanation from Anne?</u>

I was on the ladder, feeding cable through the box when I heard this and I nodded as I pulled the wire through the hole.

<u>Well, don't you?</u>

Yes, I said aloud. I was concentrating on getting enough cable through and not falling off the ladder and the fact that I was talking to myself didn't really register. Well, let's face it, using this book is just another way of talking to myself, isn't it?

It's not as if you'd been taking her for granted or treating her like dirt. All she had to do was tell you about Trisha and give you the chance to put your side of the story.

I finished with the box and got off the ladders, moved them to the window and put the worklamp over the top rung. The light cast shaky shadows on the wall but they were just shadows. I started fixing the sensors, still thinking about Anne not giving me the chance to explain. It seemed like I deserved that much if only out of common courtesy and that's what I told myself and what the whisper replied to.

Right. You didn't think it hurt as much as when you left Trisha but it hurt all right. You just forced yourself to believe it didn't. Men are like that, all pride and brave-faced stoicism.

That's true, too. It didn't hurt as much but pain's pain. It was the not-knowing to begin with and, now, the idea that Anne believed Trisha straight off without giving me the chance to defend myself. Well, that sort of thing can drive you bonkers.

And that's what I thought as I fixed the sensor and it was what the shadow answered next.

All she had to do was tell you about Trisha but she didn't. That's not right.

And I agreed that it wasn't.

That was the first night but the second night, I knew it wasn't my mind talking to my mind.

I was in the back bedroom last night, fixing the sensor there and half-wondering about the best way to wire up the floodlight I'm going to put on the back wall. And I just sort of blanked out. I don't mean I flaked out or woke up an hour later or anything like that. In fact, I still fixed the sensor and connected the wire up. But I did it all without thinking about it and without thinking about the floodlight. When I came back to myself, I was standing at the window and staring down at the swings.

<u>things were simpler then</u>

Those four words seemed to bypass my ears completely and they settled in my brain like thick oil on water. And that's how they sounded, like they were underlined, as if they wanted me to understand that whatever was said like that was very important.
Still, it seemed like something I was obviously thinking, looking at the swings where I'd played when I was a kid, I didn't immediately think—oh shit, I'm cracking up—I just sort of nodded and carried on looking out of the window.

<u>the weight of any parted relationship is the hardest to bear if it is carried alone</u>

That's when I knew it wasn't my mind talking to my mind. I mean, what the hell did weight and relationships have to do with the swings and being a kid? Nothing, right? Besides, this time I had the very firm impression that the words had come from behind me. I turned and the shadow was there. With its arms open.

Fear tastes sour. I know that because it was the overwhelming sensation when I saw the shadow with its arms open as if to embrace me. It's a sharp, acrid taste, a bit like paracetemol tastes when you don't swallow it down first time and it gets slimy in your mouth. It made me gag. Then my stomach knotted and I could feel my eyes bugging out. I grabbed the lamp off the windowsill and pointed it directly at the shadow. It should have faded like shadows do when light shines on them. It didn't. It stayed exactly where it was with its arms open and I'm sure it cocked its head at me as if asking a question.

I left the room almost at a gallop. I was scared to bloody death and just wanted to get out of there and I don't care if it makes me a coward. Who's going to know but me?

I went to work today and got through it but the thought of coming back here and having the shadow waiting for me was too much. I rang Frankie but he was busy and couldn't meet me for a pint. I thought about ringing Neil but decided against it because I don't want anybody, not even Neil, to think I'm cracking up and Neil has a way of making you tell him things even when you've decided not to mention anything.

I went swimming at the leisure centre. I dunno, I think I was hoping that I could tire myself out, that maybe the action of the water on me as I moved through it would wash away the fear of the shadow. It didn't work. I swam forty lengths and all it got me was rubber-legged and light-headed and the fear still underlay everything. I thought about going to my Mum's and staying the night but that would only put it off. And I'd still have to come back here even if I decided to leave and find somewhere else to live. I had a shandy in the bar and told myself to grow up, to stop acting like a kid scared of the dark and, for a wonder, it worked. I think it worked mostly because of the alarm system and my Dad's tools. I haven't finished fitting the system yet and his tools are still here, vulnerable to any gang of toerags who fancy kicking the back door in. I came home.

But I was only brave enough to get in the house and sit here in the living room. The thought of going upstairs is too much. I'm going to have to but not yet. If I can get through the night maybe I'll be able to finish the alarm tomorrow and maybe the shadow will have got tired of waiting or maybe I'll have got enough nerve back to ignore it. God, I hope so. The taste of fear is bloody awful.

It's no good. I can't deny it anymore. I can't ignore it because it refuses to be ignored. The only bright spot is that it doesn't seem to be trying to frighten me now. In fact, I'm not sure it ever did try to

frighten me, it might just have been me. It's real though. I'm positive of that but it's more like the shadow I thought I'd made up. What I mean is, it's whispering to me but what it's whispering feels more like what I'd probably be thinking about anyway. It's like it's vocalising my deepest thoughts.
I think I can live with that. With a bit of luck, it'll help me get through this, whatever it is I'm feeling since Anne finished it and what Trisha told me. If it stops me getting like I was when I first moved back here, if it stops me wandering round the borough like some loony, it'll be worth it.

I know it's real because of what happened earlier today, Saturday. I'd finished all the wiring and fitting the sensors late Friday night and there was no sign of the shadow, no whispers. All that was left was fixing the floodlight on the back wall and then putting door locks on the interior doors.
I'd promised my Mum I'd take her over to Oxborough this morning because she'd got some final insurance payment for Dad and she wanted to do some early Christmas shopping.
After she'd spent up, she wanted something to eat and decided on the BurgerKing over Top Shop. We had cheeseburgers and she chomped into hers with gusto like always—when fast-food took off in the seventies, my Mum was like a convert to a new faith. She can't get enough of burgers and fries and she covers the lot with ketchup the way a kid does. She looks at you, trying to look shame-faced but the twinkle in her eyes tells you the truth.

We talked and she asked me how I was, how were things and I told her about the alarm system and the toerags. She nodded and said it was a good idea, she'd felt a lot better after my Dad put the alarm in their house a few years back. She bemoaned the fact that she couldn't leave the back door on the latch anymore, the way she'd done when we lived down in The Rows, it was a shame, she said and I nodded. I was thinking about all the good jewellery she had, stuff my Dad bought her for birthdays and Christmases and anniversaries.

"There's that," she agreed. "But it's the other things, things that aren't worth anything to anybody but me. Like pictures of you when you were a baby and of me and your dad when we were courting. Snaps of us on holiday and at family parties, of my Nan and your aunties. People break in these days and stuff like that gets ruined or ripped. I think, half the time, the burglaries have nothing to do with money or stuff they can sell, they just like to break and smash things. I'd hate it if my memories got ruined because some kid wanted to know what it felt like to smash up a house."

My Mum's right. Whenever I hear about a burglary and some old person getting beaten to a pulp, it always seems to me that the beating was the real reason rather than anything the bastards stole. It was a bad thought, sitting opposite my Mum who's turned seventy and living on her own. But it was the idea of her snapshots, what she calls her memories that stuck with me while I finished fitting the alarm system this afternoon.

I fixed the floodlight on the back wall as soon as I got home because it's October now and the light fades quickly in Seapool in the autumn, especially in The Rows. I had egg and chips for my tea and checked my pools coupon, realised I'd have to turn in to work again next week cos I hadn't won again and then started putting the new locks on the doors.

I did the living room door and the door from the kitchen into the hall. All that was left was the back bedroom door where I'm keeping my Dad's gear. I'm pretty sure it was only because of my Dad's gear that I worked up the courage to go into that room. The last of the grainy overcast had gone and the setting sun was shining through the window. It was that glorious mellow light we get in late afternoon. So there were lots of shadows but they were just the kind you always get in a room where the last long rays of sunlight are coming through the window.

I'd learned from experience downstairs that a bit and brace were best for the door itself but my electric drill works fine on the jambs so the sounds I heard, I put down to settling in the frame after I'd finished. Then I caught sight of some movement out of the corner of my eye and knew the sounds had nothing to do with settling wood.

I was bent down with my left eye against the door edge, my Dad's ancient bradawl poking through to test if the hole was deep enough in yet. As I began to press, I saw something like a dark blur edge across the vision of my other eye. I turned my head to look.

The sun was lower, shining in my eyes, making shadows dance across the floor and walls as it shone through the thin branches of the tree next door. I was already telling myself that it was one of those moving shadows when I looked in the far corner and knew I was wrong.

The sunlight shone directly into the corner and it was just a large, golden blur. Except for the man-sized shadow about six inches away from the angle of the two walls.

See, that's the thing, it was standing <u>away</u> from the two walls. Not lying against them like an ordinary shadow would.

I just stared at it, still waiting for it to become one more dancing shadow and knowing it never would. It was real. Then the noises impressed themselves on me properly.

I put the bradawl down but didn't stand up. I squatted there and stared at the impossible shadow and listened to its whispers.

<u>memories are light enough to carry when they are good and the photos help make them so but without the image, you are never sure if your memory of something is perfect or just a sort of desperate wishful thinking</u>

For a long moment, I was happy to believe it was something to do with the house and not me. I've never really dismissed all that medium stuff as crap—once I learned about electricity and static electricity and storage, I thought it could be a really good explanation for all that sort of stuff. Memories and emotions and stuff stored up from the past, like static and then oozing out or something like that. Having that thought, that it was the house, leaking out whatever it had stored over the years was all right. I didn't think there was anything to really be afraid of in the past. Not that sort of stuff anyway. Then the shadow whispered again and I knew it was talking <u>to me</u>, about stuff to do <u>with me</u>.

<u>you carry weight from the time you are born and life is a course in learning to carry that weight because the load increases as you age and it is memory that helps the most but only while each memory is good. images help but where are the images of your weight?</u>

I couldn't deny the questions were directed at me after that, could I? Anyway, the shadow confirmed it by spreading its arms towards me. The build up in tension in the room was so strong, building so fast, it felt like a gigantic amount of static electricity was looking for somewhere to earth itself.
I didn't want to be that earth. I decided the lock on the door could wait till tomorrow. I gathered up my Dad's tools and heard his voice in my mind, telling me to look after my tools and they'd never let me down. I came downstairs as fast as I could, trying not to be scared but scared shitless, the image of those shadow arms opening towards me in an embrace fixed in my mind.

That was about an hour ago. I made myself a mug of tea and drank it, staring at the flicker of the gas fire as the wind down the chimney turned the flames blue and yellow-orange. I put the light on and the telly on and kept my eyes away from anywhere a shadow might form. And, for half an hour, it worked. More or less. In fact, I almost convinced myself that all I'd seen was a normal shadow cast by the sun through the tree next door. I told myself that all I'd heard was my Dad's voice talking about carrying the weight through our lives and passing stuff on, like he'd said to me after his first stroke and like he'd said to my Mum. My Mum had been talking about her snapshots this morning and my brain had mixed it all up and that's what had happened.

After half an hour, though, I knew I was kidding myself. The shadow was real and it was talking to me, asking questions of me about <u>my</u> snapshots, not my Mum's. And then I really thought about my snapshots and finally got my own small set of photographs out and sifted through them.

And that's the problem, really. It didn't take long to sift through them because I've only got a small set of photographs.

When I left Trisha, the only photos I had were the cropped snaps in my wallet. There's one of my Mum and Dad on their wedding day, one of Andrew when he started Somerville Grammar, all dolled up in his new uniform and one of me and Trisha at our wedding reception. We're standing behind the cake, posing with the knife, ready to make the cut. Back at my old house, Trisha's got several albums, full of Andrew as a baby, of her family and my family at parties. There's others of us on holiday at Butlins when Andrew was a toddler. All the usual snapshots of a shared life, the sort you look at when somebody you haven't seen for a while visits.

Or just when there's nothing on the telly and you thought your wife was out at a girl's-night-in on a Tuesday night in January but wasn't there when you rang to speak to her...

I sat here and felt that enormous emptiness I'd felt after my Dad died and again after I found out about Trisha and moved back to Oil Street.

I looked at the picture of me and Trisha getting ready to cut the cake.

And, for the first time, I noticed the expression on Trisha's face and the look in her eyes. She's smiling, the tiny spangles in the lacework of the dress picked out by the flash of the camera. That smile doesn't look to me, now, as of one of unvarnished happiness at being married to the man she loves. There's something almost smug in that smile when you see the slight narrowing of her eyes. Until half an hour ago, I'd always put that narrowing down to the glare of the flash. But I don't think so anymore. She doesn't look like a new bride, happy to be married and enjoying the reception. She looks more like somebody who's got what she set out to get and now she's trying hard not to look smug about it and only failing by millimetres.

I'm looking it now and that's still what it looks like and

Oh God, it's down here now.
As soon as I looked at the photo again, it whispered to me.

 <u>with no other images to help, you only have your memory and perhaps your memory of things past is imperfect.</u>

The whisper made all my body hair stir, like short grass in a breeze. The goosebumps that followed that are still with me, like tiny eggs full of something trying to break through my skin into the light. I'm sitting in my chair and the shadow's right there, six inches or so off the back wall of the room. Even while I'm writing this, it's whispering—it's no good, I can't write and listen and it feels like I've <u>got</u> to listen.

It's stopped whispering now but it's still standing there with its arms outspread towards me.

 <u>where are the images of you before any wedding, before any child, before a life together? where are the images to tally with your recollection of her face when it was just the two of you, getting to know each other, learning what pleased you?</u>

That's what it asked and then the whispers stopped and my body hair lay down again and the goosebumps have gone and—oh shit, it's just gone. It faded away right while I was looking at it.

I've waited five minutes but it's still gone and there's no rational explanation for anything that's just happened. It was there and it was real and it whispered to me and asked me questions I couldn't answer.
I'm going to bed. Maybe I'll wake up and the rational explanation will be that I had a dream but I know that won't happen.

I brought this book with me to work and I'm writing this at half four in the afternoon. The door's closed and I'm not expecting anybody to come knocking and it doesn't really matter if they do. They'll see me writing and they'll just think it's work.
It's been two days since the shadow appeared in the living room and asked me those questions. I haven't seen it since then but it wasn't a dream. I woke up the next morning and remembered it all, right down to the goosebumps so I know it wasn't a dream. I've been thinking about those questions ever since and I still haven't got any answers. I was thinking that writing this would help me but it doesn't really. I'm sitting here and writing and then looking out of the window and seeing the weather deteriorate by the minute and all I can think of is that there won't be any more of that glorious golden mellow light in the afternoons; autumn's really here and Seapool will start to look bleak again like it always does just before winter arrives. I don't need to be a psychologist like Neil to understand that the regret I'm feeling for that lost mellow light is only a metaphor for my deeper regrets.

Oh, sod it, if this carries on, I'll be so full of self-pity that suicide will start to look like a good idea. If I was a kid, I'd go to my Mum and she'd give me a cuddle and make it all right again. Maybe I'll go to my Mum's anyway. If nothing else, it'll stop me repeating those whispered questions, looking for answers I know I don't have.

Jesus, my life's stopped feeling like a soap and it's turning into something from Shakespeare.
I went to my Mum's. She didn't give me a cuddle but she smiled when she opened the door and we drank tea and talked and, for a while, those questions stopped echoing in my head. Then, as she was looking for a pen and some paper to leave a note for the milkman, I saw the dark red cover of her enormous photo album in the drawer of the sideboard my Dad made in his little shed in The Rows.
I asked her if I could have a look at it and I felt a strange sort of thrumming inside me that made my stomach flutter and then it was gone. My Mum looked at me and smiled and then took the album out, forgetting all about the note to the milkman. She put it on the coffee table between us as she sat on her chair and I sat on the couch.
I flicked through the book and she gave a commentary on each picture, reminding me of this holiday or that relative or some party or other. I was enjoying it and the questions in my mind seemed to have faded completely. Then the little black and white snap, tucked away in the top right corner of the left facing page, caught my eye.

It was of a baby, about a year, eighteen months old. The baby was sitting on what looked like a scale-model of a proper dining room chair. I knew that chair—my Dad made it for me so I could sit on it with my feet touching the floor and feel like a grown-up instead of sitting on the couch with my chubby legs swinging in the air.

This baby was sitting on my old chair but the baby's feet weren't touching the floor. The baby's legs were encased in Plaster of Paris all the way from ankles to hips. The legs were splayed out, kept apart by what looked like a shortened wooden brush handle, embedded in the plaster cast. The baby didn't seem too put-out by this at all and his manic grin beamed out of the old photo, milk teeth poking through his bottom gum.

I asked my Mum whose baby it was.

She gave me a long, strange look. There was a glint in her eyes as she peered over her glasses at me. Like she was amused but a bit worried at the same time. I saw all this in my quick look up at her and then I looked back at the photo. A part of me wondered if this was some long-kept secret. It even crossed my mind that she'd had another baby before me and that, for whatever reason, it had gone before I was born. God help me, I even wondered if it had been illegitimate and had been sent away. I know that happened a lot in the fifties.

"It's you son," my Mum told me quietly.

Her voice sounded far off, so far off it took a while for the words to get through to me so I could make sense of them. When they finally did, I looked and saw that there was no doubt my Mum was amused this time.

"Don't you remember?"

I shook my head.

"Well, you were only a baby," she told me. "Just turned one when it happened. That was taken about, oh, two months after it happened. Your dad got the camera off a bloke at work. One of those that fell off the back of that lorry with the broken back door. Probably the same lorry we got your radio from when you passed your 11+. You do remember that, don't you?"

I nodded. It was a Perdio with a leather case. It had tiny holes in the leather where the speaker was.

"But I don't remember being in plaster. What happened?"

"You decided to see if you could fly," she said happily and shook her head.

It felt like the room tilted to the right and I nearly fell off the couch.

"You were at the top of the stairs. You'd been toddling for a while and you'd crept upstairs. I was in the kitchen and thought you were with your dad and he thought you were with me. I came in from the kitchen to ask him to mash the spuds, looked up the stairs and nearly died of fright. You were standing on the little landing, leaning against the wall with your left hand, grinning at me. I screamed at you to stand still and that got your dad out of the living room. You saw him and made the funny gurgling noise you used for Daddy and then, before either of us could move, you put your right foot out to walk downstairs. You'd been coming downstairs for a while, doing that little half-on-your-bum, half-on-your-hands shuffle. This time, you decided to do it like you'd seen us do it. Then you toppled forwards and if your dad hadn't been so quick, you'd've probably killed yourself. Still, it was bad enough."

"What was?" I asked, my voice didn't sound like my voice.

"You broke both legs and dislocated both hips."

The rest of the time went by in a blur. I don't know what we talked about or how many red lights I stopped at on the way home. I got home twenty minutes ago and started writing this and I've been thinking about that dream I had after that poor girl had her accident. Is that what I was dreaming about? That near-fatal topple I had when I was just turned one? If it is, why was the shadow there? Something else, too—when I left junior school and went to Somerville Grammar, I stopped looking for that marvellous moment between the sky and the ground. I didn't demand to use the trampoline all the time and I didn't dash home to jump off the slide or The Dead Tree. I just got on with secondary school life and grew up.

I think that's odd, strange. I mean, that moment before gravity noticed me again and dragged me down is so wonderful, so thrilling, that I can't believe I just stopped looking for it. But I did.

Oh, God, does it matter? When there's all this other stuff to think about, does it matter?

SEVEN

"Neil, I'm knocking off now. Neil?"

Neil looked up and saw Sarah standing in the doorway, all bundled up in her coat, her black bag draped over her shoulder, car keys dangling from one long, elegant finger. He nodded and smiled.

"Aren't you going home?"

"Not yet, love. I'll see you in the morning. Just switch the phone over for me." He smiled again and stared at Sarah until she smiled back and nodded and closed the door behind her. When the small click sounded as the phone was routed through to his office, Neil was looking out of the window at the twilight as it coloured the sky purple and the empty garden filled with shadows.

"Oh, it might," he murmured. "It might matter a lot, Davy."

Yes, the fact that Davy had apparently stopped searching for that moment between the sky and the ground might matter a lot by the time all of this was over.

Neil knew he would have to give this journal to Martin and Martin would hand it over to the police psychological experts for their opinion and, if and when there was a court case, the fact that Davy had stopped looking for that moment during his teenage years would weigh heavily, Neil thought.

For the simple reason that it would add substance to the opinion that Davy suffered a breakdown or something even worse.

It was the dream that would do it. The dream where Davy was standing at the top of the stairs and the shadow was waiting at the bottom.

Davy might have given up looking for that sublime moment before gravity noticed him again in his waking hours but, Neil was sure, not in his dreams. The police psychiatrist would say that the desire to leap from high places was a physical manifestation of Davy's obsessive, addictive personality and the dream he had proved it. Even if Davy never mentioned having the dream again in this journal, the couple of mentions so far plus the fact of his near-fatal jump when he was a toddler would be enough. The worst thing would be that Neil wouldn't really be able to argue with the conclusions of any psychiatrist the police produced. God, what a friggin mess.

"No wonder he always felt like his life was running out of his control," Neil muttered to the empty garden beyond the window.

No wonder Davy had been the way he was when he was a kid. He didn't remember the accident except way down deep in his mind, where the barricades are strong and high. Oh, down there he remembered all right and he remembered how lucky he'd been. He ended up with broken legs and dislocated hips and his legs were in plaster but he was *very* lucky. And he'd always known how lucky he'd been. Davy, the grown-up Davy who lived behind those barricades and still had his kid-memories, knew he was lucky to be alive and, because he knew it he always felt like his life was running away from him. That was probably the reason why he'd always been looking for that edge, that moment between the sky and ground. If he could keep challenging life like that, keep winning each small battle then, behind the barricades, the Davy who remembered the accident could keep telling himself that he was in charge. Yes, he'd been lucky but he kept on being lucky so there was no reason to feel guilty about it. If he kept hitting life head-on then he kept earning the right to still be alive.

The changes in his life over the past two years had started to eat away at the barricades and what was behind them was beginning to peek through. Just enough for Davy to see something there and wonder about it.

Life was perverse that way—most of the time, life was humdrum and ordinary, made that way, strangely, by having things to do, ordinary stuff that you did every day because they needed doing and created the white noise most people live with most days and even years.

In Davy's case, those things stopped him really thinking about himself and his life; the white noise kept him numb and there was no need to seek out that sublime moment between the sky and the ground. That's why he'd stopped looking when he was a teenager. When you're a teenager, almost as much as when you're a kid, life is full and exciting and, when it isn't, it's boring and teenagers love that white noise because it provides the perfect vehicle for the anger and frustration when you realise that nobody else in the world understands you or what you've got to suffer because *you alone* understand how crap the world is. It changes a little when you reach sixteen or so and people keep asking you what you're going to do when you grow up, but that can be white noise, too.

Now, Davy had time on his hands and nobody to talk to but himself, or the shadow he thought he'd created. He was writing in the journal and finding out that what he was really doing was examining his life. And, as he'd said, moving back into a house not fifty yards from where you were born and brought up, moving back with just a few plastic bags, some tools and a suitcase didn't seem much to have or far to have come. Things like that would make anybody begin to look inside themselves and what Davy had found was something that would have been better if it had stayed behind those barricades.

Neil turned away from the window and looked at the phone. After reading that it had been Trisha who had made Anne call it off with Davy, Neil was even more sure that anything that might have happened to Anne was more likely to be down to Trisha and never mind the fact that Trisha was dead. Neil thought about ringing Martin again and pressing him to think about Trisha rather than Davy. No, Martin was a good policeman as well a friend. He might not do it straight away, given the fact of Trisha's death, but he would treat Neil's suggestion seriously at some point.

"Better to read the rest of this," Neil said and settled in his seat.

Davy hadn't used dates but going on what he'd written so far and the few times he'd mentioned the time lapse between entries, Neil thought he must be coming up to Andrew's accident very soon.

Would that be when the shadow started becoming overtly threatening to Davy? Neil thought it might.

I wrote that yesterday, Tuesday. I dreamed again last night. The same dream—me at the top of the stairs and the shadow at the bottom with its arms open wide.
The dream woke me up and when I woke up the shadow was in my bedroom.
The first pearly light of a misty Seapool dawn was seeping through the net curtains my Mum gave me when I moved back here and I could see the shadow by the door quite well. Mind you, if it had been four-in-the-morning pitch black, I'm pretty sure the bloody thing would have managed to be visible to me.
I sat up in bed, wide awake, my shoulders trembling and my stomach still churning with the last vestiges of the dream. I stared at the shadow and just waited. Somewhere inside me, I knew it was going to start whispering to me so I just waited.

<u>do you not remember this dream from before the recent accident? you thought you left behind seeking that moment between sky and ground when you reached puberty but you didn't. you remembered it in your dreams.</u>

As always since it began to whisper to me, the words seemed to simply settle in my hindbrain, their meaning apparent immediately without needing to be carried by my ears or decoded by whatever part of my brain decodes sound. I understood the words but I didn't know what they meant. And I actually spoke to the shadow then. I actually talked to it like it was a <u>person</u> instead of the thing I'd made up to be a sort of sounding board for my internal conversations. God, if this isn't going round the bend, I don't know what is.

"The only dreams I remember from being a teenager are the wet dreams every lad I ever knew had," I told the shadow.

It was true. Those wet dreams during puberty were wonderful and awful at the same time, filled with shameful embarrassment but also with that sneaky hope that you'd have another one when you went to bed the next night.

<u>you dreamed of that moment between the sky and the ground more than you dreamed of Miss Sandals your history teacher.</u>

That was too weird. I sat in bed and heard that and it was just too weird. I remembered the wet dreams but not their content anymore than I remembered their content when I woke up after having one all those years ago.

Now, last night, I heard the shadow say that and suddenly remembered the dream and who starred in it. Miss Sandals was my history teacher and gorgeous. She was young, maybe only twenty four when I was fourteen and fifteen and she had this amazing black, wavy hair and legs that seemed to go on forever. And when she smiled, her dark brown eyes sparkled and made everybody in the class go all dreamy. Christ, the dream I used to have <u>was</u> about her and it wasn't really all that sexy. It was just a sort of picture show where she was getting undressed in the gym changing rooms and I was hiding behind the lockers and watching. That was it, real pornographic stuff, wasn't it? But the point is,

the scary point is, if somebody had asked me what my wet dream was about, I'd've just looked at them and said I didn't have the faintest idea. Once the shadow told me, I remembered the dream in every detail. God help me, I could feel myself getting a hard on and that was too much, just too bloody much. I forced myself out of bed and forced myself to walk past the shadow and out of the door. I came downstairs and, just like after my Dad died, I started my day earlier than normal.
I went to work and drifted in and out of it, doing stuff on automatic pilot, alternating between being convinced I'm certifiable and telling myself that I just need a rest, a break, maybe a holiday. Then I came home and had my tea and washed up and read the paper and watched the news and then started writing in this book and I still don't know if I'm mad or tired and need a break or
There's the phone.

Andrew's in a coma.
Four words. I wrote them and I know they're true but even looking at them in my own handwriting, it's hard to accept them.
I got home from the hospital not long ago and now I'm writing this because if I don't, I think I might just start mumbling and pulling my bottom lip or kicking things or breaking windows or something. I might just, oh bollocks, I don't know what I might just, I just know I have to do this because I'm

Shit!

I'm babbling, that's what I'm doing. Come on, Davy, get a grip!

Even through the thickness of her voice down the phone, I knew it was Trisha and I almost put the bloody thing down—I really didn't feel like talking to her after that Sunday when I put her alarm system in. Then I thought maybe that's what she was ringing about, maybe the alarm hadn't worked and somebody had broken in. Oh God, if only it was that simple, that unimportant.

"Andrew's in hospital," she told me after I'd asked her what was up. "The university's just phoned me. They say we should get there as soon as possible. Will you drive me? I don't think…"

I told her I'd be round in ten minutes and made it there in eight.

She was standing in the doorway when I pulled up. She was haloed by the porch light and her face looked so white she might've been a ghost. She closed the door and ran down the path, got into the car and went straight into it. She didn't say thank God you've come or anything, she sat in the passenger seat and told me.

"He's unconscious," she told me breathlessly. "He was at some dance on this side of the river and got drunk or something. He fell and hit his head. They said the boys with him said he got up and started to laugh and then collapsed and the ambulance took him to Seapool General."

"Andrew? Drunk?" I sounded incredulous as I said this because I was.

the scary point is, if somebody had asked me what my wet dream was about, I'd've just looked at them and said I didn't have the faintest idea. Once the shadow told me, I remembered the dream in every detail. God help me, I could feel myself getting a hard on and that was too much, just too bloody much. I forced myself out of bed and forced myself to walk past the shadow and out of the door. I came downstairs and, just like after my Dad died, I started my day earlier than normal.
I went to work and drifted in and out of it, doing stuff on automatic pilot, alternating between being convinced I'm certifiable and telling myself that I just need a rest, a break, maybe a holiday. Then I came home and had my tea and washed up and read the paper and watched the news and then started writing in this book and I still don't know if I'm mad or tired and need a break or
There's the phone.

Andrew's in a coma.
Four words. I wrote them and I know they're true but even looking at them in my own handwriting, it's hard to accept them.
I got home from the hospital not long ago and now I'm writing this because if I don't, I think I might just start mumbling and pulling my bottom lip or kicking things or breaking windows or something. I might just, oh bollocks, I don't know what I might just, I just know I have to do this because I'm
Shit!

I'm babbling, that's what I'm doing. Come on, Davy, get a grip!

Even through the thickness of her voice down the phone, I knew it was Trisha and I almost put the bloody thing down—I really didn't feel like talking to her after that Sunday when I put her alarm system in. Then I thought maybe that's what she was ringing about, maybe the alarm hadn't worked and somebody had broken in. Oh God, if only it was that simple, that unimportant.

"Andrew's in hospital," she told me after I'd asked her what was up. "The university's just phoned me. They say we should get there as soon as possible. Will you drive me? I don't think…"

I told her I'd be round in ten minutes and made it there in eight.

She was standing in the doorway when I pulled up. She was haloed by the porch light and her face looked so white she might've been a ghost. She closed the door and ran down the path, got into the car and went straight into it. She didn't say thank God you've come or anything, she sat in the passenger seat and told me.

"He's unconscious," she told me breathlessly. "He was at some dance on this side of the river and got drunk or something. He fell and hit his head. They said the boys with him said he got up and started to laugh and then collapsed and the ambulance took him to Seapool General."

"Andrew? Drunk?" I sounded incredulous as I said this because I was.

Andrew doesn't drink like that, not enough to get rolling drunk. When he passed his GCSEs, he went out with a gang of mates and got legless. Neil's daughter helped him home and he staggered into the hall, threw up, staggered into the kitchen and threw up and then staggered out into the garden and threw up twice more. After I'd doused his head under the garden tap and then got a pot full of coffee down him, he sobered up enough to vow he'd never ever do it again. He meant it. He said he hated the idea that he wasn't in control, that somebody had to help him home and then he'd had no control over his body and had thrown up. He was so adamant that he made Nicole Judd be a witness and to promise that she'd tell everybody how he couldn't keep a promise even to himself if he ever got drunk again. Andrew's a lot like his mum in that way, he hates not being in control of himself.

"Students drink," Trisha said but her voice was low. It sounded, oh what's the word? Furtive.
I glanced at her and she was looking at her hands, picking at her thumbnail, obviously wanting to put it in her mouth and chew it—it's what she always wants to do when there's something bothering her or she's not sure how to say something that needs to be said. She always wants to do that but makes herself <u>not</u> do it because it would be like admitting she wasn't in control. I saw her picking at her thumb so I knew something wasn't right.
We said nothing else during the drive. It's only seven miles to the hospital from my old house but, Christ, it seemed to take an eternity. Then, finally, I was

parking the car in the main car park outside the main doors of the hospital. I got out and Trisha got out and, as I was locking the doors, she marched round the front of the car and stood in front of me. Her legs were slightly apart, her back ramrod straight, chin out, hands by her sides. She looked like an Old West gunfighter. She looked very old and very young at the same time in the harsh orange blur of the security lights. I suppose I looked about the same. Apart from the gunfighter bit.

"Andrew phoned me on Monday night," she said, staring right into my eyes. "He wanted to know if...there was any chance of you and me getting back together." She took a deep breath, as if she was about to dive into a pool. "I had somebody with me and...he answered the phone. Andrew asked me who he was and..."

This pause went on so long I wondered if she'd just blanked out, a delayed reaction thing or something. It also gave me time to wryly acknowledge that I'd been right about turning her down the other Sunday—it would just have been sex, not a try at reconciliation. Then I had to fill in the pause.

"So you told him who the somebody was."

She nodded. "He was angry and..." She wiped angrily at the moisture on her cheeks that might have been drizzle but wasn't. "He said some very hurtful things to me and about me and..."

"You lost your temper and told him the reason I'd left."

My voice sounded flat because I didn't want to sound angry. Does that make any sense? Yeah, I think so. I wanted to sound sympathetic but I couldn't manage that so I kept my voice flat. Trisha just nodded. I took her elbow and led her towards the doors.

"Trisha," I said slowly. "It's done. If he was going to get drunk because you had a row, he'd've done it on Monday. All that matters is that we get up there and find out how he is." And that last bit was true even if the idea that Andrew wouldn't get drunk a couple of days after a row with his mother wasn't true at all.

She let me ease her into the hospital and said nothing else. I don't know what she was thinking but I was thinking that I could well imagine Andrew being upset enough to get drunk after the row. I can imagine Trisha, who hates the thought of not being in control and not just of herself, not liking the idea of whoever it was she was with hearing her <u>son</u> having a row with her. No, Trisha wouldn't like that at all because it might give the bloke ideas. So she'd really go to town on Andrew, not really to hurt Andrew because God knows, she loves him, just to let the bloke who was there know who was in charge. And I can imagine she'd be a bit more graphic than she needed to make her point. Yeah, I can imagine Andrew hearing it and then spending two days brooding and then going out and getting drunk because of it.

But it's worse than that. We found out, from one of the lads who'd gone to the hospital with him, that it hadn't just been a simple fall.

Andrew had left the dance up in Saughall and gone round the back of the building where they're building some sort of extension. The lad told us that Andrew had climbed up the scaffolding and tried to walk across the plank in the middle. He got half-way and started farting around, tap-dancing and swinging his arms and then he'd fallen. No, that's crap. The lad said it looked like he decided to see if he could jump from the plank onto the big pile of cardboard boxes piled up about ten feet away from the foot of the scaffolding. 'sort of like stunt-men do, you know?' the lad said and then just sobbed into his hands.

See? Jesus, when I heard that, it scared me even more than hearing he was in a coma. Andrew's never been like me that way. He never seemed to go looking for the high place. He dived off the springboard at Laketon Pool when he was nine and he represented his school once in a trampoline competition but it was only once. He soon gave up acrobatics for football, much to his teacher's disgust. I stood in the corridor, listening to the lad tell us what happened while we waited for the doctor to come out of the room they've got Andrew in. I stood there and wondered if it was my fault. I know that sounds daft but I couldn't help it. What if, I thought, my love of high places had waited until now before coming out in Andrew and, because he hadn't had the practise like I'd had, he'd cocked it up and so ended up in a coma?

That's what I thought in the corridor and then, when the doctor came out and said we could see him,

I told myself to stop being a bloody idiot and go in and see my son.

We went in and I looked and saw Andrew and then looked at all the machines he was wired up to and listened while the doctor told us what was what.

Andrew was in a coma and they were still worried that the injury could deteriorate. They'd operated on two clots but they gave us no real prognosis. They were doing all they could and he was young and strong was what it amounted to.

Trisha sat down on the chair by the bed and held his hand and talked to him. She talked to him about everything but their argument, never coming close to even admitting she was wrong never mind apologising. She finally let the tears overflow her lovely dark lilac eyes, though. I sat on the chair on the other side and just looked at him and all those bloody machines. It was like all those horrible flashes I'd had when he was young had come at once, become real.

God, it's awful. They call it intensive care or therapy or something but, Jesus, it's hard to see where care can come into it. I know they do a great job and they do care but it's so hard to see anything but the bloody tubes and the monitors. And the noise is terrible. All those unearthly beeps and boops and the suck-let-go of the ventilator. It's a horrible sound. I think it's the way it makes a sort of <u>chunk</u> sound after the inward suck. I sat there and heard it and it seemed like the inward suck was Andrew, trying to get enough breath inside him to stay alive and then the chunk sound was the machine saying, sorry, *that's all, we know it's not enough but it's all there is. I remembered Johnny Simpson down in The Rows. He had terrible asthma and he sounded like that when he had an attack. I heard the sound of the ventilator and saw poor Johnny's stricken face as he tried to get enough air into him to stay alive.*

I stared at the machines and kept on staring because, I think, I didn't want to look at Andrew. But I had to in the end. I had to because he's my son.

And it was worse than all the rest put together. Worse than the low grade anger I felt for Trisha and the dislike of the machines and their noise. It was worse because Andrew doesn't look sick. He looks like he's just asleep. There's the bandage on his head but there's no other marks on him. He looks like Andrew asleep. I stared at him for a long few minutes and then I had to look away again and that was when the nightmare became darker and deeper and more terrifying.

The shadow was standing next to Trisha, about two feet from Andrew's head.

I refused to believe it, tried to make myself believe that it was Trisha's shadow I was seeing, thrown by the fluorescent bar above her head and knew I was fooling myself. Trisha's shadow was on the floor, flat and shaped like a huddled mass. The shadow was standing up, man-sized and -shaped, <u>my</u> size and shape. And then it opened its arms. It spread them out like an embrace.

But not to me. God, Jesus Christ, if only!

It spread its arms out towards <u>Andrew</u>.

I nearly yelled at it to piss off back here, to this house where it belonged but it turned its head towards me and whispered to me. I know now that it definitely bypasses my ears because I heard it loud and clear even above the horrible machine sounds and the mechanical breathing.

   <u>guilt is a terrible weight, a heavy weight, heavy enough to kill</u>

Then it turned away from me and looked down at Andrew, still with its shadow-arms spread in that awful prelude to an embrace.

We stayed until mid-morning today and even then, it took me easing her away and some almost-harsh words from the sister to persuade Trisha to let go of Andrew's hand. She'd been holding on like it was a straw and she was drowning.

There's a huge observation window in the room and I stared through it as we walked past. The shadow was still there, still standing at the head of Andrew's bed. I willed the bloody thing to leave, to follow me out but it stayed there with its arms spread.

In the end, I had to trust that the idea I'd had would work and that the shadow would leave him and come back here.

I got Trisha home and into bed and then I drove here like a maniac. I phoned my Mum and work to let them know what had happened and then came in here and started writing all this down.

It's not just so I can get it straight in my head, this writing. I'm waiting for it to get late enough for me to switch on the standard lamp without it looking funny from the outside.

The idea I had was simple and, I suppose, desperate.

While I stared at the bloody thing in Andrew's room, I suddenly saw it in the back bedroom here that night when I first saw it after moving back. I remembered pointing my worklamp at it and the way it stayed in the beam of light, like it was frozen. What I'm hoping is that the shadow is _really_ mine and that it'll have to come back here, back to me. I'm going to turn the light on and hope it freezes the thing. God knows, it's feeble but it's all that's keeping me from going completely mad at the moment.

Okay, time to do it.

My hands are shaking and my mouth feels as dry and gritty as the bottom of a budgie's cage but it's working. It took five minutes but the shadow finally appeared in this room. Maybe it took five minutes for it to travel the seven or so miles from the hospital, I don't know. Don't care, either.

It's not against the wall, it's standing off the wall behind the telly by about six inches. It really does look frozen in the cone of light from the standard lamp my Mum bought me as a moving-in present. It's just a shadow. It hasn't got its arms spread and it's head isn't cocked to one side like it's asking me something but I suppose that's what I'm waiting for now. I'm sitting here, waiting for it to start whispering again, saying things I just don't have a clue about.

It's nearly midnight now and the shadow's exactly like it was when it finally left Andrew's bed and came back here. No outspread arms, no whispering either. I wonder if the light's done more than just frozen it in place? I wonder, please God, if the light's fixed it completely so it's nothing more than a shadow that's somehow managed to make itself more than a two dimensional figure?
I'm knackered. I've got to get some sleep. Christ, the air feels heavy, like there's a storm brewing.

It's Monday night now. The Monday after that horrible day. I went to bed that night when I froze the shadow in the cone of light and actually fell asleep. I dreamed, though. It was the same dream, the one where I'm standing at the top of the stairs and the shadow's waiting at the bottom. It woke me up and I got up and came downstairs and the shadow was still frozen in the light. It didn't have its arms outspread and it didn't whisper anything.
It hasn't moved or whispered in the days in between.

I go to work each day and go to the hospital on my way home each tea-time and stay until Trisha arrives around half six. I don't trust myself to remain calm while she talks to Andrew about everything but their argument. And then I come home and ring my Mum to tell her there's no change and then I sit here and watch the shadow. I put the telly on and I try to read the paper or a book or watch whatever's on the telly but I'm really watching the shadow for any movement, listening hard for anything it might be whispering.

It hasn't moved or whispered and I'm beginning to believe instead of just hoping that the light from the lamp has not only frozen it but somehow drained it of whatever power it possessed.

I have this sort of superstitious idea that if it stays frozen and silent until Wednesday night, a week after Andrew's accident, it'll mean it's over. Please God.

There's the phone. Please, not bad news about Andrew.

It was Trisha and my heart seemed to jump into my throat when I heard her voice—I was convinced that she was ringing me to tell me that Andrew was dead and it was time for me to go to the hospital and say goodbye to him.

Shit, in a way, it was almost as bad as that would have been.

"I just rang to say they're positive there's been no deterioration in Andrew's condition." Trisha told me.

I told her that was good but I kept looking at the frozen shadow and wondering what the _real_ reason for her calling was. I mean, telling me he was no worse seemed a bit pointless.

"I think it's a good sign," she said uncertainly. "You know, with it being a week since...you know. And how worried they were about another clot and more swelling. I've been there every day and held his hand and talked to him and I think that's it, you know?"

I heard the question she didn't ask. She wanted me to tell her that she was right, that she'd apologised the best way she could by making sure there was no worsening in Andrew's condition. I mumbled something and then just waited to see if she'd say what she'd actually phoned me to say. Finally, she spoke again.

"When he's better, awake... when he comes home, I'll make things up to him properly, Dave."

There was another long pause and I saw the faintest movement from the shadow and it felt like the world was beginning to go out of focus. And Trisha couldn't wait any longer for me to fill in the pause.

"Dave, if we—"

I knew what she was going to say, knew this was the real reason for her call. I knew it the way I know how to wire a plug. And I knew it would be a mistake and I knew that I had to tell her exactly that.

"Trisha," I said. "Us getting back together for Andrew would be...wrong. Living a lie wouldn't work."

"Dave, please don't write us off. I...maybe I was...if..."

Even then she couldn't bring herself to just come right out and say she'd been wrong.

I told her I had to go, told her there was somebody knocking on the door, had been for five minutes and they were obviously not going away. I was looking at the shadow, waiting for another movement, not knowing what else to say to get her off the phone. But she saved me having to think of another lie.

"<u>It's that tart, isn't it!</u>" Trisha yelled.

I winced and held the phone away from my ear. I started to say something but she was past listening. Trisha was almost ballistic.

"God, I can't believe it! Not after I told her about you and that she was wasting her time, fawning over you like you were both a couple of randy teenagers!" Her voice could've stripped paint.

But, terrible as it sounds given everything else, it was almost funny. Wasn't it? I've got to be honest. I mean, really, it <u>was</u> almost funny. Trisha broke up our marriage because she wanted sex, <u>just sex</u> with somebody different. In other words, she was willing to throw away all those years of marriage because she felt <u>randy</u>. Now she was accusing me of acting like a randy teenager. I mean, deary deary me, it <u>was</u> almost funny.

Except, it's not funny in the least. And I had to ask her what she'd said to Anne.

"I told her she was wasting her time! What else? I told her you'd never be able to leave me behind! Why not? You said as much when you left in January!" She sounded full of righteous indignation, almost gloating.

I told her I didn't remember saying that and the shadow moved again, just a slight lift of its arms and I began to dread the moment when, I was sure, it started whispering to me. I really couldn't cope with the shadow whispering to me while Trisha was ranting at me.

"Not in so many words," Trisha said, her voice a little more normal. "But it's what you meant. You were having wet dreams about me for God's sake! That's what I told the slag! I can't believe she's still with you after that. She must be more bloody stupid than she looks!"

The only thing I could think of to say after that was that we should say goodnight. She tried to mollify me, tried to tell me she was upset over Andrew, she didn't mean to be like that, please, wait. I just said goodnight and put the phone down.

Dear God, no wonder Anne called it off.

I just sat here and stared at the shadow but it's stopped moving now, if it ever really did. God knows, it might've been just my imagination, a reaction to Trisha's diatribe. I hope so.

I'm not sure I can do this. I'm not sure I can carry on like this.

Okay, I seem to have got the shadow sorted out and that's good but I just can't see Trisha being any different than she was on the phone.

Never mind the fact we're apart and that she split us up, there's no way Trisha would confide in some bloke she's only sleeping with. We were together a long, long time and it makes you close in more ways than just sex or, in my case, love.

Until the menopause, I was the person Trisha talked to first about things. Whether it was decorating or her family or work. And I did the same. It's probably why I made up the shadow, because everybody needs somebody to talk to, to bounce things off. So, I'm the one Trisha will <u>keep</u> haranguing and I'll be expected to sit here and let her because, from her point of view, that's how it's supposed to work. And I don't think I can do that. Not anymore, not now it's about Andrew.

I used to shake my head when I heard of blokes, husbands, fathers, just walking out one day and never coming back because things got too much for them. I could never see myself doing that. I think I can understand it now, though. The idea that I could just get my coat and car keys and drive away from all of this, head into the night, chasing the sun, seems really tempting right now. I mean, even knowing Trisha like I do, it never would've occurred to me she could be so hard and spiteful, so dog-in-a-manger. It's not as if I'd walked out because I found somebody else, is it? She was the one who went looking for somebody else. Saying what she did to Anne seems so, oh, I don't know, just so bloody <u>mean</u>. It makes me wonder if I ever really knew her at all.

Oh bollocks. I'm so bloody tired. It feels like this room is making me tired, the air's so heavy. I'm going to bed and I hope there are no dreams tonight. That'd be too much.

It's still dark outside because it's only half-three in the morning. I did dream and it woke me up and now here I am again, pen in bloody hand, wondering how I'm supposed to get on with my life when it feels like it's collapsing round me like a condemned building.

It wasn't even _that_ dream. It was worse. I dreamed about me and Trisha. I suppose, thinking what I thought before I went to bed, I should've been expecting it but that's no consolation.
I dreamed about that first time we made love, in front of her parents' fire. It was so vivid, I could see the way the sweat glistened on our nakedness, like I was watching it all from a point on the ceiling. I saw the way the fire flickered and the reddish glow it lent to our skin and I could feel how we moved in time and even the look in her eyes when she came milliseconds before I did. That's when I woke up and I half expected to find I'd come for real but I hadn't. I lay there for a minute or two and then came downstairs.
Now, I've just got to find some way of filling the hours before I go to work cos it's like it's back to the way I was after my Dad died.
Christ, won't things ever change? It seems like me and Anne happened to some other bloke. I find it really hard to believe that for those couple of months, I felt and acted normal. It doesn't seem possible that I used to go to bed and sleep without remembering if I dreamed or not and got up at a normal seven o'clock.

Anne.
 It's been a while since I thought of her in that way, about how we used to be a couple. I can see her face when she came back the night she called it off. Now I know why she did it and I don't really blame her. Still, now I know why, now I know about Trisha, I

wonder if it mightn't be possible for me to explain it to Anne? Maybe we could even try again?

Why not? Shit, it's got to be worth a try, hasn't it?

EIGHT

The ringing phone made Neil jump a little in his chair and he snatched it up. "Judd? Oh, hello, love."

He leaned back in his chair while Joy asked him if he knew what time it was and was he ever coming home tonight. Neil looked at the book on his desk and shook his head.

"I don't think so, Joy." He closed his eyes and listened. "Yeah, love, I know but...it's important. I'm only going to be here, nowhere else but I need to finish this...thing. I promise, I'll tell you everything tomorrow. Tell you what, I'll meet you for lunch and tell you then. Okay?"

Four miles away, Martin Cottingham stood outside 12 Oil Street and watched the ambulancemen take what was in the boot of the car out and put it on the stretcher. He sighed. The bulge of his pager seemed even more intrusive than usual and he thought about ringing Neil.

"Any ideas where he is, sir?" Sergeant Robb stood next to his boss and watched as the ambulance drove away. He was telling himself that he'd seen worse than what had been in the boot of the car but, truth to tell, he wasn't sure.

"Eliot?" Martin asked and turned back to look at the house behind him. "None at all, sergeant. Not one bloody clue. And, to be honest, unless he strolls into the station, I really don't think we'll find out for a long time."

He didn't add what he was thinking; unless Neil Judd can come up with Eliot's whereabouts in the same way he worked out it was Trisha Eliot who had been the main threat to Anne Jordan.

Of course, technically that was still up for discussion. Until he had the medical and forensic reports, there was nothing to say that the fact the Micra now being loaded up onto the carrier belonged to Trisha Eliot was anything but coincidental; Eliot could have used the car because it was handy. Martin doubted it very much, though.

"So, what now?"

Martin shook his head and looked at his sergeant's young face. The man was a good copper, good with details and good at interrogation but there was an eagerness there that part of Martin distrusted. Robb had no doubts that David Eliot was the cause of everything they'd found so far. Ah, youth. To be so sure, to never have any doubts.

Well, youth was fine and eagerness was good but Martin had been around the block a few times more than young Sergeant Robb and something about this case was making Martin's instinct twitter; he smelled something more than an eternal triangle here. Still, trying to find David Eliot was his main concern right now.

"Sir?"

"Stay here and make sure we get everything. I'm going back to the factory and bring Patterson up to date."

Robb watched Martin walk towards his car and frowned. Robb knew Martin sometimes felt he was a bit too cocksure of himself and Robb occasionally admitted to the fact. This case, though...it looked and felt so clear-cut, Robb just couldn't understand Martin's attitude. Apart from anything else, the boss looked his age and that was something Robb had never seen before. Cottingham was nearly fifty five but he'd always looked a good five years younger. Now, though, lit from above by the sodium lights in this dingy street, the old man's bald spot and the left side of his face, in the harsh orange wash, looked like the profile of a man who'd had a stroke.

"And what about Neil Judd?" Robb muttered.

Robb liked Judd. In fact, he didn't know anybody who didn't. A lot of it was down to the bloke's manner, softly spoken and that slow smile and those grey eyes. But Robb had heard the story about how Judd and Cottingham had met and he'd talked to the sergeant who'd been in that pub. The sergeant, an inspector now, said it was the most unnerving thing he'd ever seen and not just because of the way Judd fought and won. No, it was the way he'd managed to persuade him and Cottingham to leave the teenager alone. And Robb knew that Eliot was a friend of Judd's, he'd heard Cottingham talking on the phone. What if Judd knew where Eliot was and wasn't telling? And, Robb disliked the thought so much it made his stomach tight, what if Cottingham knew that Judd knew and *wasn't doing anything about it?*

"No," Robb told himself quietly but sternly.

No, the boss was the best copper Robb knew and he'd do the job the right way. In the meantime, Robb had his own job to do. He ordered the uniforms to get some lights down here so they could go over the garden. Maybe they'd find the knife.

Neil chewed at the sandwich he'd made himself in Blackhay's kitchen and thought about what he'd read so far. It was getting more disturbing by the sentence. When the police finally had this book, it would be clear that Davy had had a breakdown and any police psychiatrist would be all over it like a cheap coat because, the more you read, the more it seemed that nervous breakdown was too small a phrase. Psychotic Break might be big enough, though.

Neil didn't like Davy talking about how tired he was, how the air in the room felt heavy. Visual hallucinations were bad enough but believing that the internal pressure of a room was dropping was too close to tactile hallucination for comfort. The whispering was the worst part. For all three phenomena to come *after* Andrew's accident was like a huge motorway sign, pointing to the fabled phrase—*while the balance of his mind was disturbed.*

Even though he was hoping to work out where Davy was by reading the journal, Neil knew the really important thing was that Andrew was still alive and, if God was good, he would come out of it. Neil needed to have something to show him to prove that his father hadn't simply lost his mind.

He was about to start reading again when the phone jangled into life again. Neil hoped it wasn't Joy again.

"Hiya, Paul...that was quick...okay, got that...yeah, it is. I'll tell you soon. Thanks, mate."

I'm living in some old black and white film, one of those B-movies they used to have before the big picture at The Gaumont.
The only good thing about what happened this evening is I got angry enough to stop thinking about walking away from everything. Andrew's my son and, please God, he's going to need me. I can't walk away from that. Still, what happened was bloody ridiculous.
I went round to Anne's and <u>I was followed</u>.
I mean, it's daft, isn't it? Yeah, of course it is. It's also true.
I got to Anne's house and then remembered that it's late-night-opening at the supermarket where she works. I sat in the car for a bit, thinking I'd wait till she got home just after seven and then go to see Andrew later on, after Trisha had left. But I thought it might look a bit funny, some bloke sitting in a car parked in the road and not doing anything. So I drove off, thinking I'd go to the hospital and come back to Anne's later. And I was followed.
I thought it was my imagination at first. Well, being followed by a car isn't the sort of thing that happens to electricians in a town like Seapool and my nerves aren't exactly in peak condition. But the little car, a Metro or Fiesta or Micra, followed me, two cars behind, all the way through the one-way system in town. When we got to the big set of lights by the precinct, I knew it wasn't my imagination and I was suddenly pissed off. I had no idea who it was or why they were doing it but I had enough on my plate without this and decided to get my own back. I

took it all round the borough and up to the embankment at Laketon.

It's not been a bad day today and the river looked good and the air was clear so, instead of turning round and taking whoever it was on another tour of Seapool, I parked the car at the end of the embankment and got out. I watched the other end of the road out of the corner of my eye and the little car turned the corner and parked, facing the river.

I leaned on the railings and looked at the river. The tide was coming in and the lights flickered as the little boats bobbed up and down. The air smelled of the river and the sand and I heard Andrew's voice in my head.

"What's that smell, Dad?"

He asked me that when we were up at the embankment one Christmas time when he was about nine. Just a boy and his dad, out for a walk while the woman in their lives was at home or out shopping. It was a beautiful day that winter's day, what my Nan always called a 'clean day'. The sky was a hard blue and the air had an edge of frost.

I told him that his granddad always called it Nature's first smell. It was what my Dad had told me when I'd asked him the same question when I was about nine years old myself. He said that after all the explosions had finished and the ash had cooled and the water started to seep into the world, the 'ozone' must have been the first real smell.

"I like it," Andrew told me all those years ago. "It smells new."

Oh for the simplicity of youth. Why do we persist in looking for complex explanations when the truth is usually so simple?

Anyway, thinking of Andrew, I realised I was late getting to see him and I got angry, really angry all over again.

I got back in the car and started the engine but I left the lights off. I was angry enough to still want to get my own back on whoever was in the car, whoever had made me late seeing my son.

I drove down the embankment and, just before I reached the little car, I turned on my full beams. The driver must've been blinded by the sudden light but I couldn't see any movement in the car, the driver was just a shape behind the wheel as I drove past.

I drove to the hospital and the little car couldn't follow me so close because I beat it to the lights at the junction on Lake Drive. I arrived at the hospital and went up to see Andrew. I wasn't thinking about the little car anymore, I was thinking about Andrew and how he'd looked and sounded when he was nine years old. I was nearly crying when I got into the room.

I've been to see him every day, just like Trisha but where she holds his hand and talks non-stop to him, all I can manage is to sit in the chair and look at him. As I sat down in the chair tonight, I thought he looked different, as if he'd moved in the bed. It was probably just that the staff had moved him to prevent bedsores or something but I prefer to think he did it himself. His left hand was lying on the sheet and I took it in my own hands.

And this time, I started talking to him.

I talked about how I'd just remembered him when he was nine. I told him about the colour of the sky as the sun dropped into the bay just before I left and about the big ship I saw sailing into the sunset. I even told him about being followed. I told him in a sort of half-comical way, two men sharing a joke. As I described the way I'd turned on my lights, Andrew's hand tightened on my own hand.

I looked down at his left hand and there was no doubt that his fingers had curled a bit round my hand. The hollowness inside me, the emptiness that had grown after Trisha's phone call seemed to shrink a bit.

"Andrew," I said softly. "Son, are you there? Can you hear me?"

The pressure on my hand increased the tiniest bit but it was real. I looked at the monitors and tried to believe I could see a difference in the slow waves as they crossed the screens. I tried to believe I could hear a difference in the sound the beeps and boops made. The truth is, it all seemed the same.

"But you tried to squeeze my hand, didn't you?" I whispered and he squeezed my hand again.

I almost squeezed back. It was so big inside me, that desire to squeeze back that, if I had, I probably would've broken the small bones in his hand. So I settled for talking to him about everything and nothing. I told him about fitting the alarm system and ripping out the old toilet. I just rambled on. I've got no idea for how long but, eventually, I found myself talking about when he got out.

"It's bound to be hard, son," I told him. "But I'll be there to help. I'll take time off and spend as long as it takes to get you back on your feet. And your mum will be there, too. Together, we'll get you through this. Well— not together like living together but you know what I mean." I licked dry lips. "I don't know what your mum's said but, well, I know she thinks that us getting back together will help you but see Andrew, the thing is, I don't think it's a good enough reason and—"

That's when he squeezed my hand again. Quite hard. I wondered if he was trying to tell me that me and his mum <u>should</u> get back together because he thought it would help him. I asked him that question and then, right then, if he'd squeezed my hand, I'd've thought he wanted us to get back together and I'd've gone back tonight. But he didn't. He just lay there, his hand in mine like a pale, sleeping bird. So I asked him if he thought I was right, that it wouldn't work. And he squeezed my hand. I nodded and thought about telling the nurse about him squeezing my hand. I even looked over my shoulder to the observation window to see if I could see anybody there.

The shadow was there, right by the door. As I looked at it, sweat broke out all over my body. The shadow glided across the room and stood at the head of Andrew's bed.

The sweat was that clammy sweat of illness and fear. Andrew's hand in mine had been cool and dry but now the sweat leaking from my palm turned his palm slick. I wanted to rip my hand away because I didn't want to make his hand feel like that, didn't want to infect my son with my fear of the shadow. I wanted to wrench my hand away but I just started to ease it from round Andrew's hand.

Andrew squeezed my hand, the hardest squeeze so far. I stopped looking at the shadow and looked at Andrew and saw something was different. It took me a few moments to work out what it was and then I realised his eyes weren't fully closed anymore. I could see the whites of his eyes peeking out from below his long, thick lashes. For that wonderful split-second, I forgot all about the shadow. Then I felt the air in the room change.

It felt like this room's felt for the last few days, since Andrew had his accident. It felt heavy and charged, like there was a storm brewing. I looked at the shadow again.

It was opening its arms and then it whispered to me.

<u>guilt is a burden but less of one than trying to share it for the wrong reason</u>

I've got no idea what it means. Well, I suppose I thought it had something to do with not getting back with Trisha but that's all. And the idea that the shadow was there at all, instead of being frozen by the lamp in this room, was too awful to think about.

Cos now, I think maybe if I don't find a way of understanding what the whispers mean, something awful is going to happen to Andrew. Worse than being in the coma.

I forced myself to look at Andrew and I told him I had to go. I gulped when I spoke, that's how scared I was. He squeezed my hand again and all I could do was sit and stare stupidly at his hand in mine. And the shadow whispered to me again.

<u>he knows and understands the truth but are you sure you do?</u>

And I don't know what that means, either.

The clammy sweat on me was worse than ever and the air pressure in the room felt like it was dropping fast. All I could think about was all the electricity in those bloody machines and monitors and the friggin ventilator.

Because it really felt like there was a storm brewing and I couldn't help thinking about all that electrical energy in a storm, looking for somewhere to earth itself. What if it earthed into those machines? Andrew could be electrocuted, charred like a piece of wood on a bonfire or simply die because the machines all blew their fuses at the same time.

The thought was so strong, the image so vivid, I looked at the monitor. The normally slow, green sine wave was spiking and moving across the screen at an incredible rate. I couldn't believe that was a good sign. If it was a reflection of his bodily functions, it couldn't be a good sign. I looked at the shadow and it moved closer to Andrew's head, its arms still open but pointing down towards his body instead of just straight out.

I almost jumped up, tearing my hand away from Andrew's. I glared at the shadow, wanted to scream at it to piss off back here and leave him alone. But I was scared to in case it just got tired of waiting for

me to understand what it was saying to me and just called down the lightning.
I tried a whisper of my own.
   "I'm leaving," I told it. "I'm leaving and I'll try to find a way of understanding you. Just leave him alone."
The shadow stepped back and lowered its arms. I sighed and looked at Andrew. I told him again that I had to go. I told him I had to figure something out and my voice sounded weak. Jesus, but terror is a really awful thing.
The jagged spikes on the monitors sailed off the screen and were replaced by the slow sine wave again. I looked at the shadow and it was gone.
I left the room and then left the hospital. I kept looking over my shoulder to see if the shadow was there but it wasn't. I got in my car and drove away and I was bloody followed again. The bastard, whoever it is, hadn't given up. I saw the car as I stopped at the set of lights outside the hospital but I still couldn't see who was driving. It followed me all the way back to Oil Street but it stopped at the top of the road.
For a minute, sitting in my car, I thought about reversing back up the street and dragging the bastard out and having it out with whoever it is. But I've got more important things to worry about now. I got out of the car and came inside the house.
I closed the kitchen door behind me and walked into the hall and then just stood there.
I was terrified. That's the brutal truth. I was just plain scared to bloody death. What if the shadow

had only been playing with me, like whoever had followed me? What if it only pretended to leave Andrew's room? What if it waited till I left and then just rematerialised in the room and was still there instead of back here, frozen by the light from the standard lamp?
But I couldn't stand in the hall forever so I took what little courage I've got left and opened the living room door.
And the shadow wasn't here. Just the bright cone of light from the lamp behind the telly and no shadow. I felt the scream building inside me. Then my brain finally got the message my eyes were telling it.
The shadow <u>was</u> here, in the light of the lamp, standing with its arms by its side, like it had been waiting for me.
And that's how it's been ever since.
Now, here I am, knowing I've got to try to find a way of understanding what the shadow's trying to tell me. I've got to think of a way very, very soon. And I don't have a bloody clue how to do that. Not one—shit, there's the bloody phone again. I don't need that right now, not while I'm trying to think of a way of understanding what the shadow's whispers mean. I'll just let it ring.
It's no good, I can't think while the phone keeps ringing. If it's a bloody double-glazing salesman or somebody trying to sell me a kitchen, I'll probably scream. I've got find a way of understanding the shadow.

It was Trisha. Oh boy, was it Trisha. And now I know who was following me.

I picked the phone up and before I had a chance to say anything, she was screaming at me.
  "<u>Why didn't you ring to tell me about the machines showing a change!</u>"
It wasn't a question, it was an accusation. Her voice wouldn't have just stripped paint, it probably would've melted steel wire.
I told her I'd only been home half an hour and had just finished my tea but she cut me off.
  "Christ, I've just got here and they tell me there was a definite change in his alpha or beta waves or whatever the hell they are and that you must've been there when it happened but you didn't say anything to them and then you get home and think of your bloody stomach before you think to ring his bloody mother!"
I still don't know how she managed all that without taking a breath but she did. I opened my mouth to defend myself, tell her it was probably a glitch in the machines or something because it settled down almost immediately and Andrew showed no sign of anything.
I didn't even think about telling her he squeezed my hand and it looked like his eyes were trying to open. How would she react to that? To the idea that her son <u>hadn't</u> squeezed his mother's hand after she'd been the one who sat and held it and talked to him every day? Forget it, right? That's when I looked at the clock on the mantelpiece.

It was nine o'clock and Trisha had only just got there? No, she'd probably been there about fifteen minutes, long enough to be told about the spikes on the monitor. Then she'd bombard them with questions to which they probably had no real answers and then she'd've charged to the phone to scream at me.

It was suddenly so clear and obvious. It takes about fifteen minutes to get from the top of Oil Street to the hospital. Add the quarter of an hour she'd been there before phoning me and it makes perfect sense. It was Trisha who followed me in her little yellow and black Micra. I almost said it to her as I thought of it but the shadow started moving.

"Are you still there you bastard! I bet that bimbo is there, probably screwing you stupid while I'm talking about our son! That's why you didn't phone me! That's it, isn't it, you bastard!"

She was really screaming and I wondered what the people in the hospital must be thinking. God, I was surprised somebody didn't rip the phone out of her hand and drag her out. She sounded like she'd have jumped down the phone line to strangle me if she could.

That was when the shadow got really agitated. Its waving arms looked like a wheatfield in a gale and I actually saw, for the first time, where its mouth is. It was opening and closing, like a fish trying to breathe on a riverbank.

"You selfish bastard!" Trisha screamed one last time and slammed the phone down.

I lowered my phone slowly, watching the shadow, waiting for the whispering to start.
Nothing. No whispers at all, just waving arms and that opening where a mouth would be.
It's still doing that and it's still not whispering. I know it wants me to understand and I want to understand but the fact that it can't even whisper at all now, not even stuff I don't understand is as scary as anything else that's happened lately. If it doesn't whisper, I won't be able to understand and what will that mean for Andrew?
Jesus Christ, what the hell am I going to do? What can I do to make myself understand what it's trying to tell me?
There must be a way, there must be. I heard it before and even had a sort of half-glimmer of understanding about guilt and Trisha. What was I doing then that I'm not doing now?
Shit, I I've got to find a way of understanding it properly!
What can I do! What the fuck can I do?

NINE

Neil made himself another cup of coffee and wished he still smoked. God, he really felt like a cigarette, even an old, stale, untipped Woodbine would do. He wanted to go home and leave this journal in the drawer of his desk. He wanted to ring Martin and tell him he had nothing else to add and it would be a waste of time asking any more questions. He wanted to be ten years old again and at Laketon Pool with the sun shining hot and strong and the water in the pool gleaming blue and silver. He wanted to be standing next to ten year old Davy Eliot on the third top board, looking down at that gleaming water. He wanted one more chance to say something to that ten year old boy who loved to jump and dive from high places. Neil wanted to say more than he'd said all those years ago, wanted to *unsay* what he'd said all those years ago.

What would he say? Oh, that was easy.

"'Davy,' I'd say as we looked down at the water thirty or forty feet below. 'Don't even think about it, mate. Don't practise anymore, don't swan-dive off this board. We've all jumped off it and we can brag about it to everybody else until we all get tired of it. Find some other way of feeling alive, Davy cos this sort of thing gets dangerous after a while.'"

Neil frowned; he rarely talked aloud to himself but that's what he'd been doing a lot since Davy's book had arrived. For a few moments there, he'd actually been in Laketon Pool with his old mates and was talking to ten year old Davy about not diving off the board. This wasn't so unusual; his memory meant that when he recalled something, it was almost like going back in time. A lot of the time, he could actually smell whatever there had been to smell at the time he was remembering. But actually changing what he'd said, actually articulating the thought or wish was something new. Something he didn't like; you could never change anything that had happened. Sometimes, if you were lucky, you might be able to change the consequences but that was all.

Was that what Davy was trying to do? Was that what he thought he'd done before posting this journal? It seemed all too plausible to Neil.

Was Davy Eliot, after leaving his comatose son in a room where the sounds were almost as bad as the fact of the coma, about to decide that his perceptions would be more acute if he started jumping again?

Neil thought so. The question was, where would Davy jump from? Did he start off small, like he had done when he was a kid, or what?

Wait a minute. Wait a minute!
The shadow started going bonkers when I thought about Trisha being enraged enough to try to jump down the phone line at me. That's right, isn't it? What if—what if—oh shit, this is so mad but what the hell, the whole thing's crazy.
<u>*What if the shadow went bonkers because of that word? Jump?*</u>
It's moving again. The shadow's moving again. Its arms are waving round again and that hole where a mouth would be is opening and closing again. God, I'm right.
<u>*Jump.*</u>
That's it. And, really, it's not so surprising, not all that crazy. Not really. I mean, I remember Trisha saying, well yelling at me really, that having sex with somebody else, somebody she knew didn't love her but just wanted her, lusted after her—that it made her feel more alive because she seemed more aware of everything. I remember thinking, after I'd left and could face thinking about it, that maybe it was something like I felt doing the bungee jump. Cos that's what it's like—it makes me feel more alive, more aware of everything around me. Oh, there's probably a posh word for it but what it amounts to is that my mind as well as my body feels sharper, feels more like it did when I was a kid who loved finding that thrill, finding that edge and walking it. And what did I do when I was a kid to get that feeling? I jumped, that's what I did.
But where can I jump now? There's no bungee jumps to go to and Laketon Pool's closed for the winter

and The Pit's got a factory on it now. So what's left?
'Ang on. Let me think a minute, stop waving your bloody arms and let me think it through, let me work it out!
Okay, okay, okay, back in a minute.

I've just been upstairs, into the back bedroom. With the floodlight on, you can see a lot out the back. You can see the swings from that room. The rides are still mostly silhouettes but it doesn't matter. I saw them and knew what they were. I stood looking out of the window of the back bedroom and saw across the seventy odd yards of ground between me and the swings and knew what each silhouette was, which ride. I stood there and remembered how fascinated I was all those years ago by the slide. Before Eddie dragged the mattresses out. And I felt exactly the same fascination just now, looking at it from the back bedroom. It was strange. It looks like the slide but it looks like something else, too, something not really of this world.
The four sets of struts supporting the chute are dark grey lines in the dimness and the railed ladder is another line at an angle. The platform looks like the wheelhouse off an old ship.
Why? Why should it look like that, so much the same and so different? I think maybe it's because it stands alone. It's the only piece of apparatus on the far side of the swings, as if it doesn't belong with the rest, as if whoever built it knew all along that it would be totally different in effect to the rest of rides. Does

that make sense? No, probably not but who cares? What matters is that I saw the silhouette of the slide and felt the same rush I felt all those years ago.
But that's all very well. The truth is, the slide's beyond me isn't it? Yeah but—but the thing is, there's something else out there that might not be. At least, I hope so. That's why I'm here again in the living room, thinking it all through; I want to see if what I'm thinking is okay and the only way to do that is write it down while I'm thinking and see what reaction I get from the shadow.

Okay, that's good. I looked at it and it was nodding its head. And it <u>is</u> a head now, not just a sort of shaped blob of darkness. It still can't make the whispers come out of its opening mouth but that shake of the head will do me for now. I'm going out into the swings.

God, this is hard and wonderful at the same time. I can hardly hold this bloody pen, I feel so wired up and alive. Shit, it's bloody marvellous but it's bloody scary, too.
I jumped. Well, dropped is what I really did but the effect was the same. Not from the slide. I dropped from The Dead Tree.
I squeezed through the gap in the railings and that made me feel good, too, just knowing I could still do that. Anyway, I walked over to the bottom gate and looked for The Dead Tree and couldn't find it. It took me a second to remember how things look

different when you're little, looked again and found it, exactly where it always was. I looked up and saw the branch was still there, too, sticking out like an accusing finger. I gave the trunk a shake and the creaking noises didn't sound much different than they did when I was a kid.

So I started to climb it and it wasn't as difficult as I'd been expecting. I got to the branch and put my hands on it but clung to the trunk with my legs. I mean, I'm a lot heavier than that ten year old I used to be and I wasn't sure the branch would take that weight. The thing was, though, would just dangling and dropping from it work? Well, there was only way to find out so I let go with my legs and dangled there for a couple of seconds. I started to swing my legs gently and the branch groaned but it held. I swung harder until my feet cleared the tangle of small branches on the trees round me and then let go.

And that wonderful moment was there and, probably wishful thinking, but it seemed to last longer than it did on the bungee jump. Whatever, it felt almost as good as I remembered it feeling when I was a kid.

Now I'm back here writing about it. It feels like that's part of it, part of trying to understand the whispers. It's like I've got to write it down, think it through and then see if it's making any difference with the shadow. So I'm going to stop now and—the air's just changed, got heavier.

It worked! Thank God, it worked. Well, up to a point. It got the shadow whispering again but I still don't understand what the whispers mean.

<u>guilt over more than one thing makes the weight intolerable</u>

That was the first thing the shadow whispered to me. I looked up from this book at the shadow and nearly collapsed back on the couch. The air is so heavy, it seemed to drain me. The sweat was all over me and it felt like somebody was pressing down on my shoulders. Then the shadow whispered to me and all I could do was think that maybe I understood about guilt, a single guilt. I can understand how Trisha would feel guilty about being the not-so-indirect cause of Andrew being in a coma. But what other guilt could she feel? And as I thought that, the shadow whispered to me again.

<u>first guilt is like first sin and the longer it remains unpurged the heavier it becomes and the harder to bear</u>

And that's where I'm up to. It isn't whispering anymore but its arms are still waving and I still don't know what the other guilt could be and I don't know what else to do. And the room feels like the inside of a thundercloud must feel and it's taking me all my time to hold this pen. I'm going to have to lie down and a have a blow for a bit.

I thought I'd actually fallen asleep and dreamed until I looked at the clock. It's only been five minutes at the most.

I saw something on the inside of my eyes. Oh Christ, that sounds so mad but it's true.

It was like watching an overexposed film clip, all the images jumbled up together, a mishmash that made no sense. Except right at the end. I saw the last thing sharp as a bell. It was The Dead Tree.

That's all I've got so that's what I'm going to do and hope to Christ it works.

It did. Thank you God.

I dropped off the branch twice this time and came back in here and just fell over on the couch. The air's even heavier but it worked. It was horrible but it worked and if it helps Andrew, I can put up with horrible.

This time, the images on the inside of my eyelids were clear. It was like one of those sepia-toned newsreels on Pathe News but it was clear. I was looking at a room, a smoky room, lit by two wall lights and a big candle on a coffee table. There was a three-seater settee against the back wall and then the image narrowed down from the whole room to that settee.

There was a woman kneeling on the floor, her head down between the legs of the man on the settee. The movement of her head left no doubt as to what she was doing. It was Trisha and I said her name aloud. She was with the man she went to for sex, just sex. Then the image was gone but I don't need anything more, do I? No, even I'm not that stupid.

That's what the shadow means by more than one guilt. She feels guilty about breaking up our marriage and she feels guilty about causing Andrew's accident and putting him in a coma. To help her get over the second guilt, she wants me back home to help her help Andrew when he comes out of it. But I won't go back and she thinks she knows the reason so she's carrying the guilt of that, too.

God, no wonder she's angry. She wants me back to make up for both things but because I won't go back, she can't make up for either. She hates not being in control of any situation and she's not in control of this one.

I could go back to her.

Whoa, okay. The shadow's going berserk again, shaking its head. The air's getting heavier still and it feels like there's a gigantic electrical storm right over my head.

Well, no way I can pretend I don't understand the shadow's opinion about me going back to Trisha. I just got another little picture show on the inside of my eyelids. It felt like the air in the room forced my eyes closed with its weight.

Trisha was in the kitchen of the house I used to live in. She was standing at the sink, her hands encased in a pair of rubber gloves. The suds of the washing up water gleamed in the sharp black and white of this little picture show. I saw myself leaning against the jamb of the kitchen door and something about our body language told me this wasn't just a sharing of news about our working days. There was a tension in her back and shoulders as she leaned over the sink and the way I was standing was so familiar, too. Trisha was haranguing me over something and I was listening, knowing there was little point in arguing because she'd decided she was right and I was wrong and had to be put straight.

Then Andrew came shuffling down the hall behind me, his mouth opening and closing, his right hand by his side, his left twitching, moving up from its place by his thigh to a spot just below his waist. Then whatever power the shadow controls got bigger and better. Or bigger and worse. I heard Andrew speak.

"Stop! Stop arguing about me!" Andrew said.

His voice didn't sound like his voice, not the voice he used the last time I spoke to him. It was quavering and not just with emotion; the coma had left a weakness there. As he shouted, his left arm twitched even more and his mouth drew down on the left side. His mother turned to him and said we weren't arguing about him.

"Yes you are! Dad wants to know why you won't even sleep in the same room with him when it was you who asked him to come back! But it's not really about that, it's about me! It's always about me! I should've gone to the rehab centre and then you could've both got on with your lives! You could've been happy!"

He slumped sideways down the wall and the image-me caught him before he hit the floor.

All in all, I think I preferred the ghost of Christmas Past. Seeing Trisha with that bloke wasn't nice but it was miles better than seeing Andrew like that.

<u>better to know it all because it won't change or go away</u>

That's just settled in my mind and all I can do is nod. It's probably true but I've had enough. Really. I've had enough of whispers I don't understand and of seeing horrible things on the inside of my eyelids and of feeling like there's a thunderstorm waiting to start in this bloody room. And there's something worse now. It feels like there's millions of microscopic ants running riot all over me, even in my hair and below my scalp. And there's a smell in this room, too. Something like old tin but more acidic and it itches my nose like I want to sneeze. The shadow's still going bonkers but I've really had enough. I'm dog-tired, right down to my toes and in my bones. I'm going to bed. My bedroom's free of all this stuff. Of the shadow and the heavy air and this new itching and smell. I'll probably lie awake and cry or something but it'll be better than staying here. It's got to be.

It's been four days since I wrote all that. There wasn't any point in writing every day because nothing is different. I go to work, I do what needs to be done and don't really know what it is I've done. I got to see Andrew and he's just the same and the shadow stands at the head of the bed and I hold

Andrew's hand. I'm hoping he'll squeeze my hand but he doesn't. Then I come home and eat my tea and read the paper and, when it gets dark and I can't hear anybody out in the swings anymore, I drop from The Dead Tree and come back here and the shadow whispers about guilt and I see the same little picture shows of me and Trisha and Andrew and the one where I have to watch Trisha with the bloke she went to for sex. The air in this room is normal till I've dropped from The Dead Tree and then it gets heavy and sticky and the itching starts and I can smell that tinny smell and I try to understand more, try to get the shadow to be more explicit but it's just the same thing over and over again and I don't know what else there is. Don't know what else I can do.

You know what I've been doing the most? Apart from scratching my head till it hurts and trying to understand until my brain hurts? I've been noticing how the weather reminds me of when I was a kid. And, right in the middle of the hollowness I feel inside me, there's this one tiny piece of something else and that something else is regret. Just a simple regret for those things and times that have long gone.

Isn't that odd? It's not regret for the way my life seems to be falling to pieces round my ears, although that's there, but simple regret for the fact that I'm not a kid anymore. I regret the fact that I can't just take things in like I did when I was a kid, soaking up the day and glorying in it. The colour of the leaves in the gutters and the sound they made when we trod on them, the sound of our own laughter when we threw pebbles into the river to make them skip, playing split-the-kipper and Japs and Commandos and Jack-shine-a-light and the long talks we had about important things like football and Christmas and Bonfire Night. The things I took for granted, like the sweet, slow way the light left the swings during the autumn. Things I took for granted because they'd always been there and, so, would always be there.

I was sitting on the bench on the little green at the back of the office today, watching the sun setting out in the bay and the light reminded me of Trisha's lovely dark lilac eyes and I suddenly remembered the first time I noticed that similarity. We were courting and we drove out to Abersoch. We walked on the beach, not talking much, just holding hands and looking at the way the sunlight danced on the waves. We sat on the beach as the sun went down and she put her head in my lap and I looked in her eyes and realised they were the same colour as the sky out in the west, where the setting sun turned it a dark lilac.

Trisha. Ah Christ.

She rings every day, just after nine o'clock, after she's got home from visiting Andrew, just after I've got back from The Dead Tree. She doesn't rant anymore, doesn't shout or accuse. She almost cries. It's the same thing every night.

"Please, Dave, for Andrew's sake. At least try for his sake. Can't you do it for him?"

She's trying to apologise without ever coming close to the word and, I know this, without really coming close to the emotion. There's a ragged edge to her voice, as if the strain of keeping her anger under control is almost too much.

And, every time, I'm about to say okay and then the shadow starts waving its arms and the air starts getting heavy and my whole body starts to itch and I just put the phone down on her gently because it wouldn't work and the shadow knows that.

The shadow knows.

I go to bed, no better off, no nearer knowing what it is the shadow knows and wants me to know. I cry myself to sleep. Yeah, that's what I do. I cry myself to sleep, just like Andrew did the night after his puppy got run over the first day it was allowed out after its injections. The puppy survived, lived for fourteen years and then died peacefully in its sleep. It's an ending we all could envy.

And that's what time it is now, time to go to bed, to sleep and dream. Cos that's what happens. I dream. Just two dreams, following each other with barely a break. I dream of me and Trisha making love that first time and then I dream about standing at the top of the stairs while the shadow waits at the bottom. Then I wake up while the dawn is still three hours away. I get up and come downstairs and wait till it's time to go to work again, time for it all to start again. It's so like I was of after my Dad died. Except, of course, below the tiredness and lethargy, the fear for Andrew is there, the terror I feel that the shadow will harm him if I don't find a way of

understanding the shadow. And I can feel it building, the way the air in this room feels like it's building into a storm. Only the fear I feel building won't be a storm with rolling thunder and forked lightning; it will be something fatal for my son.
What the hell am I going to do?

It's Friday night. I haven't been to the swings yet because something's changed. I thought it was like I was after my Dad died but it wasn't. Sleepless nights have taken their toll this time. It's affected my work.
Apparently, it's been so bad I've been scaring the young girls who work in the building. When it was pointed out to me, I realised the girls no longer stay and talk to me like they used to. And the older people in the building, the ones who've known me for years, so I was told today, have tried to find out what's up but I refuse to talk to them. Oh, they know about Andrew but they think there's more to it and they're right. Still, I don't even remember anybody asking me about anything. Anything at all.
It was Graham Settle who told me. Graham's the Borough Engineer, my boss and he's a great bloke but it shows how bad it's got. When he was telling me, being concerned because he's an old mate from way back when we both still worked the tools, I got angry with him. It was almost the pubescent anger of a teenager. When he saw that in me, his voice got cold and hard and I don't blame him.
"Yes, I've been checking up on you because I'm worried. I don't want to get a phone call from

Vanessa telling me she's found you on the floor because you've had a stroke."
And that made me smile; Vanessa Richards is sixty two and runs the admin. office like a sergeant major. If she found me on the floor, she'd phone the ambulance and then start giving me mouth to mouth in between telling me off for screwing up her schedule.

"You've got leave owing, Dave," Graham told me. "Take it. Take it now. Go home, decorate, spend all day with Andrew or go fishing or go to the Bahamas. Just don't come back till you're the Davy Eliot who does his job better than anybody I know. Don't come back till you're the bloke who saved my life when I nearly fell off the roof of the old Gorsey Lane works."

And then, right then, I saw Graham sliding down the slick slates of the Gorsey Lane works' roof and me sliding after him, my arm reaching out to him. He grabbed hold of it just before he would have flipped off the roof and tumbled the sixty odd feet to the ground. And I remembered again the feeling I used to get jumping off the slide.

It was that word—sliding—that did it.

I nodded and told Graham it was a deal. I came home just as another misty Seapool twilight was lowering itself over The Rows and now here I am writing this.

It's the slide. The Dead Tree only works up to a point and the slide is all that's left. I thought about building myself something to jump off. I thought about some sort of platform in the garden but I'm

not my Dad, I'm not a joiner. Anything I built like that would probably turn out rickety, swaying all over the place. It'd probably fling me off before I was half-way up and that wouldn't help me understand the shadow, would it? If I died falling off it, the shadow wouldn't be able to tell me what it knows and that'd just leave Andrew. No, if I built myself a jumping platform, it'd end up as some barmy roost for feral pigeons or something.
The slide.
That's all there is. Nothing else in the swings comes close. And, really, it's where it all started, isn't it? Well, The Pit was where it started but the crucibles aren't there anymore and, anyway, the slide was where the moment between sky and ground felt the best.
Trouble is, Eddie's mattresses were burned years ago so how am I supposed to do it?
Shit, there's the phone again. It's too early for Trisha but if I answer it, I won't try the slide because I'll stop thinking about how to do it. Just let the bloody thing ring and
Oh, this is so good, so simple. Why didn't I think of it before?
I'll get an answer machine. I won't have to listen to Trisha if I get an answer machine. Yeah, good.
What about the slide? How can I jump from the slide? I have to think of something to cushion the jump.
Cushion.
The best answers are always the simple ones. Who said that? Neil would know but it doesn't matter.

What matters is that it's true. And I've got loads of cushions. Well, I've got eight. I'll use the cushions. When it gets dark, I'll use the cushions. And I'll take the mattress from the spare bed in the spare bedroom where, one day if God's good, Andrew will sleep.

Okay, I think I've probably got just enough time to get this down before the air gets thicker and the itching starts. Till, Jesus I hope so, the shadow whispers to me to tell me what it knows.
I piled the cushions and the mattress under the platform of the slide and then climbed the ladder. I didn't climb onto the platform. I struggled round the ladder so I was on its backside, looking at the underside of the platform. My hands felt clammy and my feet, inside my old leather shoes, felt just as slippery. My mouth was dry but I could taste that sharp, coppery taste of adrenaline you taste when you're scared. I looked down at the stuff I'd piled up and guessed it was about a fifteen foot drop. Nothing, really. Not compared to The Dead Tree or the third top board at Laketon Pool or even the top of the platform I was beneath. Still, I was scared. I hung there, gripping the rung of the ladder with hands I knew just wanted to slide off. I tried to remember if I'd ever felt like this when I was a kid and I know I was never scared of heights then. But I had to do it.
I let myself drop. I landed with a thud and it jarred me all the way up to my teeth but I stayed on the piled up cushions and mattress. I lay there for a few

seconds, reliving the moment when I'd almost been in flight. It was just the same as when I was a kid. Exactly the same. Then I got up and dragged all the stuff back to the garden. Now, I'm here, hoping to God it worked.

It's half past three on Saturday morning. I haven't been to bed and dreamed and woke up and come down. I've been sitting here on the couch, trying not to think, trying not to keep seeing what I saw after I dropped onto the cushions and mattress.
Oh, it worked. It worked but, even though I know I had to know for Andrew's sake, I wish to Christ it hadn't worked.
I got in and half-collapsed on the couch and closed my eyes, my whole body already beginning to itch, the sweat running in little streams all over me. And the shadow told me what it knows, what it wants me to know.
I saw Anne in her living room, rubbing at her forehead as if she had a headache. She was walking to and from the phone by the window. Then I saw the hall of my old home where Trisha keeps the base of the cordless phone. She had the phone in her left hand, her right hand planted on her hip. There were no words but I knew Trisha was yelling down the phone because a vein in her forehead stood out sharply in the black and white image on the inside of my eyelids. Then the image faded and the shadow whispered to me what I'd already worked out.

<u>warning her off</u>

I nodded and repeated those three words aloud. I thought that was it, that it was over and started to get up. The shadow whispered to me again.

<u>warning her off for now</u>

I asked it what that meant and scratched at my head where the itch was the worst. Then the itch stopped, the tinny smell that had made me breathe through my mouth was gone. All that was left was the heavy air. And the images on the inside of my eyelids.
I watched Trisha killing Anne. In my mind, on the inside of my eyelids, I watched in sharp black and white, the woman I had married kill Anne Jordan.
No colours, no soundtrack, just the brutal image of one woman slaughtering another because of guilt and anger. If it was a film, I could've looked away but it was on the inside of my eyelids and all I could do was moan and then watch it played out to the end.
Anne opened her front door. The camera of my mind or whatever it is, was behind Anne and I saw the silhouette on the other side of the door and nearly called out to her not to open the door. But she did and then I was seeing things from Trisha's perspective. I saw the puzzlement on Anne's face, saw how quickly it turned to annoyance that she was being bothered at home. Then I saw Trisha's shoulders tense. She waved her arms as she began her verbal assault. Anne stood straighter, her whole body tensing animal-like as she sensed the violence in

Trisha. She gripped the door's edge and stepped back half a pace, ready to shut the door in Trisha's face.

Good salesperson that she is, Trisha put her foot against the bottom of the door and shook her head angrily. Anne pushed the door but Trisha simply jumped into the doorway. She stiff-armed Anne in the chest. Anne stumbled backwards and sat down hard on the floor. Trisha kicked the door closed behind her. Anne struggled to her feet as Trisha stepped almost genteelly over her. Anne pushed herself back against the little wall between the side window and the living room door. I could see Anne opening her mouth, obviously trying to talk Trisha out of whatever was on her mind.

Trisha smiled. It was horrible. There was no humour in it. It was fixed and her eyes had a flat, dead sheen to them. Like a hunting shark.

She was wearing the blouson jacket she bought while she was on some sales conference in London. She reached inside it and pulled out a knife. It's one of a set an old auntie of hers bought us for a wedding present. The handles are oak and the blades good, honest Sheffield steel. All the knives in the set are wickedly sharp, kept that way by Trisha's obsessive need to have everything as good as new. There would be no stopping that honed blade once the downward momentum began.

Nothing did. Anne reached up with her right arm but Trisha simply drove the knife past the arm, aiming for the wide open mouth of Anne's scream. The blade bit deeply into the top of Anne's upper arm and she slumped onto her bottom again. The blood oozed shiny black in the sharp monochrome image. Trisha leaned down on one knee, like an old fashioned suitor proposing. Then she drove the blade into Anne's neck where it met her collar bone.

And Trisha just went on and on and on, pulling the knife out and plunging it in again. The blood gushed everywhere, from Anne's neck and arm and chest, cheek, scalp. Christ, it was awful and the worst thing was that Trisha never showed any sign of tiring, or of even breathing hard and her eyes still had that flat, hard, hunting-shark sheen to them.

Then the image was gone and I let out a long breath. I felt dizzy, the lack of oxygen from not breathing properly finally taking its toll. Then the ants were back and the smell was back and I was breathing through my mouth and scratching myself everywhere. And I was moaning and shaking my head. I didn't want to see any more. I didn't. The shadow simply whispered to me again.

<u>guilt is a terrible burden and one which gets heavier and heavier until something has to give but not everything is inevitable, choice is still possible</u>

Then the air pressure returned to normal and the ants stopped biting me and the smell was gone. I opened my eyes and the shadow was just standing in the cone of light, its arms by its sides. But there was a difference. I could make out some features. It had a nose and a definite mouth and there were two faint glimmers that were probably eyes. But I didn't try to see anymore or work out if it reminded me of anybody. I just leaned forward, sure I was going to throw up, my head still spinning slowly. But, gradually, both feelings stopped and I could think.

I've been thinking ever since. I've been thinking how I wish I'd never seen any of that, how I wish I'd emigrated instead of going on holiday to Spain, how I wish I hadn't gone to the club with Frankie that night. All the usual if-onlys our lives always seem filled with. But the fact is that things are the way they are and I've got try to deal with them as they are.

The shadow said not everything was inevitable, choice was still possible and that's what I've got to think about and what I think about it is that maybe I can stop it, stop Trisha doing what the shadow is sure she will do if things stay the same.

Well, I was going to see Anne the other day when Trisha followed me and I still haven't seen her. I was going to see her and, really, I was hoping we could get back together. Now, though, now I could go and see her and tell her I'd sort it out. I can tell her I know Trisha's been bothering her but I'll see Trisha and tell her to stop it, tell her that me and Anne aren't together anymore and haven't been for more than a month. I could do that, I could see Trisha and talk to her, get her to understand that me not going back has nothing to do with Anne, tell her we have to find a way of living our own lives. It'll be hard but I can do it. I'm sure I can do it. And, if I persuade Trisha, get her to <u>believe</u> me, that'll be enough. Won't it?

The shadow's not moving. It's not waving its arms or shaking its head. The room doesn't feel like the inside of a thundercloud and I'm not itching all over. That's a good sign. If I do it, see Anne and see Trisha, sort it out then, all of us, Andrew especially, could be free. None of us would be trapped in this bloody thing anymore. Would we?

<u>only if you refuse to take the burden that is yours</u>

That whisper just settled in my brain. I think it's an agreement. It sounds like an agreement. Oh, I know it's sort of cryptic but it's been a while since I dropped from the slide so my ability to understand completely must be wearing thin now. But it sounds hopeful. We'd only stay trapped if I don't do what's necessary. Yeah, that's what it probably means.
Anyway, when to see Anne? Actually, it'd probably be best to see her tomorrow. Sunday's her day off and she stays home and pampers herself. And I could see Trisha later today. She goes to the hospital in the afternoon, after she's worked in the morning. I could get there and wait and then talk to her. Actually, that's a really good idea. I know it's sort of cowardly but I think I deserve a break—If we're in the hospital, Trisha can't really cause a scene. She'll have to listen to me and, despite the way she can get sometimes, she's an intelligent woman. If I explain it all properly and she has to stay calm enough to listen, she'll see I'm right.

The shadow must have agreed with all of that because, not only didn't it go berserk, I actually fell asleep. I've just woke up now, my head lolling over the edge of the couch, this book and pen on the floor. Amazing. I feel great, really great. Like I've slept for a week. It feels like it's been so long since I—
Oh shit, the shadow's not there. The standard lamp's not on and the shadow's not there. Oh Christ, no wonder the air's normal and I'm not scratching and the smell's gone. The bloody shadow's not here anymore. What kind of bloody electrician forgets the fundamental principle that light bulbs burn out when they're left on all the time?
Andrew. Oh shit, it's gone after Andrew!

No, it's okay, Andrew's okay. I phoned the hospital and the nurse told me there'd been no change. The neurologist is looking in him later today, this afternoon. Thank God, he's unharmed. I'm going out and I'm going to buy as many bloody lightbulbs as I can find. And I've got to get that bloody answering machine, too. If I'd had an answer machine, I could've just checked it and known right away that Andrew was okay; they'd ring me if there was any change and if I wasn't in or didn't answer, they'd leave a message and I wouldn't have to go through that fear again like just now.

Oh Christ, dear Jesus Christ, I feel like that Hollies song, King Midas in reverse or whatever it was called. Nothing works. I can't get anything right.

It's Sunday morning, very, very early Sunday morning and I've got to go through it all again. I've got to write it all down. I hope it helps me get it right, finally, but after last night, I can't really believe in that hope. I think I just kidded myself. We can always kid ourselves about stuff like that, stuff that's so important we want it to be right.

I thought the cushions and the bottom of the platform would be enough—actually, maybe that's not true either. I mean, I bought a load of mattresses when I bought the answer machine and the CDs and the hi-fi, didn't I? Like maybe I knew deep down cushions and one mattress wouldn't be enough.

I thought that whatever they helped me see and hear and then decide would sort it all out. But I got it wrong and now I've got to go through it all again and hope I can work it out right this time.

TEN

Neil rubbed his face and stretched his shoulders. The creaks and crackles sounded very loud in his office.

"No," he muttered softly but anybody hearing it would have heard an edge there, almost like anger. "The cushions and the bottom of the platform weren't enough and the mattresses you bought last Saturday weren't, either. Were they, Davy? They weren't enough."

There was never enough. That was the trouble with addictive stuff. It didn't matter what the substance was or the thing. Eventually, to get what you believe you're getting, you have to have a little bit more, do a little bit more and then a little bit more than that. Then you're hooked.

"It's a spiral, Davy. You should've known that," Neil said and swivelled the chair to look out of the window at the dark early morning outside. No moon, just the eerie glow of sodium lamps and the reflected gleam of the lights in Blackhay through the closed blinds. "You saw the girl, watched her as she spiralled down when the bungee jump ropes snapped. Of course, most of the time, it's a downward spiral but yours was an upward one. Wasn't it, Davy? Shit!"

The question was, how high would be high enough? In the end, how high?

Neil turned the chair back, nodding to himself slowly, knowing the answer, the layout of Oil Street glimmering in his mind. He picked up the phone.

Martin growled when his direct line rang. He was standing in his office, staring out at the street below, knowing he should be at home and knowing he wouldn't go until he got the preliminary results from the doctor and that would come through the internal phone. He picked up the phone and jabbed the button.

"What? Unless this is to tell me you've found Eliot, you better make sure your bloody shoes are well-heeled because you'll be...Neil? Christ, I'm sorry. I...okay, I'm listening."

As he listened, he frowned. He snatched glances at the sheaf of paper on his desk that laid out all the details they had so far about Anne Jordan and Trisha Eliot. When Neil stopped talking, Martin said, "Neil, why the hell should I look there? I mean..." He stopped and looked at the orange light blinking on the internal phone. He sighed. "Okay, Neil. I'll get somebody to look. I'll speak to you later."

Neil replaced his phone slowly. Now, all that was left was to find out the how and the why so he could answer as many of Martin's questions as he could.

And so he'd be able to answer whatever questions Andrew Eliot had when, if he came out his coma.

I suppose I had an inkling that I might not have it all worked out properly when I started the car to go and buy an answer machine. I suppose some deep part of me knew. Or maybe it was the shadow itself that made me buy the mattresses. Anyway, I started the car, thinking about lightbulbs and answer machines and I heard, very faintly, an echo of the last thing the shadow whispered to me yesterday morning.

<u>only if you refuse the burden that is yours alone</u>

I heard that in my mind and left the car in neutral and thought about it for a moment. Then I shook my head and told myself that it was just me reminding myself to do what I'd said I was going to do. That was all it was. I drove into town and parked the car in the big car park alongside the precinct.
It still seems ironic that I was feeling so good then. I got out of the car and saw that the mist was lifting and the pewter-sun was trying to shine through what was left. My breath plumed out in front of me and my fingers tingled and I felt good, felt like I used to feel when I was a kid on days like this. I went into Home and Bargain and bought every bulb they had on their shelves and the look on the check-out girl's face made me feel good, too. I put the bulbs in the car and then went to Curry's. It's only October but yesterday morning, I felt like it was Christmas and I was doing my Christmas shopping.
I bought the answer machine. It's one with all the latest gimmicks—call screening and time and date

stamp and all that. I came out of Curry's and saw the mattresses in the window of the furniture shop next door. So I went in and bought four mattresses. They're only singles but they're a lot springier than those old ones Eddie dragged out of his house. I loaded them all into the car, squashing them onto the back seats. I was sweating by the time I finished and had to press really hard to close the hatchback but I got them all in.

It was still only quarter to eleven and I decided to just have a walk round the precinct. There were no impossible shadows there, no smell but the chilly air and the cleaning fluids they use to clean the shops and I wasn't scratching at a whole-body-itch. Andrew was okay and I felt secure in the knowledge that I was going to keep him safe by getting Trisha to see reason and telling Anne not to worry anymore.

Thinking about it now, sitting here and writing it down, I'm pretty sure it started <u>not</u> being all right when I was in Menzies. I looked at the books and then just wandered up the aisle until I was standing at the music section. I just stood there and stared, feeling daft because there weren't any records. There was no vinyl at all. I felt a sort of half-sad, half-cynical smile on my face as I looked at the CDs and tapes. And I heard myself singing. It didn't strike me as funny, singing out loud to myself. I sang 'where have all the vinyls gone' to the tune of 'where have all the flowers gone'. The supervisor was next to me and she asked me if I was talking to her and I mumbled something and she walked away. Then I saw all The Beatles' stuff and just felt sad. I got a huge lump in my throat. God, Trisha loves them. I stood there, willing back the tears, remembering the way her eyes lit up when she opened the cabinet my Dad had made for her thirtieth birthday, the one I'd asked him to make. I'd bought all the records The Beatles ever made and put them in the cabinet. And I said aloud, right there in Menzies, "She really loves them."

"What?" A woman's voice sounded right in my left ear, making me jump.
I looked at her and smiled but she was frowning and I realised I'd spoken out loud. She huffed and walked away, muttering and it was too much, too like when I first moved back here and went wandering round the playgrounds, muttering to myself. God, I hope it doesn't come to that again. I couldn't stand that.
I left Menzies, almost trotting and walked back up the pavement towards Curry's and, this time, I looked in the window. As much to calm myself down as anything, I think..
And there it was, right as you walk in the doorway. They had some sort of sale on and the microsystem was part of it. It's got a CD and digital tuner and detachable speakers and double cassette and remote control and, when it's on, looks like something off a plane's flight board. I bought it. I think I bought it because the shadow wanted me to buy it, so it could finally make itself plain enough for me to understand.
Anyway, I bought it with my Barclaycard and then went right back into Menzies and bought every

Beatles' CD and three sixties compilation CDs. I know what I was thinking when I bought them—I was thinking that listening to the music I loved would bring back some good memories and I could remember how good it felt then, how good I felt then.

I took it all back to the car and jammed it in with the bulbs and the mattresses and then decided I'd treat myself to a burger from MacDonald's to round off the feeling I'd had that it felt like Christmas time. I took all the stuff home and put a new bulb in the lamp and switched it on. The shadow didn't appear and I decided that it meant it had no reason to be there because I was going to get everything sorted out, to do the necessary as my Dad used to say. Then I drove up to the hospital and I was still feeling good, safe in the knowledge that what I was going to do, talking to Trisha and going to see Anne on Sunday, would be all that was needed.

But, shit, it all came crashing down round my ears yesterday. It started in the hospital and ended in this living room while I was listening to the music playing on my new toy.

Trisha was already at the hospital when I got there. She was sitting in the chair, holding Andrew's hand, talking to him about how she was going to get him back on his feet when they finally let him go home. I stood in the doorway and some of the good feeling I'd had began to fade. But not much. I coughed, the way you do when you don't want to startle somebody. She turned and looked at me and then went right back to talking to Andrew. I sat on the chair on the other side of the bed and tried not to hear the boops and beeps and the awful sucking sound of the ventilator or see the slow green waves on the monitor.

I looked around the room, checking for the shadow but it wasn't there and what little of the good feeling I'd lost came back. The neurologist arrived and asked to see us in the office. All the good feeling went away at roughly the speed of sound. It was the tone of voice, I think.

In the office, he told us that the tests they'd done showed there was very little activity in Andrew's brain. He told us that, if they turned off the ventilator, Andrew might be able to breathe for himself but they believed that would be all he could do.

He was sitting on the chair, sideways to the desk, one leg crossed over the other. His white coat seemed too bright in the muted light of the room. He's quite a young bloke, looks a bit like Mr Gibson used to look when he taught me English. Really deep tan and bright blue eyes under a mass of dark blonde curly hair. He spoke quietly and looked serious which didn't quite go with the way he looked.

I asked him what the future held for Andrew. Trisha glared at me but then she looked at the doctor. He looked at the floor for a moment and then flicked an invisible piece of something off his knee.

"I think it highly unlikely he'll recover in any real way," he said.

I asked him what sort of chance he'd give, a percentage sort of thing.
He sighed and looked at the floor.
"At best," he said softly. "I'd say there was a seventy thirty chance that he will breathe on his own again but I'd have to reverse those figures if I was talking about the chances of him having anything else in his life."
I could feel myself frowning so I asked him what he meant.
"If he lives, I think it likely that it would be <u>all</u> he could do," the doctor told me, looking straight into my eyes.
"But you don't know for sure," I said and that's when the shadow appeared behind the doctor, just looking at me, its arms by its sides.
"No," the doctor admitted. "I don't know for sure. The brain and its recuperative powers and processes are still more of a mystery than we like to admit. However, it is what I believe very strongly. I'm very sorry."
He stood up and shook my hand. He looked at Trisha but she only stared at him, her hands twining together in her lap. The doctor left us in the office.
I watched the shadow rather than the closing door. Trisha just sat there and stared out of the window at the view of Blackhill behind the hospital. The shadow began to wave its arms at me. I assumed it wanted me to get on with getting everything sorted out between me and Trisha and Trisha and Anne.
I looked at Trisha and then at the shadow and shook my head. Well, God, it wasn't the time, was it? But

the shadow kept waving its arms and I could feel the air pressure in the room beginning to drop. My scalp began to itch and I knew the tinny smell would be next and I also knew I couldn't handle all of that after what the doctor had told us.
I took a deep breath and tried to calm myself so my voice wouldn't sound clogged.

"Trisha," I said. "Trisha, there's something I've got to talk to you about."
She turned her head slowly and looked at me. Her eyes were shining and her face was very, very pale. Her mouth was a thin, purple line. She raised her eyebrows at me.

"I know you think the reason I won't come home is because I'm still seeing Anne," I said and waited for her to jump in and rant at me for even mentioning Anne's name. Trisha only sat in the chair and stared at me. "Well, that's not the reason and, Trisha, it's no good harassing her about it. We haven't been together for more than a month. It's over. It was over before...Andrew. Trisha I can't come back. That's all. It's me. Not you or Anne or anything like that. And coming back for Andrew's sake would be—it'd just be wrong. It wouldn't work. So, please, love, leave Anne alone. Stop threatening her. Violence is never right and it'd—"
That's when Trisha jumped in. Oh God, how she jumped in.

"What?" She demanded and her voice was so quiet that, for an instant, I thought it was the shadow whispering to me. But it was Trisha. "You think I give a damn about you and your bloody bimbo?

You think I've got enough time to think about harassing her? Or the energy? All I'm bothered about is Andrew. If you want to spend your time trying to recapture your youth by humping anything in a skirt, even while your son lies in a coma, carry on. But please, please don't tar me with the same brush. I grew up a long time ago, Dave. There's no way I'd even think of doing something so juvenile as get into a catfight with some bimbo with more hormones than sense."

She said it so quietly, she was so in control. No sign of her temper, no sign that she was the sort of woman who'd phoned a woman she didn't know and threatened her. I knew she had but I also thought she'd now thought it over and, after what the doctor said, decided that it was a waste of energy, energy better spent proving the doctor wrong. I didn't care so long as she stopped thinking about Anne.

Trisha turned away from me then and stared out of the window again. I looked at the shadow but it wasn't there anymore. I sighed with relief. I'd done it, sorted it out, done what the shadow wanted me to do and it had gone because it wasn't needed anymore. I closed my eyes and sighed again. When I opened them, Trisha was looking at me. There was something in her eyes I couldn't fathom but then she spoke and it was gone.

"I'm going back to see Andrew," she said. "Then I have to go home. I've got some urgent work to do."

She stood up and left me in the office alone. I waited for a moment and then followed her into Andrew's room. The shadow wasn't there.

Trisha sat in the chair and held Andrew's hand and I sat in the other chair and watched them and tried to work out what was different. I listened to the horrible sucking sound of the ventilator and the slow beep and boop of the monitor, watched the green waves roll relentlessly across the screen and then I knew what was different. Trisha wasn't talking to Andrew.

I wondered what it meant but then she stood up and looked at me.

"I've got to go, Dave," she told me and she sounded like the Trisha I married all those years ago. There was no ragged edge to her voice, no strain from trying to control the anger bubbling inside her. For that split-second, she even looked like the old Trisha, the one whose eyes matched the colour of the sea off the Lleyn peninsula. She looked like the young Trisha who had loved me once.

I told her I'd stay for a while and she left. After the door had closed, I looked at Andrew and felt tears brimming in my eyes. It was the first time I'd cried over him and, as I cried, I heard myself talking to him. Not asking him questions like the first time I'd spoken to him, but talking to him the way Trisha had talked to him every day since he'd been there.

I talked about his Nan and about work and how I was now on holiday. I told him about buying an answer machine and what I call a hi-fi and he always calls a sound system. I talked to him for half an hour by the clock on the wall of the room and then I just dried up and sat looking at him.

The bandages are off now and he just looks like he's asleep. No marks, no blood, no bruises. Just a peaceful look on his face, eyes closed, hands outside the sheet, one with a drip attached by a butterfly needle. His chest is bare apart from the connectors for the monitors. The ventilator's still there, pushed into his mouth, making his chest move up and down which is fine except it accomplishes it by making its awful sound.

It was the tube stuck in his mouth and the sucking sound that got to me. I cried again, big, silent tears rolling down my burning cheeks. I took his hand, the one without the butterfly needle, in both of mine and just cried. I looked at my son through the prism of my tears and tried to reconcile what I saw with the Andrew I knew.

How could this be the little boy who sat on our back step with his tongue stuck out of the side of his mouth as he tried to tie his laces that long-ago afternoon? How could the person in this bed be the lad who always had to write banana on a scrap piece of paper before he wrote it in his book, to make sure he'd got it right? Was this the boy who spent hours kicking his football against the back fence, wearing the Liverpool strip I'd bought him for his birthday? How could this be the same lad who breezed through school and all that teenage angst with a smile and a joke? How could this inert body be the same one who'd had his gym teacher talking about the Olympics? Could the man lying in this bed be the Andrew who jogged to work for Paul Horne and Derek Frost the summer before he went to university and came home covered in grime and cement, grinning all over his face?

It just didn't seem possible but I knew it was true and I cried myself out of tears. When the tears dried up and the deep, wracking sobs had become hitches of shallow breath, I started talking to him again. This time, I talked about how he'd be okay, how I'd help him prove the doctor wrong, how he'd walk again and talk again and play football again and finish college.

The thing was, I told him, the doctor had admitted he couldn't be sure. Seventy thirty against weren't bad odds in something like this.

"That's what you have to think about, son," I told him. "Think about the thirty percent."

I told him I wasn't going to think about the other seventy percent. I'd concentrate on the thirty percent chance he would come out of it and that he should concentrate on that, too. And, right then, as I said it, there was a gorgeous pale green corona all round Andrew's head. It shimmered and seemed to move clockwise. It was the most beautiful pale green I've ever seen. A bit like the way the sky looks sometimes in spring at sunset out in the bay, seen from Laketon Pier. I just sat there and looked at it and smiled. Even when I let go of his hand, the corona stayed round his head. Even when I kissed his cheek, leaning my face into that wonderful light, feeling the slight tingle of it, it stayed.

I came home.

Driving home, I started to feel good again. The shadow had left without whispering to me. Trisha had told me I was stupid for even thinking she would try to harm Anne. And that glorious green corona had surrounded Andrew's head when I told him we'd beat the odds and make him well again. Something about that colour made me think of stuff that was healthy, like grass in the spring, the brightness of flowers in the sun. Just stuff that was full of life. Andrew was full of life and the corona confirmed it. When I got in, I made myself something to eat and it was only when I was sitting here on the couch that I remembered I'd bought an answer machine. I sat down and saw its little red light blinking at me. I smiled and then finished my tea. Then I played the message. It was Trisha.

"Dave," she said. "It's me. I'm just ringing to tell you I'm going to see my parents. I'm driving down tonight. I need a break. I think we all do." There was a long pause and then I heard her take a long breath before she said, "Things haven't worked out the way I hoped and some time to think, away from everything seems like…anyway, just to let you know." As the mechanical voice told me the time and date of the message, I felt a really deep sadness. I just stared at the machine and felt sad because she'd sounded so lost, almost forlorn. It saddened me that, after all the years together, regardless of what had happened, she found it so hard to tell me how bad she felt. We'd always been able to talk to each other about anything. It was something we promised ourselves, back when we were still planning our dreams, looking forward to a time when our wishes had been fulfilled, a promise that we'd never become well-acquainted strangers like so many older couples seem to become as their kids leave home.

But, now, that's exactly what we've become. I suppose it started when her menopause started. That was when I stopped being the first person she talked to about everything.

I started to turn away, thinking about turning on the telly and watching whatever the film was when the answer machine began to glow.

It wasn't the beautiful green of the corona around Andrew's head. It was a deep purple, shot through with black lines and it moved anti-clockwise. I stared at it, mesmerised by the way the black lines looked like spokes in a moving wheel. Then it faded and was gone and I thought it must've been some sort of sympathetic thing, a visual sadness caused by Trisha on the answer machine.

I took a deep breath, the way you do when you've seen or heard something sad and leaned towards the telly to turn it on. And then I smiled.

The answer machine wasn't the only thing I bought yesterday.

I made myself another mug of tea and then put the compilation CDs on the hi-fi, thinking I'd save The Beatles' stuff till later because it was still a bit soon after hearing Trisha on the phone to listen to her favourite songs. I plugged my top of the range headphones into the jack and put them over my ears, lay back on the couch and zapped the hi-fi with the remote control and waited to be transported back to the decade when _my_ music was made. Back to when I was young enough not to have to worry about anything more important than getting caught in the beam of somebody's torch playing Jack-shine-light.

There's probably a word for it, Neil would know, but it's amazing how your mind works. I mean, you start out with one thing on your mind, one direction you think you're heading and then, bang, you're off on some tangent because a word, a smell, a song makes you think about something else.

I intended just letting the music from the sixties wash over me and I'd remember all the good times we had and the good things we used to do down here in The Rows. And that's how it started.

I listened to Gerry and the Pacemakers singing 'I like it' and I remembered the last Christmas before we left junior school and the party we had in Mr Frost's room. George May brought in his electric guitar and two wooden blanks him and his dad were going to turn into electric guitars. He gave me and Neil a blank each and Mr Frost got the rounders bases out, long metal poles set in heavy round bases that looked a bit like microphones if you were eleven and The Beatles ruled the world. Frankie sat on a stool behind a pile of cardboard boxes with a set of drumsticks he must've nicked from somewhere and we mimed to the records the girls had brought in. We did them all, Gerry and his mates, The Four Pennies and The Beatles. The girls even pretended to scream like they'd seen the girls on the telly do it.

Last night, it was easy for me to see us as we were then, wearing our second-best clothes, our shoes scuffed from playing football in the yard, hair trying to be long despite our mothers' demands for 'trims' that were little better than short-back-and-sides. God, we were so young and so full of possibilities.
Then, from there, my mind took me on a trip and I wondered where those people are now. Neil and Frankie and most of the lads I know about and still see but what about George May? I can't remember anybody telling me he made it as a musician, which is what he always wanted to be. The last I heard of George was that he moved to Newcastle when he was about fourteen. And what about the girls? I know Linda Hawthorne works in a solicitor's office and Linda Delap runs the florist where I always bought the flowers for Trisha's birthday. But what about Gail Evans and Carol Wynne and Janet Hargreaves? And Mr Frost? He was a smashing bloke, what happened to Mr Frost?
The next song came on and I hummed along with it, my voice just a vibration in my throat. It was The Tornados' Telstar. It was the first record I ever bought. I actually said that to myself as I listened to the opening bars. Then, suddenly, I saw the old 45 record on the turntable of the Dansette record player my Mum bought one Friday afternoon the previous autumn. She went out for peas and spuds and came home with this box tied with baling wire and a canvas strap as a handle. It was there when I got home from school and she told me it was a present for the house, not just for me. It was three

days before my birthday and, on my birthday with my birthday money, I went down to Broadway Radio to buy a record.

Broadway Radio's still there, where Byron Row joins Oil Street, by the lights. It doesn't sell records anymore, just what those toerags who tried to break in here that night called 'white goods'. Back then, it used to sell the top twenty records. Back then, it was cool to buy the number one single and, good as Telstar was, I think I'm still a bit pissed off that The Beatles hadn't been around long enough to be number one that week.

I was still thinking about that when the last note of the song faded in the earphones and I was waiting for the next record to spark another memory when my mind took off on another tangent. This time, though, it wasn't just in my mind that the memory sparked into life. I was, suddenly, almost dizzily, actually <u>outside</u> the shop, looking in the window. The memory was so vivid, I got some idea of what it must be like for Neil.

I could see my reflection in the big window. I was all bundled up in my dark blue duffelcoat, hands in pockets, hood down. I was looking at the big orange card stuck in the window, close to the hoover display. The list of top twenty records was on the card. The road behind me was reflected, too, a ghostly image full of spectral bodies and bikes and cars and buses.

The air in the living room changed then, became heavier and my body began to get that warm feeling you get just before the itch starts. But I put it down to the incredible vividness of the memory. That day when I bought Frank Ifield's record was overcast and misty but I was toasty warm in my duffelcoat.

I didn't even open my eyes last night, I just lay on the couch and recalled that day outside the shop. If I'd opened my eyes, I might've just run out of this house and kept on running.

But I didn't and now I'm just waiting for what comes next.

I lay on this couch and remembered, for the first time since it happened, the only car crash I've ever seen.

ELEVEN

Martin Cottingham stood and watched the van drive away. He thought about ringing Neil and then shook his head. No, get the paperwork started and then leave it to Sergeant Robb. Then go home and get some sleep. Martin felt he really needed some sleep. Tomorrow would be soon enough to see Neil. When the sun was up, or at least the sky was brighter. Yes, tomorrow.

Four miles away, Neil looked at his own phone. He thought about ringing Martin, asking if they'd found Davy. Then he shook his head. Tomorrow would do. If Martin didn't ring, he'd be here tomorrow and, Neil decided, that was fine. Right now, he needed to finish Davy's journal.

Davy believed that the shadow belonged to him and, for better or worse, this journal belonged to Neil. For now, anyway. It would finally belong to Andrew and he would have questions and he would ask those of Neil. Neil needed to have the answers. This journal would give him most of them and then he would have to find the rest from the person whose name Paul Horne had given him earlier tonight.

If that person was willing to talk, of course.

But that would be tomorrow. When the sun was up or

the sky was at least brighter and there weren't so many shadows eager to creep out into the open.

I've seen the results of crashes over the years, sometimes only bare minutes after they happened. That afternoon, more than thirty years ago, as the streetlamps were coming on and the twilight was settling over Seapool with a misty calm, I actually saw the crash.

Instead of hearing the opening bars of the next song on the compilation CD, I heard the screech of brakes. Last night, just as I did all those years ago, I winced at the sound. The little boy in his duffelcoat watched the ghostly reflection of the car begin to slide sideways as its brakes bit. And then he turned, full of that grim, shameful fascination for such things.

When I was turned all the way round, I noticed the people on the pavement on both sides of the road had all stopped walking and were, like me, watching the thing happen.

The car had braked because a young mother had lost her grip on the pram she was pushing. The big pram, its hood up, had bounced off the pavement and was rolling into the centre of the road. The car had been coming round the bend, past the pub on the corner, just picking up speed as the driver saw the lights change in his favour. When he saw the pram, he braked but the day was misty, the roads greasy and, of course, there were no such things as servo-assistance or ABS brakes in those days. So the car slewed sideways, heading for the pram broadside, heading into the middle of the road. A double-decker bus was passing on the other side of the road.

A man, in his twenties maybe, dashed off the pavement next to me and launched himself at the pram. He grabbed the chromed handle and pulled back. The baby was safe but the bus and car were still heading for each other and nobody was going to pull either one of them back.

The car hit the bus' front grill and the screech of grinding metal and the cough of breaking glass was worse than the sound of the squealing brakes. I watched the bonnet of the car crumple, the windscreen crack and then smash. I watched the driver who was wearing a trilby, almost fly through the screen. I saw his face collide with the piece of jagged glass and heard the awful groan I made when I saw the blood. His body stopped half-in and half-out of the broken screen and his head hit the centre ridge of the bonnet. His head bounced once and then was still.

Then the memory or vision or whatever it was, was gone and I was listening to the songs on the CD. But with each song, instead of remembering the good times I'd had when the songs were new, I remembered all the bad stuff that happened. There seemed to be an awful lot of it. Jimmy burning his legs, Eddie breaking his arm and leg. There were others but they're the important ones.

And then I noticed that the air in the room was still heavy and I knew it had nothing to do with what I was remembering. I opened my eyes and the shadow was there, in the cone of light from the lamp behind the telly. The itching started and the smell would come next and I knew I'd just run out of here then, screaming. But the smell didn't come next. What came next was the car crash again. Exactly the same as the first time I'd remembered it.

It replayed itself and then I saw Jimmy and Eddie getting hurt again. Exactly as I saw them minutes earlier. They were real action replays, the sort Match of the Day love.

I looked at the shadow, asked it what this meant, waiting for its whisper. It waved its arms at me but there were no whispers. I shook my head and its waving arms went berserk. They looked the sails of a black windmill, blowing madly in a gale. I yanked the headphones off my head and yelled at it to tell me what it wanted.

"I've done what you wanted! I talked to Trisha, I'm going to see Anne tomorrow! It's sorted! You're not supposed to be here anymore!"

I heard the whine in my voice and didn't care. I just wanted it to stop, to bugger off and leave me alone because I'd done what it wanted. But below all that, was the fear. The fear that it obviously wanted something else, that there was still something else I needed to understand and, if I didn't get it, the shadow would just go and visit Andrew.

The weight of the air and the fear I felt made me feel like I'd been awake for days, long past sleep itself, just weary down to my very soul. I lay back again and closed my eyes, expecting another set of replays. What I got was a sharp mind-image of the mattresses I'd bought in the morning.

It was enough. I knew what I had to do.

I put an old pair of work jeans on, hunted out my old trainers and put an old crew-neck jumper on. It was as close as I could come to how we all dressed when we were kids. I dragged the mattresses down and lay them on top of each other by the outside toilet. I found some old twine and tied them together. I squeezed through the railings and walked round the swings, making sure there was nobody out there. There wasn't anybody, not even a cat or a dog. I went back and got the mattresses and got them over the railings at the second attempt. I half-carried, half-dragged them across to the slide. I put them below the slide but on the other side to where we used to put Eddie's old mattresses. On that side, all the backs of the houses were dark, not even the blue glimmer of a telly. I ran up the ladder and felt myself smiling at how little noise I made.

On the platform, I just stood there for a few moments, feeling the breeze on my face and remembering back all those years. I could almost feel myself shrinking to the four feet eleven I used to be. Then I looked over the top of the cage and down at the mattresses.

I could just make them out in the dim light shed by the security lights from the docks and the flour mills. They looked about the same height off the ground as Eddie's six had looked. I climbed on top of the platform and sat there, my legs swinging slowly, my hands gripping tightly onto the top bar, breathing deeply. There was a thin thread of apprehension; I wasn't ten or eleven now and my bones weren't so springy. I also weighed a lot more.

Still, that thin thread was soon replaced with the stomach-twitter of anticipation. I took another deep breath and pushed off and out with my hands.

Even now, scared as I am by what happened after I jumped, I can still feel that magical moment. It was so much better than bungee jumping. The fragment of time before gravity realised what I was doing felt so much longer, almost endless. Just like it used to when I was a kid. For that moment, it felt like I could, if I tried hard enough, simply swim through the air, like I swim through the baths and fly away.

Then gravity laid hold of me and I stopped looking at the way the sky was still light purple in the west and looked down at the mattresses, aiming for their centre. And I hit it perfectly. There was a thud, a small sound from me, a judder up my legs. Then I rolled and just stepped on to the asphalt. Just like I always used to.

I did it ten times. Each time was better than the last, each tiny snip of time between the sky and ground an almost endless moment of flight, filled with euphoria.

I forgot why I was doing it. It was just as well I missed the centre of the mattresses that last time or I'd've carried on till the sun peeked over the houses. But I missed the centre and rolled onto the ground and banged my shoulder hard enough to make me moan. The moan made me remember why I was doing it. I dragged the mattresses back to the garden and dashed into this room.

The shadow wasn't here. The standard lamp was still on, its new bulb burning brightly but the shadow wasn't frozen in its cone of light. The air still felt heavy and I could smell a hint of tin. My head started itching and I rubbed at it, staring at the cone of light, willing the shadow to appear.

I muttered for it to come back. I muttered through gritted teeth, gritted so I wouldn't scream. Nothing. I sat down on the couch and put my head in my hands, rubbing my head with my fingers. I kept looking up to see if the shadow was there but it was just the light. That was when I saw the glow round the phone and the answer machine.

It was a bright, vivid orange with a yellow fringe. It was pulsating and, inside it, I could see the tiny red message light blinking.

Andrew.

The message was from the hospital. They'd rung while I was out jumping off the slide. The shadow got fed up waiting for me to come back and gone up to the hospital and done God knew what to Andrew. I knew this as I pressed the button to replay the message.

"Mr Eliot," a soft warm voice said. "This is Julia Bacon at the hospital. I'm ringing to tell you that Andrew showed definite signs of increased brain activity earlier this evening. I know what the consultant told you this afternoon and I thought you might feel better knowing Andrew hadn't given up yet. The activity settled down again and it's now at its previous level but there were definite signs that Andrew was partially aware. If I'm on duty tomorrow when you call, I'll speak to you again."

Oh, it sounded like good news but I thought I knew why Andrew had been partially aware earlier in the evening. The shadow was there. While I was out reliving my younger days, the shadow had gone and stood behind Andrew and Andrew had known. Not only that, he'd known what the shadow had in mind and the increased activity was him trying to wake up so he could ward off the shadow.

I stared hard at the cone of light.

"Come on you bastard," I said. "I'm here. Come back now you bastard!"

The air pressure dropped even further and the ants made my whole body feel like it was on fire. The worst was my scalp. I was rubbing so hard at it that my fingers burned. I shook my head and half-expected a cloud of black/brown bugs to shower down to the floor. Even if the shadow came back, I didn't think I could stand the way my head felt.

I got a pair of scissors and my electric razor and stood in front of the mirror over the mantelpiece and shaved my head. I didn't care what it looked like, so long as it didn't feel like my head was about to catch fire. It doesn't look too bad actually cos I've been going bald for a couple of years and it just looks like I've owned up now.

As I was putting the razor back in its case, the shadow came back.

It didn't go pop and arrive in a puff of smoke, it just faded into existence in the cone of light, standing away from the wall, its arms by its sides. Then the air pressure dropped even more and I just fell onto the couch. It still amazes me that it happens so fast.

It just drains me, like the way long hot summer afternoons used to drain me when I was a kid only it happens in seconds. I lay here on the couch and waited for the whispers to start, waited for the shadow to explain what the replays of parts of my life meant.

There were no whispers.

I waited, feeling the fear building in me but nothing happened at all. No whispers, no action replays, nothing. I actually moaned, begging the shadow to explain and then I heard something. Not a whisper. I know what an electrical noise sounds like and it sounded like that. My eyes flew open. I was convinced the bloody lamp had burned out or the lamp itself had fused and the shadow was gone again.

The shadow was still there. But the telly, which I hadn't turned on because I'd listened to the CDs instead, was on. Its screen was flickering with that pale grey light it has before the picture arrives. And pictures did arrive but they weren't any part of any programme that was supposed to be on last night.

The itching faded slowly and the tinny smell was only there if I actually thought about it. The air pressure was still low but it didn't seem to weigh me down so much anymore. I sat up straighter and stared at the television screen. For a second, I thought I'd fallen asleep and was dreaming. But I wasn't. The telly was showing me exactly what I'd seen earlier on the inside of my eyelids.

I'd jumped from the slide ten times and, oh God, it had sharpened my senses and perceptions all right.

Even as I watched, I was thinking about the Saturday morning matinees we used to go to at The Gaumont because that's what it was like. I wasn't in the sixpenny stalls with all my old mates but it was still like watching a film. While I watched the film of my life, part of me, a part trying very hard not to be terrified and failing, remembered the films we saw when we were kids during our holidays—The Young Ones and Hercules Unchained and Help and Hard Day's Night and the rest—and how we hid in the toilets so we could watch them again for free if they were good. I remembered how grown-up I felt the time we saw Barabbas and, because we'd got there late and missed the start, we'd been able to stay in legally until we could utter the fabled phrase—this is where we came in—and leave.

But this wasn't Barabbas, it was my life and it scared the hell out of me. It was my life and it shouldn't have bothered me at all but it did because, with each scene, I saw it the way it _actually_ was and not the way I'd always remembered it.

The shadow was there each time. In every scene I watched, the shadow was there. Not just when Jimmy and Eddie and that poor girl on the bungee jump were hurt. It was there in _every bloody_ scene.

It was there when I stood in the delivery room after Andrew was born. It was there when I said goodbye to my Dad in the room where he died. It was there when Trisha admitted her adultery. It was there when I did the somersault off the board in Chamberlain Street baths and again when I dived from the board in Laketon Pool. At every bungee jump I ever made, it was there. And it was there at the car crash I witnessed outside Broadway Radio on that long-ago birthday.

I was just nodding by then and it took me a second to realise that the car crash was different than the first time I'd seen it and the second time. Not because the shadow was there but because I finally saw what would've happened if the bus hadn't been in the way.

The shadow was standing in the gutter, bare yards from where the car finally stopped. Its arms were outspread and I assumed it was Death, waiting to claim the driver after his head bounced once on the ridge of the bonnet. It wasn't waiting for the driver, it was there for me.

The car crash repeated itself on the telly screen and I watched as the car slewed across the road, heading for the pavement where I was standing. Then it was broadsided by the bus and was stopped. If it hadn't hit the bus, it would've just kept coming, right at me, out of control. It wasn't going very fast but it looked sort of ineluctable. Like, it was going fast enough to have hit me and knocked me over and then just kept rolling over me or knocked me back through the big plate glass window of the shop.

So the shadow had been with me all my life but I still didn't really understand why. So, last night, here in the living room of 12 Oil Street, I asked the shadow.

"Why are you here?" I asked and the screen went black.

The whisper oozed across the room's heavy air and into my brain where it settled just like oil on the surface of water, spreading out with its pretty colours that are, ultimately, deadly.

<u>from the beginning the end is known</u>

I shook my head, still not understanding. The screen on the television flickered into life again.
I watched one of my teenage-dreams but this time, I got it all.
It was like one of those Hitchcockian things where you see the action from the hero's or the victim's or the baddie's viewpoint. I could see the hallway, lit by the dim yellow bulb. Then the angle changed from bulb to stairs and I saw them rising up towards me. They looked much bigger and the distance much longer than they should've done to a teenager. Of course, the watcher on those stairs wasn't a teenager, was he? Oh no. He was a toddler, just turned one year old and the toddler's mother was in the kitchen and his father was in the living room.
Then my Mum appeared and I could see her open mouth as she screamed and then my Dad was in the hall and then everything rolled. I saw flashes of my arms as they pinwheeled when I lost my balance. I saw the second bottom stair and the newel of the banister. Then my left arm flashed into focus again and, beyond it, I saw the shadow waiting for me at the bottom of the stairs, ready to embrace me and take me back wherever it is we come from.
I never reached those open arms because my Dad caught me. He didn't catch me clean and I heard the wet snap of breaking bones as I rebounded off the

wood and hit the third riser with my pelvis and collided with the second riser with both legs.

The screen went black again and the shadow whispered to me.

<u>the burden was hard to carry for so long alone and what is too heavy to carry alone we pass on so the weight is shared</u>

All I could do was nod. I knew now. I knew what the shadow knew, knew why it wanted me to talk to Trisha and persuade her from harming Anne. If she continued to harass her, if she went that one step further and did what I'd seen her do in the preview of possible futures, the guilt she was already feeling would increase intolerably and the only way she could bear it would be to pass it on. Who to? Andrew. If that happened, if Andrew had to bear the weight of his mother's guilt as well as his share of my guilt, it would be too much. Much too much. When he comes out of the coma, he won't need any more weight to carry.

Well, I thought last night, it was sorted. Trisha was going to leave Anne alone and tomorrow, I'd tell Anne she had nothing more to worry about and that would remove some of the guilt I had in that direction. As for Andrew, I'd already decided to concentrate on the thirty percent chance he had of recovery and I'd help him get back on his feet.

As for the rest of my guilt, I'll just have to carry it alone. I'm not living with Trisha or Andrew anymore, Anne is out of my life, my Mum's got her own life. I'll be alone but it feels like a good deal to me. For all but one year of my life, those closest to me have had to carry some of my guilt. Not anymore. I can set them free of that, at least. Like I said, it seems like a fair swap.

That was so hard to write. I've been sitting here and writing, hoping I've got it right, the fear still rippling through me that I've cocked it up again, not understood what the shadow's been trying to tell me. Now it's done and it feels right, feels like I've got it right this time. For fifteen minutes, as I began to write it all down, the shadow was standing in the cone of light with its arms outspread and I kept looking at it, kept expecting the air to get heavy again and for the whispers to settle in my brain. But it's been motionless for nearly an hour and half now. The room doesn't feel like a cloud-chamber and I'm not scratching at myself like a demented monkey.
I think I've got it right this time.
It's nearly half three in the morning but, for the first time in a long time, I feel tired. A natural tiredness. I'm going to go to bed and get some sleep and, later this morning, I'll see Anne and it will all be done and dusted.
I've just thought of a phrase I heard a while ago. God knows who said it but it sounds like something Neil would've said. Anyway, it seems to sum up how I feel now I've finally understood things properly.
<u>Roll wheel roll.</u>
That's it and that's how I feel. Like I've come full circle. From being a toddler with nothing to carry

but myself, through all those years when I was trying to carry something too heavy for me and so made my family share it, on through what I suppose was my own mid-life crisis and waking up in the early hours, to now. All I've got to carry is my own guilt and, it's perverse but true, I feel lighter. Light enough to be able to go to bed and sleep without worrying about dreaming and waking up after an hour. It feels like it's been a long, long time.

TWELVE

"Roll wheel roll," Neil muttered and didn't really hear himself. He was remembering the conversation when he'd used the phrase that Davy remembered.

It wasn't long after Thatcher resigned and Davy and Frankie and Neil had got together after a long time without seeing each other. After the usual finding-out-where-they-were and a couple of pints, they'd wandered into a sort of discussion about mortality and immortality and Time and all the other almost-related topics. Frankie had just had to remortgage his house to keep his business afloat and was ranting on about Thatcher being the main reason and it was his heartfelt comment about her that had led to the discussion.

Frankie told them that he'd never really fancied living forever, living past his peers and mates but now he thought he had a good enough reason to do it. He said he'd really like to live long enough for History to finally tell the truth about Margaret-bleedin-Thatcher. And after the laughter and nods of agreement, they'd got into Stephen Hawking and Time and the rest of it and Neil had told them the phrase he thought best summed up how he felt about Time and, probably, Life.

Now, sitting in his office, with the journal frozen in the bright light of the anglepoise lamp on his desk, he wasn't surprised that it had occurred to Davy after he thought he'd watched a re-run of his life. But something else had happened, hadn't it?

It must've done or this journal wouldn't be on his desk now. Davy went to sleep early Sunday morning and the journal had arrived yesterday, Wednesday. Whatever had happened had happened on Monday and it had been something that had made Davy feel he needed to send the journal to Neil for Andrew's sake.

For what he knew would be the final time, he looked at the journal again. Like one half of some Scouse songwriting partnership might have said, back in the sixties when they were all young and time was something they all had plenty of, it was getting very near the end.

Then it would be time to hand it over to Martin and Neil would have to try to get somebody to talk about something they'd probably spent their life trying to forget.

How can one man get so much so wrong so bloody often? I thought it was all done and dusted and now I'm back here with this pen in my hand, writing in this bloody journal again.

It's different now, though. This journal isn't for me now, it's not a way for me to write out my thoughts or to write myself out of the depression I've been in since my Dad died. I've got to write it for Andrew now. I've got to get it all down, exactly how it happened. For him. There's only one way I know for him to get it and that's to send it to Neil. I wish I didn't have to do that because he's been one of my best mates since we were about four years old and he helped me survive when I wasn't sure I could or even wanted to. But it's the only way I can be sure of helping Andrew when he comes out of the coma like I hope he will.

I went to bed at half three yesterday morning feeling light and even woke up five hours later feeling light, almost like a new man. I came down here and the shadow was still pinned in the cone of light behind the telly and it was motionless. The answer machine was just the plain, everyday cream it was when I bought it and its red light wasn't blinking. I rang the hospital and Andrew had had an uneventful night. I did what little housework needed doing and then I went to see Anne.

Anne's road was Sunday-morning-quiet. There were two children playing hopscotch on a chalk grid outside Anne's neighbour's house but the rest of the road was empty. I got out of the car and walked up the path and rang the bell and waited.

She opened the door wearing a housecoat and she had a towel wrapped round her head. She blinked a few times when she saw me but I must've looked strange; the last time she'd seen me, my head wasn't shaved. For a second or two, I thought about asking her out again. It was the way her eyes shone and her smile looked so warm. Then I remembered what the shadow wanted from me and mentally shook my head.

What I _thought_ the shadow wanted from me.

"Hello, Anne," I said and smiled. "Listen, I just want you to know that I know Trisha's been harassing you about— us. I've spoken to her about it and she understands now that we're not seeing each other anymore. She'll stop phoning you now. You don't have to worry about her anymore. I'm sorry for the trouble she's put you to but, well, I think a lot of it's the strain of Andrew. You know?"

She looked at me and nodded, as if she was thinking about it, wondering if me saying it was the same as Trisha doing it. Then she nodded again.

"I heard about your son, Dave," she said. "I'm sorry. Listen, I'd invite you in for coffee but I'm going up to see my sister in Scotland. I have to catch the late train."

I told her that it was okay, I was going to see Andrew anyway. I told her to look after herself and apologised again for the trouble I'd caused her. I walked back to the car, feeling good, knowing I'd done the right thing. When I got to the car, I turned and waved to her and she waved back. As I opened the car door, a car turned into the road at the top end. I only noticed it because the sun flashed on its screen and by the time I'd blinked away the glare out of my eyes, Anne had closed her door.

The hospital was Sunday-quiet, too and I parked opposite the main doors. There was nobody at the desk behind the big observation window outside Andrew's room and it disappointed me a bit cos I'd been hoping to see Julia Bacon. But she'd told me Andrew had been partially aware and that was the important thing. If he'd done it once, even if was because he was afraid of the shadow, he could do it again for better reasons.

I sat on the chair by his bed and talked to him for nearly an hour, until I heard the rumble of the dinner trolleys further down the corridor. I talked to him about everything and nothing and told him it'd be okay, we'd get him well again. I held his hand as I told him that and he squeezed it twice. When he did that, I felt something inside me that was very similar to the feeling I got jumping from the slide. It was a lightness, a sense that my body weighed little more than the air around me. Then I told him his mum was away for the weekend, having a break at his grandparents' house and he squeezed my hand once.

"I suppose she called in before she left and told you," I said.

The shadow appeared behind Andrew's bed and I didn't notice if Andrew squeezed my hand again.

Now, I'm pretty sure he must've done, trying to get my attention over something to do with his mum. But then, seeing the shadow, all my attention was fixed on it.

"What the hell are you doing here?" I whispered, the fear running though me like fire in a paper factory, the panic not far behind. "I've done what I had to do, what I promised to do. Why the hell are you here?"

I waited for the whisper, the heavy air, the scurrying ants, the tinny smell. None of it happened. The shadow just stood there behind Andrew's bed, arms by its sides, looking at me. And, because there was no heavy air or maddening itch or smell or waving arms, I thought I understood. The shadow was there to witness me doing what needed doing. It wasn't there as a threat to Andrew.

Even so, I didn't like it there, so close to Andrew. It was time to leave. I said goodbye to Andrew and told him I'd see him the next day, today. I told him to concentrate on the thirty percent chance he had and left the hospital. I got home just before the football started on the telly.

I had the sort of Sunday I hadn't had in ages. I watched the football, ate my dinner, read the papers. At tea time, I started to think about getting my stuff ready for a new week at work and then I remembered I was on holiday. I didn't have to go to bed early or get up early and, better still, I wasn't expecting to wake up in the ditch of three-in-the-morning anymore. Shit, I could stay up late and—well, I didn't really know what but I could stay up late. Then I remembered the hi-fi and the CDs and grinned.

See, the thing was, I'd done what I was supposed to do, made my mind up about the rest of my life. I could listen to those old songs and, this time, just hear the music and remember the good times. No more little picture shows on the unplugged telly, no more scurrying ants or tinny smell or the feeling that I was sitting in the centre of a gigantic thundercloud. God, I felt so good.

I played all the CDs and revelled in the nostalgia of them, of those days when England was swinging and The Beatles ruled the world. I went to bed at half past two this morning and there were no dreams, no waking in the small hours and waiting for the pearly light of another misty Seapool dawn to seep into the bedroom.

I got up this morning at half eight. It's the latest I've stayed in bed for God knows how long. I woke up humming one of the tunes I listened to on Sunday night and stood in the shower trying to remember the words. God, I wish I hadn't remembered that old Mamas and Papas tune or its words.

Monday, Monday, can't trust that day.

Still, at ten o'clock this morning, well yesterday morning really since it's now nearly ten past one in the morning—anyway, at ten o'clock, I was still feeling good and didn't know you can't trust Monday, Monday. I just knew I was on holiday with no calls on my time, nothing to do but please myself. I had no places to be and no promises to keep because I'd kept them all. I stood in the kitchen and saw how

the early mist was still eddying on the grass verge of the swings but the sky was a soft blue and it looked exactly like the days I used to love when I was a kid. I decided to go for a walk round The Rows, visit a few places I hadn't visited for years, those places I'd remembered while I listened to the old sixties songs last night.
Would it have been any different if I'd stayed in yesterday morning? Only the details, not the main events. Still, I wish I'd stayed in. That way, I wouldn't have had to see the terror on the children's faces or the awful mix of anger and fear on the faces of the young mothers. I wouldn't have had to hear the question the lad asked, the lad who looked to be about ten years old, which feels like the age I was the last time I was really happy
But I did go out and everything happened so I've got to write about it. For Neil to read and understand, for Andrew to read and, please God, understand.
I walked down Shakespeare Row and onto the dock road. I stopped and looked at the pair of magpies that were perched on the big gate of the flour mill there. They looked at me and made that clacking noise in their throat, scolding me for disturbing their mating or whatever they were doing. Then they took off, flapping gorgeous, iridescent black/blue wings and another old song flitted through my mind.
I hummed the melody of 'Fly on my sweet angel' and walked off down the curving road. Now, I'm surprised the tune didn't just clang in my mind, like a door closing in some huge castle. But I was so sure I'd done the necessary like my Dad used to say.

I walked round my old haunts, feeling good, not really thinking about anything. I bought a hot-dog from the van opposite The Stump pub and ate it leaning against the railings of the dock. The slow tide lapped against the dock walls and I remembered being eight years old and standing in exactly the same place. My Dad stood next to me that day and gave me a brief history of the docks and the shipbuilding industry there used to be here years ago. I finished my hot-dog and bought a Styrofoam mug of tea from the lad in the van who looked younger than Andrew and made me feel older than God. Then I walked down towards the ferry.

And that's when it all started to go bad.

I walked through the kids' playground behind the block of flats by the ferry. It's a short cut and that's all I was thinking about when I crossed the little half-circle of rides. I went into some sort of blank-out. A fugue state I suppose.

When I came back to myself, there were three young mothers yelling at me. I was standing at the bottom of the little chute of the slide and looking up at the three year old boy who was waiting to come down. I blinked and looked at the women.

"What the hell are you doing, you maniac!"

"Bugger off and leave them alone or we'll get the police."

"People like you should be locked up or put to sleep or something!"

"Mummy, make him go away! I don't like him Mummy! Make the dark man go away now Mummy!"

I winced at the screeching noise of the women and the plaintive howl of the child on the slide. I shook my head and held out my arms to the women, asking them wordlessly what was wrong.

The shadow was standing next to me, mimicking the way my arms were held out. All the spit in my mouth dried up and my stomach rolled sickeningly. My legs felt like they were about to just tumble me on my backside and that would have made things worse. The women wouldn't have bothered with the police, they'd have just fell on me like the wrath of God. And would I blame them? Oh no, not me.

The shadow turned away from me and looked at the now sobbing child. The boy's face looked like an uncooked pancake with two huge raisins for eyes. His little mouth was still open in a silent scream as he looked at me. No, not at me. He was looking at the shadow, seeing what his mother and her two friends couldn't see. The little boy saw the shadow and knew it for what it was and was so scared he couldn't even scream.

Then all the other children came running to their mothers, all crying, all begging their mothers to make the dark man go away. The tallest of the women, dressed in jeans and a pale blue top, her hair in a loose ponytail, finally got tired of waiting for me to leave. She stepped forward and aimed a kick at me. I stepped back but she kept coming and one of the others came round to my left and swung a big black bag at me, catching me on the shoulder.

I finally found enough strength to run away. Not from the women; God knows, the way I felt then, the look of anger and fear in the women's faces was enough for me to want to fall down and let them kick me to death. No, I ran because the shadow had started to move towards the chute of the slide and wasn't standing on the floor anymore. It was floating above the ground, getting ready to float all the way up the slide to the little boy, frozen by his terror at the top.

I ran out of the playground and kept running until I reached the ticket office of the ferry terminal. I bought my ticket and, thank God, a boat was in. I ran so fast down the slipway that I nearly fell twice but I got onto the gangway and made my way to the top deck. I sat on the wooden bench in front of the funnel and put my head in my hands. I cried into my cupped hands and tried to work out why the shadow was still with me and, worse than that, why it now followed me round instead of being pinned in the cone of light from the lamp in 12 Oil Street.

I didn't know, couldn't work it out, didn't have a bloody clue. I felt like wailing into the wind that blew off the river, smelling of the water and the sand, of the ozone my Dad called Nature's first smell. I even lifted my head to do it but the sight of the shadow in front of me closed my mouth.

It stood in front of the funnel with its arms still outspread but it made no movement. I waited for the whisper but none came. I waited for the air to get heavy, for the terrible burning itch and the tinny smell. Nothing. Just the shadow and its arms open in an invitation to embrace.

I didn't even try to ask it any questions. I just sat there and stared at it as it was staring at me and blanked out again. It was another insistent voice that brought me back to myself.

I blinked stupidly and turned my head. The boy looked about ten, his jeans were dirty, his trainers muddy, he had one of the shaved-head haircuts they all have now. He stood a good two yards away, leaning against the rail but I could see his whole body was tensed, ready for flight if necessary.

"Why is that thing there mister?"

I frowned and shook my head.

"That thing you've been talking to for the last ten minutes," he said. "There, right in front of you. It's just a shadow you know." He said this kindly, as if I was a loony and needed treating kindly.

"You can see it?" I asked him. "Doesn't it frighten you?"

"What, a shadow? Nah, why should it? There's loads of shadows all over the place. I just want to know why you're talking to it like it can answer you?"

I looked back at the shadow and it lowered its arms and turned slowly towards the boy. It began to float across the air to him, slowly raising its arms towards him. He stood on the deck and stared at it, just like the toerags had done in my garden that night. I watched the colour drain from his face and watched his hands begin to shake uncontrollably and then watched his whole body shake. He was making a noise, a horrible murmuring noise and still he couldn't stop staring at the shadow as it moved closer to him.

I stood up and dashed between the shadow and the boy. I flung my arms up, as if I was shying away a maddened horse and I yelled at the lad to run, get the hell away from here right now.

The boy screamed and took off towards the stairway.

"Keep it away from me mister! I don't like its face! Stop it!"

The shadow stopped and dropped its arms slowly, the features in its face clearer now. When the ferry docked at Seapool Ferry I realised that I'd been on the boat to Oxborough and stayed on it for the return trip, like we used to do when we were kids. It'd been fun in those days. Not today.

I got up and waited at the top of the stairs until I was the last on the boat. Then I got off and trudged up the gangway and up the slipway, glad that the boy hadn't brought anybody running after me to grab me and keep me till the police arrived.

The shadow walked ahead of me all the way up Ferry Road. It walked backwards, its arms outspread all the way. Where I side-stepped to let people pass, the shadow simply moved backwards and the people walked through it, oblivious to it. Then, just as I reached the bottom of Shelley Row, it was gone. Gone home, back to Oil Street, I thought and put my head down and kept walking.

I walked and didn't try to think about why the shadow was still with me or why it was now out of doors and able to be seen by other people. Well, by kids anyway. I was out of ideas and out of energy for anything like that. I just wanted to get back here and sleep and maybe wake up and find it was all a horrible dream.

When I reached the delicatessen on Byron Row, I looked up. The road was starting to get ready for the rush hour. There was a queue of traffic at the lights and the bus was third in line. I noticed it the way you notice most things like that, peripherally. I was outside Broadway Radio when the lights changed and the bus entered the junction.

The car came round the bend fast. Too fast for the road conditions. A patented Seapool twilight, all misty and lowering, made the road a bit greasy and the orange glow of the streetlamps looked like thin daubs of paint smeared on the air. There was a young woman looking in the window of Broadway Radio, one hand holding the handle of a pushchair loosely. The baby in the pram was gurgling happily at the colourful mobile hanging from the top of the rain cover.

The bus was moving toward the bend in the road when the car came round the same bend. The car was straddling the white line. I was waiting for the sound of the car's brakes but they didn't come.

I didn't think of the first and only accident I watched all those years ago, I really didn't. My mind was past thinking about anything much by then. I just stood there and absently wondered why the car hadn't braked. Then I heard the electronic buzzer on the door of Broadway Radio as somebody left the shop.

It was a young lad, about seventeen, and he came charging out of the shop. He must've seen the bus through the window and didn't want to miss it. He banged into the pushchair, knocking it out of the loose grip of the young mother. The pushchair rolled towards the road. <u>That</u> was when I thought about the other crash.

My mind left off being too tired or too lost to think then. I looked up and the car still wasn't braking. I waved my hands but the car just kept coming, about forty yards away from the pushchair.

"Oh shit!" The young lad yelled.

He leaped past me, his hands clutching for the handle of the pram. The pushchair rolled off the pavement and kept on rolling into the middle of the road. I started to run towards it, still watching the car. I thought that what I saw was something to do with the misty air and the dim light of the twilight, a reflection caused by one or both of those things. Behind the screen of the car, I thought there were two bulky shapes. Whatever, the car was still coming. The bus braked, its air brakes hissing loudly as it tried to swerve away from the car but it just made its rear end fishtail. And the car was still coming.

The child's mother must've seen this and she screamed. It seemed to go on for a long time that scream. The car turned its headlights on, full beam, blinding me and the lad who put his left hand up in front of his face, still reaching out for the pram with his right. The bus slewed and caught the back end of the car, not much but enough to keep it coming sideways towards the pram. I shouted something, knowing I wasn't going to get there in

time. Maybe it was a prayer that the young lad would get there, I don't know.
If it was, Somebody must've been listening. The lad caught the handle of the pushchair and yanked it towards him. It hit him in the shins and he sat down with a bump in the gutter. The car was still heading for him and, God knows why, I ran in front of him.
The car caught me on the hip, not hard but it knocked me out of the way. It hit the pram and knocked it flying up onto the pavement where it landed right next to me. It reeled back on its little wheels and then rocked forward again. The baby tumbled out and landed in my lap. The mother screamed again and then, even above that awful sound, I heard the crunch of the car's tyres as they rolled over the lad's legs. His agonised howl was the loudest sound yet.
Then the car drove on, tyres squealing, through the lights and into the misty distance. I watched it, trying to get the numbers on the back plate but they were obscured by something. Then I looked down at the baby. It was looking up at me and gurgling, completely unhurt, not bothered at all. I got up shakily and limped towards the young woman who was just standing on the pavement with her hands plastered to her face. I handed the baby to her and she almost squeezed the life out of it, making the baby cry where the near-fatal accident hadn't.
My hip was throbbing but it didn't feel wet with blood and my legs worked fine. I rubbed it and went to see if the young lad was all right. A couple of the shopkeepers had phoned the police and ambulance.

The police arrived first and the ambulance arrived a couple of minutes later. The lad lay half-in, half-out of the gutter, his face white, his eyes scrunched up in pain, his hands hovering over his legs like birds, wanting to touch but scared to. The ambulancemen told him he'd broken both legs and he told them he knew that and, for Christ's sake, could they just hurry the fuck up.

The police took statements from me and the lad and the young mother and a few others but nobody had been able to get the car's numbers. All anybody knew was that it had been a small car.

When the police let us go, I walked home, reliving the accident and remembering the other accident when I was just turned ten But, mostly, I thought about the fact that the shadow was still with me and, worse than even that, that I was back to the way I was after I first moved back to Oil Street—I was blanking out and muttering and frightening mothers and terrifying their children. Well, the <u>shadow</u> was terrifying the children and it seemed I was doomed to have it walking with me for the rest of my life. It seemed to me, as I opened the back door, that the only thing left for me would be to leave Seapool altogether. But, if I did, what about Andrew and the promise I'd made him? And there was no guarantee that the shadow would leave the town with me. It might just remain here in Oil Street.

The shadow was waiting for me when I came into the living room. The atmosphere in the room felt so full of static electricity that the fillings in my teeth jangled. But worse even than that was the itching that began the second I walked into the room.

I staggered to the couch and sat down heavily, staring at the shadow. It was waving its arms wildly. The tinny smell came then, almost overpowering and the itch was worse than ever, like the microscopic ants were trying to eat their way out through my skin, or maybe trying to eat their way in. I was rubbing so hard at myself, I was probably helping them.

Eventually, the smell and the itch backed off enough to become just about bearable and I had enough breath to ask the shadow why it was still here. Why, when I'd done everything it had wanted me to do, when I'd made it right, for Anne and Trisha and Andrew?

Nothing. No whispers, just more arm-waving and the maddening itch and awful smell and the feeling that the air in the room weighed more than the bloody house. It felt like it weighed enough to crush me, bone by bone. I yelled at the shadow, pleaded with it, cried and moaned. I even threatened it which I knew was bloody ridiculous. Or maybe it wasn't because then, the shadow managed one, weak whispered word.

<u>Jump</u>

The word oozed across the storm-like air and settled into my brain and it all stopped. The feeling that an electrical storm was about to crash around me, the terrible itching of the ants, the smell of tin.

I went to get the mattresses.

I've no idea how long I was out in the swings. I know there was nobody there again and I know it was twilight when I went out and full dark when I finally stopped but that's all. I was lost in time again, like in the afternoon at the playground and on the ferry. I just kept on jumping and landing and jumping and landing again and again.

To begin with, I knew I was jumping so I could understand what the shadow wanted me to know but then I got swallowed up by the moment between sky and ground. It just filled me up and made me lighter at the same time. Then I landed awkwardly on my injured hip and came back to myself.

I dragged the mattresses back to the garden, came in and just collapsed again on the couch. My legs were like rubber, my hip singing some aria or other about pain and the sweat was dripping down my flanks.

The air in the room was storm-like again and the ants started in on me again, relishing the sweat maybe. The smell was terrible. And the shadow whispered to me.

look at the machine

I sat up and looked at the answer machine. It was throbbing. It looked like a cartoon, like one of those bumps on the animal's head, angry red and orange and pulsating. Incandescent. That's the word, that's what it was. Dreamily, I pressed the button.

Trisha's voice, even tinny through the speaker, seemed to boom into the heavy air of the living room.

"You bastard!"

There was a long pause and the two words shot out of the machine and into the air in coloured streaks. They were both dark purple, like the bruised way the clouds look before the lightning strikes and the thunder shatters the air. I followed those two strident swatches of colour as they shot up to the ceiling. Then Trisha was screaming again.

"You lying bastard! Did you think I'd just take your word for it? Did you really think I was that stupid? I saw you! I watched you making your plans with that cow! I saw you smile and wave at each other! <u>Bastard</u>!"

It all came out of the glowing speaker in bursts of purple and livid yellow, surrounded by a sullen, infected red. I shook my head, trying to work out what she was talking about.

"<u>You fucking bastard</u>!"

I stared at the colours in the room as Trisha yelled this, astounded by the venom in the words and in the air, a horrible slimy green/yellow that looked like the eye of a mad cat. I'd never heard Trisha use what my Mum always called the 'f-word' in all the time I've known her. Not even when she was so angry she was almost speechless. But she wasn't speechless when she made the call to let me know that she'd followed me and seen me at Anne's. She hadn't gone to Crewe, she'd followed me, saw what she'd seen and made five hundred from the two and two.

"Andrew deserved more than that, you bastard! He won't be able to tell you but I know he would've done! Well, I'm telling you! Telling you that you're a sick, selfish bastard who never deserved a son like Andrew!"

The phone was slammed down and the sound it made filled the air of my living room with a miasmic stream of colours, shot through with black. I was so dumbstruck by the tirade and the terrible colours it produced, it took a few minutes for what Trisha had said to clear my circuits and make sense. And then it did. Dear Jesus, it did.

She'd been talking like Andrew was <u>already</u> dead. Trisha had listened to the doctor and, instead of thinking about the thirty percent chance Andrew had of making it, she'd decided the other seventy percent was more or less a hundred percent and he was never going to recover. She'd gone over the edge and, because her guilt was so overwhelming, because she is the way she is, has always been, she was lashing out and blaming everybody and everything else.

The enormity of it hit me then, the possibilities. It felt like my stomach was going to come out of my mouth at the speed of light and the room began to spin like the Waltzer on Laketon Pier. I groaned and leaned forward.

<u>almost too late</u>

The shadow whispered to me and I forced myself to look at it. It wasn't moving at all, just holding its arms open in that awful welcoming gesture that just scares me shitless. It stood there in the light of the standard lamp, staring at me. The features were clearer still and it looked like a man's face. A man who was frustrated, a man trying to get me to make things right.

"For what?" I murmured.

The floor under my feet steadied as the room stopped spinning. My stomach stayed where it was and I breathed in at last.

The shadow moved and I thought it was going to start waving its arms at me and answer me but it only dropped its head. It dropped it the way somebody who was tired and frustrated about something would drop their head. And that's all it did.

I ranted at it for five minutes but, really, I knew what I had to do. I knew the only thing I could do.

I went back out to the slide.

I dragged the mattresses across the darkened ellipse of the swings, muttering to myself, telling myself not to forget why I was doing it this time. I told myself not to get lost in that moment between the sky and ground this time, just jump and then find out what it was almost too late for.

I put the mattresses on the far side of the slide and then climbed the ladder, still muttering to myself, like a mantra. I got to the platform and looked over the cage. Something was standing by the mattresses but it was just a bulky shape. I decided it was the shadow, there to make sure I didn't blank out again and get lost in the moment.

I nodded. That was fine, that was good. I swung my legs over the top of the cage and checked to make sure the shadow was still there. It was. I pushed off and out and the moment was still there. The endless second or so between the sky and ground was still there. I sucked it up and in, breathed it in, lived it like I'd never done before because I knew the real reason I was doing it. This wasn't like all those other times when I did it for the thrill.

I hit the mattresses with a thud and rolled and thought the sound I heard was me, groaning as my hip throbbed beneath my jeans. It wasn't me.

"Bastard!" Trisha screamed at me.

I was on one knee, looking up to see if the shadow was still there, to see whether one jump was enough. I saw Trisha standing over me, her right arm raised to shoulder height.

"Trisha?"

My voice was low, disbelieving. She brought her arm down and I raised my own left arm to ward off what I thought was a punch. Our two arms hit each other and the pain jarred right up to my shoulder. Trisha snarled, a mixture of rage and pain but she kept coming. She raised her arm again and, this time, I saw the thin flicker as the moon came out and glinted on the blade of the knife. She stabbed me in the shoulder and the burning was intense, like those old-fashioned tetanus booster jabs. I rolled on the mattresses and rolled right off, hitting the asphalt with my injured hip. I got to my feet just as she stumbled over the mattresses. That's what saved me.

They're still quite springy and her feet turned bandit on her. She staggered to one knee and looked up at me. Her face, in the thin moonlight, was awful. Her eyes were wide and her mouth was open in a line, like a slit in her face. She snarled again, struggling to stand up.

"You were lucky this afternoon, you bastard," she growled and finally got to her feet. "Some poor bastard got it instead but not this time. This time, I'm going to kill you."

Even as I backed away, I was trying to work out what she was talking about and then, of course, I knew. Trisha had been driving the little car that nearly killed the baby and broke the lad's legs. She was trying to run me over because she'd seen me saying goodbye to the woman she thought was stopping me going back home.

Trisha screamed. It sounded like a wild animal, a big, female cat, one whose young was dead and now she was going to kill whatever had killed it.

That's what I thought in that mad second and it still seems apt because Trisha thinks of Andrew as dead. She came across the mattresses and the knife glinted again in the moonlight. I turned and ran up the ladder of the slide. I had nowhere else to go.

I got to the platform and the shadow was there. It had its arms by its sides but something about the angle of its head reminded me of a questing animal. Then I heard Trisha clanging up the ladder behind me. I sidled round the bar you use to give yourself a good push-off and pressed myself against the caging.

I glanced down once at the mattresses and then Trisha was on the platform.

I made the mistake of trying to talk to her but she'd learned the lesson from down by the mattresses. She wasn't going to take time talking, she was coming at me with the knife aimed at my throat.

The shadow stepped between us. I could still see Trisha through it but it was like looking through a thin sheet of black cotton, one that's not far from turning into a lot of holes. Trisha stopped. Her arm was still raised, holding the knife, but the wired, steely intent on her face faded and puzzlement took its place.

For one mad, manic second, I almost asked her what the shadow looked like to her, could she see the features, did it look like a man to her? But then I realised that Trisha wasn't really seeing it. She just knew there was something between her and me and she was trying to work out what. Finally, after an endless few seconds, she decided she didn't need to know, she just needed to get past it or through it. Trisha charged the shadow.

The shadow opened its arms, just like it's always opened them to me, in an embrace. The shadow embraced Trisha, its arms opening so wide I thought it might actually enfold the entire swings. Trisha's face looked through the thin curtain at me, her eyes full of questions, her mouth opening in a wide O of bewilderment.

jump

The shadow whispered to me and I nodded but I couldn't stop looking at Trisha. It was like she'd hit an invisible wall of energy, like in those science fiction serials we used to watch on Saturday mornings at The Gaumont.

<u>now</u>

There was an urgency in this whisper and this time I jumped. I did it the way Eddie did it all those years ago. I vaulted over the caged platform but all those years I'd practised meant I kept my control. As I hit that moment of wonderful almost-flight I called back to the shadow that I was clear, I was clear now.
I hit the mattresses and looked up towards the platform. The shadow detached itself from the top of the slide and simply floated up and out over the swings. It did what I've been trying to do all my bloody life and it did effortlessly. I looked to see if Trisha was coming down after me but the ladder and the chute were both empty.
I think she was probably sitting on the floor of the platform, trying to work out what the hell happened. I dragged the mattresses across the swings—in case I got it wrong again and needed them. Then locked myself in the house.
I spent an agonising ten minutes waiting to see if Trisha tried to break in, going from front door to back door to front window, the burning in my shoulder settling into a pounding thud and my hip

complaining each time I put my weight on that foot. Finally, I decided that Trisha had gone.
I picked up the phone to ring Anne and warn her that Trisha was still in Seapool and then I remembered that Anne had left hours ago and would be safe in Scotland.

<u>none of that matters</u>

The shadow whispered to me and I looked at it, replacing the phone slowly, still wondering how I could keep Anne safe until I'd had the chance to get Trisha to understand the truth.

<u>triangles have three sides and stand because of them remove one and the others fall and that is what she understands</u>

The ants were back and the air pressure dropped and the smell was everywhere. I sat on the couch and shook my head, still not understanding.

<u>love and hate are separated by a line that is almost invisible and the line causes obsession when the one turns to the other</u>

And the television clicked on again.
I looked at the screen and groaned when the picture flickered into life. It wasn't sepia-toned anymore, it wasn't even the sharp black and white of a good print. It was Cinemascope and in glorious Technicolor and no matter how much I groaned and

pleaded, nothing dislodged the scenes from the screen just as nothing had dislodged them from my memory since they'd happened for real all those years ago.

I watched myself and Trisha making love for the first time, watched our sweat glisten in the reddish flicker of Trisha's parents' fire. I watched us move together and apart with such ease and pleasure. But then, instead of moving on to us lying next to each other and floating on the high of our climaxes, the way the memory always had in my mind, the film paused on the screen.

I was looking at a close-up of Trisha's face, her gorgeous dark lilac eyes in the centre of the screen, just after she came. I knew that look so well, didn't I? It was the thing I regretted most about us breaking up, that soft look, the way the firelight glimmered in the corners of her eyes, the way the lids were almost closed. It was the look that had told me she loved me, the one that had told me we were together and it was right, it was the way it was meant to be.

<u>can you be sure that your memory of that look is the same as her memory of the feeling she had, that what you took for love was nothing more than contentment in the moment for her?</u>

No, I couldn't. After everything, how could I? And, if that was right, could there be love now? Or had what she felt for me reversed itself into hate *because she no longer had what she always wanted, that total control over any situation?*

   <u>but it's not too late to make sure her hate harms nobody else because triangles have three sides</u>

That was the last time the shadow whispered to me but it wasn't the last thing I watched on the screen of my television. The scene on the television changed from that look in Trisha's eyes.
I watched myself walking round the playgrounds of Seapool. I watched myself standing to one side as the children played and laughed and their mothers sat and talked and kept watch.
I watched myself walking to each ride and muttering to myself. I couldn't hear what I muttered but I could see the terror on the children's faces as they looked at me and heard me. I saw what they saw when they looked at me.
The shadow stood next to me with its arms open, its facial features so clear now, so like my own as it looked at the children.
And I watched as the mothers in each playground left off their chatter and ran towards me, and now I could hear the soundtrack. They yelled at me to get away, to leave their children alone, to stop frightening innocent children with my loony talk and the strange look on my face. It happened at each playground I walked through. I watched myself coming back to 12 Oil Street and going to bed and I watched myself getting up and dressing in old, tatty

clothes and going out to the playgrounds and doing the same thing every day.

I watched in horrified fascination as the Davy Eliot on the television grew old, his face turning grey, his eyes staring wildly around him, his beard growing white, his hair growing back but not much. I watched as the rest of my life became a horrifying round of doing nothing but frightening children and their mothers.

I didn't have the strength to close my eyes against this horror show, nor to scratch any longer at the ants as they scurried all over my body, nor to wipe the sweat from my face and hands as the storm-laden air of this living room weighed me down and down. I just sat on the couch and cried and cried. Then, when I thought there was nothing worse I could watch, I watched the worst of all.

I watched Andrew, alone in my old house, reading a newspaper whose front page headline said it all.

LOCAL WOMAN GAOLED FOR MURDER OF LOVE RIVAL

Then he put the paper down and left the house. I watched him walk, limping slightly as he made for the swings at the back of this house in Oil Street. He had piled four mattresses below the slide and I watched him climb the ladder and vault the cage and thud into those mattresses. He stood up shakily and did it again. When he stood up the second time, he shook his head but there was a smile on his face that I recognised. Oh God, I knew that smile.

Andrew had found that magical moment before gravity noticed him, that wonderful moment between sky and ground. But it wasn't enough. The shake of his head told me that. He wanted that moment but he wanted more, he wanted it to last longer.

For the next half an hour, I watched my son as he found bungee jumping and sky-diving and none of it was good enough. Then, the final scene began and I still couldn't look away.

The day was bleak, the sky streaked with grey and purple as afternoon was replaced by evening, the plume of breath from his mouth showing how cold it was. Andrew was alone, looking up at the skeleton of the building not far from this house in Oil Street. They're going to start to build another factory there very soon. The framework of the building was stark against the grey sky, like a massive gibbet. The site was empty of other people and the two security lights made Andrew's face look gaunt and harshly orange, like a child's Halloween mask. I watched my son pile up sacks and flattened boxes and the mattresses he'd brought with him. Then he walked to the ladder at the base of the skeleton and started to climb.

At each level, he stopped and looked down once, shook his head once and then climbed to the next level. Finally, about fifty feet up, he was satisfied. He stepped off the ladderway and walked across the boards until he was over the landing pad he'd built for himself. He took a deep breath and stared up at the twilit sky. Then he spread his arms out and I watched my son swan-dive off that stark skeleton as he went in search of the moment between sky and ground.

And then the shadow granted me a favour. The television screen went black before I had to watch Andrew land.

The air in the living room returned to normal, the only smell was Dettox air-freshener and the ants stopped their maddening forays.

I was all cried out, all emotioned out really, beyond thought, beyond trying to work out what the shadow wanted or what I could do. I lay on the couch until the throbbing in my shoulder became too much and forced me to remember that I had been stabbed.

I staggered upstairs to the bathroom.

I eased myself out of the jumper and looked at the wound Trisha had inflicted. There was a lot of caked blood down my arm and blood still seeped out of the shoulder. I cleaned it up and it didn't look bad enough to need stitches.

And that was when I finally understood, when it all became crystal clear in my mind.

I looked at the slightly gaping wound and decided it didn't need stitching and was pleased. Not because I didn't like the idea of somebody jabbing me with needles but because I've always felt guilty when I've had to go to casualty, always felt there were people there more in need than me.

It was that word, <u>guilty</u>, that did it.

Because it's all guilt. Guilt and regret, the second evolving from the first. Trisha feels guilty for so many things and it's turned into a sort of obsession with her.

I feel guilty about Trisha and Anne but, I realise now, mostly, for not having died in the tumble down the stairs when I was a toddler.

The shadow's right. Triangles have three sides and Trisha was right, too. She's convinced that I'm still seeing Anne and that the triangle she perceives is the reason that Andrew has only a thirty percent chance of making a full recovery—in her mind, no chance at all.

But I'm pretty sure I don't have to worry about Trisha harming Anne now. I think, after what happened on the slide, Trisha probably went home. She would've been confused, emotionally drained. She probably went home and fell into a sleep that was probably more of a blackout. Even if she woke up and still felt she had to go after Anne, Anne's in Scotland. By the time she gets back, it'll be done and Trisha will know that there's no point in harassing Anne anymore.

I've owed the shadow a death for over forty years and my life has been filled with that regret for just as long. The guilt and regret have been so profound that those closest to me have suffered by having to share the weight of it. Well, I can do what Trisha failed to do on the slide. I can remove one side of the triangle she perceives and, by doing it, I can make sure that nobody else has to carry the guilt of that removal.

It's the early hours of Tuesday now and I've been writing since that last, terrible scene on the television. I've thought about going to see Andrew again but it would be too tempting to stay there. Sometimes, the time comes and you do what you have to do or the time goes and it's too late. Besides, I said all I needed to say the last time I saw him. I told him to concentrate on the thirty percent chance. Anything else, well, I've written it in here and Neil will help him. The main thing is that he feels no guilt for anything that's happened.

We bequeath some terrible things to our kids, like the love of high places for instance, but I don't want to him to think any of this was his fault.

It's Tuesday and it doesn't seem strange that it was a Tuesday in January when I found out about Trisha's adultery or that my Dad died on a Tuesday. I bet that, if I phoned my Mum and asked, she'd probably tell me that it was a Tuesday when I took that tumble down the stairs. It's just another click, just the symmetry of the circle finally closing for me.
I'm just an ordinary bloke, my story wasn't much different to anybody else's. Then the shadow made itself visible to me and I realised that, really, I'd been dreaming all my life.
And now I've woken up to find that, like all dreams, mine tattered and scattered.
Yeah, I woke up here in Oil Street, where all shadows come to whisper, where all rainbows finally fall and dreams come to die.
Oil Street, where all flights come to rest.

I've got a lot of regrets but now I've made up my mind, I'm strangely at peace. I know where and when and, more importantly, why. Not many people can say that, can they?

I'm closing the circle at last.

I'll take one last look over Seapool, remember my life and where it led me. And, now, I think I'll be able to remember all the good times. Cos despite everything, there _were_ good times.

Then I'm going to find that wonderful moment when my body is almost at rest, when the outward motion dies just before gravity takes hold of me again. One last time, I'm going to live in that sublime moment between sky and ground, when it feels like I could really fly.

I'm going to pay the debt I owe and set my family free.

And you know what? I'm going to make my final leap with my arms wide and my body flat on the air and my head up, looking towards the sky.

I'm going to do a swan-dive, like I did off the third-top board in Laketon Pool, the swan-dive I could never do off the slide in Oil Street swings.

I'll be too high and it'll be too dark to see the whispering shadow when I make that final leap. Maybe it'll cushion me on the way down, happy that I've paid my debt at last. It might but, even if it doesn't, I know it will be there somewhere, its arms outspread, waiting for me.

It always has.

THIRTEEN

The morning sun was pale in the soft denim blue of the early morning sky. The sparrows in the hedges at the bottom of Blackhay's garden twittered and flapped in and out of the bushes. Downstairs, breakfast was underway and its clattering, cheerful noise drifted up into Neil's office. It was like this yesterday and would be like this tomorrow but everything had changed, just the same.

Martin Cottingham had arrived just as the sun peeked over the houses. He'd slumped down in the chair and taken the coffee Neil gave him and drank it. Then he'd taken off his overcoat and put it on the floor at his feet. He looked up now, his face showing how much he hated having to do this, opened his mouth and then looked at what Neil pushed across the desk.

"Read it," Neil told him. "Before you tell me anything, read it Martin. Just do me one favour and read it here. I've got to ring Joy and take my bollocking for staying out all night and then I've got things to do downstairs. You can stay here and nobody will bother you." He smiled. "Not even Charlie-bloody-Patterson. I'll get Sarah to deny she even knows you. It'll probably take till late this afternoon to finish it and then I'll come back and you can ask me whatever you like and tell me whatever you've found and worked out."

Martin nodded and opened the blue-backed book. He didn't even hear the door close as Neil left the office. At first, he made notes in his little book but then he just read the book Neil had given him; Neil could summarise it a lot better than Martin could. The more he read, the more it felt like the office closed in around him, that the world had narrowed down to the neat handwriting on the pages of the book and the strange, unnerving story it told.

He read the final page just as Neil opened the door and came back in. Martin wasn't surprised that Neil had known exactly when Martin would finish; it was just Neil being Neil.

Neil sat down and leaned back in the chair. "Okay, Martin," he said. "Whenever you're ready."

Martin took the manila folder out of his briefcase and put it on the desktop. He looked at Neil and wondered where to start. How the hell did you do this? The gut feeling he'd had about this case had been right but, Christ, your gut didn't tell you how to deal with...whatever this was.

Neil smiled at him. "Martin," he said quietly. "Usually, there's just one main question. Anything else sort of follows on from it. You know that."

That was Neil all over. He could slip into your mind and then tell you what you needed to know to get it done. Martin nodded. "Okay. This book, journal or whatever, will be evidence. You know that but the thing is, I haven't got a clue what it's going to be evidence *of*. All I do know is that the trick-cyclists are going to be all over it. I suppose what I want to know is what they're going to tell me."

Neil nodded. "That's the one. Okay, first off, I need to know what you found yesterday."

Martin opened the folder, took a breath and poked his glasses up to the bridge of his nose. "Trisha Eliot's body was discovered in the bushes at the eastern end of Oil Street swings. It looks like she might've been murdered. Anne Jordan's body was discovered in the boot of a car registered to Trisha Eliot. She *was* murdered. David Eliot's body was discovered in the enclosed courtyard of the old water tower in Oil Street. Just where you said to look." Martin put the page to one side and looked at Neil.

Neil closed his eyes and rubbed at the scar above his right eyebrow. He took a long breath and let it out slowly, like a sigh; he'd known but, Christ, he'd wished he was wrong. "Yeah," he said, mostly to himself. He opened his eyes. "Given what you've just told me, that journal will probably be used as evidence that Davy had a complete breakdown. What started as a mid-life crisis brought on by grief after his dad died, deepened into a clinical depression. This lasted right through Trisha's admission of adultery. What they'll say, I think, is that moving out and living on his own pushed Davy right down. Down far enough for clinical depression to feed on itself until it mutated into something which, for want of anything better, they'll call a psychotic break." He shrugged. "If I was an objective party, I'd do the same. It's all there, Martin. Visual, auditory and tactile hallucinations, phantom smells. It's not classic but it's close. Close enough for them to think about schizophrenia actually but Davy was a bit too old for that to present in any concrete way. No, it'll be a murderous psychotic break, I think."

"Eliot killed his wife during, what, a blackout?"

Neil shrugged again. "I imagine somebody will say that he killed Trisha during a fugue state, that he perceived the shadow as real and put all the blame onto it. I think they'll probably say he killed himself in a fit of remorse when he came out of it and realised what he'd done," Neil told him. "It's feasible. And the journal will support it." He smiled but it wasn't a slow one this time. This time there was a hard edge to it, cynical. His voice matched it when he spoke again. "It's a bit like The Bible, that journal. You could use it to support an argument for or against. But, since there's not likely to be anybody contesting the result of the inquests, I don't suppose it matters."

"While the balance of his mind was disturbed," Martin said.

"I think so, yeah."

Martin nodded but Neil could see the doubt in the older man's eyes and smiled to himself; Martin had read Davy's journal and read more than the convenient confession of a man who finally fell off the ragged edge of his sanity.

"Neil..." Martin began.

"I know. But, whatever it is, it's not going to change anybody's mind. Especially not Charlie Pattterson's," Neil said and poured them both another mug of coffee which they drank in silence.

"I'll take this and see where they're up to with the forensics and medical stuff," Martin said after he'd drained the mug. He put the journal and the folder in the slim briefcase and stood up. "I'll see you when I know, okay?"

Neil nodded and showed him out.

*

"Forensic investigations and the pathologist's preliminary findings," Martin told Neil early Friday morning as he put the five sheets of single-spaced A-4 on the desk. He cleared his throat and chewed his bottom lip. "Anne Jordan was stabbed at least twelve times with a carving knife. We found the knife on the platform at the top of the slide in Oil Street swings. It's one of a matching set that belonged to the Eliots. Traces of blood on the knife and on the jacket Trisha Eliot was wearing match Anne Jordan's blood type. We believe that Anne Jordan was murdered by Trisha Eliot. We've got a witness who says she saw a woman, dressed similarly to Anne Jordan late Sunday afternoon. She was arguing with a woman wearing a jacket similar to Trisha Eliot's jacket and then they both got into a small car outside the main train station in Oxborough." Martin laid the paper on top of the others and then simply sat in the chair, his hands on the desk.

"Martin?" Neil said and frowned.

"Neil, I...look, tell me what you think happened. I've got all these bloody facts and there's no doubt in anybody's mind, especially Charlie Patterson's, that in a fit of jealous rage or some sort of breakdown brought on by the prognosis she heard from the neurologist concerning her son, Trisha Eliot killed Anne Jordan. She probably persuaded Anne Jordan into her car so that they could both see Eliot to sort things out. Then she tried to kill David Eliot and he killed her and dumped the body in the undergrowth of Oil Street swings. There's even some support for the idea that he might even have believed it was the shadow who was trying to kill him with the knife and, because he believed that the shadow was real and meant some harm to his son, he killed his wife by mistake. I think, given the knife wound that was found in Eliot's shoulder, that there's even support for the idea that he killed her in self-defence. And, then, like you said, killed himself in a fit of remorse. But...shit, Neil, just tell me what you think happened to David Eliot." He wiped his forehead and grimaced at the thin film of sweat on his fingertips. "The trick-cyclist said, more or less word for word, what you suggested about the journal and Eliot's state of mind. But I know you don't believe it and I know you know I've got my doubts. Oh, not enough to change the verdict of the inquests but, still." He looked at Neil and was met by the relentless gaze from those dark grey eyes. Martin tried to match it but couldn't. He picked up the mug of coffee and stared into that instead.

"Martin, what's happened? You knew there was something not right, something that didn't gel, but nothing to make you look like you look now. The verdict of the inquests is more or less guaranteed and, normally, you'd take that and move on, even with your slight doubts. Now, though, you look like there's something bothering the hell out of you. What is it?"

Martin nodded. Even now, there were times he was prepared to believe that Neil was psychic. Then what he was about to tell Neil resurfaced and the thought faded like...well, like a shadow fades when the sunlight moves across it. He took a deep breath and asked, "Neil, what would you expect to find if somebody took a header from nearly a hundred feet and landed on cobbles?"

"Depending on how he landed, massive internal trauma. Lots of broken bones."

Martin nodded slowly. "More or less what we found with Trisha Eliot. Extensive internal injuries, they say. The consensus is that David Eliot threw her off the slide and then hauled her body to the bushes." Martin paused and chewed his bottom lip again. "The top of the slide is nothing like a hundred feet off the ground," he said and looked at Neil and waited.

Neil's face showed nothing. "And Davy?"

Martin took another deep breath. "David Eliot broke both legs and dislocated both hips."

They looked at each other for a few seconds that felt like a lot longer. The silence was thick with possibilities. Finally, Martin broke the silence.

"Just like the injuries he describes in the journal." He took another breath. "His heart stopped. The doctor told me that Eliot died of heart failure, probably about half-way down, from fright or stress. It was the only explanation he could come up with for the lack of damage. He said that Eliot's body, in death, had likely become very similar to a toddler's. 'Martin', he said to me. 'You know what kids' are like. They bounce where we'd break. God looks after little babies and drunks the same way.' Then he signed off his report and I left."

Neil rubbed at his scar. "Your trick-cyclist would have to know about those apparent anomalies and he must've wondered," he said, almost to himself, thinking it through. "There must've been something else to support the idea of Davy's psychosis being bad enough to kill." He looked at Martin and then, before Martin could say anything, he went on. "Ah, the fact that there was no message on the answer machine from the hospital and the fact that there's nobody working at the hospital called Julia Bacon was the clincher, wasn't it? The telephone call Davy said he got from her proved that when the shadow was whispering to him or he was seeing things, he was in a fugue state. That's it, isn't it? Without that, there'd only be a second-hand evaluation based on the facts and the journal but, once there was a non-existent phone call, the medical facts could be ignored. The pathologist's throwaway line about drunks and babies would do as an explanation."

"How the hell did you know that there wasn't any message from the hospital or that there's nobody at the hospital called Julia Bacon?" Martin tried to sound harsh to hide the unease he felt about the way Neil could do this sort of thing.

"Before hormones turned every kiss into an exquisite agony, Julia Bacon was the first girl Davy ever went out with. They were about thirteen. She had the longest, blackest hair I've ever seen and eyes almost the same colour. She's a music teacher in Surrey now," Neil told him.

Martin was about to ask him how he could remember that and then gave up; Neil just could. "Yes, that's right, Neil. Everything you said is what they said and, like I told you, that's how it's going to come out. That's what the verdict will be. While the balance of his mind was disturbed. Now, tell me what you think."

"I think I've got to talk to somebody," Neil said slowly. "I hoped it wouldn't be necessary but I had the feeling that it would be anyway."

"Who?"

"Somebody who's probably spent half a lifetime trying very hard not to talk about something. Probably trying not to even think about it." He shook his head slowly. "Martin, I'm sorry but that's all I can tell you for now. There's no guarantee the person will even see me never mind talk to me but I've got to try. Until I know one way or the other, I can't tell you anything. Can you trust me a bit longer?"

Martin nodded and shrugged; Neil would tell him and Martin was prepared to wait. After all, it wasn't going to make any difference to the outcome of this case. And he had no doubt that the person Neil needed to talk to would talk to Neil. People did. "Okay, Neil. But why? It won't make any difference."

"It might to Andrew Eliot," Neil said and rubbed at his scar again.

"Oh." Martin nodded and then stood up. "The inquests will be finished in a week or so and I'll give you the journal back. The CPS have agreed that a copy will be acceptable for the files." He smiled. "I know you don't need it to jog your memory but maybe the boy will need it."

"Oh, he'll need it, Martin. Thanks."

FOURTEEN

The house stood alone at the end of the street. Even from the car, parked twenty yards away where the actual road ended, Neil could see how large the upper storey windows were and that there were no curtains on them; they all had vertical blinds and they were all open. There was an ornate iron gate built into the high stone wall. A large floodlight bent over the gate, like the single eye of some alien monster in a film.

Neil got out of his car and locked it, still looking at the large, uncurtained windows, still frowning as he had been since turning into the road. He hated the idea of doing this but he knew he had to because Davy had asked him to help Andrew.

On the stone, above the gate's lock, was a grill and a button. Neil pressed it.

"Yes?" A woman's voice, not young but not the frail voice of an old woman either.

"Miss Leather? My name's Neil Judd. I phoned you earlier today."

"Oh." The voice sounded disappointed, as if the woman was sorry Neil had come. Neil wasn't surprised.

There was a low hum and then a buzz. The gate swung back on well-oiled hinges. Neil walked through the opening and then walked up the curved path of raked gravel. The sound was loud in the quiet of this out-of-the-way place, nine miles away from the hustle and bustle of Seapool. The front door to the house was open. Light shone out of the hallway even though it was only one in the afternoon.

"Miss Leather?"

"In the back room at the end of the hall."

The hall was lit by concealed fluorescent lights, the light cast by them diffuse and soft. The wallpaper was white and so was the paintwork. The floor was wood, blonde oak, clear-varnished; Neil cast no shadow. His footfalls echoed dully as he walked to the room at the end. He looked through the open door and squinted at the brightness of the sunlight beaming through the huge, sliding patio windows.

"Come in and sit down Mr Judd."

"My name's Neil, Miss Leather," he said and stepped into the room.

"And mine's Emily."

The woman sitting on the recliner chair to the right of the door looked to be in her late-fifties. She was thin but not gaunt and her pale green eyes shone in the light from the windows. Her thick, dark brown hair was parted in the middle and framed the oval face. She looked a bit like Nicole, Neil's youngest daughter. She was wearing a long, floaty skirt that looked like it belonged in the late sixties, all pastel colours and permanent creases. The blouse was pink, low necked but buttoned all the way up to a wide, penny-round collar. She wore no shoes. Her hands lay in her lap lightly, the fingers intertwined but still.

"Thank you for seeing me," Neil said and sat on the armchair opposite the woman. Between them was a low coffee table. On the table was a thick book, a photo album or a scrap book.

"Seeing you doesn't mean I will talk to you, Neil. Listening costs me nothing but time and time is something I have plenty of. Would you like some tea?" She raised one tapered hand and pointed to the teapot in the ingle where the living flame gas fire burned blue and yellow.

Neil smiled and poured himself a cup and asked her if she wanted one. She nodded and took the cup from him with one hand. When she leaned forward, Neil saw the slight wince of pain that she quickly controlled. When she leaned back, the stiffness of her back was only noticeable because Neil was looking for it.

"Now, Neil. You mentioned Mr Horne and a house that he looks after for me. I have two houses in which Mr Horne acts as my agent."

"12 Oil Street," Neil said and then sipped his tea and waited.

Emily Leather dropped her eyes and looked in the china cup as she sipped her own tea. But not before Neil saw the shine in those eyes fade slightly and the way the vein in her neck pulsed before she swallowed to hide it. There was a long beat of silence and then she looked up from the cup, obviously expecting Neil to say something else. Neil leaned back in the chair and waited.

Finally, Emily Leather put her cup down and sighed. "Perhaps it's about time I found another agent to deal with my property," she said.

"Not on my account, Emily," Neil said and smiled. "Paul is a friend of mine and did me a favour because I asked and because I told him it was important. Unless you gave him explicit instructions concerning the house, I don't think you can blame Paul."

Emily smiled. "You have a nice voice, Neil Judd but it can't disguise the sharpness of your mind. No, I gave no instructions about 12 Oil Street. Still, I can't imagine Mr Horne giving out my name with abandon or on a friend's whim. What about 12 Oil Street, Neil?"

"You used to live there," Neil said. It wasn't a question.

"Mr Horne didn't know that," Emily said and sat up straighter in the chair which tilted slightly as she moved. "Nobody knows that. Not anymore. How did you find out?" There was the merest hint of accusation in her voice and the narrowing of her eyes told Neil that this was a strong woman.

"I didn't. I guessed."

"Well, what about it? Everybody's got to live somewhere. Even if it's only in a cardboard box under a railway bridge."

Neil saw the way her whole face seemed to close in on itself when she spoke the last two words. Emily Leather hadn't meant to do that, hadn't meant to mention anything about bridges or railways.

"Emily," he said softly. "It's all right, I know. You don't have to keep forcing yourself to hide it from me. I'm not here to lay blame. I'm here to help somebody who needs help."

She looked at him sharply and a muscle ticked angrily in her cheek. "I don't need help, Mr Judd."

"I wasn't talking about you, Emily. I was talking about a young man who, if he wakes up, is going to find out that he's an orphan. And worse things than that. And my name's Neil." He smiled again.

"If he wakes up? An orphan? What could be worse than that, Neil? Being an orphan is the worst thing there is."

"And you'd know that, wouldn't you Emily?"

She wiped at the two errant tears on her cheeks and shook her head. "How..." Emily swallowed past the unexpected lump in her throat. "How can you know that? Nobody round here knows anything about me. I'm just the refugee from the hippie years, the woman who lives in the big house on the hill and never speaks to anybody. How can you *know*?"

Neil sighed and put his cup down on the tray next to the teapot. He'd said he was here for somebody else, for Andrew and it was true. But her voice, thick with emotion and memory, had been the voice of a child, maybe fifteen years old and Neil had never been able to *not* help a child.

"I remember your father, Emily. George. It's George I need to know about. And about 12 Oil Street. If you say no and ask me to leave, I will. But you'll still be here, Emily and so will your memories. I saw the pain mentioning railway bridges gave you and how startled you were by the fact that you actually spoke them. Sometimes, Emily, sometimes—"

"The mind makes its own mind up," Emily said and nodded.

Neil smiled. "Yes. Maybe your mind's decided it's time to talk about it. To somebody other than itself and your reflection in a mirror. What d'you think, Emily?"

She leaned back in the chair again and stared at Neil. Only one other person had ever stared at Neil like that, with the sort of relentlessness he himself used. When he was finished here, Neil would tell his wife what had happened and she would look at him like that until he told her everything.

"What are you, Neil? Not an estate agent."

Neil shook his head. "No, Emily. I'm a psychologist. I work with children."

She nodded. "Yes, and you are very good at what you do, aren't you?"

"Yes," Neil agreed.

"What do you know?"

"I know your father used to talk to himself. Usually on the old railway bridge down in The Rows," Neil told her. "I imagine he was diagnosed as paranoid schizophrenic. Or perhaps he was never diagnosed. We're talking about the fifties and, since he wasn't really a danger to anybody, he was probably classed as the local loony by more than just us kids."

Emily nodded. "Yes, that's right. Just the local loony. But the local loony was my father and I loved him and he loved me. He loved his family, Neil. His wife and his daughter and... and..."

"His son," Neil said and then rubbed his scar.

"Yes. My brother was three years younger than me and my father doted on him. He loved the bones of Robert. I never felt left out. I was older, at school and then out with my friends and my father never ignored me." She took another deep breath. "He was a brilliant man, my father. He was a lecturer at the university across the river. He taught Mathematics and I inherited his love of the subject so we spent lots of time together. My mother was a teacher and, once Robert was in school, she taught part time at the local junior school. Her name was—"

"Jane," Neil said. "Jane Leather. She had dark blonde hair and rosy cheeks. Her favourite poem was Kipling's 'If'. She used to recite it to us every Friday afternoon before we went home. But I don't remember either you or your brother, Emily."

Emily just gaped at him and leaned back in the chair again. "You remember that?"

Neil nodded. "I liked her and it was probably your mum who made me like poetry almost as much as I liked football."

"That's..." She shook her head. "Well, Robert and I both went to a public school. As day pupils. They called us gifted and my parents decided that the money would be better spent on our education rather than moving out of 12 Oil Street." She shrugged. "It didn't bother me. I liked it down in The Rows. I had good friends and there was still plenty of money for toys and clothes and a holiday to Wales each July. My father loved..." Emily swallowed and sipped at her tea again.

"He loved high places," Neil said gently. "Or was it that he loved the idea of flight?"

"Are you sure you're only a psychologist, Neil?" She smiled but it hardly touched her eyes. "It was the idea of flight. His hobby was trying to invent a flying machine. You know, those things they try to fly in or on or with off long piers and things on Bank Holidays. He was convinced that he would do it one day. It was all in the maths, he said. He spent years, literally years, working out the formulae. He had books full of numbers and letters and diagrams which even I, loving the subject as he did, could make neither head nor tail of. Finally, when Robert was ten, my father set about building his flying machine. Robert was born in July and we always spent his birthday on holiday. I used to tease him that it was like having two presents instead of one and he used to tease me with the same idea. I loved him," she said and finished her tea.

Neil waited, having a terrible idea that he knew what happened. But Emily needed to tell it if for no other reason than she hadn't told it to anybody since it had happened.

"We were in a caravan in Wales, not far from Pwhellhi and my father brought the wood and canvas and struts with us. He and Robert constructed the thing in the field behind the caravan while my mother and I visited the local market and shops. On the Thursday, we all went out to walk up the mountain nearest the site. The machine was finished and my father intended trying it out on the long pier jutting out over the bay. We walked up the mountain and marvelled at the view and the taste and smell of the air and my father said that, if he had the nerve or more confidence in his machine, this would be the perfect place to take off from. So, we went back to the caravan and my father tested his machine."

"And it worked," Neil said. "It must have been something similar to a hang glider."

"Yes, almost exactly and it worked." Emily clasped her hands together tightly in her lap and Neil knew she wanted to bang the arm of the chair but it would hurt her back too much. "That night, while we were all asleep... Robert got up... he got up and..." She took a deep breath, so deep, it looked like she might just forget to breathe out again. Then she did, letting it out slowly and closing her eyes. "He was only eleven years old that day but he was strong. He carried the machine to the mountain. Not as high as we'd walked that afternoon but high enough. He jumped. And he died. He..." The sudden eruption of sobs made her whole body shudder.

Neil got up and held her hands. She squeezed his hands and he waited until she ran out of tears. She looked up and smiled at him.

"He didn't have your love of maths," Neil said. "He didn't think about the weight differential. Or about the method of control your father had yet to work out. It took him up and, what, some gust of wind drove him down, out of control?"

Emily nodded. "It must've been something like that. Even so, it must've been wonderful. For a few seconds, it must've been a marvellous sensation. He would've thought he was flying for real and well-able to control it. His father had built it and, so, it must be perfect."

Neil gave her hands one last gentle squeeze and then sat back in the chair. "You came home and your father blamed himself."

She nodded. "It happened so suddenly. We buried Robert and the next day, my father began to talk to himself. My mother called the doctor in and he gave my father Vallium that he never took. He was asked to resign from his job because it didn't look good and, worse, some of the younger students were afraid of him. My mother had to work full-time after that. He spent his days...well, you know. I was fourteen years old and it was very hard on me. What kept me going were those friends I mentioned. When we were walking home, if he was in his usual place on the bridge, they would help me get him home. He'd be lucid for days and then my mother and I would wake to find he was gone. Eventually, we realised that, without having him locked up, there was nothing we could do. And, as you said, he never caused anybody any harm so he was left alone." She smiled, just a small one and shook her head once. "Apparently, the children in The Rows had more backbone than those young students at the university. The kids in The Rows were never afraid of him." She sighed. "It was like that for nearly eight months. Then it, my father, deteriorated." She eased herself forward in the chair, as if she wanted to be as straight as possible when she finally said it, to show she was strong enough to bear it. "His voices talked to him all the time and, when my mother begged him to tell her how she could help, he only ever said the same thing—"

"The shadow knows," Neil said quietly.

She gasped and the pulse in her throat beat hard twice. "How could you know that?"

"Emily, please, tell me. I promise, I'll tell you everything when you've finished."

"Finally, it got too much for my mother. She...cracked, I suppose. She was in the kitchen, cooking our tea and my father was sitting on the back step, muttering and answering and asking and she couldn't take it anymore. She was peeling potatoes and the paring knife was in her hand when she ran at him, yelling for him to shut up. He turned and stood up and the knife cut his arm. She didn't mean it and it wasn't a deep cut but my mother was lost by then. She ran upstairs and I followed her. After she stopped crying, she told me we would have to leave, we couldn't go on like this. She was scared that, if we stayed, she would kill him and it wouldn't be an accident. I tried to talk her out of it but, deep down, I knew she was right. I waited up that night, hoping my father would have a lucid moment or two when I could explain. After the incident on the step, he went on his wanderings and didn't come back until very late. But he was lucid.

"He saw me still up, in the living room, with the standard lamp on. He came and sat by me and put his arm round my shoulder. He told me he knew what I was waiting for, what I wanted to tell him. He told me he understood, that it was the right thing to do. He loved us both but he didn't want to harm us and if we stayed, he would, one way or the other. He knew he would. We left the next day. We moved into my mother's house in Oxborough. My father rang once a week and I was sure that was the only time he was lucid. We talked about how I was, how my mother was, how I was doing at school. We never talked about him. He always finished by telling me not to visit him. He said he hoped he'd be well soon and then he'd come and see me.

"Then, one week, he didn't ring. I was worried but I didn't want to worry my mother. She was only just finding her feet. She still loved him and her heart was breaking. I went to see my father in Oil Street. He wasn't there. The back door was open but he wasn't there. The standard lamp was lit in the living room and so I waited there for him to come home." She sighed again and wiped another tear off her cheek.

"He never did. The police came the next morning and found me asleep on the couch. They'd found my father on the railway tracks, underneath the bridge where he used to sit and talk to himself. My mother died the next year. They said it was pneumonia after an operation but I knew it was really a broken heart. 12 Oil Street had been left to him by his great uncle and my father left it to my mother and she left it to me. My grandmother looked after me until I was eighteen. She died when I was in my final year at college and left me her house. I spent the years between my twenty-first birthday and my twenty-fifth, spending the money I was left and moving from commune to commune, hoping I could find some sort of explanation for what had happened. I took a great many drugs, sampled a great many religions and philosophies and none of it worked. I eventually worked out that life was life and if you tried to live it, you had to take what it threw at you. I decided that it wasn't really a life I wanted anything to do with. I rented out the two houses and invested the money I hadn't spent. It bought me this house and it pays my way." She opened her arms slightly and smiled at Neil.

Neil poured them both another cup of tea but said nothing. After drinking some of the tea, Emily rested the cup and saucer on the arm of her chair.

"So, Neil, I've told you everything and, I must admit, I feel better. Will what I've told you help?" Her voice was as bright and brittle as her smile.

Neil saw the smile and saw, too, that it didn't reach her eyes where the sunlight now made them seem hard. "I need to know everything Emily," he said quietly but there was an edge to his voice.

"I have..." Emily said and the cup fell off the arm of the chair. She looked at it and bit down on her bottom lip. She started to cry silently as she watched Neil pick the cup up and put it back on the saucer.

"Emily," Neil said gently as he sat back in the chair. "Letting out part of it's no good. It just makes it harder to lock away again. Tell me what happened the night you spent in the living room of 12 Oil Street, waiting for George to come back."

"Why don't you believe me?" Despite the tears, it was a demand. The demand of a woman used to having her own way because there was never anybody to argue with her. Behind the demand, the tears were those of a child.

"Oh, I believe that your brother died in a fall and that your father's illness drove your mother away. I even believe that he was found below the old bridge over the railway. But I don't believe that he didn't come home that night, Emily. George had no reason to kill himself, he'd been living a sort of half-life for months but he *was* living it. No, when he came home that night and found you there, something happened to make him decide that suicide was the best thing he could do. The safest."

She looked at him through the prism of her tears, trying to find the words to deny it all, as she'd tried to deny it since the morning it had happened. But this man, with his dark grey eyes and his soft voice, seemed able to look beyond all the elaborate barriers she'd erected. He looked at her and saw the truth and then told her what he saw and it could be nothing else but the truth. The truth was something she'd tried to bury so deep that there were times she could almost convince herself that it had never happened. But this man knew it and wanted her to tell it. Finally, to tell it. Emily wasn't sure she could handle the truth.

"Neil...I... please, leave now. There is nothing else I can tell you."

Neil sighed and leaned forward. "Emily, did you see the shadow that night?"

She heard herself gasp but it still sounded like something else, like the whisper she'd heard all those years ago. The whisper of something she knew was impossible.

"Emily, it's been long enough. Somewhere inside, you know that. Otherwise, why would you let me come here and talk to you? You've spent years here, with the gate locked, having your groceries delivered and talking to nobody if you could help it. This house has more square footage of clear glass than any other house I've ever seen.

The lights must cost a fortune on their own. Tell me about the shadow, Emily."

It was impossible. That this man could know so much was impossible. But then, so was the thing she'd seen in 12 Oil Street yet she'd done everything she could to make sure she never saw it again. Why would you try that hard if it was impossible?

Emily Leather looked at Neil, saw in his eyes that he wasn't about to leave this thing alone and, too, saw in his eyes that he wanted to help. All the years of fear and pain cried out for help.

So Emily told him about that last day and night.

She phoned her mother to say she was staying behind at school to do some work on a project and she would be home by eight o'clock. It was the only lie she'd ever told her mother but the worry about her father was stronger than the small shame she'd felt at that. She got the five to five ferry from Oxborough Pier Head and was walking up Oil Street at twenty past five. She let herself into the kitchen of 12 Oil Street at twenty five to six, already calling out to her father and getting no answer.

She made herself something to eat and drink and then sat in front of the tiny black and white television and tried to watch whatever was on. Outside, early March blew wild and wet and she decided to light the fire to keep her mind off the idea that her father was out in that wild weather, muttering to himself, totally oblivious to the weather and the askance looks from passers-by. When it got to half past eight, Emily began to get really worried; even during his really bad days when she'd lived here, her father had never stayed out in this sort of weather after the sun had gone down.

She stood at the front window and willed him to come home. She stared into the dimly lit street and prayed to see him walking down the road, heading for home. She didn't care if he wasn't lucid, just so he came home now. And he did. She could see him come round the bend in the street, his upright walk so familiar, his long arms swinging, like a soldier marching. As he came closer, Emily could see that he was shaking his head, almost angrily and then, outside the front gate, he stood still. His head was cocked to one side, as if listening to somebody and then he shook his head again and waved his arms wildly.

The worry she'd crossed the river with and which had turned to fear when he failed to arrive home earlier now deepened into a kind of low terror that made her mouth dry up and her body to start to itch and sweat. She could even smell something more than the burning smokeless fuel and the Pledge polish on the furniture. It was something faintly like the smell of the thin sheets of tin her father had used when making the first struts for his flying machine.

As her father stopped his agitated waving and head-shaking, Emily turned away from the window to go to the kitchen and greet him as he came in.

There was a shadow in front of her.

She knew it was impossible because there was nothing but herself to cast a person-shaped shadow in the room and there was no light behind her strong enough to cast her own shadow. More than this, though, was the fact that the shadow was free-standing. It didn't lie against any surface, it simply stood in the middle of the room, between her and the door. Even when Emily moved, convinced it was some trick of the light from the standard lamp and the television, the shadow stayed where it was. Then it opened its arms towards her, like an embrace and Emily screamed.

The scream should have given her the impetus to run but, instead, it seemed to freeze her in place. The sweat on her body increased, the itching became almost unbearable and the smell intensified. She screamed again when the shadow made a movement towards her and still she couldn't move.

Her father came running into the house and into the living room. He saw Emily and yelled something she didn't understand, something about the guilt being his and his alone. Then he was hugging her close to him, still yelling and not looking at her, looking at the shadow.

Emily didn't want to look but her eyes seemed to have ideas of their own. She peered over the top of her father's arm at the shadow. It was still in the middle of the room, still with its arms outspread but no longer moving towards her. As she stared, still trying to convince herself that it was impossible, the shadow turned its head and looked at her father instead of at Emily. And, as it did, Emily was sure she saw features in that darkness where its face would be. The expression on those features seemed vaguely familiar to Emily. Almost...almost like her father.

She whimpered against her father's arm and asked him what it was, begged him to send it away. Her father shushed her, never taking his eyes from the impossible shadow in the room. He eased her round the couch and sat her down and held her even more tightly, still hushing her gently and telling her not to worry, to close her eyes and the dream would soon fade from her mind. That's all it was, he told her, a dream. She'd fallen asleep while waiting for him to come home and the dream had woken her up and she was frightened. But her dad was here now and he'd keep her safe, not to worry, go back to sleep.

Emily closed her eyes and, as the first grey wave of sleep rolled towards her, she thought she heard her father say that he would do it, all right, he would do it, just leave her alone. Then Emily dived under the incoming grey wave.

"When I woke up," Emily told Neil. "It was to the sound of urgent banging on the front door. I was groggy and stumbled to the front door and opened it. It was the police. My father had dived off the bridge and was dead."

Neil held her while she cried again, careful not to press too hard and hurt her injured back. Eventually, the tears tapered off and she eased herself out of his arms. He went to the kitchen and made another pot of tea. The windows in the kitchen were as large as in the upper storey and looked out on a lawn and a flower bed. No sheds, no small fountains and no trees. A wide, long expanse of grass and one circular flower bed. Nothing to block the sunlight or throw shadows.

"So," Emily said after she'd taken the cup from Neil. "D'you see why I would want to lock myself away, Neil?

The thought that I could end up the same as my father wasn't a pleasant one."

"No," Neil agreed. "But why don't you finish the story, Emily? There's not much more and it's better telling it all. We can deal with what we see, it's the stuff we don't see, the stuff we try to keep hidden, that makes life hard." He smiled at her.

Emily saw the smile and shook her head. "How did you know?"

"You've got a bad back," Neil said simply. "You control the pain by sheer force of will most of the time but when your mind's on other things, the stiffness is there and so is the pain. You said that you're father dived off the bridge. If you were told by the police, they would've said that it looked like your father jumped off the bridge. Tell me, Emily. Tell me what happened and set yourself free. You didn't fall asleep on the couch, Emily. Not even the heavy air and the maddening itch could've made you do that. Not while the shadow was still in the room and your father was talking to it. This was your chance to find out what had made your father change from the brilliant, kind man who loved all his family, to a man who spent his days sitting and talking to himself. The chance to know that, to maybe help him beat it and come back to you and your mother was there and you wouldn't've been able to sleep through that."

She nodded but there were no tears now; this man was right, it was time. "I pretended to sleep on the couch. I nearly did fall asleep because my father sat next to me and held me until he thought I was asleep. Then I felt him let go and then I heard him leave the house. I opened my eyes and the room was empty. I followed him. I had to keep ducking into the front gardens of the houses because he kept looking over his shoulder and I didn't want him to know." She shook her head. "I don't know, I thought if I followed him and waited to see what was going to happen, I could stop it, help him see there was no need. I never thought that he was going to do what he did. I thought he was just going somewhere to sit and argue with the shadow and, if he did, I could help.

"He walked round The Rows for half an hour and I could see that he was still arguing with the shadow. I could just make out the shadow in the light from the streetlamps. It walked with him, next to him, its arms still held out from its sides. Finally, he walked across the bridge and sat down. I smiled to myself.

"That's the thing that always wakes me up. I dream of him sitting down and then I see myself *smiling* because he was going to argue and I was going to help him. I crept up on them, my father and the shadow. I sidled along, hugging the railing of the bridge, keeping my head down. I was about two yards away from them when my father stood up. He..." She moaned and looked at Neil. "I can't do this, Neil, not even for you. I can't."

"Not for me, Emily," Neil told her and took her hands in his. "Do it for you. Because it's eaten away at you for too long."

She took a long, deep breath, her chest heaving as she tried to control the breath and her sobs. Then she let it out and spoke. "I smiled again and started to walk towards him. I thought he'd beaten it and was going to go back to the house. Instead, he climbed onto the railing and balanced, his arms out to the sides. And the shadow was with him, exactly the same stance. I screamed and he looked at me. He shouted something but I was deafened by my own scream. Then the shadow floated off the railing and came towards me. I could see my father through it. It was like looking through black gauze. I screamed again and waved my arms at the shadow, put my head down and charged it. I ran through it, felt nothing and wouldn't have stopped if I had.

"I got there just as my father pushed off. He dived out and for a second, an endless second, it looked like he was going to flap his arms and fly away. He seemed to be suspended, as if gravity had forgotten him. Then he fell and..." She paused and took another breath but Neil saw the slight shake of her head before she said, "I turned away and ran towards the side-street where the fence was broken. I scrambled through it and started to slide down the steep ramp of soil and grass but it had been raining hard all day and it was treacherous. I slipped and rolled and did a somersault. I landed on my back on the first rail of the track. I screamed again and tried to roll over, still wanting to go to my father, praying he wasn't dead and I could do something to help him."

She looked at Neil and squeezed his hands again, almost begging him to let her stop now. Neil smiled and squeezed back.

"Last inch, Emily."

She nodded. "The shadow was there. It was floating above the track, barring my way. I swore at it and crawled towards my father and the shadow stayed between me and him all the way. And then...then I got to him and looked at him through the shadow and... God, he was..."

"He looked like he had simply fallen asleep," Neil said.

She gaped at him."Yes. I expected him to be broken into little pieces, his head at least just a squash of blood and bone. He'd *dived* off the bloody bridge! He didn't look hurt at all and...and...there was a smile on his face. I must've blacked out then and when I came to, there were torches shining in my face and a policeman was asking me how I was.

"I spent three months in hospital in traction. I cracked a vertebra and tore the muscles so badly they thought I'd never be able to walk properly again. The bone healed but the muscles have never really got better." She seemed to run out of words then and just sat in her chair, still squeezing Neil's hands, breathing deeply.

"But you walked," Neil said. "You walked and went to college. You beat it then, Emily. You can beat it properly now. It's out and you've dealt with it. You've told somebody the darkest thing you know and you can live again now, love."

"How did you know that my father...that his injuries ...?"

"What did you think you saw," Neil asked in reply. "In that moment when you father looked like he might actually fly away?"

Emily shook her head. "Nothing. I...it was..." Then she tutted—how stupid was it to have told Neil everything, told him about the impossible thing she had seen and balk at this? "I thought I saw another shadow," she said. "A smaller shadow."

Neil nodded and smiled. "Okay," he said. "I thought it might've been something like that. Maybe that's the reason your father's injuries weren't as severe as they should've been." He shrugged and smiled at her again.

Emily looked at him for a long moment, then said, "Will you tell me why I had to tell you all of that, Neil?"

Neil told her about Davy Eliot.

*

"Won't it ever end? Dear sweet Jesus, that poor boy. If he wakes up. Doesn't anything ever end?"

"It's ended for you," Neil told her. "And, if God's good, it will be ended for Andrew, too."

She looked at him, her mouth already framing the questions—how, when his father and mother are dead because of the shadow? Why, when it didn't end when her own father died? But she didn't ask the questions. She saw the look in his dark grey eyes and said, "Because you'll tell him about my father and you'll tell him there's no need for him to wonder why or try to find out."

Neil nodded. He took a card out of the inside pocket of his jacket and handed it to her. "Both my phone numbers are on it. I don't think you will but, if you want to talk about it anymore, just ring me." He smiled.

She took it and smiled back. Then she leaned forward and opened the thick book on the coffee table. She turned the book so the photographs were facing Neil. "That one," she said, pointing to a small colour snap of a man and woman and two children. "Is of us on holiday the year before Robert was killed. The one next to it," she moved a long finger across the page. "That's of my father's great uncle. The one who owned 12 Oil Street. His name was Elias Leather."

Neil looked at it and saw the vague similarity in the men's faces. The old sepia-toned photo was of a man dressed in the clothes of the last century. His hair was shiny, parted in the middle. He had a thin moustache and his dark eyes were almost hypnotic. There was something about the light in those eyes that Neil didn't like. "He looks like a hard man," he said, almost to himself.

"Apparently, he was. He was a bully who drove his wife to suicide and killed his daughter, so they said. There was no proof and he was never charged but he was shunned by his neighbours after the child's death. His daughter died when she fell down the stairs in 12 Oil Street. Neighbours said they heard screaming and crying a good half an hour before she fell." Emily shrugged and closed the book. "I heard it from my mother's mother and I used to think it was merely the sort of story that gets passed around over the years. Certainly my father never mentioned it and neither I nor Robert ever felt anything...inimical in the house. Until the night my father died." She sighed and leaned back in the chair.

"Well," Neil said. "It's over for you Emily. You have nothing to feel guilty about. You tried to save your father and hurt yourself. That's pain enough without spending your life locked away, trying to keep shadows at bay."

She nodded. "I am half sick of shadows," she murmured and looked at Neil.

"The Lady of Shallot," he said. "Rather fitting, really."

Emily frowned and then smiled and then laughed out loud. It was a good laugh, honest and true, the first time she could remember really laughing for years. "Of course, Alfred Lord Tennyson. The three streets in The Rows named after him." She laughed again. When she'd finished she said, "I hope your friend's son comes out of it, Neil. Will you tell me if he does?"

"Yes," Neil said.

When he got home, Joy was home, waiting for him. She made him a cup of tea and just sat in the chair opposite him and looked at him with the same firm gaze Emily Leather had. Neil smiled and then told his wife both stories.

The following afternoon, Neil left work early and drove to the small area of sheltered housing close to the ferry. He parked the car in the small car park close to the children's playground. He looked at the small kids playing on the swings, being watched by their mothers. He smiled and then frowned, remembering what had happened to Davy here just a few days ago. He turned away and walked to the main entrance of the single block of low-rise flats.

There was a security man sitting in the little office to the left of the doors and he looked up when Neil pressed the button for the number eight flat.

"Hello?" The voice was frail, a woman's voice.

"Dolly? It's Neil Judd, sweetheart. Can I come up?"

"Neil? Bugger me! Okay."

When the buzzer sounded, Neil pushed the door and went inside.

The door to the flat was open and Dolly Sedgely was already shouting to Neil to come in and put the wood in the hole. Neil closed the door behind him.

Dolly was in the neat living room. The big window looked out across the ferry terminal to the river and the skyline of Oxborough. The room smelled of Mentholatum that Dolly rubbed on her chest because it was, she said, the only thing that worked for her bloody lungs.

"Sit down," Dolly told him and stubbed out the untipped cigarette in the ashtray on the arm of her chair. "Sit down, Neil and let me look at you."

Neil did as he was told and Dolly looked at him like he was a prospective boyfriend for one of her seven daughters. She didn't look any different to the way she'd looked when Neil and his parents were at her ninetieth birthday seven years ago. Her hair was permed and covered in a brown net. The net was dark brown, about the same colour as Dolly's eyes and the hair under it was dark ivory. The lines on her face were delved deep but Neil was sure most of them were laugh-lines. Her hands were small, liver-spotted, the fingers stubby with clipped nails of nicotine yellow. She was thin but she'd always been thin. Sitting down in the chair, she looked swallowed by it. She was only about four feet eleven inches tall but, when she stood up, she stood straight, her chin out and her eyes flashing.

"You look too thin," Dolly told him and pushed a plate of cream cakes across to him and then leaned forward to pour him a cup of tea so strong and sweet, the spoon almost stood up in the cup on its own. "So, why are you here, Neil? It's not my birthday and I see you haven't brought me any flowers. Come on, you young bugger, what's up?"

Neil sipped the tea but left the cake alone. "D'you remember a man called Elias Leather, Dolly? He lived—"

"That old sod," she said, almost spitting the word. "Lived in Oil Street, he did and a right nasty piece of work he was, too. Oh aye, I remember him. Why wouldn't I? I'm old but I'm not senile. And I worked in his sweat-shop when I was eleven. A right bastard he was." She chomped into her cake and drank some tea and then leaned back in the chair. She squinted at Neil. "Why d'you want to know about him? Even you wouldn't've liked that miserable wife-beating, child-killer, Neil." She shook her head angrily.

"I need to know what he was like, Dolly. You remember Davy Eliot? From Oil Street?"

"Aye, little Davy's a nice lad. Always came and asked me if I wanted any shopping doing on a Saturday morning. Met his wife once and his son. The lad was just like his dad but I wasn't struck on her. Looked a bit bossy to me. Anyway, what's Davy got to do with Elias Leather?"

Neil told her about Davy and Andrew and she nodded and tutted and drank her tea. When he'd finished she sighed and shook her head.

"Well, Leather lived in number 12 right enough," Dolly told him. "Owned it, which was really unusual them days. He wanted to be close to the factory and that's why he lived there. His factory was built on the field all the kids called The Pit. We made sheets of tin for other factories. He worked us to bloody death did old Elias. Not even when he got married did he stop being a miserable bastard. She was lovely was Olivia. Lovely girl. Lot younger than him, of course. She had lovely thick hair, very pale and her eyes were like yours, Neil, dark grey. She had lovely hands, too. Long fingers. But she was thin. Thin hips. Probably why she had so much trouble when the old sod got her pregnant. He was always going on about getting a son and heir, another miserable bastard to pass the business to. Mind you," she poured herself another cup of tea and spooned the sugar in like she was ladling soup. "We were all pretty sure the old bugger thought he was never going to die. Out of spite. Anyway, Olivia got pregnant and I think it was the only time we saw Elias smile. Me, I think it was wind but never mind. He paid for the best, I'll give him that. Best doctor and best midwife and everything. Olivia gave him a little girl." Dolly drank the tea and shook her head. "She had a terrible delivery and it meant she couldn't ever have another child. Shame."

"Elias wasn't very happy about that, I imagine," Neil said.

Dolly shook her head and made a raspberry noise with her gummy mouth. "I should cocoa. The day after she had the baby, he stormed into work and walked round the shopfloor like a bear with a sore head. Yelling and kicking the tin sheets. Sounded like a bloody thunderstorm in there that morning. He sacked two men for being too slow to straighten the sheets he'd kicked over himself. The bastard."

"He didn't change his mind even when the baby started to grow?"

"Not him. He had a face like a burst boot as it was, after the baby, it was even worse, like he'd spent all his money on lemons and spent all night sucking on them. Olivia came to the factory with the little chick, to say thank you for the toy we all clubbed together to buy. She looked awful. Her face was as pale as her hair and she was thinner than ever. Elias walked behind her and you could see her sort of cringing whenever she heard him say something to somebody. You know, sort of leaning forward, shoulders hunched up. I remember Nellie Parsons whispering to me that it looked like Olivia was trying to keep the baby so close to her because she was worried that Elias would hurt the little mite."

"And he did," Neil said.

"Oh, nothing was ever proved but I lived in Oil Street and I'd heard the poor little bugger crying. Olivia called her Elisabeth. I've always thought it was the closest she could get to Elias and it was her way of trying to mollify the old sod. Anyway, Elisabeth lasted until she was just turned two. I remember that day like it was yesterday. It was a Sunday and we only worked half-days on Sunday. I was home, playing in the little field where the swings are now. Me and my friends. Elisabeth was standing in the back garden of Oil Street, peering between the railings and you could just tell that she'd've loved to come and play with us. Then old man Elias came out and shouted at her to get back in the house and the poor little toddler just, oh, just folded up. Like a piece of paper. She just crumpled onto the grass and that miserable bastard yelled at her about the dirt and then yanked her up by one arm and marched back in the house. Elisabeth cried for an hour solid that Sunday while we were playing in the field. And then she stopped. All of a sudden like. Like something cut her off in mid-cry." Dolly took a big breath and wiped at something on her cheek. Then she looked Neil straight in the eye. "Something did," she told him and her voice, even frail, was angry. "They said Elisabeth fell down the stairs in Oil Street but we all knew that miserable sod pushed her. Probably *flung* her down them stairs."

"What about his wife, Dolly?"

"She went into what used to be called a decline," Dolly said. "Lasted another five months, till just before Christmas that same year. They found her under Laketon Pier. Said she jumped off. Hah!"

Neil nodded. "You don't think so?"

"Nobody did," she said. "Everybody who lived in Oil Street saw Elias taking her out that afternoon. He even hired a pony and trap and that wasn't him. That miserable bastard wouldn't spend a penny if he could help it and nobody believed he was doing it for his wife's health. It was bloody freezing that day. We all watched them leave Oil Street and I saw how scared Olivia was. Her face was all pinched and there was a big yellow bruise on her cheekbone. She looked down at her hands when the trap started off but, just before they turned the corner, she looked up at us and her eyes were awful. Like a trapped animal. Course, nobody doubted that Elias did for her but nobody said nothing because he was a big noise. Knew the mayor and the police and everything and..." Dolly looked at her hands and Neil saw the faint blush on her yellowed face. She looked up at him.

"People needed to work," Neil said gently.

Dolly nodded and wiped at another something on her cheek. "Yes, that's right. So the old bastard got away with it. I tell you, Neil, the day they buried him, we had a street party. The factory was long-gone by then and there weren't nobody to tell us not to."

"How did he die, Dolly?"

She smiled. There was nothing nice in that smile despite the obvious pleasure Dolly felt at the memory. "He broke his neck when he fell out of his back bedroom window. He was too tight-fisted to get a proper glazier in and he was fixing the window himself. He overbalanced on the ladder and broke his miserable, murdering neck. And good riddance, too!"

Neil stayed for another half hour, just talking with Dolly, remembering old times. Dolly was the oldest living resident in The Rows and knew everybody and everything from virtually the time they were built. Neil made her another pot of tea before he left and she kissed him and told him to eat more, he was too thin.

"It's not going to change anything," Martin said when Neil had finished. They were in Martin's back room sharing a single malt. He lit his pipe and shook his head slowly. "I know something peculiar happened to Eliot in that house and I can almost believe that this Emily Leather saw something similar when she was a child. Maybe her father saw this shadow and that's why he was the way he was. But it's still not going to change anything, Neil. You've known that all along. I mean, even if I believed it completely, I can't go down to 12 Oil Street and arrest a shadow. Assuming it's still there." He puffed on his pipe and looked at Neil who just sat in the old rocker and looked back. "D'you think it's still there? If it made this George Leather kill himself and made Davy Eliot kill himself, wouldn't that be enough? Wouldn't that be what it wanted? It's got what it wanted and now it'll have gone."

Neil nodded slowly, something percolating in his mind. "Probably," he said and then nodded again. "Yeah, probably. And I know it's not going to make a difference in the coroner's court but it might make a difference to Andrew."

"If he wakes up," Martin said, saw the expression on Neil's face and wished he'd kept his mouth shut. Then he shrugged; it was done, best to get on with things. "Fancy a whiskey, Neil?"

FIFTEEN

Teresa Grogan smiled and took the sheets of microfiche the young man handed her. He thanked her and Teresa nodded, noticing again the lovely dark blue eyes.

"Get everything you wanted?" Teresa asked, knowing she was too old for him but not really caring.

It had been a long time since she'd seen anybody who looked nice. Not just good looking, not just a hunk, but nice, too. But he was nodding and already turning away. She watched him as he walked to the door. He limped slightly to his right and she could see how thin he was beneath the fleecy jacket he wore. He paused in the corridor outside the reference library and Teresa saw his shoulders move up, as if he was sighing. She wanted to go to him, ask him if he was all right but there was already a small queue forming at her desk and she'd have to help Muriel deal with it. Then the young man let out the breath he'd taken and went downstairs.

Five minutes later, just after four in the afternoon, Teresa took her break. She looked out of the window above the stairs in the corridor as she always did, just to remind herself that the world was still there. Down below, the road was quiet as twilight darkened the clear sky. The streetlights were coming on and, standing below the one near the main doors, she saw the young man with the lovely dark blue eyes.

He had his hands jammed in the pockets of his jacket, his shoulders slightly hunched, looking at the ground, like he was thinking hard about something. Then, just as she was about to go downstairs and out of the library to ask him if he was all right, the young man looked up and headed off down the road. Teresa watched him till he turned the corner and then went to make herself a cup of coffee.

She spent five minutes trying to read the magazine and gave up; she couldn't get Andrew Eliot out of her mind. That was the name on his library ticket and he looked about twenty, maybe twenty one. At least, that's how old his face looked but his eyes looked older and the way he held himself made him seem older. That's what had made her think about him as something other than a student using the library, that sense that he was older, maybe old enough for her to think about as somebody to go out with. Then she'd checked his details on the computer while he worked the machine, found he was only just turned twenty, a resident of Seapool and too young for her. And now, she couldn't get him out of her mind, couldn't stop seeing his thin face and those lovely dark blue eyes. And the way he blew the fringe of his dark auburn hair off his forehead when he spoke, the way his broad hands trembled slightly when he took the sheets from her. He was tall and she had the feeling that he was normally very fit and healthy but, just now, he was or had been ill. He looked tired, as if he'd been up all night.

He'd wanted the local papers, both of them, back as far as last autumn. She'd assumed he was doing some project work for his course. When she passed behind him later on, though, she realised he had no notepaper or folder and was simply sitting at the machine and scrolling through the papers, reading them. Almost as if he'd been away and was trying to catch up on what had been happening.

"Act your age, girl," she told herself and drained her mug. She put the magazine back on the small table and picked up her keys.

"Teresa, this is for you." Muriel handed the phone across the desk and then went back to helping the woman who was trying to trace her family history.

"Hello? Oh, hi, Neil. How are you?" Teresa smiled, like she always did when she talked to Neil Judd. "Yes, as a matter of fact, I did." She turned so her back was towards Muriel and lowered her voice. "To be honest, I've been thinking about him all the time, like a bloody schoolgirl with a crush. It's embarra...oh, well, the local rags, Neil. Both of them...what? As far back as last autumn...no, didn't seem to be anything in particular. One thing, though, he didn't make any notes, like it was some work for college or anything...he left just before four, just before I went on my break. Neil, he looked tired and, oh, like he had something on his mind...okay, Neil. Take care. 'Bye." She replaced the phone and frowned.

Neil sounded worried and that was unusual. Still, whatever the problem was, Neil was the best person to sort it out. She'd ring him at work tomorrow and find out the details. Maybe she'd ask him whether *he* thought she was too old for Andrew Eliot.

Neil put his phone down slowly and looked at the clock on the wall of his office. It was quarter past six. He picked the phone up again and rang home.
"Joy? Listen, love, I've got to go somewhere and I'll be a bit late. It's about Andrew. I'll tell you when I get home. See you later."
He broke the connection and then phoned Grace Eliot at Andrew's house. He'd phoned Teresa at the library because Grace had phoned him, worried about Andrew. Grace had been at the Eliot house all week, making sure it was aired and warm and cosy for when her grandson came home after nearly four months in hospital. Neil had picked Andrew up at the hospital two days ago and taken him home.

Andrew had started to come out of his coma at about the same time his father must have dived off the water tower in Oil Street and, once he was awake properly, Neil had spent every evening at his bedside in the ward, talking to him. He told him what had happened to his parents and then held Andrew while he cried. After that, Neil had talked about Davy, about the man he was as Neil knew him. Andrew listened and, slowly, began to talk himself. About his dad and his mum and about himself, what he hoped to do with the rest of his life.

Neil had taken him home the day before yesterday and, outside the house, had handed Davy's journal to Andrew.

"You know the outcome of the inquests," he said. "That's what your dad wrote about it. About what he did with himself during the last year or so of his life, about what happened. He wrote about his hopes and dreams and then he wrote about your mum and Anne Jordan. Read it, son. It's what your dad wanted. When you've read it, give me a ring and we can talk about what it says and how you feel. Okay?"

Andrew had nodded and then went inside the house where his Nan waited for him. Neil had spent yesterday and today, up till Grace had phoned him ten minutes ago, waiting for Andrew to ring. In fact, when the phone buzzed at him, Neil thought it was Andrew. When he heard Grace's worried voice, Neil had rubbed at the scar above his eyebrow and called himself an idiot for waiting for Andrew to ring instead of ringing the lad himself. Especially when she told him that Andrew had spent most of morning, before going to the library, asking her about Davy's family history and about whether anybody else in the family had been ill like his dad.

"Grace?" Neil said now as Davy's mother answered the phone. "It's Neil. Andrew's not at the library. He left about four this afternoon...I'm going to see if I can find him, love. Don't worry, I'm sure he'll be okay. Probably just needed some time on his own. I'll find him and bring him home. He'll probably be starving and really fancy a bowl of your peewack soup." He chuckled as Grace laughed on the other end of the line and asked him how he knew she'd made the soup. "That's what nans do, Grace. They always know the right thing to make. I'll see you, love. Try not to worry."

Neil put the phone down, knowing that Grace would spend the rest of the night, until Neil brought Andrew home, doing nothing *but* worry about her only grandchild.

"Should've rung him this morning," Neil told himself as he put his jacket on and picked up his keys.

Yes, he should've phoned Andrew this morning and invited him down to Blackhay. He could have had his lunch and then Neil could have given him the half-crown tour and shown him the kids who had problems, just like Andrew. Then they could have sat in the office and Neil could have listened to Andrew talking about the guilt he felt. Neil could have told him about Mad George and Emily and Elias Leather and made the boy see that nothing was his fault.

"But you didn't and now all you can do is find him," Neil told himself as he left the car park.

Where to start looking? Well, it didn't need a detective did it? When Grace told Neil that Andrew had left home at half past one, telling her he was going to the library and wasn't home yet, Neil had a fairly good idea what he was at the library for. He'd hoped he would catch Andrew still there but he hadn't and now Neil was turning off Paradise Avenue and heading for The Rows.

Andrew wished he'd taken his dad's car instead of walking to the library. His left leg was aching and his pulsing head felt like an overripe tomato. He was cold, too. His fleecy jacket might be the height of fashion and look good but it didn't keep out the chill of late January once the sun had gone down. Walking, limping, through the crust of snow was hard work and it made him warm but not warm enough. Still, things were the way they were and he had to get on with it.

"I've got to get on with it," he told himself as he finally crossed the invisible barrier between the rest of the town and The Rows.

He was at the top of Shelley Row, the road that used to be where all the local shops had done thriving business, so his dad had told him. Andrew remembered his father telling him that the café used to do the best fry-up breakfast in Seapool when the brake linings factory was open at the bottom of Oil Street. Andrew had never been in The Rows before.

He stepped into the doorway of the café and leaned back against the bars of the railing protecting the door. He was tired and not just in his body. For the first time he could remember, his brain actually felt like the muscle it was and it was tired, weary, full of stuff he didn't want to think about at all.

Like the fact that his mother had killed a woman she didn't even know. His mother was the woman who'd helped him do his maths homework the first night he came home from Somerville Grammar because his dad was working overtime. She'd sat next to him at the dining table and coaxed him through the equations and kissed him on the cheek when he worked out the answer to the last problem on his own. How could that woman kill somebody? His mother was the woman who'd taken him into town to buy him his first suit for the second year dance when he wanted to look smart because Shirley Mottram was going and Andrew thought she was gorgeous. How did that woman turn into a murderer? His mother was the woman who'd sat and held him the night his new puppy was at the vets after getting knocked over. She'd held him and hushed him and told him the puppy would be fine. And the puppy was fine. His mother was the woman who taught him how to sew— 'so you won't ever go out with a button missing, Andrew.'— and taught him to smudge his drawings to create the illusion of shadow.

Andrew bent his head; he definitely didn't want to think about shadows. But, of course, that's all he'd been able to think about since reading his father's journal.

He'd started reading it in bed, the night he'd got home from hospital. He'd read it until he'd fallen asleep and then he'd spent all yesterday reading it while his Nan was out shopping and then while she was in the kitchen getting tea ready. It was something else he didn't want to think about, like his mother and his father.

How could his father, the man who'd taught him how to kick a football, who'd bought him the Liverpool strip and a new pair of boots for his fourth birthday, possibly be dead? How could the man who'd shown him how to wire a plug and how to read a schematic be nothing more than a stone in the Garden of Remembrance at the crematorium? How could that man, the man who'd been his best friend, possibly have committed suicide? More than that, how could that man have thought he was doing it for his son?

"God," Andrew muttered and wiped the tears off his cold cheeks.

He took a deep breath and rubbed at his left leg and then stepped out of the doorway and started making his halting way towards the bottom of the road. He had a vague idea where Oil Street was but, mostly, he was just heading towards the docks. That was where the street ended and he hoped the road sign hadn't been prised off the bricks.

Why was he here, in this strange little corner of Seapool where, the old joke went, you really needed a passport just to walk around?

"Because I have to know," Andrew told the frigid air of this January night.

He had to know if his father's madness was genetic, if the seed of the illness was already beginning to grow in Andrew himself.

He'd read the journal, finishing it at one this morning, and then just lay in his bed, staring at the ceiling. Neil had told him what had happened and that had been a low time. It had been so bad, Andrew believed that it was the worst time in his short life.

Listening to Neil, Andrew felt the ward beginning to shrink, that the air had somehow turned to concrete and was crushing him slowly, breath by breath, heartbeat by heartbeat. That was when Neil had started talking about Andrew's dad and, because he'd talked about Davy Eliot as Neil had known him, Andrew felt the weight lift. Then he'd started talking himself, about his dad and mum and himself. Andrew had no doubt that it was the listening Neil had done that was the real reason for what the doctors called Andrew's astonishing recovery.

Then Andrew read the journal and knew that *this* was the worst time in his short life. He'd fallen asleep, eventually, last night and he'd dreamed. It was the dream that had brought him to The Rows tonight.

In the dream, Andrew was asleep. He knew he'd been asleep for a long time and he wasn't in his own bed. He had vague recollections of muttered voices and the feeling of somebody holding his hand but that was all. Then, in the dream, the sleeping Andrew had felt a change in the air around him. It seemed to become heavy and sultry, the way the air did just before a storm broke. That was when the sleeping Andrew felt the approach of something awful.

He knew that whatever it was bore him no good will. It felt hard and deadly and it was in the room with him. He moaned or thought he did but nobody came to help. He struggled on the bed, trying to lift his arms but they weighed almost as much as the air seemed to weigh. It felt like he was tied down by wires attached to both hands and his chest. He moaned again, louder and still nobody came. Except the thing in the room with him.

Lying on the bed in...in hospital...Andrew prayed to the God Nan Eliot believed in, prayed that he could at least find the strength to scream. If he could scream, the people in the hospital would hear him and come to help him. He couldn't scream.

Then the thing in the room was with him and, somehow, it managed to pierce the billowy cloud of sleep that was all Andrew could see. Through the gauzy cream of the thinning cloud, Andrew saw the thing that had sneaked into the room with him.

It was a shadow. A person-sized, person-shaped shadow.

It floated across the room and stood at the bedside. Andrew watched, terrified, longing to be a child again so he could put his hands up or grab a cushion and hide behind it, like he'd done when Dr Who was on the television. He couldn't move at all, except his traitor-eyes which swivelled in sockets that felt gritty and brittle, to fix on the shadow by the bed.

The shadow opened its arms.

It looked like it wanted to embrace Andrew, give him a hug, the way his mother had done the day he got his exam results. But Andrew sensed nothing of that love and pride in the shadow's embrace. Those open arms looked like they simply wanted to enfold Andrew and smother what little life there was left in him.

Andrew prayed again for the strength to scream but all he could manage was a strained 'help' that sounded weak in his mind so he knew nobody could have heard it. Then he could do nothing but wait for the shadow to lower those open arms and swallow him up.

That was when the shadow stopped moving. It was bent towards Andrew, the arms beginning to move inwards and then it stopped dead. It cocked its head to the side, as if it was listening to something or for something. Slowly, it raised its head and let its arms drop to its sides. It looked down at Andrew on the bed and Andrew saw that it was no longer just a shadow. He could see features where a face would be. There was a line that looked like a mouth, a mouth that looked as if it was closed in frustration. And a lighter, greyer smudge above that hard line that could only have been a nose. And, to either side of the nose, eyes. There was a hard light in those eyes and Andrew could see the truth of the shadow's dislike for him and the frustration at being thwarted in that hard light. Then the shadow floated away from the bedside and was gone. There was no puff of smoke, no sudden pop of imploding air. The shadow was gone the way a shadow goes when the light moves across it.

That was when Andrew woke up last night, in his own bed. He woke sweating but cold, a terrible headache already starting behind his wide eyes. He stared at the ceiling, unsure where he was, feeling the blockage in his chest that he felt sure was the scream he hadn't been able to manage in the dream. Good job, too. If he'd woken himself by screaming, he'd probably have given Nan Eliot a bloody heart attack.

"What was that all about?" Andrew murmured and pulled the duvet up to his chin.

God, what a terrible dream. What the hell had brought it on?

"The journal," he told himself.

It must have been the journal. Reading it, reading about the shadow in his father's life, the precursor to his madness. That was it, like eating cheese before bedtime or something. That and the fact that he was home after almost four months in hospital, more than one in a coma.

He rolled over and closed his eyes.

are you sure that was a dream and not a memory?

He opened his eyes and felt his heart give a sudden jolt that throbbed in his throat. Memory? Of what? He'd been in a coma.

"I was in a coma, how could I remember anything?" His own voice sounded unfamiliar and far off.

you had vague recollections of muttered voices and somebody holding your hands.

Try as he might and he tried very hard, he couldn't argue with that. He lay awake until the orange-wash on his bedroom ceiling turned to a pearly glow as dawn replaced the streetlamp's light.

He got up and ate the porridge Nan Eliot made for him, read the paper and did the crossword. He sat in the chair and tried to convince himself that the dream had been just a dream but he couldn't. The more he thought about it, the easier it was to remember every horrible detail.

And as he remembered those horrible details, he started to have an idea that was even more horrible than the dream had been.

Finally, he knew what he had to do. He asked Nan Eliot about his granddad's family and her family, asked her quietly while looking at his hands, if there had been anything like his dad's illness in either family in the past. Then he told her he was going to the library, he'd see her later.

At the library, he'd read every report there was about the three inquests. There were a lot of articles which, he supposed, wasn't surprising. In a relatively small town like Seapool, two murders and one suicide via the old eternal triangle was bound to be big news. Andrew read everything there was to read—he read about what the papers called his mother's savage revenge attack on Anne Jordan. He read about what the papers called his father's slow but sure descent into madness. Andrew read about what the papers called the shadow of death that had stalked David Eliot and, ultimately, the two women in his life. He even read about himself, the coma, his astonishing recovery.

Then, instead of ringing Neil and talking to him, he'd started to make his limping way down to The Rows.

And, now, here he was. At the bottom of Shelley Row, feeling like a shadow himself. Except for the pounding headache and the dull grinding ache in the muscles of his left leg.

Why hadn't he got in touch with Neil?

Andrew stood at the bottom of Shelley Row and looked at the glow of light on the sky reflected from the mills and wondered why he hadn't been in touch with Neil. Neil would have helped him, would have talked it through, listened to Andrew while he tried to explain the way he felt about the journal.

"He would've talked me out of...this," Andrew said and nodded.

Like his father said in the journal, Neil was the best at what he did and he would have talked Andrew out of coming down here and doing...whatever it was he was doing. Andrew didn't really know what he was doing, he just knew he had to do it. He had to know, that was all.

Had to know what? He shook his head, reluctant to articulate the thought but not saying it aloud didn't put it out of his mind.

It had been there ever since the dream and going to 12 Oil Street was the only way he could think of to find out whether the answer was yes or no.

He sighed and pushed his hands deeper into the pockets of his jacket. Then he bent his head and began to walk up the road, hoping he'd find Oil Street before his leg packed up or before the cold finally turned him into a bloody icicle.

Neil turned into Shelley Row and stopped the car. Andrew had left the library around four o'clock and now it was nearly seven.

"A lot can happen in three hours," Neil said and rubbed at his scar.

Neil had no doubt Andrew was down here in The Rows, the question was where, exactly. Logic said it would be 12 Oil Street. After all, that was where Davy had spent his last months and where he'd written the journal and it was the journal that had sent Andrew down here. Neil had hoped the lad would be in touch after reading it, logic said he would.

"Sod logic," Neil muttered angrily.

No, there was more to it than the journal. If Andrew had simply read the journal, contacting Neil would have been the obvious thing, the emotional reaction, not just the logical one. After reading what had happened and knowing the verdict of the inquest, Andrew would feel guilty. Never mind that his father had made it plain in both the journal and his letter to Neil that no blame attached to Andrew, the lad would have felt guilty. Feeling like that, he would need somebody to talk to about it. Not his Nan but to somebody who knew his father and mother in a way that Grace Eliot didn't know them.

"Something happened to make Andrew decide there was more than just guilt in all this. Otherwise, why ask if there'd been anything like Davy's illness in the family before," Neil said and shook his head; he was talking to himself again and that would get him nowhere.

No, think about it but move. The house seemed the obvious place, especially after three hours. If Andrew had felt the need to look at the places where Davy had learned to love high places and to jump from them, he would have done that first, building himself up to the actual house. Neil put the car in gear and headed for 12 Oil Street.

Andrew stood in front of the gate and looked at the house. It was just an ordinary house, the same as the other houses in the street. Even when you passed the row of garages half-way up the road, the houses were the same even if the street somehow felt different. And the street *did* feel different. It was almost as if the air at this end of the road was different and somehow lent an odd skew to the houses and the gardens and the few trees.

Andrew could almost think that, like The Rows was a different country compared to the rest of Seapool, Oil Street was another county in that different country. The way that the dock road seemed deserted when he finally arrived there, only increased that feeling. Or maybe it was his tired mind, seeing and feeling things that weren't there.

It had taken him a while to find the road. He'd headed towards the docks, keeping an eye on the glow of light on the sky. In fact, Shelley Row led straight to the dock road and he'd come out there and wondered which way to go next. He wanted to look at the roller-blind factory because that was where The Pit had been when his father was a kid. He wanted to find the swings and look at The Dead Tree and then he wanted to look at the slide. Standing on the dock road and wondering which way to go, Andrew hoped to see somebody he could ask but the place seemed as deserted as the dark side of the moon. Didn't anybody come out at night down here? Wasn't anybody walking the dog or going for a pint?

He'd stood opposite the main gate of the flour mill, shivering with the cold, his hands, still feeling like blocks of wood, jammed in his pockets. And nobody had come. Finally, he'd decided that the ferry terminal was to his left and turned right. Fifty yards later, he saw the little alleyway between two houses and a graffiti-scarred sign on the wall. He bent down and peered at it. He could just make out the word Oil behind a black and red heart with the words Jack and Sonia burned into its centre.

Andrew walked down the alley, his eyes wide, his ears burning with the effort of trying to hear every sound, his hands clenched and out of his pockets. When he was small, his mother had made it very clear she didn't want him spending any time in The Rows and now, half-remembered stories from infant and secondary school about the place still held a place in Andrew's mind. He hadn't felt deprived by his mother's admonition; his dad's occasional recollections and his granddad's funny anecdotes did him fine and all his friends lived close to him but his mother's stern voice and the stories he'd heard in school had stayed in his mind.

After what felt like an endless walk, Andrew emerged into Oil Street and it turned out to be a street like any other street. He looked at the number on the house next to the alley and then crossed to the even side of the road. The first house there was number sixty two, the one to the left sixty four. Andrew walked up the street to his right.

Now, here he was in front of 12 Oil Street and he felt an odd sort of anti-climax. You expected the house your father had gone mad in to look ominous at least. Maybe you weren't expecting gargoyles or high eaves or leaning chimney stacks but, still, shouldn't there have been more than this common three-bedroomed semi in a street full of them?

Or perhaps it simply confirmed the fact of his father's madness. His father hadn't been a raving psychopath or blood-sucking monster or a giant with a bolt through his neck. He'd been an ordinary man with ordinary hopes and dreams who, when those dreams and hopes died, slowly lost his mind. And didn't that, because of its very ordinariness, mean it was more than likely that what Andrew had been thinking since the dream was true? That he had inherited his father's madness?

Worse than that, his mother had had her own sort of madness, hadn't she? It wasn't the deep, psychotic madness of his father but, when she finally cracked under the strain of worrying about Andrew, the moment she'd killed Anne Jordan must have been a moment of insanity.

If his mother had gone mad, even for an instant, and his father had been profoundly mad, what chance did he have of staying sane?

Andrew sighed and wiped the tears off his cheeks again and heard an echo of his granddad's voice in his mind.

Sometimes, you do something because it's time and, if you don't, the time's gone and you've missed the chance.

George Eliot had said that to Andrew one afternoon when they were talking about football and how George had chosen to become a joiner instead of going for a trial as a professional footballer. It applied to most things, Andrew now believed. He put his hand on the latch of the front gate, lifted it and walked into the front garden of 12 Oil Street.

He didn't have the keys to the house and maybe there was a cowardly part of him that was hoping he couldn't get inside the house. He shook his head and tried the handle to the planked gate at the side of the house. It turned and the gate opened on a push. Andrew stood there for a moment and then walked into the back garden and closed the gate behind him.

He could see well enough because next door's kitchen light was on and he felt nothing but the chill air as he walked up the L made of the side of the house and the little oblong patch of grass. When he reached the end of the L, he stopped and looked at the square of the back garden.

The kitchen light next door went out and the garden was in darkness. Andrew's night-vision went with the light and he was left with the after-image of the railings he'd been looking at. Then, replacing this, he saw the garden as it must have looked when his father caught the toerags planning to burgle the house. He was beginning to smile at that when his eyes refocused and he could see normally.

And wished he hadn't.

By the railings, by the gap in them, he saw a shape. He tried to remember if the shape had been there before the light had gone but he couldn't. The shape looked like a person, somebody who was either coming in or going out through the gap in the railings. Andrew opened his eyes wider and, for a second, he thought the shape was moving towards him, approaching him but to one side, his left. Then it was gone.

Well, probably just another after-image, gone now that my eyes have adjusted.

He tried to take a full breath so he could stop his thighs trembling and turned away from the garden and looked at the back kitchen door. He stepped onto the stone step and looked at the door to the outside toilet. He smiled again, remembering how amazed he'd been when his father told him about outside toilets and baths in front of the fire. He saw the big padlock on the door and wondered if his father's tools were still inside the closet-like toilet. Then he looked at the back kitchen door again.

The handle was one of the old brass types, big and round. Andrew put his hand on it, feeling its cold sink into his hand as he turned it. It turned but the door didn't move in its frame. He let go, that cowardly part of him breathing a sigh of relief; okay, he'd tried, he could go home now.

There was click. It seemed very loud in the still, freezing January air. Andrew frowned and put his hand on the handle again. He turned it and, this time, it turned all the way and the door opened.

"I just didn't turn it far enough," he told himself but didn't really believe it.

Andrew pushed the door open and stepped inside the house. He felt around on the wall for a light switch but couldn't find one. He could see the reflection of a streetlamp at the end of what must have been the hall and walked towards it. Two steps into the hall, he saw the door to the living room. It was open.

He stood in the hall for a moment, asking himself if he was sure he wanted to do this.

"No but I have to," he said and stepped into the living room.

The light switch was on his right, just beyond the doorframe. He pressed it but nothing happened. The curtains were drawn and, by the orange-glow of the streetlamp outside, he saw the couch and, in the far corner, a bulky shape that could only be a television.

Why hadn't the kids from round here taken it? If the back door was open, they didn't even need to break in. Why was the television still here? And the couch and the standard lamp and the video and the sound system and the single armchair? The room looked like somebody still lived here and had just nipped to the upstairs toilet.

Andrew blew into his numb hands and, almost dreamily, walked across the room to the television and the standard lamp. He bent down awkwardly, his left leg still struggling to do what it had been doing for twenty years with no effort at all. He felt the base of the lamp and found the cord. He reached beneath the television and video unit and found the socket. He pressed the switch. The lamp came on.

He eased himself up and back and sat on the couch. He looked round the room. In the shadowy, yellowy light of the lamp, the room looked cosy, even more like somebody had just nipped out for a minute. Andrew shook his head, frowning. The light in the ceiling didn't work but the thirteen amp socket did. Did that make any sense? Well, he supposed the five amp fuse could have blown. He looked at the socket behind the television unit and saw that the plugs for the telly, video and sound system were lying on the floor. Andrew sat back on the couch and blew into his hands again. The tingle in his fingertips felt good. He looked at the sound system and remembered what his father wrote in the journal about listening to all that sixties music. Andrew quite liked that old music and he smiled as he thought about his dad listening to it and remembering when it had been brand new.

From that, Andrew remembered so much about his dad and his mum. The way when he was little they always seemed to be looking at each other, how the only way he could get their attention was to pull at his mum's dress or his dad's trousers. He remembered how they always seemed to be laughing and joking. He remembered the holidays they had when he was allowed into the pubs on the campsite and saw them getting slightly tipsy and singing and doing daft things because they were having fun. Why did that have to stop? What happened to make those people turn into the people they were last autumn? Surely it must have been more than Granddad Eliot dying and Trisha Eliot's menopause? There must have been more to it than that, more to turn them into a woman who killed another woman and a man who killed his wife and then committed suicide.

Andrew thought about everything he'd read and heard, everything that happened last autumn and before. He sat on the couch and remembered it and remembered how it had been when he was a child, a little kid. The memories got all mixed up and he didn't even try to stop the tears.

Finally, he remembered how he'd felt when Neil told him what had happened. Andrew remembered the deep guilt that seemed to fill him up and that deep guilt was with him now. Because he *was* guilty. The thing that had made his mother...do what she'd done and made his father kill himself was the fact of Andrew's coma. And the coma was Andrew's fault because he'd been angry enough to get drunk and do something really stupid. So it was his fault. All his fault.

The air in the room changed.

It had been cold in the room when he'd come in and his breath had fogged the air in front of him as he entered the living room. Now, he could feel the tingle in his fingers and the way the lobes of his ears were beginning to glow. He breathed out and watched for the little cloud of breath. There wasn't any little fog coming out of his mouth. A thin line of sweat insinuated itself down his left side and he shifted on the couch to let it run away instead of making him itch. But even after the moisture was gone, the itch was still there.

And everywhere else.

"Oh God," Andrew moaned and put his head in his hands.

His head itched, right below his scalp and he rubbed at it.

"It's true," he muttered, still rubbing at his head. "I'll smell tin next."

He did and he moaned again, louder, more forlorn, the moan of a child lost and alone with nobody to turn to.

It was true then. His father's illness, his madness was something else he'd passed onto his son. Andrew had his father's hair and build, he had that way of blowing his fringe off his forehead and the little kink in the little finger of his left hand. And he obviously had a mind that was only half an inch away from madness. Just like his father.

If he opened his eyes, he'd see the shadow. It would be there in the room with him, its arms open, waiting for him to cross the line from his brittle sanity and into that dark land where his father had finally gone mad.

you cannot hide from it forever

The words just echoed in his mind. There had been no change in the heavy air, no sense that a vibration had altered it for his ears to pick up on and transform that vibration into the words. They had just been in his brain, their meaning clear. Andrew closed his eyes tighter and rubbed harder at his head where the itch alone seemed capable of turning him into a dribbling idiot.

would you force others to share your weight because you are too cowardly to acknowledge it?

Andrew shook his head and moaned. The air weighed down on him the way it had done when he first heard what had happened to his parents. The sweat on his body made the itch worse and he could feel the tips of his fingers burning. The smell was everything and everywhere. He could smell its acrid underhint in the back of his nose and almost taste it in his throat.

will you deny what is yours and make others suffer because of your cowardice?

He moaned again and wondered why, *how* all this happened so fast to him. With his father, it had taken weeks, months before it got this bad. How was it possible that it had happened so suddenly?

there are degrees of guilt like everything else

Of course. It was simple. Awful and terrifying but simple. His father's guilt had been less than Andrew's. His father hadn't known that his illness had had to be borne by other people, by his family. Not until the very end when the shadow made it plain to him.

"I've known how guilty I am since the beginning," Andrew murmured and sobbed.

It was true. Even when he was at the dance, brooding about what his mother had told him, drinking like it was going out of fashion, Andrew had known it was stupid, the wrong thing to do. Yet he'd carried on. Now, he could actually remember the scaffolding and how he'd thought, even as he climbed it, that if he fell, his mother would know why. Yes, even then, Andrew had thought about how bad his falling would make his mother feel. Childish and spiteful. And everything that happened afterwards was a direct result of that childish spite.

His father had been unaware of his guilt, if there had ever been any. Andrew had known all along. No wonder this madness came so quickly.

"What can I do, though? I don't know how to make things right," Andrew said and knew he was talking to the shadow even though his eyes were screwed up tight so he wouldn't see it.

look or you will not know how to understand

Andrew opened his eyes and looked.

The shadow was frozen in the cone of light thrown by the standard lamp. It was exactly how his father had described it and how Andrew had seen it in the dream last night. The dream that was really a memory. The shadow opened its arms and Andrew saw its face, no longer a dark blur but a real face. The mouth was a tight line, the nose like a blade, the cheekbones high and cruel, the eyes flinty, staring at him.

"I don't understand," Andrew said. "Tell me."

*

Neil was still twenty yards away from the house when he saw the dim yellow glow as it filtered through closed curtains.

"Shit," he said and steered the car into the gutter outside 12 Oil Street.

He got out of the car and jumped the low fence. He didn't bother looking through the window. The curtains were drawn and it didn't matter anyway; he was going inside. He opened the gate into the back garden and ran up the L. He stepped onto the back step and nearly brained himself on the open toilet door. He stared inside and saw three tool chests and the coil of cable to a worklamp.

"Still here? After three months?"

It was hard to believe. After all, this was The Rows. He shook his head and reached for the handle of the kitchen door and turned it. It didn't matter that Davy's tools were still here, Andrew was all that mattered now.

Neil pushed on the kitchen door and it opened. He stepped into the kitchen, looked briefly down the narrow room and then went into the living room.

Andrew watched the shadow waving its arms, watched the tight line of its mouth opening and closing, watched the hard light in its eyes flash. And he didn't know what he could do.

"Please, tell me," he groaned and rubbed again at his head where the ants of his insanity were running riot. "I don't understand what you want!"

The shadow stopped its waving and stopped opening and closing its mouth. For a second, Andrew thought the smell of tin abated and his head felt less like it was covered in itching powder from Ali's Joke Shop.

jump

The word crossed the heavy air and settled in Andrew's mind and he knew. Of course, what else could he do? It was making that stupid, drunken jump that had caused everything and led him here. He stood up.

the key is on top of the cooker in the kitchen

Andrew frowned and turned to ask the shadow what key, why? But the shadow was already waving its arms at him.

time is getting short

Andrew closed his eyes and, on the inside of his eyelids, he saw four springy mattresses and nodded. He went into the kitchen and found the key. He opened the padlock on the toilet door and pulled the door open. The mattresses were squashed together in the corner, still tied with the twine his father had used.

He hauled the mattresses across the garden and pushed them onto the top of the railings. He kept one hand on them as he squeezed through the gap and then pulled them down onto the snow-crusted grass verge. He looked up and saw the outline of the slide across the swings and took a deep breath. He rubbed absently at his left thigh and then began to drag-carry the mattresses behind him.

*

The change in the air-pressure as he stepped into the living room made Neil stagger and he had to sit on the arm of the couch. He smelled tin and his head began to itch. He ignored both and fixed his eyes on the shadow pinned by the cone of light behind the television.

The shadow was waving its arms and Neil could see its face. It was the face of the man in Emily Leather's sepia-toned photograph.

"Where is he? Where's Andrew?" Neil demanded.

gone

Part of Neil felt strange as the word settled in his mind. He'd known it was real but to hear it, to feel the storm-laden air, smell the acidic hint of tin and feel the burning itch was something else.

"Where?"

The shadow stopped waving its arms and stood still. The mouth became a line and the eyes glared at Neil. Neil matched it with his own relentless gaze.

"Where?"

Nothing. Neil rubbed at his scar and told himself to think, bloody think!

Then he knew. He saw the open door to the outside toilet, saw the toolchests and the worklamp and he knew. He got up, struggling against the weight of the air that wanted to drive him down to the couch and, he didn't doubt, make him see him things and hear things from his past.

At the door, he turned to the shadow. Its mouth wasn't a line now, it was open in what was almost an O of surprise. The thick brows above the eyes were raised quizzically.

"You won't win this one, Elias. You won't win this one, you bastard," Neil told the shadow.

As he began to turn towards the door, the shadow faded away.

Andrew got to the top of the ladder and almost fell onto the platform. He'd been climbing this ladder, clambering over the cage of the platform, hanging on with numbed hands and then letting himself drop for God knew how long. He was tired. His head was aching like a rotten tooth and his left leg seemed as numb as his hands. But he kept climbing the ladder and dropping down onto the mattresses because...because...oh, because it felt *wonderful*.

That endless moment between the sky and the ground was exactly what his father had said it was and it filled Andrew with a sense of lightness and freedom that he'd never known before.

He struggled up and leaned against the iron bar you used to give yourself a good push off when you were going down the chute. He breathed in deeply, feeling the cold of the night air making his throat burn and then moved towards the cage again.

The shadow was suddenly there. Not as dark as in the living room of 12 Oil Street because it didn't have the cone of light as a contrast. It was a dark grey and its features, that hard face and harder gaze locked on Andrew. Despite the cold, Andrew's head began to grow warm, ready to start itching. Instead of smelling the clean chill and the faint sweetness from the additives factory further up the dock road, Andrew smelled tin and its acidic underscent.

"What? What are you doing here? I've been jumping and...and..." Andrew realised that he had nothing else to say. He'd been jumping and that was *all* he'd been doing. The reason for jumping, the *only* reason for doing this was to find out what the shadow wanted him to know. Instead of remembering that, Andrew had been lost in that magical moment between the sky and the ground.

like your father before you and you know the consequences of that

The words settled in his mind and their meaning spread like oil on water. Andrew dropped his head. Yes, he knew. Because his father had forgotten why he was jumping, three people died. He forgot and only learned what the shadow knew when it was too late and three people had died.

there is little time now and you must decide if you want to know or if you will simply revel in the moment between sky and ground and let whatever happens afterwards happen

Andrew looked up and saw that the shadow's arms were outspread towards him. Andrew nodded and suddenly thought he knew what the consequences might be this time.

"My guilt could kill those closest to me if I don't accept it?" he said softly, the rise in inflection on the last word making it a question.

But the shadow only opened its arms wider and no words settle in Andrew's mind. Andrew wanted an answer but it was obvious that he needed to jump again before he could understand what the shadow wanted him to understand. He braced his legs and arms and then bent his knees slightly.

If this was to be the jump that would make everything clear, he would make it the best jump he could. He would vault over this caged platform, just as his father had all those years ago when he had been a child of ten, unfettered and free.

Neil saw the dark shape of the piled mattresses below the platform of the slide, saw that the top two were misaligned and looked up. He saw Andrew and the shadow. Neil started to run, his eyes still on the two shapes on the slide.

"Andrew! Wait! The mattresses are all skewiff!" Neil yelled, just as he'd yelled all those years ago. The only difference was that Eddie wasn't about to vault over the platform, Andrew was.

Andrew heard something and started to raise his eyes from looking at the mattresses below but the shadow's urgent whisper stopped all thought of that.

jump

Andrew swallowed and felt his knees begin to lock.

now

Andrew vaulted.

He kept his eyes open, looking up at the sky and hit the marvellous moment his father had found all those years ago. Andrew felt it somewhere deep inside himself, a place he thought might have been his soul. He felt the frigid air push against his face as his outward motion continued for a second. Then, instead of simply falling down, it was as if gravity was looking the other way and Andrew was suspended in the air. It felt like he would just hang there, long enough to count every one of the billion points of shimmering light in the dark velvet-like blue of the winter sky above him. Maybe he would be able to fly like this all the way up to the nearest shimmering point of light.

Then the air was rushing past him, making his hair blow upwards, turning his wide eyes into narrow slits. He looked down at the mattresses, feeling like his mind had expanded, as if, in that endless split-second, all his perceptions had been heightened. *This* time, he would have no trouble understanding the shadow.

Neil saw Andrew vault the rail of the cage and cursed. He pumped his legs and arms harder, feeling the burning in his throat as he yelled at Andrew again, knowing it was too late. Another part of his mind was praying to Anybody who was listening that, this time, he got there in time to get the mattresses straight.

Andrew saw somebody running across the swings and heard his name cutting through the air like a jagged knife. Neil? What was Neil doing here?

Neil reached the mattresses and dived at them. He hit the top one with his hands and yanked it towards him. He looked up and saw Andrew only half a foot away. Neil rolled and hit the asphalt on his hip.

Andrew hit the mattresses and his left leg bent underneath him. He heard it crack and he groaned. But he stayed on the mattresses. The pain sent terrible, burning arrows all the way up to his groin and the sky above seemed to tilt to the left. He groaned again and tried to move his leg from under him. He couldn't. The pain retreated from his groin and settled into a burning pulsation that made his lower leg feel like it was on fire.

Neil got up and saw Andrew's leg was bent underneath him.

"Andrew, I'm going to ease your leg out from under you. It's going to hurt but it's got to be done. Okay?"

Andrew wanted to say no, wanted to *scream* no but the pain in his leg was too much and all he could manage was another groan. Then the pain went up in an enormous spike as Neil lifted Andrew's bottom upwards with one hand and eased his left leg out. This time, Andrew managed to scream.

Neil took his jacket off and covered Andrew with it and held him until the last of the shudders stopped wracking the boy's body. Then Neil stood up.

"Tell me when you think you can put up with some more movement, son," Neil said. "And we'll try to get you to the gate."

The pain was back to being only almost-unbearable now and Andrew could think. What he thought was worse than the pain.

"No! I've got to find out what the shadow wants!"

"No, you don't. You need to get to hospital and get your leg fixed," Neil told him gently.

Andrew shook his head, knowing he didn't have the words to explain, knowing that whatever he said would only confirm his madness and Neil would try to help him and that was the last thing Andrew needed.

Neil leaned forward. "Andrew, look at me."

Andrew opened his eyes and saw Neil's face only inches from his own. That close, he could see the hard edge to Neil's mouth and the way the starlight seemed to spark in his eyes.

"Whatever you think you have to do will have to wait. That leg needs seeing to. I'm going to move you and it's going to hurt like a bastard. Get ready."

Andrew looked up at the slide and there was nothing there but the grey silhouette of the platform and ladder and the struts. The shadow was gone. Oh God, where had it gone? Then Neil moved the mattresses and everything turned grey and the pain took over the whole world.

SIXTEEN

A week later, the snow still covered the grass verges of Oil Street swings as Andrew settled himself on his crutches in the back garden of 12 Oil Street and looked across at the slide. There was nobody in the swings and the slide was throwing back lances of sunlight from its metal struts and the glare of ice that was the chute.

"Ready?" Neil asked from the step by the kitchen door.

Andrew turned and nodded. He followed Neil inside the house.

In the living room, the only things still there were the couch, the standard lamp and the television.

"Where's everything else?" Andrew asked.

"At your Nan's house. Till you decide what to do with them," Neil said and saw the way Andrew's face closed in on itself as he closed his eyes. "Sit down, Andrew. This is what you wanted and you're here. It's time we sorted this out."

Andrew sat on the couch and, as Neil sat next to him, he took a deep breath and looked at his father's old friend. "Neil, I've...if I...oh Jesus, Neil! I'm like my Dad, I'm insane!" His voice cracked on the last word.

Neil put his hands against Andrew's cheeks and turned his head towards him. "No," he said gently. "You feel guilty. You're not insane any more than your dad was. And you have nothing to feel guilty for anyway."

"I know my Dad said none of it was my fault but if I hadn't got drunk and jumped off that scaffold, maybe my Mum wouldn't've been...and if she hadn't got like that then maybe Dad would've just got on with his life and none of what happened would've happened and that poor woman..."

Neil let go of Andrew. "Andrew, it happened. And none of it's your fault. None of it. I know it's easy for me to say because it didn't happen to me but, still, it's true. Your mum did what she did and your dad did what he did. There were reasons for it all, all of them human. That's what they were, Andrew. Your mum and dad were both human. If you could speak to them now, they'd both tell you they regret things. Mostly, what happened to you then and what's happening to you now. They can't but I can. That's why your dad sent the journal to me. He wanted me to know what happened so I could make you understand that none of it was your fault.

"See, the problem with people is, we're always ready to take things personally. You think about what happened and you see it from your perspective. You were angry with your mum, got drunk and ended up in a coma. After that, from your perspective, everything that happened was your fault."

Andrew nodded and wiped at the tears he'd cried. "Exactly. My fault."

Neil smiled. "What about your mum? From *her* point of view, the reason you ended up in a coma was because she got angry. You knew her and you know she wasn't the type to admit she was wrong easily. But we can't hide from ourselves and deep down, she knew she was wrong. So, what happened to you was her fault. From *her* perspective. And your dad? If his grief for your granddad hadn't taken such an odd turn, maybe your mum wouldn't've done what she did, maybe she'd've talked to him about what she was going through, how she felt. If that had happened then, from your dad's point of view, everything else that happened wouldn't've happened." He raised his eyebrows.

Andrew thought about and finally nodded. Yes, he could see that now but it didn't mean anything really, did it? Compared to him being as insane as his father, it didn't matter much.

"Yes," he said slowly. "But it doesn't alter the fact that I'm going insane, too. Like my Dad did."

"Why d'you think you're going mad, Andrew?"

"Because I saw the shadow, too," Andrew said and looked at his hands.

Then he told Neil about the dream that was really a memory and about what had happened in this house before Neil saw him on the slide. And he told him that, even though the last jump hadn't been perfect, he knew that if he didn't...do something, then the people closest to him would suffer. His three grandparents would suffer because of Andrew's insanity.

When he'd finished, he looked into Neil's grey eyes, expecting to see the look of a man who was about to phone the loony bin and tell them to bring the white canvas jacket. Instead, he saw Neil smiling.

"The shadow was real," Neil said.

"What?" Andrew didn't know whether to burst out laughing or try to hobble away on his crutches.

"I saw it, too," Neil told him and then told him about Mad George and Emily Leather and about Elias Leather.

Andrew listened and, at first, wondered why Neil was doing this, was he just humouring him until he could get him admitted to the psychiatric ward? Then, slowly, Andrew began to realise that Neil was telling him the truth. Neil only ever told you the truth.

"And you really saw it? When you came here last week looking for me? You really saw it?"

Neil nodded. "Yeah, and three days ago when I came to get your dad's stuff. It was there, in the light of the standard lamp." He pointed to the corner of the room and then stood up. He put his hand underneath the fringed shade of the lamp and pressed the switch. The light came on, forming a cone of light against the wall.

Andrew winced when the light came on. He wanted to close his eyes but couldn't. All he could do was stare at that cone of light while another part of him wondered at the idea that Neil had come alone to this house when he knew what he knew about the shadow. Then, as he stared, he saw a subtle change in the cone of light.

"Oh God," Andrew moaned. "It's still here."

"Yeah, it is but it's not the same," Neil said.

Andrew looked at Neil and then back at the shadow in the cone of light. He frowned. Yes, he knew there was something different but he couldn't work out what. Well, it was a bit smaller than he remembered but that could've been just because he didn't remember it properly. The shape was there and its arms were outspread and... then he gasped.

"It doesn't look...its...it doesn't look like the same...face."

Neil nodded and smiled. He sat down again. "When I came back the other night, the shadow you saw was there. It was the shadow your Dad saw, the same one old George Leather saw and the one his daughter saw. But it wasn't alone."

Andrew looked at the shadow and then back at Neil and shook his head—he couldn't get his mind round the idea that Neil had been here, on his own and had seen not one shadow but two and was still willing to be here now. "Two shadows? I...what does that mean? And why's there only one now? And who, what is it if it's..."

"What does it look like to you, Andrew? Have a proper look and tell me what you think it is."

Andrew reluctantly turned to look at the shadow, the *smaller* shadow. It still had its arms outspread and Andrew didn't like that at all but he forced himself to look and...actually, that wasn't really true. It was reaction to what he'd felt the last time he'd been here, to what his father had written in the journal. Now, those outspread arms didn't make him feel bad or scared at all. Why was that?

Neil was watching Andrew and saw the change in the lad's face as something occurred to him. "What, son?"

Andrew turned and looked at Neil. "The other shadow...the one in my dream and the one I saw...its arms..."

"They scared you?"

Andrew nodded. "I didn't like the way they seemed to be, oh, reaching for me?"

"And now?"

Andrew looked again at the shadow pinned by the cone of light in the corner of the room. "They... God, this is going to sound stupid."

"I've heard lots of stupid things," Neil told him. "Said a few, too. Come on, Andrew, tell me."

Andrew smiled. "Well, it's like you do when you're sort of saying, you know, like 'there you go, easy, nothing to worry about.'" He looked at Neil and shrugged. "See? Stupid."

"No, I don't think so, Andrew. I think that's exactly right. Remember the smaller shadow Emily Leather saw? And Elias' daughter?"

Andrew nodded but slowly, not sure where Neil was going.

Neil looked at the shadow and Andrew watched the slow smile at the corner's of Neil's mouth. "Is that you, Elisabeth?"

Andrew gaped at Neil—how could he do this sort of thing? How could he just sit there and talk to a shadow that might *still* be the same shadow that had sent Andrew's dad mad? He was about to tell Neil that it was enough, it was time to go, he didn't want to be here anymore but, from the corner of his eye, he saw a flicker from the direction of the shadow. For a second, Andrew thought the shadow was about to move towards them, finally embrace them both in those outspread arms, but when he looked properly, he saw that it was nothing like that.

The shadow was still in the cone of light from the lamp but, where before its arms were outspread, now they were down by its side. And, more than that, Andrew could see proper features on the shadow's face. They were no longer suggestions of mouth and nose and eyes, they *were* mouth and nose and eyes. Andrew looked at the face and there was no doubt that he wasn't looking at a man's face at all. The face he could see was that of a child, little more than a toddler, maybe two years old. And with this realisation, Andrew watched wide-eyed as the shadow dwindled until it stood no higher than two or three feet off the ground.

"Has he gone now, sweetheart?" Neil asked.

Andrew's sharp intake of breath sounded very loud in his ears as he watched the shadow's head incline forward and then back twice, nodding.

"And what about you, Elisabeth?"

Andrew suddenly understood what Neil was doing and he waited for Neil to finish the question so the shadow could nod or shake its, *her* head. But Neil didn't qualify the question, he just sat on the couch, smiling at the shadow.

"Neil, it can't..." Andrew began but Neil cut him off by lifting his right hand, palm out.

The television came to life and Andrew almost squealed in shock.

The screen flickered and then settled and Andrew watched as a figure emerged from the pale background. It was a girl, two years old, dressed in a white dress with puffy sleeves. There was an ugly bruise on the girl's left arm and an uglier one above her left eye. But the girl was smiling and Andrew had to swallow past the lump in his throat as he understood what, *who* he was seeing. Then the little girl spoke and he had to blink so he could see her properly because his eyes were full of tears when he heard what she said and the pleading tone she used.

"Sad but happy. I couldn't stop him but I helped the people. Did I?"

Neil leaned forward, looking at the shadow in the cone of light rather than the figure in the television. "Yes, sweetheart, you did. You helped them all. If they could, they'd all thank you. They can't so I will. Thank you for helping them all." He turned and raised his eyebrows at Andrew.

Andrew nodded and said, "Thank you for...helping my Dad. Thank you Elisabeth."

"Welcome," the girl in the television said and smiled again.

"Can you leave now, little one?" Neil asked.

The shadow nodded and the little girl on the screen said, "Yes, Neil. Thank you. Bye bye."

The television flickered and died. The shadow in the cone of light waved at them and then faded, the way shadows do when light passes over them.

Andrew blinked away more tears and swallowed twice before he could find his voice. "The shad...the little girl...cushioned them? My Dad and George? So they didn't..."

Neil nodded and turned the standard lamp off. "So, still feel guilty, son?"

Andrew shook his head. "No. No, I don't." He took a long breath and let it out through pursed lips. "That poor little girl," he said and shook his head again. Then, as he began to get his crutches in the right position before lifting himself off the couch, he frowned and looked at Neil. "How did she know your name?"

Neil smiled. "The same way the shadow your dad saw knew his I suppose. Now, come on, let's get you back home."

Andrew settled back on the couch. "No," he told Neil. "That's not how she knew. And why did she thank you. Come on, Neil, tell me."

Neil sat on the arm of the couch. "It doesn't matter, Andrew. We came here for you and to help you realise that you aren't to blame for anything. So you can get on with the rest of your life. Now come on, let's go."

"You talked to her the other day," Andrew said, almost to himself. "That's right, isn't it? You talked to her and...helped her somehow." He shook his head again. "How? What did you do? Come on, Neil. I don't feel guilty and I know I can get on with my life but I want to know."

"I just persuaded the other one, Elias, to go. And I wanted Elisabeth to know that what she'd done was good, that it had helped. Once she knew that, she could go, too. And now we can go. Your Nan'll be wondering where we are."

Andrew stared at him. "You just *persuaded* the other shadow to go? Just like that? Neil, he was evil. He killed his own daughter and drove at least two other people mad and made them kill themselves. I might be young but I'm not stupid. You don't just *persuade* something like that to go and it goes."

Neil stood up. "That's what I did, Andrew. I just showed him that he couldn't do any more damage and he went. Elisabeth saw you and you thanked her and now she's gone because there's no need for her to be here anymore."

"Yeah, but how did you—"

Neil shook his head. "Let's go," he said and left the room

Andrew thought about staying, forcing Neil to come back and tell him exactly what he'd done or said but then he remembered who it was he was dealing with and knew it would be a waste of time. He got up from the couch, took one last look at the standard lamp and the television and said, "Thank you, Elisabeth. I hope you can be happy now."

As he reached the door, Andrew paused as words seemed to bypass his ears to settle in his mind.

welcome and thank you too bye bye Andrew

Andrew smiled but didn't turn round. He followed Neil out of the house. Outside, he looked up at the hard, blue winter sky and felt something else seep into his mind. No, more than just his mind, it filled his entire being, a lightness; it made him feel the way he had when he'd vaulted over the caged platform of the slide. Unfettered and free. He smiled at Neil.

Neil saw the smile and recognised it as the same smile Davy Eliot used to smile when he was a kid about, oh, ten years old. "Ready to go?" Neil asked.

"Yeah."

Neil closed the front gate and pocketed the keys he'd got from Paul Horne that morning. He turned and watched Andrew making his careful way to the car. When he reached the car, Andrew looked up at the diamond-hard blue sky again and smiled his father's smile again. The sun threw the lad's shadow behind him and pinned it to the ground.

They got in the car and drove away from 12 Oil Street.

THE END

WALLASEY
DECEMBER 2009

www.ingramcontent.com/pod-product-compliance
Ingram Content Group UK Ltd.
Pitfield, Milton Keynes, MK11 3LW, UK
UKHW041258180426
11947UKWH00008B/556